NIGHTHAWK

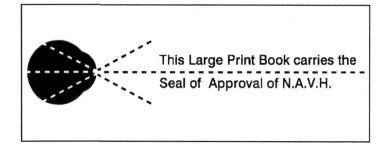

This Large Print Book carries the
Seal of Approval of N.A.V.H.

a NUMA field team,
dent left her unable to
d the computer technol-

member of the Special
at six foot eight, married
Ph.D. in Ocean Sciences.

ne biologist, married to
fitness aficionado, an ac-
and an excellent marks-

in of the NUMA vessel

ECURITY AGENCY
ad of Ex-Atmospheric
SA, director of the *Night-*

Former NASA scientist,
ert, integral part of the
am. Coworkers refer to
Emma.
field agent.
NSA field agent.

ATES AIR FORCE
nsen Commander of the
tions Squadron, based at
Force Base, California.

NIGHTHAWK

A NOVEL FROM THE NUMA® FILES

CLIVE CUSSLER
AND GRAHAM BROWN

LARGE PRINT PRESS
A part of Gale, a Cengage Company

 GALE
A Cengage Company

Farmington Hills, Mich • San Francisco • New York • Waterville, Maine
Meriden, Conn • Mason, Ohio • Chicago

LIBRARY OF CONGRESS CATALOGING-IN-PUBLICATION DATA

Names: Cussler, Clive, author. | Brown, Graham, 1969- author.
Title: Nighthawk : a novel from the NUMA Files : a Kurt Austin adventure / by Clive Cussler and Graham Brown.
Description: Large print edition. | Waterville, Maine : Wheeler Publishing, a part of Gale, Cengage Learning, 2017. | Series: A Kurt Austin adventure | Series: Wheeler Publishing large print hardcover | Series: The NUMA Files ; 14
Identifiers: LCCN 2017016335 | ISBN 9781432838881 (hardcover) | ISBN 1432838881 (hardcover)
Subjects: LCSH: Austin, Kurt (Fictitious character)—Fiction. | Marine scientists—Fiction. | Large type books. | BISAC: FICTION / Action & Adventure. | FICTION / Suspense. | GSAFD: Adventure fiction. | Suspense fiction.
Classification: LCC PS3553.U75 N54 2017b | DDC 813/.54—dc23
LC record available at https://lccn.loc.gov/2017016335

ISBN 13: 978-1-4328-3889-8 (pbk.)

Published in 2018 by arrangement with G. P. Putnam's Sons, an imprint of Penguin Publishing Group, a division of Penguin Random House LLC

Printed in Mexico
1 2 3 4 5 6 7 22 21 20 19 18

supposed to joi
before a car ac
walk, instead joir
ogies departmen

Paul Trout Talles
Projects division
to Gamay. Has a
Quiet and steady

Gamay Trout Ma
Paul, Gamay is a
complished diver
man.

Ed Callahan Cap
Catalina.

NATIONAL S

Steve Gowdy H
projects at the N
hawk program.

Emma Townsend
astrophysics ex
Nighthawk prog
her as *Hurricane*

Agent Hurns NSA

Agent Rodriguez

UNITED S

Colonel Frank Ha
9th Space Oper
Vandenberg Air

Russian Federation

Constantin Davidov Special executive at the FSB, successor to the KGB, in charge of *technology retrieval* for the Kremlin.

Rear Admiral Sergei Borozdin Old friend of Davidov's, commander of the Russian 1st Salvage Fleet (Pacific).

Victor Tovarich Captain of the TK-17 Typhoon-class submarine.

Major Yuri Timonovski Commander and pilot of *Blackjack 2*.

People's Republic of China

General Zhang Highest-ranking officer at the Chinese Ministry of State Security.

Daiyu (Black Jade) Special operative for the Ministry, one of the "children that were never born."

Jian Daiyu's partner, also one of the "children that were never born."

Li Ying Liaison officer, Beijing.

Lieutenant Wu Field officer for the Ministry of State Security.

Falconer Code name of an anonymous asset connected with the NSA's *Nighthawk* program.

MS *Reunion*

Buck Kamphausen Captain of the MS *Reunion*.

PERU

Urco Archaeologist studying the origins and disappearance of the Chachapoya people.

Vargas One of Urco's volunteers.

Reyes Another of the volunteers.

WASHINGTON, D.C.

Collin Kane Bomb disposal expert.

Prologue:
The Burning Point

South America
January 1525

The spear hit Diego Alvarado in the chest. A jarring blow that knocked him to the ground but failed to puncture the strong Castilian armor he'd carried all the way from Spain.

He rolled, took a position on one knee and leveled his crossbow. Spotting movement in the trees, he let the bolt fly. It sliced into the foliage, drawing an anguished scream.

"In the trees to the right!" he yelled to his men.

A cloud of blue smoke exploded over the narrow trail as several large-bored muskets, known as harquebuses, fired simultaneously. The shots tore into the forest, severing small tree limbs and ripping through the lush green leaves.

A wave of arrows flew back at them in

response. Two of Alvarado's men went down and he felt a spike of pain in his calf as an obsidian-tipped dart punctured it.

"They have us surrounded," one of the men shouted.

"Hold your line," Alvarado ordered. He limped forward instead of back, ignoring the pain and reloading his weapon.

After a long hike into the foothills, they'd been ambushed, lured down a path and attacked from both sides. Another group of men might have broken ranks under the assault, but Alvarado's men had once been soldiers. They stood like a wall and didn't waste their precious ammunition. Several drew their swords while the others steadied their heavy firearms.

The natives were drawing themselves together to attack once again. With a shrill cry, they charged from the trees. They broke into the clearing only to be struck down by Spanish thunder as a second wave of black powder explosions shook the air.

Half their number fell, others turned and ran, only two continued the attack. They rushed toward Alvarado, charging through the smoke, their dark, reddish faces and blazing white eyes highlighted by streaks of war paint.

Alvarado took the first one with the crossbow, dropping the man in his tracks, but the second lunged with a spear. The tip of the crude weapon deflected off the angled chest plate of Alvarado's silver armor. Impervious to such crude blades, Alvarado reached toward his assailant without fear. He grabbed the man, shifted his weight and flung him to the ground.

Falling on him, Alvarado finished the native with a dagger.

By the time he looked up, the rest of them had fled.

"Reload," he shouted to the men. "They'll be back soon."

As the men began the laborious process of packing powder charges in their weapons, Alvarado tried to remove the native's arrow from his calf. He dug at his own flesh with the tip of his dagger and then eased the arrow out. He looked at it and then tossed it aside. It was nothing new. He'd been told these "people of the clouds" were different than the Inca and the other tribes of the area. That they were brave in combat, there was no doubt, but they had no greater weapons than any of the other natives. They had nothing to their advantage but raw numbers.

Alvarado poured some wine from a small flask on the wound. It stung, but helped numb the pain — and, he hoped, clean out any poison. He then wrapped his calf in a cloth and watched as the blood soaked it, spreading from a central spot, until the entire cloth was stained crimson.

"We have to fall back," he said, struggling to get up on his feet.

"How far?" one of his men shouted.

"All the way," Alvarado said. "Back to the village."

None of them argued. In fact, they looked relieved to hear the order.

They formed up and began to move. Alvarado managed to walk for the first mile, but the heavy armor and the pain in his leg soon became too much. One of his men came to help, supporting him and leading him to the sturdy packhorse they'd used to carry in supplies. The strap was loosened and the goods dumped on the ground. With a boost, Alvarado was lifted up onto the horse. He held on tightly, and the entire party continued quickly, heading downhill, back toward their camp.

After several hours Alvarado and his men reached the village they'd left early that morning. Night had fallen, but warm fires stoked by the soldiers he'd left behind welcomed them.

A nobleman named Costa helped Alvarado down from the horse. "What happened?" he asked, blanching at the wound.

Costa was an aristocrat of the middle tier. He'd agreed to fund the expedition in return for a third of all treasure recovered. Why he'd come along personally was anyone's guess, perhaps for the adventure, or more likely to ensure he wasn't cheated out of his profits. So far, he'd done little but complain.

"We've been tricked," Alvarado said. "These people of the cloud are not amenable to our presence. They would rather kill us than join us even if it means they remain enslaved to other masters."

"But what about Pizarro?" Costa asked. "These are his marks. He came this way. He said we would find allies."

Alvarado knew all about Pizarro's marks. The would-be conquistador had carved inscriptions into some of the trees alongside the trail so that Alvarado and his reinforcements could catch up with Pizarro and his advanced guard.

He knew about Pizarro's plans as well, to turn other natives against the ruling group. It had worked in other places, but not here.

"Something must have happened to him," Alvarado said. "Either Francisco has been killed or . . ."

He didn't have to finish. None of them really trusted Pizarro. He kept talking of gold, which no one had yet seen, kept promising wealth, which had yet to appear. He was a little man with big dreams. He'd been turned down by the Governor twice when requesting funds to assist his expeditions and in desperation had finally turned to Costa, and to his rival: Alvarado.

While Alvarado didn't like or trust Pizarro, he did understand the man. Both of them were cut from the same cloth. They were men of inauspicious birth, both had come from Spain to make a name for themselves. But they'd been enemies only months before, and it was entirely possible that Pizarro had agreed to partner with them only to lead them to their doom.

"We must leave for the coast immediately," Alvarado said.

Costa looked sick, at the thought.

"Something wrong with that order, my friend?"

"No," Costa said. "It's just that . . ."

"Spit it out."

Costa hesitated. "Some of the men have fallen ill. Fever. It may be the pox."

Alvarado could not imagine worse news. "Show me."

Costa led him to the largest of the native

huts, made of mud and grass, that might have been a communal gathering place. A fire in the center burned brightly, venting smoke through a hole in the roof. A group of Alvarado's soldiers lay on the dirt floor around it, each of them in various states of distress.

"When did this begin?"

"Shortly after you left to find Pizarro."

In the flickering light, Alvarado kneeled beside one of the men. The soldier was little more than a boy; he lay on his back with his eyes closed and his face toward the thatched ceiling above. His shirt was soaked with perspiration and small red sores had begun to appear on his neck, face and chest. His temperature was so high that kneeling over him felt like standing too close to an open flame.

"Smallpox," Alvarado said, confirming the diagnosis. "How many are like this?"

"Eight are in the grips of it. Three others are less ill, but they can barely stand. They certainly can't walk ten miles to the coast."

With eleven of his men sick, several wounded and two dead, Alvarado had only twenty left who could fight. "We'll have to leave them."

"But Diego . . ."

"They're too sick to walk and too heavy

15

to carry," Alvarado insisted. "And we're greatly outnumbered. I count thirty huts around us. Each big enough for a large family. There must have been more than two hundred people living here before Pizarro came through. Even if half are women and children, we'll never hold out. And who's to say other villages are not allied with this one."

Costa took the estimate grimly. "Perhaps Francisco will turn back and bring help."

"It's too late to pin our hopes on rescue," Alvarado said. "You and the others must go while there's still time."

Me and the others," Costa repeated, suspiciously. "Surely you don't intend to stay?"

Alvarado put a hand to his forehead and wiped a sheen of sweat from it. It might have been the heat or the wound in his leg, but he suspected it was the beginnings of the disease that was ravaging his men. "I would only hold you back. Now, round up the men and head for the ship. Sail with the current until you're clear of the coast, then turn north and head back to Panama."

Costa stared for a short moment, then abruptly turned to leave.

Alvarado grabbed him by the wrist, gripping it with such strength that Costa thought his bones might break. "Pay my family what you owe me or I will haunt you till the end of your days."

Costa nodded. It might have been the only promise he'd ever made that he was honestly afraid to break.

As the men departed, Alvarado grew feverish. He'd armed himself with two pre-loaded muskets and his crossbow. The other men who could hold weapons were each given a loaded pistol and several helpings of rum.

With the fires still burning in the night and the smoke drifting thick and low, they waited and watched. It seemed forever, but eventually the natives appeared.

Through a gap in the thatched wall, Alvarado saw them approach. When they were close enough, he fired into the nearest group.

The blast scattered them, but others came from different directions. They burst into the huts from all sides.

The pistols fired and several natives went down, but the horde raced across the bodies of their dead brethren, while others crashed through the flimsy walls to join the attack.

Alvarado fired the second harquebus, killing two more natives. He clubbed a third attacker with the smoking barrel, but was knocked to the ground an instant later.

Resorting to his crossbow, he fired the bolt into the melee. He was reaching for his dagger when a stone axe came down upon his wrist and hacked off his hand.

He shouted in agony and gripped instinctively at the bleeding stump. But a spear through his back paralyzed him, ending his cry and leaving him on the ground unable to move or to even call out to his men.

Lying there, Alvarado watched as the natives massacred his sick and dying men; hacking at them and stabbing them repeatedly. The frenzy lasted for several minutes, with blood, sweat and saliva flying in all directions.

In the aftermath, Alvarado was left for dead. As the light faded from his eyes, he watched the natives dragging a few surviving men into the forest. He would never know what became of them.

Invisible and unseen in the mayhem, the tiny pathogens that carried smallpox and measles had been spread with every breath and every splattering of blood and saliva. The natives of this New World had never been exposed to them before. They had no resistance to the invisible enemy.

In a week, most of the warriors involved in the attack would be sick and dying. In a month, their entire village would be stricken. By the year's end, scores of other settlements would be suffering as well, and, in a decade, the entire region would be wilting under the strains of the epidemic.

Unchecked, smallpox would ravage the Incan empire, pave the way for the Spanish conquest and ultimately kill over ninety percent of the native population of South America. An entire continent laid to waste by a weapon no one could see.

1

Vandenberg Air Force Base, California
Present day

Steve Gowdy sat in a comfortable chair on the top level of a darkened control room in the heart of Vandenberg Air Force Base. The setting resembled the NASA command centers in Houston and at Cape Canaveral, but was smaller and stocked with military personnel instead of civilians.

Gowdy was in his late forties. He wore a gray polo shirt and black slacks, his thin covering of sandy brown hair perfectly coiffed but too thin to conceal his scalp beneath. He looked like a golfer ready to play eighteen holes at the local country club, a visitor on a day tour or a bored middle manager stuck in another endless meeting. Only the tightly bunched wrinkles around his eyes and the unconscious drumming of his finger on the arm of the chair suggested he was paying close attention.

Gowdy hadn't come to Vandenberg for a tour of the place, or to marvel at the technology, but to oversee the final stage of a mission so secret only forty people in the entire world knew of its existence.

The project was called *Ruby Snow,* which meant nothing, of course, but had a poetic ring to it that Gowdy appreciated. It involved an aircraft funded by the National Security Agency and operated by the Air Force and other members of the Defense Department.

Aircraft was the wrong word, he reminded himself. The *Nighthawk* was a hybrid vehicle, part aircraft, part spacecraft. The latest in a long line of platforms descended from the space shuttle. It was the most advanced machine ever flown and was finally returning to Earth after three long years in orbit.

A large storm brewing over the Pacific had caused the NSA to move the reentry up by a full week, but, other than that, everything had gone according to plan.

Watching the reentry live, Gowdy stared at the huge, high-definition screens that made up the front wall of the room. One showed a column of numbers and symbols that honestly meant nothing to him, except that all of them remained green.

A second display showed a chart with a

line that dove sharply from the upper-left-hand corner before leveling out across the middle and then beginning to drop again on the right side. Labeled *Nighthawk Descent Profile,* the chart had something to do with the altitude, speed and distance of the aircraft. But he kept his attention glued to the central display, where a global satellite map showed the Pacific Ocean and the west coasts of North, South and Central America.

Icons representing the *Nighthawk* and lines tracing its path were drawn in bright colors. Because the *Nighthawk* flew in an unusual polar orbit, the reentry path originated over Antarctica, cutting across the globe at a diagonal angle. It had flown past New Zealand, passing to the east by less than a hundred miles, and from there it drew a line directly over the top of the Cook Islands and Tahiti. It passed south of Hawaii, and its projection continued toward Vandenberg and the high deserts of California. It still had several thousand miles to go, but traveling at over five thousand miles per hour meant less than forty minutes before touchdown.

An echoing call rang out over the loudspeaker system, known as the loop. "Vehicle has cleared Max Q," an anonymous voice said. "Heat shield secure. Temperatures dropping."

Max Q. That was a term Gowdy knew. *A danger point — the point of maximum aerodynamic stress on the craft. A point where any weakness or damage would likely result in structural failure and loss of the craft.*

Hearing that the *Nighthawk* had passed Max Q reduced Gowdy's anxiety a bit. Many things could still go wrong, catastrophically wrong, but the largest hurdle had been cleared.

He glanced down to the middle tier of the amphitheater-style room. That level was the domain of the flight director. In this case, an Air Force Colonel named Frank Hansen. Hansen was a steely-eyed veteran of thirty years, a former fighter jock and test pilot who'd survived two ejections and a crash in his time and was now head of the 9th Space Operations Squadron.

Hansen turned, made eye contact and offered a nod. So far, so good.

Among all the controllers and system specialists and experts, Hansen was the only man in the room — aside from Gowdy himself — who understood just what a monumental risk they were taking. And if Gowdy measured him right, Hansen was just as nervous.

Hansen pressed his intercom switch. "Give me a status update," his calm voice called out.

Down on the lowest level of the room, the individual systems controllers went into action. Each of them had one thing to worry about; guidance, telemetry, propulsion, etc. . . . Like the front row in a movie theater, their positions made watching the main screen a neck-craning exercise, but since every bit of information they needed was displayed on smaller monitors directly in front of them, they rarely looked up until their tasks were done.

Gowdy sat back and listened as the stream of replies poured in over the loop, his finger continuing to drum.

"Telemetry: Go."

"Electrical: Go."

"Flight controls: Go."

On it went, each man or woman reporting, confirming good news, until all the controllers had reported in but one.

An awkward pause ensued. Down below, Hansen waited and then pressed the button on his transmitter. "Guidance, what's your status?"

There was no response.

"Guidance?"

The room went deathly quiet. Gowdy's

finger stopped its tapping. In all the simulations, he'd never heard a delay, not even a few seconds. He stood up, gazing down over the rail toward the bottom row, where the guidance controller sat.

A young airman with a crew cut was working furiously, typing and tapping things on his keyboard, switching screens.

"Guidance?" Hansen called out. "I need a response."

"Guidance is go," the airman finally replied, "but we're seeing a delay in the repeat."

Because the *Nighthawk* was a pilotless craft and controlled remotely from Vandenberg, the system had been designed to repeat every instruction back to control center before executing a maneuver, much in the way a pilot repeated the instructions to air traffic control to make sure everyone was on the same page.

Gowdy tapped his own intercom button, which went directly, and privately, to Hansen. "What's happening? What does it mean?"

"A delay in the repeat could be anything," Hansen replied. He spoke with a practiced indifference. "It could mean a problem processing the command, an error on our end, or even —"

Before anything else could be said, the Telemetry controller spoke up. "Telemetry is yellow. Signal intermittent."

On the big screen with the numbers, two boxes had begun flashing yellow alarms; a third began to flash red.

"Course deviation detected," the tracking controller said. "Two degrees south and turning . . . Five degrees and turning . . ."

Gowdy felt his throat clench up. He buzzed Hansen again. "What's happening?"

Hansen was too busy to reply and Gowdy turned his gaze back to the screen. The *Nighthawk*'s projected line had begun to curve, angling to the right, away from California and toward Central America.

"Eleven degrees south and still turning," the guidance controller said. "Speed dropping, descent arrested. Altitude maintaining nine-one thousand."

Gowdy could hardly believe his eyes. Instead of descending as planned, the *Nighthawk* was leveling off at ninety-one thousand feet and losing speed because of it. Since the craft was a glider at this point, it was imperative that it maintain the proper descent profile; otherwise, it would bleed off so much speed that it would no longer be able to reach California.

Gowdy felt his legs shaking. He gripped

27

the rail in front of him with one hand while the other went into his pocket, fumbling for a key.

"Reissue directional commands," Hansen called out tersely.

"No effect," the controller said.

"Reboot command program."

"Reboot initiated . . . Stand by."

Gowdy descended the stairs to Hansen's level and held his position. He was sweating now, his hands trembling, his fingers on the key he hoped never to use.

How could it all be going wrong now? A decade of research and three years in space. How could the effort possibly be failing here at the end?

"Twenty-one degrees south," the guidance controller said. "Altitude still nine-one thousand, speed dropping to four thousand."

"What's happening?" Gowdy shouted to Hansen, no longer bothering with the intercom or the pretense of calm.

"We've lost control."

"I can see that," Gowdy replied. "Why?"

"Impossible to tell," Hansen said. "It seems to be a constant right turn. There may be damage to the wing or vertical stabilizer. But that wouldn't explain the telemetry problems or the delay on the command repeat."

Gowdy fumbled with the key in his pocket, turning it over and over in his hand. It was his responsibility to terminate the mission if it became too dangerous; his call. To act early before all hope was gone would be a mistake, but to act too late . . . could be disastrous.

He stepped forward, barging into Hansen's personal space. "Get this damned thing back on track."

Hansen pushed past him, all but shoving Gowdy into a seat. The two men had never liked each other. Hansen felt Gowdy didn't know enough about physics and astronautics to be attached to the program, and Gowdy considered the Air Force Colonel to be arrogant and condescending to his authority. The higher-ups had ordered them to get along; it had worked for a while, but not now.

"Transponder data intermittent," the telemetry controller said. "We're losing the signal."

"Reboot the transponder," Hansen called out. "If the transponder goes out, we'll lose track of the vehicle. It's not in primary radar coverage."

Gowdy sat, immobile. His body went numb and he listened to the desperate exchange as if in a trance. It wouldn't matter if they were in radar coverage, the *Nighthawk* was designed with a complete stealth covering. Unlike other spacecraft, it was black in color, invisible to telescopes. It was covered with the most advanced radar-absorbent material ever developed.

He looked up. The vehicle was now streaking toward the coast of South America at thirty-five hundred miles per hour. Its turn was moderating, its speed continuing to drop. Its maximum glide path, marked by a shaded orange circle on the map, was shrinking with each second and moving south. It no longer reached the United States.

Gowdy knew what he had to do. There was no more reason to wait.

He pulled the red key out of his pocket and inserted it into a slot on the panel in front of him. A turn of the key opened a compartment just above it and a small pedestal rose up and locked in place. The pedestal was marked with yellow and black chevrons. In the center loomed a red button protected by raised metal bars that prevented it from being pressed by accident.

Gowdy looked up at the screen. They were now getting erroneous position data indicating the *Nighthawk* was in several different places at the same time. Returns blinked on and off, but the main line continued to head south, heading straight for the Galápagos Islands and the coast of Ecuador beyond.

"Guidance reboot completed," the controller said.

"And?!" Hansen asked.

"No response."

"That's it," Gowdy whispered. He turned the key to the right and the red button lit up.

"Self-destruct, armed," a computer voice called out.

Letting go of the key, Gowdy reached for the button.

A firm hand intercepted him, grabbing his wrist and yanking it away.

Hansen had appeared at his side. "Are you insane?" the Air Force Colonel growled.

"It's gone off course," Gowdy said. "We can't have it coming down in a populated area, the risk is too great that the worst will happen."

Hansen continued to hold Gowdy's arm back. *"The worst* has already happened. It happened the moment we brought the *Nighthawk* and its cargo back into the atmosphere. Destroying it now will only trigger the catastrophe."

Gowdy blinked, confused. He felt a sense

of vertigo. He truly didn't understand. But then, this was what Hansen had complained about all along. The science was beyond him.

The *Nighthawk* suddenly vanished from the screen. The graph showing its descent profile went blank and all the numbers in the far screen froze and began to blink red.

"Telemetry is down," another controller reported with little emotion. "*Nighthawk* contact lost."

A murmur swept through the room. It sounded like fear. Gowdy stared at the screen, waiting and hoping the course line would reappear. He sat in silence as repeated attempts to reestablish the link between Vandenberg and the aircraft failed.

Eventually, a new number appeared on the screen and began rapidly counting toward zero.

"What's that?" Gowdy asked.

"Surface interface time," Hansen said with grim honesty. "The longest possible time the *Nighthawk* can remain aloft before reaching zero altitude."

The number ticked down without mercy, going from minutes to seconds and then stopping implacably at 0:00:00.

"Now what?" Gowdy asked.

"Give me live satellite coverage," Hansen

ordered. "Wide-angle. South Pacific and western South America."

The controllers did as ordered. No one asked why.

One by one, the satellite views came up. Gowdy stared at the peaceful scene. Clouds drifted over the Pacific. The west coast of South America ran hard against the blue waters of the ocean. The tropical disturbance in the Pacific swirled like a peaceful merry-go-round.

Everything appeared calm.

"What are you looking for?" Gowdy asked.

The stern Air Force Colonel turned to the NSA bureaucrat he'd put up with for so long and exhaled. It was more relief than frustration.

"Absent a command from the ground, the *Nighthawk* will enter an autonomous mode, thinking for itself. When it determines its own position and computes that it can't reach Vandenberg, the craft will execute emergency descent procedures, slow to an appropriate speed and then land safely . . . by parachute."

"How do you know it hasn't broken up already?" Gowdy replied, trying to reassert his aura of authority. "How do you know the autoland system hasn't failed like everything else?"

"Because," Hansen said, "we're still here."

It took a moment, but Gowdy began to understand. He looked up at the live satellite view and all the normal things it displayed. "How long do we have?"

Hansen performed a quick mental calculation. "Seven days," he said. "Less, if the fuel cells, solar panels or the battery packs were damaged."

Gowdy turned back to the screen and the massive expanse of the South Pacific on display. Seven days to search all that ocean and find a needle in its watery haystack. Seven days to find and shut off a ticking bomb that could shake the very foundations of the Earth.

2

Kohala Point, Hawaii

Kurt Austin straddled a surfboard in the tropical waters a half mile from the Kohala Lighthouse on the Big Island of Hawaii. The strong Pacific sun warmed his tanned skin and the swells rolled beneath him in a constant rhythm. His muscles were taut and his mind quiet as he watched a fifteen-foot wave build toward the beach and then curl into a perfect left-hand break.

White foam zipped along the top of the wave, racing to catch up to the surfer riding it, but he kept his speed up, turned out and accelerated toward the beach just before the crest surged and crashed down behind him.

The sheer power of the wave sent a thunderclap echo off the lava rocks at the south end of the beach. There was a timbre to that symphony. "I could listen to that sound forever," Kurt said.

"That's because you're *Kaikane*," a surfer

beside him replied in a distinct Hawaiian accent. *"Born from the sea."*

Kurt glanced to his right, where a solidly built Hawaiian man straddled a short board. Polynesian-style tattoos on his arms and chest nearly matched a pattern painted on the board. He had shaggy black hair, a warm smile and a soft face. His name was Ika, but everyone called him Ike.

Kurt grinned. "You might be right about that."

Now in his thirties, Kurt Austin had grown up in the Pacific Northwest where he'd spent most of his time boating, fishing or swimming. Years working in his father's marine salvage business meant he learned to dive as a teenager. He spent countless hours underwater since, working for his father first, before a stint in the Navy and several years with a special CIA unit that did subsurface recovery and engineering.

Since leaving the CIA, he'd been with NUMA, the National Underwater and Marine Agency, a branch of the federal government focused on the exploration, study and preservation of the world's oceans.

Strangely, the farther he'd gone on his journey, the more technology came between him and the water. Skin diving gave way to wet suits and then to dry suits. Those layers gave way to hard-shelled, deep-diving units, which encased him like an undersea astronaut. More often than not, he now used submersibles, either robotic units piloted from the surface or manned subs that were pressurized and heated and comfortable enough to wear shorts and T-shirts. And so, after finishing a project on Oahu, Kurt had decided to get back in touch with the water and the rhythms of the sea.

Being in Hawaii, that meant surfing, and over a period of weeks Kurt pushed himself to tackle larger and faster waves with a relentless desire to improve.

After several weeks, he was almost as good as the local guides he'd grown to be friends with. His skin was so tanned, he might have passed as a Hawaiian — except for a mop of prematurely silver hair.

"The rhythm of the sea is changing," Ike said, turning and gazing out behind them. "Can you feel it?"

Kurt nodded. "Swells coming through faster. Closer together."

There was a storm out there. It was beyond the horizon but growing toward cyclone strength. The waves pushed ahead of it were starting to line up.

"Gonna get too rough to ride soon," Ike said.

"Let's make the best of it, then," Kurt said.

He dropped forward on his board and began paddling toward the break zone.

Ike did the same and they moved closer to shore, increasing their pace and separating. One huge swell after another rolled beneath them until Kurt sensed a monster wave, the largest of the day.

This was the wave he wanted, the one that carried danger and power in equal measures. He paddled faster, began to roll up the face of the swell and got to one knee. He stood and turned with perfect timing, dropping in and accelerating just as the top of the wave began to curl.

Ike was up ahead of him, already slicing a white wake in the water as if his board were powered by rockets. Kurt cut across the wave behind him and couldn't help but grin at the incredible feeling that poured through him as if he'd tapped into the power of the sea itself.

Accelerating down the face and cutting to the left, he stayed just ahead of the curling top that was forming a pipeline behind him. He dropped his hand and trailed his fingers in the water, drifting back until all he saw around him was a tube of translucent blue, a sheet of liquid glass.

The wave roared like a living thing and began to close on him like Scylla and Charybdis. Just before it was about to crush him, Kurt turned out and zipped into the open again.

He saw Ike up ahead and another surfer who'd picked the same wave. They maneuvered a little too closely and Ike had to cut back. His turn was sharp enough to avoid contact, but the other surfer was over-matched by the speed and power of the breaker and he went down.

Kurt turned to avoid him, but then the sea surprised them all as the wave peaked suddenly and closed out all at once.

The entire front crashed simultaneously, a change from the long, curling break they'd been enjoying. A mountain of water landed on Kurt's shoulders, knocking him from his board and driving him under.

He was forced deep and slammed into the sand. An outcropping of lava rock gashed his arm and he felt the snap of the surf leash attached to his ankle as his board was ripped away.

The huge wave held him down, but Kurt's experience diving prevented any panic. He steadied himself as the undertow returned and the swirling sediment around him cleared enough to see the light from above. He planted his feet and pushed off the bottom.

Breaking the surface, Kurt immediately glanced around. Another wave was barreling down on him and his board had been flung into the shallows and tossed onto the beach. Ike was there in the shallows as well, pulling himself back onto his board and paddling frantically to get back out into the water.

Kurt quickly realized why: the other surfer was nowhere to be seen. He'd gone down and stayed down.

Kurt took a deep breath and dove just as the following wave crashed over him. He felt the surge rushing by, lifting him and then releasing him as if he was just beyond its grasp. He heard the muted rumble of the wave crashing up ahead and fought to see through the sand that exploded and swirled back toward him.

In the gloom ahead, he spied a flash of color, yellow and red, dimmed by the water's hue and blurred by the limitations of human vision underwater. He kicked hard and used his arms in a powerful stroke, lunging forward, until he grasped the surfer's board. It was wedged into a gap in the lava rock, stuck tight. Feeling along the board, Kurt found the leash, used it to pull the unconscious wave rider toward him and ripped the Velcro cuff that held him.

The undertow returned. The next wave was coming. He pulled the limp surfer to him, pushed off the bottom once more and emerged beyond the crest of the wave.

He swam toward the shore; the next wave crashed behind them and shoved them forward in a burst of foam and spray.

As they cruised into the shallows, several other surfers rushed out to help. They grabbed the injured man by his arms and legs and hauled him onto the sand.

Ike helped Kurt to his feet and onto the beach, where he stood with his hands on his hips, drawing in as much oxygen as his lungs would allow. "Is he okay?"

A few feet away, the other surfer was on his side, coughing and spitting out water. One of the men with him nodded.

Ike grinned and held up the broken end of Kurt's leash. "Look at this. You broke your leash. You're a *real* big-wave surfer, now."

Ike laughed at his own joke and gave Kurt a playful shove.

"Not exactly how I wanted the ride to end," Kurt said. "What happened with that wave? Everything seemed fine and then . . ."

Ike shrugged. "Every wave is different, bro. It's part of the deal. *Moana* will let you play, but from time to time she reminds you *I'm dangerous. I'm unpredictable. One day, I'll turn on you. And in that moment of truth, you'll find you can't control me. You'll find you're at my mercy and only I will decide whether to hold you down or set you free.*"

Kurt enjoyed the poetry of the statement, enough that he didn't labor the point with anything but a respectful nod and a glance back out to the sea. The waves were still growing, the storm was coming on. Moana *would not let them play anymore today.*

A shout from higher up the beach broke his reverie. "Kurt Austin," a voice called.

There was an official tone to the address, sharp and clear. A tone very out of place on a beach with so much local flavor.

Kurt looked up and saw a man coming down from the road. He wore black slacks, dress shoes and a white, button-down shirt. He had narrow shoulders and hips but stood ramrod straight and moved with a purpose. He'd come from a white SUV parked on the road up above.

"Kurt?" the man shouted, getting closer.

Ike leaned in. "I wouldn't answer, if I was

42

you," he whispered. "Looks like Five-O to me."

"I should be so lucky," Kurt said. He recognized a government official when he saw one, and he recognized this one in particular. "Rudi Gunn," he said, extending a hand to NUMA's number two official. "I didn't know you were on the island. I'd have brought you surfing with me."

"I only arrived a few hours ago," Rudi said, shaking Kurt's hand, "but, considering the wipeout I just saw, I'd have to consider any future invitations as part of a plan to get rid of me and take my job."

"And handle paperwork all day long? No thanks. What are you doing here?"

"I've been trying to reach you," Rudi said. "Must have left a dozen messages on your phone."

"Phones and surfing don't exactly mix," Kurt said. "What's the emergency?"

"Who says there's an emergency?"

Kurt offered an incredulous look.

"Okay," Rudi said. "There probably is an emergency — otherwise, they wouldn't have sent me to pick you up — but I don't know what it is. I'm just lucky the valet at your hotel remembered you loading up a surf-board and heading this way."

"That kid just lost his tip," Kurt said.

"He'll survive on what I paid him," Rudi said. "Trust me."

Kurt knew it was time to go. He looked over at the surfer he'd pulled out of the sea. The young man was smiling now; he offered the hang-loose sign: a twist of the wrist with his thumb and pinky extended.

Kurt returned the gesture and then turned to Ike. "The sea isn't the only thing that's unpredictable. Looks like I have work to do."

He pulled a black T-shirt over his shoulders and grabbed the backpack he'd brought with him. Hiking up toward the waiting SUV, he asked the obvious question. "So what can you tell me? Now that we're out of earshot."

Gunn shook his head. "Only the obvious," he said. "That time is of the essence."

Kurt figured Rudi knew more than that, but he was as tightlipped as anyone at NUMA. Being number one in your class at West Point tended to come with that kind of self-discipline. "Don't suppose I have time to shower and change?"

Gunn shook his head. "No, I don't suppose you do."

3

Rudi drove to Upolu Airport, a small strip on the northern tip of the island. A gleaming turquoise Gulfstream waited on the tarmac with engines running. It was a NUMA aircraft, one Kurt recognized as a model with extended range.

The aircraft was buttoned up as soon as Kurt and Rudi took their seats. Moments later, they were screaming down the runway. After a long takeoff roll, the Gulfstream clawed its way skyward and turned east.

As they climbed, Kurt stared out the window. Off in the distance he saw the dark clouds of the tropical depression that had sent the swells barreling to the shore. After a tip of the imaginary hat to the storm, he turned his attention back to Rudi.

Of all the men at NUMA, Rudi was the closest thing to an enigma. Now in his late forties, he had lost none of the intensity and precision that were his trademark. Fiery but close-lipped, Rudi could be jocular and fun but never quite let down his guard. His mind was always active. Even now, as he sat in silence contemplating whatever it was they would soon talk about, Kurt could sense that Rudi was planning, coordinating and rearranging things. He was a logistical genius with a knack for getting things set up in the most efficient order.

Kurt let him be. Twenty minutes went by before either of them spoke. "Are we going to see a flight attendant sometime soon? I could use a drink."

"You know alcohol is not allowed on NUMA aircraft anymore," Rudi said.

Kurt chuckled. *By the book, as always.* "I was thinking a bottle of water or a nice, cold Coke."

"Oh," Rudi said. "Sorry. Help yourself." He pointed to a fridge.

Kurt unbuckled his seat belt and went to the mini-fridge. He opened it and plucked two bottles of Coke from the back, where they'd be coolest. Glass, not plastic, and he noticed the fine print on the label. It was written in Spanish, suggesting the plane had been restocked somewhere south of the border. Turning the bottle in his hand, Kurt found the bottler's address, nodded to himself and closed the fridge.

He returned to his seat, opened both bottles and slid one toward Rudi. "Time to talk," he said. "Judging by the long takeoff roll and the slow climb, I can tell we're carrying a lot of fuel. By our course, I can safely assume we're not going to Oahu or Los Angeles; and by the wrinkles in your shirt, I'm assuming you've been on this plane a long time. Just came to get me and to bring me back, I'd suspect. So where are we headed? Somewhere in South America?"

Rudi was in the process of pouring the Coke into a glass as Kurt spoke. "South America?" he said. "Is that your guess?"

"It is."

"A rather large place," Rudi replied with a grin. "Maybe you'd care to be more specific."

Kurt hemmed and hawed for a second as though thinking deeply on the subject, though he already knew exactly what he was going to say. "Ecuador."

Gunn's eyebrows went up.

"Guayaquil," Kurt added, "to be precise."

Gunn looked truly shocked. "With all due respect to the great Johnny Carson, Carnac has nothing on you."

"Not really," Kurt said, grinning and pointing to the Coke bottle. "These were filled in Quito. But that's a landlocked city.

47

The largest port in Ecuador is in Guayaquil. And we tend to work on the sea."

"Hmm," Gunn said. "Not sure whether to be more impressed or less."

A red phone buzzed beside Gunn's chair. He picked up the receiver and listened for a moment. "We're ready," he said. "Put them through."

"If you're not giving the briefing, who is?"

"A colleague in the National Security Agency."

"Am I working for the NSA now?" Kurt asked. He'd been loaned out before.

"Not just you," Gunn replied. "Every NUMA ship and team member within five thousand miles."

Now Kurt's eyebrows went up. There could be only one reason for that. "They've lost something."

Gunn didn't confirm or deny. "I'll let them explain."

A flat-screen monitor on the bulkhead wall came to life. It displayed the confines of a briefing room with two men at a desk. The first was an Air Force officer with multiple ribbons on his blue jacket. The second wore a shirt and tie.

The man in the tie spoke first. "Good afternoon," he said. "My name is Steve Gowdy. I'm the director of ExAt projects for the National Security Agency."

"ExAt?" Kurt asked.

"Extra-atmospheric," Gowdy replied. "Basically, anything that takes place above the stratosphere. Including our satellite and maneuvering vehicle projects."

Kurt nodded to indicate he understood and Gowdy leaned toward the camera like a TV reporter on the evening news. "Before I begin, you have to understand that this project is of the utmost importance and is compartmentally classified on a highly restricted basis."

Kurt had heard this speech before. "There's not much in the NSA that isn't. But I understand."

Gunn cracked a smile, but Gowdy didn't seem to get the joke.

"We've had our project go off the wire at the last moment," Gowdy continued. "An experimental craft on a reentry profile over the South Pacific."

Kurt knew something about the NSA's space operations. "X-37," he said, referring to the well-known NSA craft that was launched on a rocket and returned to Earth by gliding back down similar to the space shuttle.

"No," Gowdy said. "A vehicle we call the *Nighthawk*. Its official designation is VXA-

01. It's the first of its kind. In a way, the X-37B was a prototype, a test bed used to develop certain technologies. The new craft is twice the size of the X-37 and far more capable."

"I'm impressed," Kurt said. "I've never heard of it. Not even a rumor."

"We've done our work keeping it quiet," Gowdy admitted. "By flying the X-37 under mysterious circumstances, we've been able to occupy the public's attention and give them something to be suspicious about. In the meantime, we've built *Nighthawk* and had it up in space for over three years. Unfortunately, it went off course on reentry and failed to answer commands."

"So . . . are we worried about losing the warp technology to the Klingons?" Kurt asked.

Gowdy sat in stony silence before answering. "There are no warp drives," Gowdy said without a trace of humor, "but the *Nighthawk* is the most advanced aircraft ever built. It was constructed with materials and technology that are two generations beyond anything the European, Chinese or Russian space agencies are using. It's a revolutionary aircraft. I say *aircraft* because it looks like a plane, but, make no mistake, it is a spacecraft, capable of maneuvering in orbit, acting autonomously and completing missions the shuttle never dreamed of. And while it doesn't have a *warp drive,* it does possess a revolutionary *ion propulsion system* that could be used for Earth–Moon travel and cut our transit time to Mars in half."

Kurt nodded. "And you want us to look for it."

"You'll be part of a team responsible for a specific sector in the search zone. Naval assets from Pearl and San Diego will be working close by."

As Gowdy spoke, Rudi Gunn unlocked a briefcase, pulled out a file and passed it to Kurt.

Using the edge of his palm, Kurt broke the imprinted seal. Inside, he found information about the *Nighthawk:* trajectory data, time sequencing and a map.

"As you can see," Gowdy continued, "we lost track of it halfway between French Polynesia and the South American coastline. Based on the last telemetry response, and the vehicle's speed and altitude, we believe it came down somewhere east of the Galápagos Islands."

Kurt studied a satellite photo with red lines overlaid upon it. The lines showed a widening cone of probability that began just east of the Galápagos. It stretched and widened in a sideways V toward Ecuador and Peru. A scale suggested the calculated odds of the *Nighthawk* coming down in any particular section.

"Does it have an emergency beacon?" Kurt asked, still studying the map.

"Yes," Gowdy replied, "but we're not receiving a signal."

"So we'll be looking for debris," Kurt concluded.

"No," Gowdy said firmly.

Kurt looked up.

"We have reason to believe the *Nighthawk* landed intact," Gowdy said.

Gowdy went on to explain the autoland system and how the internal processors would take over the flight controls once commands from the base at Vandenberg were cut off. He mentioned the word *confidence* at least three times but never gave a reason why the autoland system should be working when so many other systems on board had failed.

Kurt let it go. "What resources do we have for the job?"

At this point, Gunn took over the conversation. "Everything we could get our hands on," he said. "NUMA has three vessels in the area. One coming up from the Chilean coast and two coming through the Panama

52

Canal from the Gulf of Mexico."

Another sheet of paper came Kurt's way. It listed the various ships.

"Paul and Gamay Trout are already on the *Catalina*," Gunn said, referring to two of the most trusted members of NUMA's Special Projects team. "They were down off the coast of Chile doing an ecological study. They'll be within range in about fifteen hours."

"That's fortunate," Kurt said.

Rudi nodded. "The *Jonestown* and the *Condor* will transit the canal and arrive thirty-six hours later."

"Thirty-six hours sounds a little optimistic," Kurt said, looking at the relative positions of the ships. "It's nearly thirty hours' sailing time and the canal looks like a freeway at rush hour this time of year. Ships can wait as long as two days to transit."

"They're getting a priority hall pass," Rudi said. "Since NUMA helped prevent the destruction of the canal a few years ago, we've had a gold star status anytime we stop by."

"Ah," Kurt said, recalling hearing about the operation from Dirk Pitt himself. The fact that NUMA's Director had been personally involved in thwarting the destruction paid dividends to them all.

Gowdy broke in. "NUMA will be in charge of the southern and eastern patrol areas. In three days, a salvage fleet from the Navy's 131st Salvage Squadron will arrive from San Diego to search the western half of the target zone, while additional vessels from the Pacific Fleet will cover the western edge of the search area."

Kurt was looking at the list of vessels. Aside from two auxiliary ships out of San Diego, they were all warships. Destroyers and frigates. "What's with all the firepower?"

"Unintentional consequence of logistics," Gowdy said. "This section of the Pacific is a long way from everywhere. Forty-five hundred miles from Pearl. Twenty-nine hundred miles from San Diego. These were the closest, fastest ships equipped to search for underwater targets. Additional salvage vessels are following, but they can't keep up and are being left behind. In addition, P-3 Orion and P-8A aircraft are crisscrossing the search zone, dropping sonobuoys and other autonomous units to assist the search."

There was some logic to that, but it suggested panic. "That's a large fleet," Kurt said. "Are you sure that's the best way to do this?"

"What do you mean?"

Kurt closed the folder and leaned back in his chair. "I have to assume you want to keep this quiet. A dozen American ships and a swarm of aircraft surrounding the Galápagos Islands might be tipping your hand. The tortoises might think we're invading."

Gowdy nodded appreciatively on-screen.

Kurt made a suggestion. "We could always publish a story that NUMA's doing an ecological study. Put that out in the press and no one would think twice about a few extra research vessels moving into the area. Once they're on station, we could deploy their helicopters and survey boats and search to our hearts' content. All without drawing any attention to ourselves."

"Not a bad idea," Gowdy said. "Except we think the Chinese and Russian intelligence services are already clued in. Within hours of the *Nighthawk*'s vanishing, we noted course changes from several vessels belonging to each country. We're tracking them. I think you can figure out where they're headed."

"The Galápagos Islands," Kurt said.

"Exactly," Gowdy replied. "Right for the heart of our search area."

That suggested other complications. "Do you think they'll interfere?"

Gowdy shrugged. "I've given up trying to

55

predict what our Chinese and Russian friends will do. My job is to keep them from doing it. But after that mess in Ukraine and all the problems in the South China Sea, I don't put anything past anyone. And once you understand how badly they want what we have, you'll come to the same conclusion. According to our studies, the Russians have fallen so far behind in technology that they're in danger of getting lapped. The Chinese are a little better off because they have an army of engineers over there and more spies than you can shake a stick at — but they still operate without much ingenuity and are probably a full decade behind our latest designs. Add in the fact that both countries prefer to catch up by stealing what we have rather than coming up with their own ideas and you can imagine them licking their chops."

Kurt understood that concept quite well. Spying and stealing have always been a big part of Russian and Chinese research efforts. "There's a reason the Russian space shuttle *Buran* looks exactly like the one we designed. A reason their *Blackjack* bomber is almost indistinguishable from the B-1."

"Yes there is," Gowdy said. "In a way, I can't blame them. In their shoes, I'd do the same thing. But we're not in their shoes and there are no circumstances under which they're going to be allowed to get their hands on this vehicle."

"What if they find it first?" Kurt asked, wondering if Gowdy was talking about a shooting war.

"No circumstances," he repeated.

The words were cold and unyielding and Gowdy didn't bat an eye as he spoke them, but that brought to mind another question.

"So why didn't you just blow it up?" Kurt said, putting the folder away. "Prevent any chance of them finding more than a fragment of the hull?"

Gowdy looked stricken.

"I have to assume it had a self-destruct mechanism?" Kurt asked. "Why not blow it to pieces and avoid all this?"

"We tried," Gowdy croaked. "The self-destruct command failed. A review of the telemetry data shows a complete loss of communications just before the command was initiated."

"A game of inches," Rudi Gunn added. "Or fractions of a second."

Gowdy nodded.

Kurt turned his attention back to the effort. "How many ships are the Chinese and Russians sending?"

"We count nine Russian vessels, including

a few warships. Twelve Chinese ships. All military. Including their newly built aircraft carrier."

"Thirty ships, from three different countries," Kurt noted. "All desperately looking for the same thing in a fairly restricted area. What could possibly go wrong?"

"Anything and everything," Gowdy grunted. "We're in a race against time. Every day that craft is missing, the danger increases."

Something in Gowdy's tone struck Kurt oddly, as did the stony silence of the Air Force officer, who hadn't said a single word.

"We're the closest," Gunn said, jumping in. "NUMA will be on scene days before anyone else. I'll bet you a bottle of Don Julio tequila that NUMA locates the *Nighthawk* before either our Navy or the Russian and Chinese fleets."

Gowdy nodded appreciatively. "I'll see your bottle of Don Julio and raise you a box of Cuban cigars if you can find it before our adversaries arrive."

Kurt was listening and thinking at the same time. With only three ships, two of which wouldn't be there until at least a day after his own arrival, chances of success were slim. But then, Kurt had spent a lifetime figuring out ways to change the odds. As he studied the map, an idea jumped out at him, a way to up his chances and deal a blow to the Russian and Chinese fleets all at the same time.

He looked up with a roguish grin on his face. "In that case, someone better call Fidel and ask him to start picking out the best tobacco leaves on the island. Because if the *Nighthawk* is out there, I'm going to find it for you. And I'm going to do it before we see any foreign flags on the horizon."

Gowdy looked on blankly, probably considering Kurt's boast nothing more than a false bravado. But Kurt had an ace up his sleeve. An ace and an elephant.

4

Beijing, China

Constantin Davidov sat in the back of an American-made sedan as it moved along a crowded Chinese highway through a canyon of high-rise office towers built from Brazilian steel, Korean glass and cement imported from Australia.

Throngs of people moved along the sidewalks. Armies of them massed at each intersection like opposing battalions. They surged toward each other at the changing of a light but mixed and meshed and passed on through without incident as they traveled to a hundred different destinations.

Street vendors and shops by the hundreds catered to them with food brought in from the countryside. Construction engineers dug up the road to bury new pipelines that would feed the city's ever-growing need for water and natural gas, while smog from exhaust pipes and coal-fired power plants choked the air, blotting out the light of the noonday sun.

"How can you stand it?" Davidov muttered to himself.

A Chinese man sitting beside him overheard and looked appropriately offended. Li Ying was a liaison officer in the People's Liberation Army, a captain in a pea-green uniform with gold stars on his shoulder boards and a smattering of ribbons above his breast pocket. "This is globalism," Ying said. "The engine that drives the Chinese economy."

A look of disgust settled on Davidov's face. As far as he could tell, *globalism* and the interlinking of the world's economies was nothing but a disaster in the making, a disease slowly infecting the cells of the world's collective body. *Everything, everywhere, all the time.* At least that seemed to be the motto. Personally, he longed for simpler days.

The Chinese officer continued. "China has transformed in a single generation from a backwater land to a global powerhouse. We're very proud of what we've built."

"Pride goeth before the fall," Davidov said.

The sentiment was lost on his host. And why not? Why should Ling worry? He was twenty-eight. A captain in the army of an ascending nation. Like his country, Ling was bold and brash at this point in his life, undaunted by decades of work that might lead nowhere.

"At least we move forward," Ling said. "Russia seems to do nothing but regress these days."

Davidov couldn't argue with that. Forty years prior, he'd come to China with a group of Soviet officials. They found no cars on the street, few working phones and nowhere decent to stay — even by Moscow standards, which at the time were dreadfully low.

Back then, the Chinese bought Russian MiGs and patrol boats with borrowed rubles. Back then, Russian oil, coal and financial aid were a lifeline for Mao's hermit kingdom, but now . . . Now, even a pitiful, junior-grade officer could be rude to a Russian emissary.

The sedan pulled up to a modern, angular building. Walls of gray cement, broken by narrow, vertical bands of glass. The design was dramatic; it brought to mind a medieval castle, complete with slits in the wall for archers to fire through.

A white-gloved soldier stepped forward and opened the door. He stood at rigid attention as Ling climbed out and Davidov followed.

"This way," Ling said.

"I know where to go," Davidov said. "Stay with the car."

"Excuse me?"

"Trust me. This won't take long," Davidov said. "You can even keep the engine running," he suggested, glancing up to the brownish sky. "Add to your precious globalism."

A minute later, Davidov was inside the building, his shoes making distinctive clicks on the cultured granite floor of the Ministry building. He was ushered into a conference room. The man he'd come to see waited for him.

"You're free to speak in here," General Zhang, of the Chinese Ministry of State Security, insisted.

"Thank you for the reassurance," Davidov said. He was quite certain the room was bugged. It didn't matter. He had no intention of disclosing anything General Zhang didn't already know. "We have word on the American space plane," he announced. "Confirmation."

"And?" Zhang said excitedly. "What happened? Did the Americans regain control?"

"They tried," Davidov said. "But our

transmission was closer and more powerful than theirs. We overrode their commands. Unfortunately, it becomes difficult to ascertain what happened after that."

"Difficult?" Zhang crossed his arms. "Did the *Nighthawk* reach California or not?"

Davidov offered a subtle smile. "You know the answer to that as well as I do, Zhang: the craft did not make it home. But our team was unsuccessful in tracking it to a final location."

The two men stood quietly. The tall, lean Russian on one side, his shorter, stockier host on the other.

Davidov was a horseman whose ancestors had ridden the frozen tundra. He had long, flowing limbs and preferred speed and stealth over massed strength — a cavalryman at heart.

Zhang was shorter, stockier. His muscular build, thick neck and heavy hands creating the look of a powerhouse who could break down walls. A bulldog who moved with the grace of a tank, slowly but inexorably, grinding and pulverizing anything in its path.

Neither was superior or inferior to the other, but they were so different as to be opposites, unable to mix for long without combustion. It made everything tense.

"You expect me to believe that?" Zhang

said, a practiced edge in his voice.

Davidov sat down. "Not really. Though it is the truth. You had ships on the flight path. Spy trawlers in the area. You know as well as I do that the *Nighthawk* is invisible to radar."

"You must have some data," Zhang proposed, trying to pry anything out of the Russian. "Some suggestion to the ultimate outcome."

Davidov shrugged. "Perhaps. But if there is anything else, the men in Moscow have not seen fit to share it with me."

"Then why have you come?"

"To inform you that our partnership is over."

This time, Zhang seemed surprised. Score one for the swiftness of the cavalry.

"The mission has failed," Davidov added. "All our efforts have been for naught. So, I've been sent to officially dissolve our joint enterprise."

"Surely we don't need to part ways so quickly," Zhang said. "We could talk some more. Smooth out our differences. Over dinner, perhaps."

"I would enjoy that," Davidov said. "Except that, as we speak, your salvage vessels continue at flank speed toward the possible crash site."

"I don't know what you're talking about," Zhang replied.

"Then I suggest you contact your naval chief of staff."

Zhang's posture stiffened. "Perhaps you're right. It seems this latest *bout* of teamwork has outlived its usefulness."

"It was doomed from the start," Davidov said. "At least this way we have no spoils to argue over."

Zhang moved to the head of the table and slid some papers together in a folder. In truth, he was pleased. Freed of the Russian shackles, his men could go to work immediately with no need to hide in the shadow of the Bear. "So it's every nation for itself," he said. "I assume your ships will be looking for the wreckage?"

"Of course."

"As will ours," Zhang replied. "I can only hope there will be no conflict."

"I wouldn't expect any," Davidov said, standing and drawing himself up to his full height. "By the time your fleet reaches South American waters, the *Nighthawk* will be in a crate on its way to Moscow with a large red ribbon tied around it."

Zhang scoffed at the boast and pressed an intercom button on the conference table. It buzzed his assistant. "Comrade Davidov will be needing a ticket back to Moscow," he said. "Make sure it's first class, China Air."

Davidov offered a bow of thanks and then turned for the door. Both of them knew he wasn't going to Moscow.

5

Hiram Yaeger walked through the air-conditioned computer bay on the eleventh floor of the NUMA building before heading for home. He made the same checks every night and thought of himself as a ship's captain inspecting his vessel, but it was really just a habit born from the early days of computing when things were not as reliable.

Back when he'd first started, Yaeger had to check and reset huge reel-to-reel tapes and inspect processing connections by hand. When they first looked for bugs, it meant actual insects that had a habit of seeking out warm, dark places, getting themselves zapped on fragile micro electric circuitry and burning out what passed for microchips in the process.

Years later, it was all about mainframe processing loads and hardwired connections. Now the computers did it all themselves, speaking to each other through Wi-Fi, checking and rechecking their own performance against preset parameters. All Yaeger *really* had to do was to make sure no one had unplugged the system from the electrical outlet.

He checked anyway.

Satisfied that everything was in order he made his way toward the outer office. "Good night, Max," he said, speaking to the computer.

"Night and day are the same thing to me," the computer replied. *"Unlike you, I work twenty-four hours a day."*

Hiram had designed Max and the rest of the computers in NUMA's state-of-the-art processing center. Years before Siri had begun talking, Yaeger had given Max voice processing and interactive capabilities. Why he'd ever added a sense of humor, he didn't know.

"No one likes a computer with a smart mouth," Hiram said, pulling a light jacket over his shoulders and adjusting his wire-framed glasses.

"I don't have a mouth," Max pointed out. *"But your point is well taken. FYI: You have a visitor in the outer office. My sensors indicate Priya Kashmir has just used her badge to*

enter the room."

"Thanks, Max. See you tomorrow."

Hiram continued toward the outer office, grinning that he'd stumped Max by saying good-bye in a way Max could not correct or elaborate on. A small victory for the human race.

He stepped through the door and spotted a figure in a wheelchair waiting for him.

Priya Kashmir was Yaeger's new assistant. Born in southern India, raised in London, and schooled at MIT — where she'd graduated at the top of her class — Priya had been set to join one of NUMA's field teams when a three-car pileup left her paralyzed from the waist down.

NUMA had honored her contract despite her injuries, paid for her medical treatment and given her a pick of assignments including working in the field if she wanted, insisting they'd find a way to make it work.

By then, she'd already decided on a different path, asking if NUMA could use her skills in the computing department.

"Hello," she said cheerfully. "How are you this evening, Mr. Yaeger?"

Her accent was a mix of British and Indian, with the slightest hint of a Boston Yankee thrown in for good measure.

"Please stop calling me that," Hiram said.

"It makes me feel old."

"Because your father was Mr. Yaeger?"

"My grandfather."

She laughed, brushed a strand of mahogany hair from her face and handed him a note. "This just came in."

Hiram took the note. It was written in flowing script that could have passed for calligraphy. "Your Post-its should be in an art museum."

"I had a few minutes on my hands while I waited for the elevator," she said.

Hiram read the note. The message was far simpler than the writing. It was from Kurt Austin.

" 'Need you to make Dumbo fly,' " Hiram read aloud. " 'Use those big ears and find me a splash-down site. And I need it quickly. Otherwise, you're going to cost Rudi Gunn a bottle of Don Julio and box of hand-rolled Cuban cigars.' "

A puzzled look settled on Hiram's face. "Curious."

Priya had to agree. "I didn't understand when Kurt rattled it off in the first place," she admitted. "And I don't honestly understand it now. But Kurt insisted you would know what he meant. I assume it's some type of code."

Hiram sighed, took off his jacket and

71

draped it over the back of the chair. "Sort of. It's Kurtspeak for: can you pull an all-nighter and find me a miracle?"

"Really? What's the Dumbo reference? Isn't that a flying elephant from the Disney cartoons?"

"*D*ynamic *U*nderwater *M*onitoring *B*and," Hiram said. "We added the *O* for fun. It's a series of highly sensitive subsurface listening posts NUMA has set up throughout the Pacific. There are several hundred major stations and five thousand tethered buoys. They listen for seismic activity."

"P-waves and S-waves," Priya said.

Hiram nodded. "With DUMBO, we can detect a large earthquake and pinpoint its location far earlier than the existing tsunami monitoring network, but we're also able to monitor the smallest tectonic movements. Deep earthquakes that wouldn't wake a light sleeper if he was dozing next to the china cabinet. We learn a lot more about deep-earth geology that way. We can even predict when a big one is coming by the prevalence or absence of tiny tremors."

Priya nodded, but she still looked confused. "What does that have to do with his mission and why does he want DUMBO to fly?"

"The flying part is just Kurt being Kurt,"

Hiram explained. "He thinks he's funny. I warn you: *Do not laugh at his jokes.* It'll only encourage him and you'll never hear the end of them. But the idea is top-notch as usual."

From there, Hiram went on to explain about the missing *Nighthawk* and the rapid naval buildup to search for it. He tied the DUMBO project in as he finished. "Kurt wants us to listen to the tapes in case the seismic sensors picked up any sign of the crash. If they did, we can triangulate a location and save everyone a lot of time searching the South Pacific."

Priya's eyes seemed to catch the light as she smiled. "That's brilliant," she said. "If it works. Can seismic detectors really be that sensitive?"

Hiram hedged. "The network is far more sensitive than we thought it would be. We learned shortly after setting it up that other sounds from the ocean were being recorded. Subsurface mining off Taiwan, torpedo and artillery explosions at military test sites around the Pacific and even the last desperate groans of sinking ships. As those go down, they tend to break up, often accompanied by subtle explosions as the hull ruptures and trapped air is released. We were able to pinpoint the exact location of nine missing ships in the first six months of operations. But the *Nighthawk* is much smaller than your average seagoing vessel."

"Better than nothing," Priya said, grinning.

"Exactly," he said. "It's just unlikely to be easy, especially given this time frame."

She eased her chair forward. "How can I help?"

"The first thing we have to do is download all the recorded data," Hiram said. "Then we have to cross-reference it and begin the slow, painful process of weeding out the background noise, the magma and seismic activity that the sensors are designed to pick up and anything that doesn't emanate from the search area. After that, we have to identify and remove shipping static, biological sources of interference like whale songs and schools of tuna, and at least a hundred other extraneous forms of underwater vibration."

The lights in the office brightened and the coffeepot in the corner switched on automatically and started brewing.

"More precisely, he means I have to do all that," Max announced over a speaker. *"Looks like we're all working through the night together."*

Priya laughed. "I swear, sometimes she

misses you," she said.

Hiram noticed a sense of glee in the computer voice that he'd have sworn he never programmed into it. "Eavesdropping again, Max. That's another bad habit."

"All in the name of efficiency," Max replied. *"Seismic data accessed, commencing download. Also, please advise Kurt that machine-rolled cigars are every bit the equal of — if not superior to — human, hand-rolled products."*

Priya laughed. "Have you been smoking again, Max? You know that's a bad habit."

"No," Max said. *"Just stating a verifiable factual principle."*

Hiram chuckled. "You're an expert at most things, Max, but I'm going to leave cigars and liquor to Kurt."

"Very well," Max said. *"Beginning audio analysis."*

Hiram walked over to the coffeepot and poured two cups. When Max finished the grunt work, he and Priya would have to make the final choices regarding what frequencies would be allowed to remain in the recording. Not much to do until then.

"Cream and sugar?" he said to Priya.

"Two cubes, please. And, thank you."

Hiram dropped a sugar cube into the dark liquid. It made a tiny splash and almost no sound at all. The way he reckoned it, the *Nighthawk* parachuting into the ocean would do something similar, although it would be the equivalent of tossing a sugar cube into an Olympic swimming pool. He put their chances of hearing it, even with the network of sensors, at ten-to-one.

He dropped the second cube in, stirred the coffee and watched the small block of sugar dissolve and disappear. At least the *Nighthawk* couldn't do that.

6

After touching down in Ecuador, Kurt checked into the hotel and allowed himself a quick shower and a change of clothes. Refreshed, he caught a cab to a dockside warehouse on the outskirts of Guayaquil's bustling port.

Passing through a security checkpoint, he entered the cavernous building and quickly found his way to the section NUMA had taken over. There, hidden among towers of stacked shipping containers, he found a rack of hard-shelled diving suits, stacks of torpedo-shaped sonar emitters, a pair of small ROVs and several sleds with cameras and lights on them.

Perched in the center of this collection, like a mad scientist amid his creations, was Joe Zavala.

A few inches shorter than Kurt, Joe had dark, close-cropped hair, high cheekbones and deep, brown eyes that seemed soft and contemplative at times, fierce at others. As Joe moved among the crowded stacks of equipment with a checklist in his hand, he displayed the qualities of a cat. Never once looking up from the clipboard and yet never putting a foot wrong or hitting his head on the overhanging arms, jutting fins or brass propellers that surrounded him.

Joe had been Kurt's closest friend at NUMA for years. He was an amateur boxer, the most gregarious member of the Special Projects team and an avowed bachelor. He was also a mechanical genius and had built many of NUMA's more advanced submersibles.

"You look like the proverbial kid in the toy store," Kurt said, alerting Joe to his presence.

"It's a *candy store* in that proverb, amigo."

"So I did a little rewrite," Kurt said. "Looks like Rudi really came through. Where'd he get all this stuff? Aside from the hard suits, I don't recognize any of this equipment."

"You shouldn't," Joe said. "Those submersibles came from an oil exploration firm. These sonar buoys are cast-offs from the Ecuadorian Navy — I have no idea if they even work yet — and those camera sleds came from the movie company that produced *Megalodon Versus the Giant Squid.*"

"A classic, if ever there was one," Kurt said.

"So I've heard," Joe replied.

Kurt turned serious once more. "Rudi told me he'd chartered a group of fishing boats to supplement the fleet. I assume this equipment is for them?"

Joe nodded. "And I have twelve hours to get it all ready and send them out. At least we've got our own people flying in to run the systems once they're on board; otherwise, I'd have to teach everyone, too."

"The more ships we have in the water, the faster we'll cover the search area," Kurt said. "But we're going to need more than a fishing fleet to make this work."

Joe checked one more thing off of his list and put the clipboard down. "What do you have in mind?"

"How much do you know about the DUMBO project?"

"Big ears in the sea," Joe replied. "You think you're going to hear the *Nighthawk* going down?"

"I was told those sensors could hear a pin drop," Kurt said. "In this case, a fifty-billion-dollar pin that fell from outer space."

"That sounds like another bad movie,"

Joe said.

Kurt laughed. "The way I see it, if the *Nighthawk* hit the water hard enough, we might hear it. Even if it parachuted down and then sank, there are compartments that would implode from the pressure. The central core covering the cargo bay, fuel cells and control unit have been built to withstand a thousand atmospheres. Something about sending it to Venus one day. But there are other cavities that might rupture. Hollow spaces in the wings and tail. The wheel wells around the landing gear."

"Good point," Joe said. "On top of that, parts of the heat shield would have been hitting a thousand degrees or more shortly prior to touch down. There might be an identifiable hissing and cavitation as that surface came into contact with the water."

"Never thought of that," Kurt said. "This is why you're in charge of building and repairing things."

"So who's listening to the tapes?"

"Hiram and Max. I told him to contact you if he needs any more information."

"Contact me?" Joe said. "Why? What are you going to be doing?"

"I have to go meet a specialist from the NSA who'll be riding shotgun with us."

"Are we really getting a chaperone?" Joe asked.

"Looks that way."

Joe picked the clipboard up once again. "Well, that ought to slow our progress by at least fifty percent. What the guy's name?"

"Emily Townsend," Kurt said.

Joe's eyebrows went up. "Strange name for a guy. Bet he got teased a lot growing up."

Kurt laughed. "From the profile they gave me, I don't think *Ms.* Townsend gets teased much. Around the NSA, her nickname is *Hurricane Emma.*"

"You know what that means," Joe said. "Either we got stuck with her because we're the problem children or we got stuck with her because she is one and the Navy didn't want her on one of their ships."

"She's got a background NASA would kill for," Kurt said. "A job with Rockwell right out of school, designing propulsion systems. Three years with Jet Propulsion Laboratory, and then the last five with the NSA. She's definitely an expert in her field."

"An expert," Joe said sarcastically, "okay? I'm upping my estimate to a ninety percent reduction in progress."

Kurt checked his watch. "I'll do my best to charm her and turn her into an ally instead of an impediment. With a little luck, and some fine wine, all will turn out well. Trust me."

"You seem to be in a very good mood," Joe said. "Nothing gets your blood up like a challenge."

"Especially when someone else is doing all the hard work," Kurt said. "And all I have to do is charm an attractive woman."

"Good luck with that," Joe said, turning back to his inventory of equipment. "But be careful. Some icebergs can't be thawed."

Kurt left the warehouse and passed through the security gate unaware that he was being observed. Perched high in one of the over-sized mobile cranes that moved the shipping containers around the port, two men were watching, one through binoculars.

He lowered them, revealing dark eyes and little else. A filtered mask covered his nose and mouth, the kind some athletes wore while training in high pollution areas. His voice was muffled as he spoke through it. "When did they arrive?"

"Within six hours of the *Nighthawk* disappearing," the man beside him said. "They're already gathering equipment and chartering vessels to help them search."

The masked man stared at the activity

below him, like a chess master looking over the board. A slight wheezing could be heard in his lungs even with the filtered air to protect them. "The Americans reacted faster than even I expected."

"But you wanted them here," the second man said. "Didn't you?"

"Of course, but it'll do us no good if they learn too much too soon."

"We could slow them down," the second man suggested. "Damage some of their equipment, scare off the charters, so they have to find new boats."

The masked man pondered this and then shook his head. "Not the kind of delay we need. In fact, I think giving them a push rather than holding them back would better serve our plans. Are you still in contact with the Chinese?"

"Yes."

"Alert them to the presence of these Americans, suggest that they know something vital. Point out the array of equipment they've gathered. The Chinese agent's imagination will take it from there."

"And if the Chinese kill them? What then?"

"The American government will send replacements and the race will begin anew."

7

Emma Townsend sat in a cozy booth in the recesses of El Caracol, the four-star restaurant Kurt Austin had suggested as a meeting place.

Despite Joe's assessment, there was little about her that suggested ice or frost. In fact, warmth was the first thought her appearance brought to mind. Her auburn hair fell straight to her shoulders and shimmered with a copper hue in the subdued lighting. Her eyes were a soft, hazel color, flecked with green, her lips full and her skin just sun-kissed enough to bring out a smattering of freckles that made her look younger than her thirty-three years.

Entering the restaurant early and waiting for Kurt, she'd already garnered her fair share of second glances and lingering stares. She noticed the gazes but ignored them. It was no worse than Washington.

The restaurant itself was an architectural

delight. Its design brought together several styles much the same way the menu did, and the clientele was a mix of hip, bohemian customers, obvious tourists and refined Ecuadorian couples. Perhaps that was due to its location in the hills of Las Peñas, a four-hundred-year-old section of Guayaquil, where brightly painted houses had been turned into art galleries, restaurants and wine bars.

Tourists and locals alike flocked there on warm evenings. They strolled the boulevards and galleries and enjoyed the views, which overlooked the city and the coastline. As night fell, the lights of the Malecón, a restored promenade on the waterfront that had once been the historic Simón Bolívar Pier, came into view.

With only a glass of water in front of her, Emma waited for Kurt and reread the NSA bio that had been sent to her phone.

A quick look told her Austin was a man of action. He and his second-in-command, Joe Zavala, were listed as the principal figures in a series of high-profile missions. They'd averted several international catastrophes, including the recent events in Egypt, where they'd prevented former members of the Mubarak regime from co-opting the sub-Saharan aquifer and establishing authority across all of North Africa.

Further reading made it clear that despite this record, both Austin and Zavala had rubbed plenty of officials the wrong way. It seemed they were not fond of authority, chains of command or doing things by the book. Perhaps that explained his position with NUMA, she thought. NUMA had always preferred to shoot from the hip, right from the day James Sandecker had founded it. Men like Kurt thrived there, while in other agencies they were shackled and held back.

Just as well, she decided. She preferred results over protocol. In fact, she preferred results over everything, including personal friendships, alliances and rules. This had made her something of an outcast in her years at the National Security Agency. It had also vaulted her up the chain of command as quickly as it made enemies. She knew her reputation. Few in the agency wanted to work with her. They were governed by fear, afraid to fail. Afraid to take a chance. In her opinion, it made them ineffective. Which made it far preferable to work with a man like Austin.

If she found the *Nighthawk* with his help, she would be untouchable. She could name her next position, most likely becoming the youngest department director in the agency's history. And if she failed . . . well, the odds were stacked against her anyway. And she could always blame it on NUMA.

She spotted Kurt as he entered the restaurant and spoke briefly with the host. From there, he walked directly to her table, seeming taller and more handsome than his photographs. It wasn't that his features were any different; if anything, they were a little more careworn and weathered, like a book cover that was slightly tattered and broken-in.

She put her phone away and introduced herself. "Emily Townsend. You can call me Emma. Pleased to meet you," she said. "Finally."

Austin sat down. "Sorry to keep you waiting," he said. "I was checking on the preparations."

"How much equipment do we have?" she asked.

"I meant, in the kitchen," he said. "I was making sure the chef was up to standards."

He grinned at his own comment and Emma found his self-assurance a most attractive quality. One that could be used to manipulate, if need be. The small talk continued until the waiter arrived.

"Any preference?" he asked, perusing the

wine list.

"Surprise me."

He closed the list. "We'll have a bottle of the 2007 Opus 1."

"Excellent choice," the waiter said, moving off to retrieve the selection.

"An extravagant bottle of wine on the first night," Emma noted. "Your expense account or mine?"

"I'll pay this time," Kurt said. "Save yours for the big stuff."

She couldn't resist smiling at his easy way and had to keep reminding herself why they were there. Before anything else was said, she pulled a small device from her purse. It was triangle-shaped, several inches long. She placed it on the table. At the touch of a button, it began emitting an audible hiss of static.

"Active noise cancellation," she said, easing the device to the edge of the table. "It listens to our words and distorts them with interfering frequencies as they pass out of this cozy little booth. Anyone trying to record or eavesdrop on us will pick up nothing but garbled static."

"What about a bug on or under the table?" he asked.

"I've already swept for it. Trust me, we can talk freely."

He seemed only half convinced, and based on their conversation throughout dinner, perhaps less than that.

She noticed that he kept glancing around, eyeing everyone in the restaurant, in particular a Chinese couple who had arrived shortly after he had and were now sitting directly across the main room. Every time she was about to get into specifics, he changed the subject to something innocuous. At one point, when she was ready to force the subject, he offered her a bite of his entrée, holding out a fork toward her.

She accepted and changed the subject. He must have his reasons.

"So how did you end up in NUMA after working for the agency?" she asked.

"Admiral James Sandecker shanghaied me," he said. "That's how he gathered all his best people."

Sandecker was now the Vice President. She was impressed that Austin knew him well enough to joke about him. And that he hadn't name-dropped him earlier.

"And how did a sworn pacifist end up at the NSA?" he asked.

"I see you have your own sources."

"In low places," he insisted.

"I was a pacifist," she insisted. "That's why I joined NASA. To better the state of humanity by exploring the universe in the name of peace. Unfortunately, life doesn't conform to the ideas of a naïve twenty-four-year-old. Not for long anyway."

"Something go wrong in paradise?"

"Doesn't it always?"

He offered a wry smile, obviously waiting for more.

"After a year at NASA, I was selected for a new team," she said. "A follow-up to the relatively famous Daedalus project, which hoped to use nuclear explosions or some other form of exotic propulsion like matter-antimatter combustion to power future spacecraft at tremendous speeds. Much faster than we can achieve with chemical rockets. It was exciting. Intoxicating, really. The project demanded long hours, at close quarters. And as you might expect, with eight people spending almost all their waking time together, we became a very tight-knit group. Then, out of the blue, we began receiving threats."

"Because of the work?"

"Apparently," she said. "A fringe group I'd never heard of began accusing us of militarizing space. At first we thought it was a bunch of nonsense. But the threats became deeper, more personal. We were sent pictures of ourselves in vulnerable areas, in our houses, in our cars, at restaurants with our colleagues. Whoever these people were, they were obviously stalking us."

"I assume the FBI got involved," he said.

"They did. And they were able to link the threats to an anti-American group that had killed two scientists in the Arctic and sent letter bombs to several high-tech companies. We thought with the FBI on the case, we'd be safe. Two weeks later, our team leader and a friend — a man named Beric — was killed."

Across from her, Kurt nodded thoughtfully but said nothing.

"Beric was an incredibly kind man," she told him, surprised at the emotion it brought up after all these years. "If anyone needed anything, right down to the cafeteria workers and janitors, he made sure they had it. If there was an underdog cause without much hope, he championed it. And he was brilliant. A genius in several fields, everything from software development to astrophysics. Above all else, he was committed to NASA's mission of peace, committed to a world where all men and women treat each other with decency."

She took a deep breath, gathered herself and then continued. "That someone would target him, accuse him of being a militarist and kill him for it, was a disgusting irony. It affected me. Lifted the blinders from my eyes. It proved to me that the pacifist mind-set is nothing but a childish dream. Peace is fragile, not a natural state. It can only be secured through strength. And when that strength fails, disaster ensues."

"In many ways, I'd agree with that," he said. "Mind if I ask how it happened?"

"Like many of us at NASA, Beric loved to fly. He owned his own plane. Took it up every chance he could. If we had to go somewhere, he'd fly himself instead of going commercial. One day, on the way to an astrophysics conference, his plane exploded. From the wreckage, the FBI was able to determine what we already knew: the explosion was caused by a bomb. Three of us were supposed to be on that plane. But, as it turned out, Beric went alone."

"I'm sorry," Kurt said.

"Anyway," she continued, "the propulsion study was cancelled a short time later and the whole project was eventually shut down. Feeling like I was drifting, I began casting around for something else to do. When the National Security Agency began recruiting scientists for their space program, I jumped at the opportunity."

He nodded thoughtfully and then changed

the subject to something more cheerful. But even as he spoke, her mind lingered on Beric. She hadn't thought of him in years. He wouldn't have approved of her career change.

She shook off the thought and focused on Kurt once more. They continued to chat and enjoy the meal. Halfway through the second glass of wine, he paused midsentence and then pulled his phone from his pocket to study a text that had just come in.

"Checking your phone," she said. "Am I really that dull?"

"Anything but," he said, putting the phone away. "In fact, I think it's time to see how adventurous you truly are." He slid the triangular, noise-cancelling device toward her, pulled out several hundred dollars in cash and flagged the waiter down. "For the meal. And a tour of the kitchen."

The waiter examined the cash briefly. Then he smiled and said, "This way."

Emma stood and went along with whatever Austin was up to. If anything, she was interested in seeing how his mind worked.

They followed the waiter through the kitchen and out the back door, where Kurt gave the waiter another instruction. "Block this door for a few minutes, if you can.

Don't let anyone follow us."

The waiter nodded and Kurt led her out into a dimly lit alley behind the restaurant.

"I think you've got this backward," she said. "People normally sneak out of a restaurant when they realize they can't pay, not after overpaying. And never before dessert."

"We were being watched," he said, leading her down the alley toward the main street.

"We're American agents operating without cover in a foreign country," she said, "of course we're being watched. I'm sure the Ecuadorian government is following us, especially considering our last-minute travel and sudden arrival."

"These weren't Ecuadorian police or federal agents," he insisted. "It was a young Chinese couple. They were waiting at the door and took a booth directly across from us. They never touched their food."

"Chinese couple," she said, remembering their features. "I saw them. Not a big surprise either. We know the Chinese are looking. But I promise you, no one could hear what we were saying as long as the interference processor was running. Our best people haven't been able to crack it."

He stopped. "They didn't have to hear what you were saying. They were reading your lips."

She froze for a second, trying to remember anything she might have accidentally said and suddenly thankful that he'd interrupted her at every turn. "I was wondering why you kept asking me to try your dinner, even though we ordered the same thing."

"Less talk, that way," Kurt said. He continued to lead her down the street.

"I'm still not sure why we left," she said. "If you knew they were watching us, it might have been a good chance to plant some false information."

"Not a bad idea," he admitted, "but I'm more concerned with real information, some of which I've just received. And I'm not interested in letting them get their hands on it."

"What kind of information?" she asked.

"The whereabouts of the *Nighthawk*," Kurt said. "I know where it landed."

She looked at him suspiciously. "Impossible."

"Not the exact point. But I can narrow it down to less than a hundred square miles."

"How?" she said.

He stopped in his tracks but didn't say a word. At the end of the alley, a trio of men had suddenly appeared. They stood there implacably, waiting under a streetlight and

95

blocking the path.

Emma eyed them. "Something tells me they're not tourists."

"I'd have to agree," he said, looking around. "And they seem to have brought some backup."

At the sound of a commotion, Emma turned around and glanced down the alley. The rear door of the restaurant had come flying open. The Chinese couple came rushing out, the man shouting something at the kitchen staff. The argument ended when he pulled out a gun and fired into the doorway. The staff scrambled to safety and the door was slammed shut.

"Didn't count on them having backup," Kurt said, "and probably shouldn't have counted on a waiter keeping two armed agents from making it through the back of the house."

"Are you armed?" Emma asked.

"Afraid not," he said.

"Me neither," she replied. "Not exactly an auspicious start to our relationship."

In simultaneous precision, the two agents at the back of the restaurant and the three new arrivals began to close in on them from opposite sides.

8

Kurt held on to Emma's hand — as he had since they'd left the restaurant. He'd hoped to outflank the Chinese and get back to the boulevard and hail a taxi. But the additional Chinese agents had cut them off.

"Now what?" Emma asked.

The two groups were closing in slowly, moving relentlessly toward their prey, as if they were afraid any quick action might offer a weakness or a break in their lines for Kurt and Emma to escape through.

"I almost wish they'd rush," Kurt said. "At least we might be able to throw them off balance."

"Think they'll shoot us?"

Kurt shook his head. "Not to kill. More likely, they'd rather capture us and torture us until we reveal everything we know."

"How comforting," she said. "Tell me you have a plan?"

Kurt's eyes darted around. He saw a thin

gap between two of the buildings almost directly across from them, but it was so narrow that he'd have to squeeze through to make it. And even from this distance he could see obstructions and cables in the way. If they were held up, they'd be instant easy targets.

He glanced to the left, where a trash dumpster with a closed lid stood in the dark. The roof of the building behind was reachable. "Can you climb?"

"And run and punch, if I have to."

"Perfect," he said. "Follow me."

Kurt raced to the dumpster with Emma right beside him. He gave her a boost and then climbed up beside her. Out in the alley, the Chinese agents delayed for a second and then started to charge.

"Keep going," Kurt said.

Emma kicked off her shoes, reached for the edge of the low-slung roof and pulled herself up without needing any help. Kurt came up beside her.

"Get to the front. Look for a cab," he said.

"What are you going to do?"

"A holding action."

She left Kurt and sprinted up toward the peak of the building, staying low in case the Chinese agents started shooting.

Kurt lay flat on the roof and waited for

their pursuers to arrive. The loud metallic banging of someone climbing on the dumpster came a few seconds later. Hands appeared on the edge of the rooftop, and then a face, as one of the Chinese men pulled himself up.

Kurt thrust a foot forward, slamming his heel into the man's face. Blood spurted from a shattered nose and the man's head jerked back. He fell, taking his partner to the ground in the process.

Without waiting for a rematch, Kurt turned and raced up toward the top of the roof and went over the other side. Emma was crouching there, waiting for him.

"I don't see any cabs," she said.

"A little late to call Uber."

They jumped down together, landing solidly on the deserted front walk. Almost immediately, the trio of men who'd been at the far end of the alley came racing back out onto the main boulevard and sprinted toward them.

"Go," Kurt yelled.

They ran across the street and this time several shots came their way. No loud concussions, just soft pops from well-suppressed handguns, the impacts marked by a sudden shattering of car windows parked on the far side of the road.

Kurt dove across the hood of a classic BMW 2002 and took cover as the well-preserved machine took the brunt of a minor onslaught.

At the sound of the shooting, the few people still out on the street raced for cover.

"I thought you said they wouldn't shoot us?" Emma asked.

"It must be plan B: Target elimination."

To see without exposing himself to a well-placed shot, Kurt ripped the mirror off the side of the car. "Sacrilege," he whispered as he vandalized one of his favorite old machines.

Using the mirror as a periscope, he said, "They're surrounding us again."

"Can you hot-wire a car?"

"Not in the blink of an eye," Kurt said. "Especially with people shooting at me."

He looked down the street. A pair of buses idled at a quiet stop beside the next intersection. "How to feel about public transportation?"

"It'll do in a pinch."

"Let's see if we can make the crosstown express," Kurt said.

They darted from the cover of the old BMW, cut diagonally across the lawn of a small church and ran toward the idling buses.

"Yuck," Emma gasped as she ran.

"What?" Kurt said.

"Wet grass, bare feet."

At least she didn't slow down.

They reached the bus stop just as the lead bus began to move out. Kurt crashed through the door with Emma right behind him. The driver instinctively slammed on the brakes.

Kurt lunged forward, pulled him from the seat and stomped on the gas pedal. The big diesel engine roared and the bus lurched forward and began to pick up speed. Kurt grabbed the wheel and steered to the left.

Behind him, the driver had pulled a can of Mace and aimed it. Kurt shut his eyes, turned away and kept his foot on the gas. A commotion followed and a loud thud. When Kurt looked up, Emma had disarmed the bus driver, flung him to the ground and taken possession of his spray can.

"Nice work," Kurt said.

She brandished the Mace in the driver's direction and pointed. He looked and then moved back to the first open seat.

"No vamos a hacerle daño a nadie," Emma said in fluent Spanish. *"Estamos trabajando para el gobierno."*

Kurt continued to drive the bus, swinging wide around a corner and down the next street. The crowd stayed put. The murmuring didn't end, but there were no uprisings. "What did you tell them?"

"I said we're not going to hurt anyone and that we're working for the government," she explained. "It's true, if you think about it. I just didn't specify which government."

"Works for me," Kurt said, rotating the big steering wheel and guiding the bus down the road. The big rig was surprisingly easy to drive as long as he went straight. How the drivers traversed narrow cobblestone streets without taking out parked cars and the corners of buildings, Austin couldn't imagine.

And after a mile, they'd reached the outskirts of Las Peñas. Kurt figured they'd left the Chinese agents far enough behind. He began to slow, easing over to the shoulder and looking for a place to park.

A sudden jolt from behind whiplashed his neck and sent shivers through the bus. The passengers screamed and several were thrown from their seats. Emma fell against the front window before regaining her balance.

Stomping on the gas instinctively, Kurt checked the mirror. The problem was obvious: a second bus had raced up behind with its lights off and rammed them. It was now maneuvering to pull alongside. Kurt swerved to cut it off and kept accelerating, but they failed to leave the other bus behind.

"Modelo nuevo," the bus driver shouted to Kurt. *"Más rápido."*

Emma explained. "He says that the other bus is a newer model and much faster."

"I got the gist," Kurt said, trying desperately to keep the other bus from getting beside them.

The two traveling monoliths continued to accelerate, roaring down the dark street and away from the brightly lit Las Peñas section of town. Other cars swerved from the road to get out of the way and Kurt accidentally took out a line of newspaper machines on the edge of the sidewalk, scattering a hundred copies of *El Telegrafo, El Universo* and *El Metro* into the air.

They careened through an intersection to a chorus of horns and onto a more deserted stretch of road that led down the hill and out toward the coast. With the pedal floored and heading downhill, the bus began to shudder; it wasn't built for speed.

"They're coming again!" Emma shouted.

Another hit from their pursuer rocked the bus. A third ramming attempt almost forced them off the road.

Fighting for control, Kurt had to slow

down. In response, the other bus raced up beside them and swerved. The two buses crashed together, windows shattered and the passengers screamed. Some dove to the floor, others began to pray.

If there was going to be a beating, Kurt preferred to dish it out rather than take it. "Get everyone on the left side," he shouted.

Emma waved the passengers over. Once they'd taken new seats, Kurt rolled the wheel to the right. The buses crashed together again and separated and the newer model fell back.

As they reached a long straight section of road, it came up once again. This time, Kurt glanced at the driver. It was the Chinese man with the bloodied nose.

"Hang on," Kurt said, expecting another cross-check.

Instead of hitting him, the other driver just pulled close and held formation. Two heavy thumps sounded on the roof above them.

"We've been boarded," Kurt said.

One set of dents appeared directly above him and Kurt knew what was about to happen. He dove from the driver's seat as a collection of holes appeared in the sheet metal above and a spray of bullets perforated the seat and the dashboard where he'd been sitting.

Lunging to the floor, he slammed his palm into the brake pedal.

The air brakes clasped the wheels at full strength and the bus went into a skid. The man flew off the roof and landed on a spiked fence. Skewered, he passed from view.

Kurt jumped back into the driver's seat as a second man swung down from the roof, his hands grasping the luggage rack. He came in from the side, kicking the door open and grabbing for Kurt's throat.

Emma nailed him in the thigh with her knee. He fell back and she blasted him in the eyes with a burst of the pepper spray. He covered his eyes and dropped into the fetal position. She promptly kicked him out through the door.

"Cambio exacto," she said.

To Kurt's surprise, the passengers cheered.

"Exact change," she said. "He didn't have it. So I had to kick him off the bus. Get it?"

Guiding the bus through a sweeping, high-speed turn, Kurt laughed. "We're going to have to work on your delivery. But great work."

For the next mile, Kurt was able to keep

the other bus well behind them, but when the road straightened, the bus closed in once again. Another slam from behind almost sent them down the embankment, while the lights of the Malecón, and a sign depicting a boat being pulled out of the water by a trailer, whipped past.

"We're running out of road," Emma said. "Unless you can make this thing swim, we're going to need an exit strategy."

"That's a brilliant idea," Kurt said.

"No, actually, it wasn't," she said.

"Seriously, it's genius," Kurt replied.

"But buses don't swim."

"Exactly!"

Kurt slowed around the next turn and edged to the left. The other bus pulled up once again, dutifully taking the right side. It came over and hit them once. Then did so again. Kurt held his ground and waited until he saw the opening for the boat ramp.

Spotting it, he turned hard and held it. The two buses locked together, sections of sheet metal tearing loose and scraping the road.

Racing forward with a trail of sparks flaring out behind them, they came to the Y junction and the boat ramp.

Kurt gave the other bus a final shove and then spun the wheel back to the left. As the two buses separated, the one driven by the Chinese agent went down the boat ramp. The driver locked up the brakes, but the bus skidded on the wet, angled surface and slammed into the bay. A sheet of water flew up and crashed down around it. When the bus came to a stop, two-thirds of it was submerged.

Kurt brought his vehicle under control and continued down the road. Less than a mile later, he pulled into a bus stop on the outskirts of the Malecón.

Several people scattered, in shock at the condition of the bus. As Kurt parked, one of the front tires blew and the entire bus tilted to the side. Broken windows and paneling swung back and forth while chunks of glass dropped to the floor. When the air brakes hissed to release their pressure, the old bus gave up the ghost.

Kurt opened the door and waved a hand toward it as if delivering his passengers on a daily run. "Welcome to the Malecón. Watch your step."

The passengers just stared at him with blank and confused expressions. "Tough crowd," he said, switching the sign up front to: *Sin Servicio — Out of Service.*

He and Emma stepped off the bus together and made their way toward the crowd of tourists down below on the promenade.

"Think they'll be back?" Emma asked, looking toward the boat ramp.

"Not tonight," Kurt said. "If they're not injured, they're probably running and hiding, like we should be doing. But I'm assuming your NSA friends can get us out of any trouble we encounter."

"I think we'll be okay," she said. "So how'd I do?"

"Not bad, for a rookie," he said.

"Not bad?" she replied. "I totally saved you from some Mace in the face. *And* I got rid of the guy who tried to Tarzan into our crosstown express."

Kurt laughed and the two of them eased into the flow of people, disappearing into the crowd and making their way to a secluded spot farther down on the pier.

"Okay, you did great," Kurt admitted. "Just don't let it go to your head."

"I won't," she promised. "As long as I get appropriate credit in your report."

"I'll make you look good," he said, "which won't be hard to do. But if you really want a gold star, you're going to have to take another risk. One that most of your NSA coworkers would have a meltdown even contemplating."

She narrowed her gaze, looking suspicious and excited all at the same time. "And that step would be . . ."

Kurt pulled out his phone, double-checked the message from Hiram Yaeger and made up his mind. "We need to steal our own equipment and go rogue for a while."

"Because stealing a bus wasn't enough excitement for one night?"

"We're being watched," he said. "The group we met tonight aren't the only agents we're going to have to deal with. And our problems won't end when we get to the open sea. According to a few satellite photos I looked at before dinner, some awfully suspicious-looking trawlers are already following the *Catalina* and our other vessels."

"Chinese spy trawlers with tall masts and lots of antennas," she said. "I already know about them. But none of that matters if we can find the *Nighthawk* and pull it off the bottom before their salvage fleet gets here."

"Which would be great if it was just sitting down there ready to be picked up like a stuffed bear in a carnival game. But I have information suggesting it didn't come down in one piece like your people think it did. In fact, it's probably sitting on the bottom in several large pieces and a thousand small ones."

She folded her arms across her chest, a faraway look that suggested she was calculating something. "Our people are adamant that the *Nighthawk* did not break up."

"And my people have audio recordings from underwater listening posts that pinpoint an impact four minutes and seventeen seconds after you lost track of the *Nighthawk*. The particular sound signatures suggest a high-speed surface impact, midfrequency noise consistent with sudden generation of superheated steam — which is to be expected when a thousand-degree surface touches seventy-degree waters — and low-volume implosions at deeper depths consistent with wreckage breaking up."

"Where?" she asked.

"Approximately fifty miles east of the Galápagos Islands chain," Kurt said. "Right in the heart of your probability cone."

"How sure are you?"

"Certain enough to risk a case of Don Julio tequila and a box of Cuban cigars," he said. "Trust me, this information is not wrong. Our subsurface listening posts are more advanced than the Navy's SOSUS line and our computers, and the guy who built them, are one of a kind."

She seemed almost convinced. "Share it with the NSA's central office and we'll confirm. I promise you'll get the credit."

"I don't care about credit," he said. "And telling anyone at the NSA would be a major mistake."

For the first time, she looked angry. "You're working for us, remember?"

"Sure," Kurt said. "But what about everyone else who's working for you? Are you willing to bet no one's moonlighting?"

By the look on her face, she obviously got the implication. She clenched her jaw and stared at him, and Kurt wondered if Hurricane Emma was about to make an appearance. "What are you getting at?"

"We've only been here for six hours, we've already been followed and attacked. There's a Chinese spy trawler following the *Catalina* and it's officially still doing an environmental survey. By the look of things, the Chinese are aware of every move we make almost before we make it. That tells me we have a leak."

"It might not be the NSA," she suggested. "How can you be sure NUMA doesn't have a mole hiding in the woodwork somewhere?"

"I can't," he admitted. "That's why we tell no one about our next move. Not

NUMA, not the NSA, no one. It's the only way to be sure this information doesn't end up in the daily briefing in Shanghai."

She looked him in the eye. Once she'd accepted his logic, the path became clear. Her lips curved into a knowing smile. "Okay," she said. "So we go rogue. I must admit, it has a certain appeal. Count me in."

"Fantastic," he said. "Now . . . all we need is a helicopter and a ship big enough to operate from. One they would never suspect us to be using."

9

The NUMA vessel *Catalina* continued through the night on a northerly heading, traveling at full speed. Two hundred and sixty feet long, the *Catalina* was sleek for a research vessel and she took to the high-speed run well, cutting through the waves and rolling only slightly with the crossing swells.

Gamay Trout was thankful for the ship's stability as she walked from the communications room to the bridge with an odd message to deliver.

Five foot ten and willowy in build, Gamay had dark red hair with a rich and ever-changing luster; her eyes and easy smile suggested a tough playfulness, brought about from growing up as a tomboy. She

113

spoke in a clear, concise way, with few wasted words, a pattern she'd been told came from an uncluttered mind that moved with effortless speed.

At any rate, she had a never flagging sense of urgency that had earned her several degrees, including a Doctorate in Marine Biology and a Master's in Marine Archaeology.

Most men found her attractive, but not in a superficial way that faded over time. The more time they spent with her, the more impressed they were, partly because she put them at ease. It was a gift, one she was trying to summon as she approached the bridge with a directive that had just come in from Kurt Austin.

She smiled as she entered the bridge, spotting Ed Callahan, the *Catalina*'s captain, his executive officer — or XO — and her husband, Paul, conversing near the radar scope.

"Good evening," Callahan said. "Sorry I've kept Paul up here for so long. We're discussing the scuttlebutt surrounding our change of plans. The fact that we were ordered off a study we'd spent five months prepping for has a few people concerned."

She raised a single eyebrow. "Gossiping around the watercooler and I wasn't invited?

Shame on both of you."

"Inexcusable," Callahan replied. "Consider this an official request to join our party."

The captain made space in the group for her to join and she slid in next to her husband. Paul was a towering man of six foot eight who spoke seriously and quietly. Gamay had met him at Scripps Institute, where Paul was getting his own Ph.D. in Ocean Sciences. They'd married soon after and had been inseparable ever since. After joining NUMA together and becoming part of the Special Projects team on the same day, rumor had it working together had been written into their employment contracts.

"Any idea what's going on?" Callahan asked.

"Not really, but . . ."

Ever the voice of reason, Paul spoke up. "I told everyone to expect the unexpected when Kurt's involved. Though I'm sure it won't be anything too crazy."

Gamay took a deep breath. "I wouldn't put money on that."

Callahan noticed the dispatch in her hand. "What have you got for me?"

She handed Callahan the printed request and explained the order that had come in as calmly as possible.

His tone changed instantly. "They want us to do *what?*"

"To dump our best submersible overboard and leave it behind," Gamay repeated.

Callahan looked at Paul for some assistance. Paul held up his hands as if to say it had nothing to do with him.

"But that's absurd, on the face of it," Callahan said. He was a two-year NUMA veteran, with stints in the Navy and Merchant Marine before that. He'd been on the receiving end of strange and questionable orders before, but this topped them all. "The *Angler* is a thirty-million-dollar machine," he reminded everyone. "It's not some old rust bucket you sacrifice to Poseidon."

"Did anyone explain why?" Paul asked. "Are we getting a tax write-off?"

Gamay shook her head and read out the order word for word. "Per Kurt Austin, Director of Special Projects. Immediate directive. Under cover of darkness, submersible NSV-2 (*Angler*) is to be launched unmanned. Ensure all systems are fully charged and set depth to one hundred feet. Program the autopilot to surface the vessel in two hours. Immediately upon launch of *Angler, Catalina* is to change heading and proceed east, directly toward the Guaya river mouth, and await further orders. Be aware, *Catalina* is under surveillance. Make all efforts to conduct launch without drawing attention to your actions. Do not report launch of *Angler* to NUMA HQ. Do not reference this order on standard radio channels."

"Are we sure this came from Kurt?" Callahan asked.

Gamay nodded. "When I double-checked, I was told to *Make sure the lid was screwed on tight and don't get the velour seat covers wet.*"

Paul laughed. "That's Kurt, all right."

The XO chimed in. "Maybe we should check with Rudi Gunn anyway. Just to be safe."

Gamay shook her head. "Trust me. You could call Rudi Gunn, Director Pitt or Vice President Sandecker himself and you'll get the same answer from all three: *If that's what Kurt wants, that's what Kurt gets.*"

Callahan glanced at the navigation panel and the chronometer. It was after ten p.m. The Moon would be up in an hour.

"No time like the present," he said, turning to the XO. "Issue the men night vision goggles and keep the deck lights off. Check the tech manuals and make sure dropping the *Angler* over the side at our current speed won't damage her. Otherwise, we'll slow down, make our turn and drop the penny then."

"Yes, sir," the XO said. "I can only imagine what they'll ask for next."

"I'm sure it won't get any crazier than this," Callahan insisted.

Neither Paul nor Gamay commented, but they shared a knowing look. If history was any guide, Callahan would probably be proven wrong.

While Gamay returned to the communications room, Paul went with the deckhands to oversee the launching — or perhaps discarding — of the submersible.

Working on the fantail of the ship moving at full speed was not an easy task under the best of circumstances. Operating under blackout conditions with night vision goggles made it a surreal sight. The view was slightly distorted, and the sky was now lit by thousands of stars the naked eye could never spot, but the sea remained black and cold.

Despite the conditions, the crew operated smoothly and efficiently, with Paul stepping up to work the heavy crane himself.

The XO soon joined him. "The quick-release hooks have been set. Feel free to lift away. Also, per the specs, the *Angler* should be fine dropping into the water at this speed."

"Expected nothing less," Paul said, "considering Joe Zavala designed it."

Joe was a top-notch engineer, he tended to overbuild, making things far stronger than they had to be. A fact that had saved NUMA crews on more than one occasion.

The crane came to life and the white-painted submersible with a broad red stripe across its back rose up off the deck. As the boom extended, Paul noticed a problem. "We're going to get creative with the launch."

"How so?"

Paul pointed toward the rail. "If you look over the side, you'll see that the slipstream of the bow wave curls back toward the ship at our position. If we drop the *Angler* straight down, it might get caught in the slipstream and be slammed back into the side of our hull or even get swept into the propellers."

Paul extended the crane to its maximum length and began to raise it up, increasing the angle to thirty degrees.

"I'm not sure that's going to help," the XO said. "The sub is up higher but also closer to the side of the hull."

"Haven't done much fly-fishing, have you?" Paul said.

"You're not serious?"

Without answering, Paul retracted the boom a few feet and then extended it. The *Angler* swung in and then out, moving farther each time Paul manipulated the controls.

"I don't know about this," the XO said.

"Trust me," Paul said, timing his motions perfectly.

He used a flashlight to signal one of the crewmen, who picked up a phone and called the bridge. Paul had already set up the plan with the captain. Upon receiving that call, Callahan would idle the props. They would reengage thirty seconds later. The reduction in speed would be almost unnoticeable. But with the props idled instead of spinning, a bulge of water would deflect off of them and out instead of being drawn through them.

A subtle change in the vibration told Paul the propellers had been feathered. The stern rode a little higher. The wake was smoother.

Paul pulled the controls back once more and the *Angler* swung toward them like a four-ton bob on a pendulum. The crane groaned, and the strain on the boom was noticeable, but it was designed to hold three times the weight.

Paul allowed one more arc and then, just as the *Angler* was swinging outward, he hit the release button. The cable disconnected with a sharp crack and the fish-shaped submersible flew outward, seeming weightless for a second, before dropping down.

It hit the water fifty feet from the ship's hull. A baritone thud resonated and its impact drew up a tower of water that spread out and splashed down behind the ship.

As the spray fell and the impact zone disappeared behind the *Catalina,* the engine vibration picked up once again.

The First Officer was standing with his mouth open. "Very impressive. Crazy but impressive."

Paul grinned. "It's all in the wrist."

By the time Paul had retracted the boom, the ship was turning east and the multimillion-dollar submersible they'd dumped out behind them was nowhere to be seen.

Twenty miles behind the *Catalina,* a figure stood on the top deck of a small vessel made up to look like a fishing trawler. Tall, for a Chinese woman, though no more than five foot six, her black hair fell straight to her shoulders and cut across them in a perfect horizontal line. Her eyes were nearly as dark as her hair, and the skintight clothing she wore made it easy to see the lean, muscular build of a distance runner. Her given name was Daiyu, which in Mandarin meant *Black Jade*. She was twenty-eight years old and already a skilled and experienced operative for the Ministry of State Security. She was also one of the "children that were never born."

It was an awkward euphemism given to her and others who were victims — or perhaps beneficiaries — of China's drastic stand on procreation. Amidst the fervor of the infamous "one child" policy, most couples who conceived second children were strongly encouraged, if not forced, to endure abortions. If they skirted the state rules and hid the pregnancy, punishments were harsh and lasting.

When officials in Guangdong discovered that Daiyu's mother was pregnant for a second time, they initially insisted on the standard remedy: threatening prison for the deception if an abortion was not agreed to. Appeals for mercy fell on deaf ears until a mysterious man named Zhang arrived from Beijing carrying special paperwork and granting them an exception at a very high price.

It was a mixed blessing. By signing the papers, Daiyu's parents would be allowed to carry the birth to term, but only under the harshest condition imaginable: the child would be taken from the family at eighteen months and raised anonymously in a government orphanage.

With little choice, her mother and father had agreed to the terms. A year later — six months earlier than they'd agreed to — Zhang had returned to her village and taken Daiyu away.

She was sent inland, to an orphanage run by the military. Some might have thought it odd to see hulking sergeants and stern-faced officers caring for gaggles of young children, but the orphanage was in a forbidden zone carved out for military purposes. There was no one around to see anything that went on there.

Daiyu grew up in the military's care, never learning the real names of her parents. She was told they were special. Her mother had been a world-class athlete who'd competed for China in the Olympic Games. Her father was an athlete himself and a decorated soldier. After his military career, he became one of China's leading scientists.

It was explained to her that her parents' blend of attributes were the only reason her birth was allowed. In a godless country, her existence was a blessing bestowed upon her by the state. From birth, she and the others like her literally owed the nation their lives. This fact was drilled into their heads while they learned at the hands of their masters.

By age twenty, Daiyu was an expert marksman, a trained survivalist who could live off the land and a lethal opponent in hand-to-hand combat. She was also an electronics expert and was fluent in five languages.

She proved less adept at the more subtle arts of charm and deception. With rough edges that the Ministry could not sand off no matter how hard they tried, she was assigned to the field instead of a consulate position; she was tasked with projects that required physical work and lethal skill.

After a series of missions to Africa and Europe, she was transferred to South America, where Chinese influence and investment were growing by the day.

Now, standing on the top deck of the trawler, she stared at the distant navigation lights of the NUMA vessel they were following. It was dark, and the wind blew with a chill.

Behind her loomed a seventy-foot-tall mast that carried a radar dome, several antennas and a powerful set of cameras, which were watching the American ship for things no human eye could see.

On a video screen to her left, a tiny flare of white appeared and vanished. It looked to her as if it was a large splash, but it did not repeat itself, and all else remained normal.

"The Americans are up to something," she said.

The statement was addressed to a man standing in the dark behind her.

Jian Feng had a sturdy, muscular build, a square face and short, dark hair. He had a very plain look except for his right ear, part of which had been torn off in a fight years before.

Another member of the unborn children, in an odd way Jian was her brother. Like her, he'd been raised to serve the state. "They're turning," he said.

"Turning?"

"Look at the radar track."

Daiyu glanced at a separate screen. The Americans were indeed turning to the east. "It makes no sense. The search area is to the north and west."

"Maybe something's gone wrong," Jian said. "The nearest port is due east."

Daiyu could only hope that the American ship had suffered a mechanical problem.

Perhaps that was the cause of the brief flash she witnessed. "They're continuing at full speed," she said, noticing the new data on the radar plot. "They've noticed us."

Jian shook his head. "I don't think so."

"And why is that, Jian?"

"We're too low in the water and our signature is too indistinct. The vessel we're following is not equipped with military-band radar, only a simple weather-tracking set. There's been no radio traffic beyond the banal chatter that seems to permeate American culture. They know nothing of us."

There were other ways to be spotted. Her instincts told her the Americans had done just that. She resisted the urge to argue and instead checked the time. Her watch was over. It had been for almost an hour. She took a final look at the American ship and then turned to go inside.

With a curt good night, she left Jian to his ignorance, walked back along the deck of the dilapidated-looking trawler and entered a hatch.

The vessel itself was filthy. It smelled of diesel oil and fish guts — discomforts she took little notice of. Passing through the wheelhouse, she entered the control room, where the façade of the aging trawler gave way to a modern command center, complete with flickering screens, climate control and a row of technicians in military uniforms sitting at various consoles.

She looked over the latest reports and then put them down without comment. Only one of them was of any consequence: the operatives in Guayaquil had been given a tip regarding the American named Austin. Something to act on. But they'd failed to corral either Austin or the rather unimpressive woman (in Daiyu's opinion) named Townsend.

"Contact General Zhang," she told the communications specialist. "Inform him of the new course. And wake me if anything changes."

The man nodded and Daiyu continued to her cabin.

She closed the door behind her and stripped off her outer layer, revealing a pistol in a holster, strapped across her flat stomach, and a series of tattoos across her back.

She removed the pistol, sliding it under her pillow on the narrow bed in her quarters, then placed the holster with her clothes.

Half dressed, she stood in front of the tarnished mirror and struck her first pose.

With almost inhuman precision, she moved through a series of martial arts steps that were beautiful, well balanced and deadly.

As she turned from position to position, the ink on her skin seemed to change color with the light. On one shoulder blade, she wore the Chinese symbol for love; on the other, the symbol for punishment. In the middle, centered on her spine, a pair of black and white forms swirled together — a stylized version of the famous symbol for yin and yang.

In Chinese mythology, yin and yang were supposed to be complementary forces, each providing what the other cannot. But Daiyu rejected the notion. In her mind, they were antagonists. Yin would destroy yang, if it could; and yang would murder yin, if ever they met — for that's what opposites did. Because of this, she'd directed that an almost invisible line be left between the two curving symbols. A sliver of her own natural skin color remained there as if she was the buffer between the two warring forces, the only thing preventing the great destruction.

As the moves progressed in speed and intensity, the sweat began to trickle from her skin. A kick, a turn, an upward thrust of the hand that could break a neck. After a time, her hair, body and clothing were soaked. Her last move was a turn and sudden punch with an open palm that could kill any opponent it caught. She held it for several seconds, realizing she was staring directly at herself in the mirror, and then turned away.

The dance was over. She stripped off the rest of her clothes, threw them in the corner and stepped into the shower, blasting the water at its most icy cold.

10

Ecuador

The sleepy airport on the coast of Ecuador
appeared abandoned in the middle of the
night. A chain-link fence topped with razor
wire and a few perimeter lights were the
only efforts at security. Occasionally, a
guard in a white pickup truck with a yellow
rotating beacon on top would drive the
taxiway and runway, but more out of boredom than anything else.

"Not exactly Fort Knox," Emma noted
from the driver's seat of a car she'd rented
under an assumed name.

"Why do you think I chose it?" Kurt said,
stepping out and walking to the gate. "Under normal circumstances, there's nothing
here worth stealing."

Kurt found the gate unlocked and eased it
back. He waved Emma through, closed the
gate behind her and hopped back in the car.

"Over that way," he said, pointing to the left.

Emma drove carefully, navigating by the moonlight and sticking to one side of the crumbling taxiway. They passed a few small planes tied down at the edge of the ramp: single-engine Cessnas and Pipers. Judging by the weeds growing up between them, few of the planes had moved in weeks, if not months.

"How did you even know about this place?" Emma asked.

Kurt pointed across the runway. "On the other side of that fence, the waves of the Pacific are pounding the beach with rhythmic precision. This is one of the better surf spots in all of South America. I was going to come here when the season begins in a few months."

They continued on, passing a small hangar and pulling up beside a mammoth orange helicopter that looked more like a giant mutant insect looming in the dark than a machine made by human hands.

The helicopter stood on spindly, outstretched legs, its long rotors drooping like a dragonfly's wings. A thin, pointed tail stretched out into the dark behind it, while its large, bulbous head bent near to the ground, giving the appearance of a locust

131

gnawing the grass.

The Erickson Air-Crane was a modernized version of the famous Sikorsky Skycrane. It was seventy feet long, sported a huge, six-bladed rotor and was powered by two Pratt & Whitney turboshaft engines. It could carry a crew of five and a ten-ton payload. Most of the working models were used to haul heavy loads to places no truck could possibly reach or to battle forest fires. Its heavy-lifting capacity and precise maneuverability allowed it to drop tons of water or flame-retardant on hilltops, in box canyons and other tight spots normal firefighting planes could not target.

Since Erickson had taken over the design, each newly built helicopter was christened with a distinct name of its own. One named *Elvis* fought fires in Australia. Another named *Jaws* ferried parts to oil rigs in the Gulf of Mexico. The craft sitting on the tarmac in front of them was named *Merlin* and had a small caricature of a wizard painted on the nose.

As Emma parked beside it, a light came on inside the cockpit and a figure stepped out through the door.

"About time you got here," Joe Zavala said. "This must be Hurricane Emma."

Emma shot Kurt a suspicious look and

then shook Joe's hand. "I've been down-graded to a tropical storm. But don't make me angry."

"Duly noted," Joe said. "Care to step on board?"

"I thought we'd have some loading to do," Kurt said. "Did you get all the equipment on the list?"

"Of course," Joe said. "It's stored away in the aft cargo container. We also have a drop tank filled with extra fuel."

He pointed at two pods attached near the tail: the cargo container was black and had the aerodynamics of a brick; the drop tank was sleek and tapered, with the appearance of an orange bomb.

"Did you run into the security guard?"

"Of course," Joe said. "Who do you think helped me load this stuff?"

Kurt laughed. "Joe has a way with people," he explained to Emma. "He was once pulled over for speeding and instead of getting a ticket, he wound up with a police escort to the Boston Pops."

"I was late for a date," Joe explained. "The officer was very understanding."

Kurt checked his watch. "Getting late here, too. If we're ready, let's go."

They boarded the Air-Crane through a door in the back of the cockpit. To reach it one had to walk under the fuselage, which was like walking beneath a small bridge. Even standing straight up, the backbone of the craft was several feet above their heads.

Joe took the pilot's seat in the surprisingly tight cockpit and began to go through the start-up checklist. He had almost a thousand hours in helicopters of various types, but this was the first time he'd flown one this size.

"Are you sure you know how to fly this thing?" Kurt asked.

"They're all the same, more or less," Joe replied.

"It's the *less* part that I'm worried about."

"Trust me," Joe said. "Have I ever let you down?"

"I'm not going to answer that," Kurt said.

He sat down and strapped himself into the copilot's seat while Emma took the third seat just behind them. As Joe finished his checklist, he turned on the navigation lights and a flashing red glow became visible out in the dark. He held the starter switch down and the rotors began to move slowly above their heads. Seconds later, the engines came to life with a throaty roar.

"Welcome aboard Zavala Flight 251 to nowhere," he said. "Please put your tray tables in the upright and locked position."

"Should we call the tower?" Kurt asked.

"They went home hours ago," Joe replied.

"In that case, I'd say you're cleared for takeoff."

Joe ran the throttle up to full power and pulled steadily back on the collective, controlling lift. The weight came off the wheels and the helicopter began to roll forward. It lifted from the ground and turned into the wind.

Accelerating and climbing, Joe turned the Air-Crane toward the sea, and they crossed the beach and climbed out over the Pacific.

An hour later, they were nearing the spot where the *Catalina* had dropped off its submersible.

"I've got it," Kurt said, looking through a set of night vision goggles. "Two miles ahead, ten degrees right, bobbing up and down on the surface, right where it should be."

A low-intensity light on the *Angler*'s hatch — no brighter than a handheld flashlight — appeared like a magnesium flare through the goggles.

"I see it," Joe replied. He brought the helicopter down to fifty feet and hovered directly above the submersible.

Kurt removed the night vision goggles and

switched positions. He moved past Emma to an aft-facing seat at the back of the cockpit, surrounded by a clear Plexiglas bubble, reminiscent of a tail-gunner's position in a World War II bomber.

The payload specialist's station offered a clear view of everything behind and beneath the Air-Crane. With the flip of a switch, several floodlights came on, illuminating the scene below. The white submersible with the broad red stripe rode low in the water, surrounded by a spiraling pattern created by the downwash of the Air-Crane's rotors.

"Back ten feet," Kurt called out.

"Roger that," Joe said, easing the helicopter backward.

Activating the winch controls on a panel in front of him, Kurt released a heavy steel hook and lowered it toward the *Angler*. His target was a prominent bar on top of the submersible's hull that resembled the roll cage of an off-road vehicle. The thick red band painted across the top of the submersible marked the attachment point.

"Right five," Kurt said. "Forward two."

As Joe maneuvered the Air-Crane, Kurt made several attempts to hook the *Angler*, but the task wasn't as easy as it looked. If the submersible rose on a swell at the wrong moment, the hook bounced off its hull.

Other times, the hook swung and missed as the attachment point dropped beneath it like a boxer ducking a slow punch.

Kurt was seriously considering getting wet and placing the hook by hand when a solid click and tension on the line told him he'd nabbed his catch.

"Got it!" he said, reeling in the slack. "Dropping second cable."

The second cable didn't attach to the submersible; it was already connected to the first cable, and also to a hardpoint near the nose gear. Its purpose was to act as a guide and keep the payload from twisting in the swirling downwash from the main rotor.

"Second cable locked."

"Pull it up," Joe said. "Can't have NUMA getting fined for littering."

Kurt set the winch control to retract and the braided steel cable went taut. The strain of lifting the four-ton submersible was felt instantly and the helicopter dipped several feet before Joe countered the effect. As the roar of the engines grew, the *Angler* came free of the Pacific and was soon locked in place, snugly up against *Merlin*'s belly.

"Outstanding," Emma announced. "Never let it be said that the men of NUMA fail to impress."

"It's what we do," Joe replied, a false tone

of bravado purposely evident in his voice.

Kurt made one last check of the winch controls and turned back toward the cockpit. "Onward."

At Joe's command, the Air-Crane began to move forward once more, picking up speed and altitude more slowly this time as it thundered across the sea toward their next destination.

"How far to the ship?" Joe asked.

Emma checked the handheld GPS unit she carried. "Ninety miles from here."

"That gives us time to practice our sales pitch," Kurt said.

"Have you decided what you want to tell them?"

"I was thinking I'd appeal to the most basic universal desire."

"I don't think love is going to help us here," Joe said.

"The *other* universal desire," Kurt said. "Money. Everyone wants to be rich."

"But we have no money to give them," Emma pointed out.

Kurt nodded. "Who says we have to use our own?"

Both Emma and Joe gave him a quizzical look, but Kurt said no more; he was still working out the details.

11

MS Reunion
Refrigerated cargo carrier
En route from Chile to San Diego

The MS *Reunion* was running with a full complement of lights as it steamed north at eleven knots. Lit up like this, the ship was visible from miles away, a white beacon alone on the dark mat of the sea.

After a brief conversation with the *Reunion*'s night watch, the Air-Crane was cleared to land. Joe maneuvered toward the elevated pad near the bow of the ship and planted the big helicopter in the exact center of its yellow circle.

One of the ship's officers watched the landing and couldn't help but be impressed at the pilot's skill, especially since there was no more than ten feet to spare on either side and only two feet of clearance between the helipad deck and the bottom of . . .

whatever the big orange machine was carrying.

With *Merlin* tied down, the officer led the new arrivals toward the bridge, stealing several glances at the attractive woman with auburn hair. It wasn't often they had female guests on board, and he couldn't recall ever having one this striking here for a visit.

In the lighted confines of the bridge, introductions were made and pleasantries exchanged. That the captain of the *Reunion* was an American played into their hands. That he'd been woken in the middle of the night weighed against them, but that couldn't be helped.

Captain Buck Kamphausen arrived on the bridge dressed in his boxers and a T-shirt, with a jacket thrown over his shoulders. Six foot three, sporting a patchy brown beard with plenty of gray creeping in, he wore rectangular glasses, which he was constantly adjusting, often with a glance at Emma.

Kamphausen was an affable fellow; he knew of NUMA and considered himself a big fan. As they spoke, though, he looked like he might agree to anything as long as Emma promised to stay on board and dine with him.

"What we need," Kurt summed up, "is to

use your ship as a floating base for a few days."

Kamphausen scratched his beard. "For what purpose?"

"I can't tell you that," Kurt said.

Kamphausen's demeanor changed instantly. "Let me get this straight," he said gruffly. "You land on my ship in the middle of the night, bringing god-knows-what on board; you ask me to change course, fake a mechanical problem and possibly miss my delivery schedule — but you won't tell me what you're attempting to do or explain what I'm getting involved in?"

"I know it sounds odd," Kurt began.

"More like, downright lunacy."

"The thing is," Kurt said, trying to keep the meeting on track, "we — and by *we*, I mean the United States government — can make it worth your while."

"Not worth my while to get fired or busted down to seaman first class," the captain said.

"I don't know about that," Kurt said. "Depends on how much we recover."

Interest sparked up in the captain's eyes. "Recover?"

Kurt nodded.

Kamphausen's gaze narrowed. He adjusted his glasses once more and focused on

Kurt. "Go on."

"You're familiar with NUMA," Kurt said. "You know what we do. We find things on the bottom of the ocean. At the risk of saying too much, that contraption we've got tucked up under our helicopter is a specially designed submersible, built to search for something that is extremely valuable."

He was stretching it a bit here, but he needed to sound confident.

"Something the United States government wants to find very badly," Emma added.

Kurt cleared his throat to get the captain's mind and eyes focused back in his direction. "It's been my experience that the monetary rewards of helping the government can be quite substantial —"

"If I recall correctly," Joe busted in, "everyone who helped us find that lost U-boat received a percentage of the diamonds we recovered or the equivalent value in cash, if they preferred."

"Diamonds?" Kamphausen said.

"On that mission," Kurt cautioned.

"Percentage?" the First Officer asked eagerly. "What kind of percentage?"

"Like in the old pirate days," Joe said. "One share for each crewman, two shares for the NCOs, three shares for commissioned officers and four for the captain."

Kurt nodded in support of Joe's ad-lib as if it were standard practice. Captain Kamphausen and the First Officer exchanged a knowing look.

Emma chimed in to help the process. "As the saying in government goes, a billion here, a billion there, and pretty soon you're talking real money. You don't need a large cut of that to buy a summer home in Tahiti."

"But you can't tell us what you're looking for," the captain repeated.

Kurt shook his head. "I can't. But think about this: Would we be here, in the dark of night, asking for your help, if it wasn't something *extremely* important?"

Knowing the plan would work best if the crew convinced themselves, Kurt let them run with their fantasy, until a voice of reason interrupted.

"Hold on a second," a new arrival said. "I'm supercargo on this run. I'm responsible for the entire shipment. We're carrying fresh fruit. Limes, apples, oranges and kiwis. If we're more than four days late, the shipment will be rejected. My company will be out several million dollars and I'll be out of a job."

Kurt looked at Joe. "What do you think?"

"I believe we can swing it," Joe said.

Kurt nodded. "We only need a couple of

days," he said, turning to the fruit company's rep. "But if we are delayed more than forty-eight hours, the United States government will buy the cargo. Lock, stock and barrel."

"Or in this case, limes, apples and oranges," Joe added.

"Don't forget the kiwis," the representative said.

"How could I?"

The captain stroked his beard. "Diamonds?"

"I didn't say that," Kurt reminded everyone.

"Barrels full of 'em," the First Officer said. "I saw it on TV."

"We'll need to have papers drawn up," the captain added.

Kurt glanced at Emma as if she were in charge of such things.

"Of course," she said. "There will also be confidentiality agreements and required radio and electronic silence until we release the ship back into your custody. Any violation of which will terminate the profit-sharing agreement and result in criminal charges."

The winds of Hurricane Emma had suddenly blown cold. But it did nothing to dampen the mood.

"We can keep quiet for a couple of days," the First Officer said convincingly.

The fruit company rep looked suspicious. "I want papers ASAP."

"I'll contact Washington and have the papers drawn up first thing in the morning," Kurt insisted.

Kamphausen grinned and offered Kurt a hand. "I've always wanted to get in on an adventure like this one."

"If history's any guide, you'll get more than you bargained for," Kurt said. "In the meantime, we should all get to work. We need to change headings."

The captain took one last look as if wondering whether he might be losing his mind. He glanced out the window to the orange helicopter sitting on his deck and the high-tech submarine nestled beneath it and reminded himself of everything he knew about NUMA. "Helmsman," he called. "Lay in a new course."

"What heading?"

He turned to Kurt. "Whatever direction our new partners want us to go."

12

Kurt gave the helmsman a new heading and the ship veered to the northwest. In the interest of secrecy, Kurt had the captain shut down the AIS beacon so their position would not be reported automatically to the satellite system that tracked the world's seagoing vessels. That done, he returned to the main deck and used an encrypted satellite phone to call Rudi Gunn.

Rudi was still in Guayaquil, working the political angle and hoping to get some assistance from the Ecuadorian defense forces without telling them why. Despite it being the middle of the night, Rudi answered on the second ring. "One of these days, you'll call me during normal business hours," he grumbled.

"These are normal business hours," Kurt said. "NUMA never sleeps."

"NUMA doesn't, but I do," Rudi replied. "What can I do for you, my insomniastricken friend?"

"I just wanted to give you an update," Kurt said. "I've left Ecuador, Joe and Emma are with me, but don't put it in any reports. The Chinese have agents everywhere, and we're not sure about the NSA right now. They may have been compromised."

"Great," Rudi said. "Maybe I'll start sending them false information."

"Not a bad idea," Kurt said. "At any rate, we're on our own. And we're not going to be checking back in for a while."

"Then why bother to tell me?"

"I didn't want you to worry," Kurt said as warmly as possible.

"Where are you?"

"On a refrigerated cargo ship. Only, don't bother looking for us. We're temporarily invisible."

Kurt heard what sounded like movement and a soft click. He imagined Rudi throwing back the covers of his bed, sitting up and switching on the light. The tone in Rudi's voice perked up instantly. "You've found something?"

"Maybe," Kurt said.

"Hot damn," Rudi replied. "Wake me with that kind of news anytime. What's the probability?"

"Fairly good. Check with Hiram for details

and stand by. Also keep the rest of the fleet doing their thing. The busier they look, the less likely anyone is to notice that we've gone off the map. Might even want to pretend you've found something back that way, it'll draw the heat in your direction."

"Great idea. I'll get something in the works. I'll even put it in a report to the NSA."

"Perfect," Kurt said. He was about to sign off and hang up when another thought occurred to him. "One more thing. If you happen to get any calls from the Malabar Shipping Line or the Golden Fruit Company of Valparaiso, Chile . . . I wouldn't answer them right away. Probably just a telemarketer."

The gloom returned to Rudi's voice. "Do I even want to know?"

"Put it this way," Kurt said. "If I don't find what we're looking for in the next two days, there will be no shortage of limes for your margaritas."

Rudi acknowledged with a soft grunt and then hung up. Kurt switched off the phone and turned to see Emma approaching him.

"You have them eating out of your hand," she said. "But how do you intend to pay for this ship? Not to mention the cargo and the pirate's booty Joe promised them?"

Kurt shrugged and put the phone away. "I figured we'd use that expense account of yours. I took care of dinner, remember?"

"Very funny," she said. "But, I'm serious. We're either going to end up walking the plank here or being drawn and quartered on the Capitol steps."

Kurt didn't think so. "There's a ten-hour difference between here and Malaysia, where the shipping company has its headquarters. They're closed now. They won't be open again until tomorrow morning, Malaysian Standard Time. By then, it will be dark in D.C. and the phones will be forwarded to the answering service. Between that and the normal speed of bureaucracy, it'll be a week before anyone starts sorting out this mess. By then, we'll have found what we're looking for."

"And when it doesn't turn out to be filled with barrels of uncut diamonds?"

"I never mentioned diamonds," Kurt said.

"No, but the cargo you vouched for is worth fifty million dollars. And this ship is worth twice that much."

"And how much did the *Nighthawk* cost?" he asked. "Fifty *billion*? A hundred? How much would the NSA pay to keep it out of Russian hands? You're worrying about the pennies and forgetting about the thousand-dollar bills. Trust me, by the time this becomes a problem we'll have the *Night-hawk*'s actual position locked down and the most important parts of the aircraft on board. Instead of complaining about the cost of this ship and the cargo, someone will be pinning a medal on your chest and calling you a risk taker and bold leader and buying Captain Kamphausen and his friends their own ships, crewed by beautiful mermaids."

She took a deep breath and looked away out over the dark sea. "You really are crazy," she whispered, before turning back to him with a smile. "What sort of Pandora's Box have you opened for me?"

"Must be your inner rebel," he replied with a grin.

"All I can say is, you'd better be right or we're going to end up partners in a fruit stand for the rest of our natural lives."

"I could think of worse fates," Kurt said. "But, trust me. It's going to work out just fine."

13

NUMA vessel Catalina

Paul Trout thought his wife was playing a practical joke on him as she read the latest order, this time from Rudi Gunn. It made as little sense as the previous one.

"Proceed to specified coordinates and begin dropping sonar buoys on north–south line. After three hours and twenty-seven minutes, begin concentric circles. One hour later, at the captain's leisure, come to a full stop. At this point, make obvious preparations for deep-sea recovery operation, including launch of ROVs. Send coded transmissions and continue recovery operations until further orders."

"Recovery of what?" Paul asked.

"It doesn't say," Gamay insisted. "Just that we need to make it look good."

"With what?" he added. "We just dumped our only manned submersible over the rail."

"I suppose we'll have to improvise,"

Gamay said.

Paul shook his head. "Ours is not to reason why," he said. "Let's go give Callahan the news. Hopefully, his head won't explode."

Four thousand miles away, Constantin Davidov thought his head might do just that. He'd been traveling in the passenger compartment of a Russian Mi-14 helicopter for the better part of a day. The huge blue-gray-painted craft was the newest, extended-range model, stripped of weapons and armor and given two large auxiliary fuel tanks. It was known to its pilots as the *Carrier Pigeon,* since it was used to ferry men and equipment over extremely long distances. The men on the ground called it the *Clay Pigeon* because it was filled with so much jet fuel that it was ponderous, heavy and slow, making it an easy target.

All Davidov knew was that nineteen hours in such a craft, including several air-to-air refueling passes, qualified as torture and should have been banned by the Geneva convention.

When the ungainly craft finally touched down on the deck of a Russian guided missile cruiser, he all but jumped from his seat to get off the torture machine. Not waiting for permission, he stepped through the door out into a pouring rain.

The weather was deteriorating in all directions as the guided missile cruiser *Varyag* and several other ships continued headlong into a storm halfway between Hawaii and the South American coast. Davidov didn't care. A ship in a Category 5 storm was preferable to another minute in the oversized eggbeater.

As the Mi-14 was strapped down, Davidov was led inside and shown to a cabin. By the time he'd showered and pulled on a clean uniform, the ship was pitching noticeably. He found he had to grip the rail to keep from losing his balance as he moved down the passageway.

He was escorted through "officer country," to the quarters of Rear Admiral Sergei Borozdin, whose door was guarded by two Spetsnaz commandos. After displaying his credentials, he was shown in immediately.

Borozdin was sitting behind a desk, pretending not to notice the arrival of his old friend. It was a game they played. The two men had come up together, one through the Navy, the other in the party machinery itself — KGB, NKVD and the consular services. They rarely met these days but, when they did, the liquor flowed.

Despite the stereotype of vodka-drinking Russians, both men preferred scotch, specifically single malts from the highlands of Scotland, preferably aged at least fifteen years.

Davidov had brought with him a fine example. He offered it to Borozdin. *"Aberlour,"* he said. "Gaelic for *Mouth of the Chattering Burn.* It's only a twelve-year-old, but it was aged in a Spanish sherry cask."

Borozdin looked the bottle over with reverence. "The least you could do for sending my fleet into this cyclone."

Despite the gruff words, Borozdin was pleased. He grinned and reached for two glasses, pouring a taste. "I swear to you, Constantin. If Putin ordered me to destroy Scotland with a nuke, I would refuse and take my chances with the firing squad."

Davidov laughed and Borozdin filled both of their glasses. The aroma was unique, with a hint of raisins. The first sips were heavenly.

Even then, Davidov swore he could still hear the helicopter blades hacking at the air above him, could still feel his body shaking from nose to feet. "It's too bad about this storm," he said as the *Varyag* rolled appreciably to starboard.

With each swell, the ship rolled and nosed down and then came back up. The waves were hitting the fleet from the front quarter, and they were getting worse by the moment.

"If we weren't so far behind," Borozdin said, "I would let it pass and proceed in its wake. We've already had to send one of the tenders back; two of its hatches were damaged."

The *Varyag* was shepherding a fleet of salvage ships and auxiliaries toward the search zone. It was larger, faster and heavier than the other ships. It was faring better, as a result.

"We must press on," Davidov said. "At least the storm is delaying the Chinese as well."

"But what about the Americans?" Borozdin asked. "They're our real problem. This damned cyclone has done nothing but aid them and ruin our plans. If it hadn't appeared, they wouldn't have brought the *Nighthawk* back early. We would have been in position to catch it when it fell. Now the storm delays us even as the Americans steam south from California in good weather."

"Yes," Davidov said wearily. "I know. Not to worry. It shouldn't matter."

Borozdin cocked his head and looked at his old friend suspiciously. "Why wouldn't it?"

"It's true, the Americans seem to have this cyclone on their side," Davidov said, smirking. "But we have a Typhoon on ours."

A few seconds passed before Borozdin got the reference. "TK-17," he said, referencing the ID number of the vessel in question.

Davidov nodded. "She's gone right under the storm and is almost in position. By this time tomorrow, the *Nighthawk* will be in her hold and on its way to Kamchatka. The Chinese and Americans will never know we've taken her and her precious cargo. They will search forever . . . in vain."

Borozdin looked pleased, but the smile quickly left his face. "Then why are we plowing directly into a Force 5 gale?"

"Appearances," Davidov said, finishing his tumbler of the Aberlour. "They must be kept up. Otherwise, the Americans and the Chinese might begin to suspect something."

Davidov finished, pushed his empty glass toward Borozdin and waited. His old friend broke into a toothy grin and gladly poured a second helping of the liquid fire. "To the Typhoon," he said, raising his glass.

Davidov did likewise. "To the Typhoon."

14

MS Reunion
*Seventy miles east of the Galápagos Islands
  chain*

Kurt stood on the starboard bridge wing of the six-hundred-foot cargo vessel looking through a pair of large binoculars. In the distance, he could just make out four red-hulled boats on the blue ocean. They were lifeboats from the *Reunion,* repurposed to search for any sign of the *Nighthawk.*

Taking a page out of Rudi Gunn's plan, they'd put four boats in the water and sent them to the east in formation. Traveling abreast of one another and two miles apart, the small fleet covered an eight-mile-wide swath at a single pass. Each of them trailed a pair of *fish:* torpedo-shaped tubes packed with the most advanced sensing equipment in the NUMA catalog, including top-of-the-line side-scan sonar emitters and a sensitive magnetic alloy detector NUMA had only recently developed.

The new detectors were far more precise than the old magnetometers that simply scanned for iron content. According to Joe, they could tell not only what alloys it was examining but where the alloy was produced and the name of the shift supervisor on duty during the mixing.

The fact was they were using the most advanced equipment in the world and covering forty square miles of ocean floor each hour. The pace had led Kurt to predict they'd locate the missing craft by lunchtime, though at half past breakfast they'd yet to find a thing.

Patient as Job, at least for now, Kurt turned to Emma. She sat in front of a high-definition screen, studying the results. As the four lifeboats moved in unison, they transmitted the data from the sonar emitters and other instruments back to the *Reunion,* where a special laptop computer processed the signals from all the different sensors into one image.

The resulting picture was a comprehensive, detailed view of the ocean floor, far sharper than any standard sonar scan. It was comparable to switching from an old tube TV to a modern high-definition display.

"This is incredible," Emma said, using the

controls to pan and zoom in on different sections of the image. "No wonder Steve Gowdy wanted NUMA on the job."

Kurt lowered the binoculars down and took a seat beside her. "Something tells me our proximity and availability had more to do with it than our expertise. Had the seven sisters of the poor been out here with a fishing boat, he'd probably have hired them, too."

"Maybe," she said. "But you definitely bring more than proximity to the table."

Kurt accepted the compliment, sat back in the chair and watched the computer screen along with her. He knew the software would point out and highlight anything that didn't belong on the seafloor, but he liked to keep an eye on the scan as much as he could. For one thing, computers were not infallible. For another, until they found something, there was literally nothing else to do.

He leaned back and craned his neck around to alleviate the soreness that had set in. As he did, Captain Kamphausen strode over. He, too, was sensing the tedious nature of the search. "Somehow, I thought looking for sunken treasure would be a little more exciting than this."

"Mowing the lawn isn't my favorite exercise either," Kurt replied. "Never liked it as a kid and I don't like it any better now."

The captain laughed, moved to the radio and checked in with his crew. Meanwhile, Joe came in, juggling three cups of coffee; he placed one in front of Kurt, handed one to Emma and kept one for himself. "Find anything yet?"

"Nothing interesting," Kurt said. "The only real excitement turned out to be an old anchor that must have fallen off a ship sometime recently. Other than that, nothing but a few outcroppings of lava rock jutting from the abyssal plain."

"That's to be expected," Joe said. "The Galápagos Islands *are* volcanic."

Kurt reached for the coffee cup. He tested the heat and swallowed some coffee down, wincing in the aftermath. "How much sugar did you put in there?"

"Only seven packets," Joe said.

"*Only* seven?" Kurt replied.

"I figured a sugar rush would keep you on your toes."

Kurt placed the cup into a holder. "I'll be bouncing off the walls if I drink any more of that."

Before Joe could reply, a soft tone and a flashing red highlight on the screen suggested they'd found something new.

"What is it?" Emma asked.

Kurt leaned over the keyboard and used the touch pad to zoom in on the highlighted area. "I'm not sure."

He adjusted the angle and allowed the computer to extrapolate the data. They soon got a closer view of the targets. In a wide swath there were several objects and a series of small craters and gouge marks in the otherwise flat expanse of sediment.

"Looks like something rained down from above," Joe suggested.

Kurt nodded and checked the magnetometer. "Can't be sure what we're looking at, but it's definitely man-made."

Emma was not as easily convinced. "How can you be sure? I don't see anything but holes in the mud."

Kurt pointed to the reading of the alloy detector. "Because those holes are hiding something built of high-strength stainless steel and magnesium."

He pressed a button and the printer came to life, spitting out a chemical profile of the target in question. It was approximately twenty percent magnesium and fifty percent aluminum, with lower concentrations of iron and other metals.

As the boats continued to move along, the image on the screen changed slowly. Several additional targets appeared, but they were too small and too far off to be rendered in any kind of detail.

"Can we get in closer?" Emma asked.

Kurt was about to zoom in when the image blurred and a large swath of the screen went dark.

"What happened?"

"It's a shadow," Joe said from behind them. "The side-scan sonar is sending its pulse across the seafloor at a nearly flat angle, like the sun getting low on the horizon. When something gets in the way of the echo, it creates a long shadow, like those you see stretching across a street in the late afternoon."

Kurt zoomed out and a jagged shape appeared. A ridge of volcanic material jutting up from the seafloor. Everything beyond it was invisible.

"We could have the boats circle back and get another scan from a different angle," Joe suggested.

"I've got a better idea," Kurt said. "Let the boats continue on until they reach the edge of the search zone and then have them make the turn as planned. While they do that, we'll take the *Angler* down and check out what we've found. If it turns out to be anything important, we'll be able to confirm. And if not, we won't have brought the whole search to a halt in the process."

"Makes sense," Joe said. "And it gives you something to do."

Kurt grinned. "There's a method to my madness."

"You keep thinking that," Joe quipped.

"I'm going with you," Emma said. "If it turns out to be debris, it's likely to be in rough condition: mostly small pieces and mangled and bent fragments. I'm the only one here who'll be able to make a positive ID."

"You don't have to come down to do that," Kurt said. "You can watch on the monitors up here."

"I prefer to see things in person," she said. "Besides, when am I going to get another chance to dive to the bottom of the sea in a high-tech submarine?"

"The lady has a point," Joe said.

Kurt didn't mind the company. "Okay," he said. "You've got one ticket to the bottom of the sea."

Twenty minutes later, Kurt and Emma were sitting in the command seats of the *Angler* as Joe used the Air-Crane to lift them off the deck and carry them toward the target zone.

Though the submersible was hooked on

securely, it still swayed beneath the fuselage of the orange-painted helicopter.

"I'll be glad when we get into the water," Emma said. "How close are we?"

"Approaching the drop zone," Joe's voice replied over the intercom.

"You mean the *Lower us gently into the sea zone,* don't you?" Kurt replied.

"Of course," Joe said. *"Wouldn't want to give you too much frustration for one day."*

As they neared the drop zone, Joe slowed the helicopter to a hover and brought it down toward the surface. At the same time, Kurt ran one last check to ensure the *Angler* was watertight and that all systems were go.

"Ready for our bath," Kurt said.

"Roger that," Joe replied.

The submersible lurched downward as the cable began to unwind. It descended the rest of the way smoothly and then settled into passing swells, rising and falling softly, once it reached the sea.

A metallic clink sounded as the hook was detached and the line reeled in.

"Catch-and-release program completed," Joe called out. *"You two are on your own."*

"Roger that," Kurt said. "Deploying communications buoy and beginning descent. See you in a couple of hours."

As Kurt flooded the ballast tanks, seawater

crept up the curved glass of the canopy, bathing the cockpit in a blue-green light. As they submerged completely, the thundering racket of the helicopter diminished to a muted staccato beat.

Kurt vented the forward tanks and the nose of the *Angler* tilted downward to begin the submarine's plunge into the deep. A fiber-optic cable, connected to a floating buoy, trailed out behind them. All radio and video communications would be transmitted through it.

The water grew darker, and the pitch steepened until the nose was pointing downward at an eighty-degree angle.

Though she was strapped in, Emma instinctively put her hand on the console to compensate for the sensation of falling forward. "It's like we're on a roller coaster and we just went over the crest of a hill."

"I didn't want to bore you," Kurt said.

"Is this why they call it the *Angler*?" she asked. "Because it dives so steeply?"

"No," Kurt said. "But we are nose heavy. It's designed that way. By descending almost straight down like a raindrop, we travel faster and save on power and oxygen."

"And sacrifice a little bit of comfort," she said, hanging forward in the straps of her seat. "How fast are we going?"

Kurt pointed to the depth gauge and a digital readout that noted the rate of descent. "About three hundred feet per minute. We could go faster, but this is a nice, safe speed. We'll level off before we hit the bottom, I promise."

The submersible continued to dive. Aside from the odd creak and groan, all sounds vanished and the world outside the canopy grew rapidly darker, changing from sea green to indigo blue to a deep violet color. Finally, it became an impenetrable black curtain.

Kurt dimmed the interior lights to help their eyes adjust and soon they needed only the glow of the various switches, indicators and gauges to see comfortably inside the sub.

"There's a certain ambiance to this," Emma said. "Almost like candlelight."

"And I forgot to bring the wine."

"A huge oversight, in my opinion," she replied.

With an eye on the depth gauge, Kurt began to trim the submarine. By using the ballast controls to pump air into the forward tanks, he raised the nose and decreased the rate of descent at the same time. "Coming up on the seafloor. Or should I say down?"

"How about turning on the porch lights?"

she said.

"Afraid of the dark?"

"No. Afraid of running into things in the dark."

Kurt reached above his head and flipped a series of switches. A battery of lights around the base of the *Angler* came to life. Initially, they lit up nothing but the sedimentary particles flying upward past the windows.

The particles were actually stationary or moving slowly downward, but as the *Angler* was dropping at a much faster rate, the particles were more like snowflakes moving in the wrong direction.

A yellow light began to flash. *"Terrain detected, one hundred feet,"* a computerized voice said.

Kurt pumped more air into the tanks and slowed the descent further. The gray sediment layer of the seafloor began to appear in the cone of light beneath them.

"Terrain, fifty feet," the computer voice said.

"So much for *ambiance*," he said, looking around for a way to switch the voice off. He'd never liked talking cars and he didn't want a talking submarine either.

"Terrain, thirty feet," the computer said. *"Descent stopped."*

They were now suspended in the water at

a depth of nine hundred and seventeen feet.

Kurt pressed the radio switch. "We're on the ground floor," he said. "Give me a bearing."

Joe's voice came back, slightly distorted. *"Target should be no more than three hundred yards from you, on a heading of one-five-zero degrees."*

Kurt dialed up the heading and the *Angler*'s inertial navigation system took over. The batteries kicked in and small thrusters on either side of the sub began to spin. Instead of propellers at the stern, which could only drive them forward, the *Angler* had two compact propulsion pods jutting out on stubby wings near its tail. They could be rotated to point forward, back, up or down, making it easy to move the sub in any direction.

For now, they drove the sub across a carpet of gray silt that stretched unbroken into the dark like a field of dirty snow.

"It's so bleak," Emma said.

There were no colorful reefs or schools of fish, only the occasional tube worm and small outcroppings of volcanic rock that hadn't yet been buried by the marine *snow.*

"It always makes me think of the Moon," Kurt said as he flicked another switch and the telescoping boom began to extend from the top of the submersible.

"What's that?" Emma asked.

"*That* is the reason they call this sub the *Angler,*" he said. "Joe named it after the anglerfish. A well-known denizen of the deep with a very particular method of getting food."

"I know all about those fish," Emma said. "They trick other fish into swimming near their mouths using a lighted antenna. When a smaller fish is attracted to the lure, they open their big mouths and chomp on it."

"Exactly," Kurt said. "In fact, I'm fairly certain *chomp* is the exact term marine biologists use to describe it."

She laughed.

Outside, the boom locked in place with a dull click; its tip was now extended out in front of the sub by fifty feet. Kurt flipped a switch and a slight electric buzz became audible in the speakers of the intercom system. But aside from the static, and an almost invisible halo around the boom, nothing else happened.

"Looks like someone forgot to change the lightbulbs," Emma said.

Kurt flipped another switch and a pair of cameras on a lower part of the boom came to life. The video was displayed on a flat screen in the center panel between the two seats. It showed a view of the terrain stretching several hundred feet ahead of them. Undulations in the sediment were clearly visible; mounds of lava rock appeared here and there. In one spot, a deep-sea crab flared white and then vanished as it buried itself in the silt.

Looking through the canopy with the naked eye, none of this was visible.

"High-intensity violet and ultraviolet light," Kurt said. "It penetrates seawater far better than the visible spectrum, but since human eyes are not sensitive to UV frequencies —"

"You use cameras tuned to pick it up," she said, finishing the thought for him. "Ingenious."

"It allows us to explore the dark much more efficiently," he said. "And if you're feeling a little pale, it doubles as a tanning salon. Though a minute or two in the beam would leave you burned."

They continued across the flat expanse, dividing their attention between what they saw on the screen and the view through the curved front window. As they neared the target, Kurt took manual control of the sub and brought them in closer.

The first thing they came in contact with was a flat piece of metal that had been bent and twisted. On the screen, a second piece could be seen nearby, complete with a hinge and some wires attached to it.

Kurt moved closer and the two pieces of debris became visible in the normal light.

"You were right," Emma said. "Definitely man-made."

Kurt eased up to the first target and held station against the current. "See if you can grab it with the claw," he said, pointing to a pair of joysticks in between the two seats.

"I warn you," she said. "I never get anything when I play this game at the carnival."

"No one does," he said. "That's why the stuffed animals are covered in an inch of dust."

Emma tested the controls, which resembled those of a miniature remote-controlled car. Pushing one of the sticks forward, she extended a metal arm with a claw-like pincer on the end. Manipulating the claw until it was directly over one of the targets, she plucked the four-foot strip of metal from the silt on the first try.

"Great job," Kurt said.

"Now what?"

"Drop it in the bin," he said, pointing to a twelve-foot-long bin attached to the *Angler*'s port side.

With a twist of the joystick, she drew the

arm back in and positioned it over the recovery bin. "Good?"

Kurt nodded.

She pressed the release button and the metal strip fell from the claw into the bin, hitting with a soft bump.

"If you fill that one up, we still have a second bin on the starboard side," Kurt told her. "They're detachable. We can send them topside by using inflatable air bags, if we need to, or we can keep them in place and carry them home when we surface."

"Perfect for cleaning the ocean floor," Emma said.

She retrieved the second piece of metal and then found a hydraulic strut.

"What do you think?" Kurt asked.

"I'm not sure," she said. "I have to admit these appear to be aircraft parts, but there's nothing definitive. Let's keep moving."

Kurt nodded and took them farther to the south, tracking along a trail of small scars in the sediment.

"Are those impact points?" Emma asked.

Kurt nodded. "A metal rain fell here. The smaller items buried themselves, leaving these marks. Only the bigger ones or those that came down with less speed remained on the surface."

"So this is a debris field?"

He nodded.

Emma looked grim. "If this is the *Night-hawk,* we'll need to find the core. All the technology our adversaries are after is hidden there."

Kurt bumped the throttle, adjusted course and guided them forward. They passed by a smattering of small parts and additional gouges in the silt, stopping only when they found another large section of shredded metal, which looked like torn and tattered paper.

"This isn't good," Emma said. "That looks like a fuselage section."

"It must have hit the water at high speed," Kurt said.

She shook her head. "It shouldn't have," she replied. "Every simulation we've run suggests the onboard computer was still operating. It should have flared as it descended and then deployed its parachutes and come down softly."

Kurt paused. He found it odd how strongly convinced everyone in the NSA was that the aircraft was in one piece. "The evidence doesn't support that," he said, tired of hearing about what *should have happened.*

"The core *must* still be intact," Emma said urgently. "Keep going. We need to find it."

It sounded like wishful thinking to Kurt, but he moved on, guiding them in a zigzag pattern. Once he'd established the width of the debris field and the direction it ran, they made steady progress, with more and more debris appearing out of the darkness, eventually stopping when they discovered several large sections of what had to be an airframe, lengths of wires and insulation wafting in the current, and the unmistakable shape of a wheel still attached to a hydraulic strut.

"Landing gear assembly," Emma said dejectedly.

The wheel hub lay on its side. Every shred of its tires had been ripped free and the hydraulic strut had been bent at a forty-degree angle. A curved section of blackened sheet metal that looked like part of the fuselage lay just beyond it.

"So much for the core being in one piece," Kurt said.

Emma didn't respond. She was staring into the dark. The look on her face suggested anger and confusion. She focused on the wheel, squinting until a small furrow appeared in her brow. "Go in closer."

Kurt nudged the throttle and guided the *Angler* gently into position, trying not to stir up too much sediment.

As they closed in on what appeared to be

the nose gear, Emma moved to the edge of her seat. The anger vanished. "It's too big," she said.

Kurt could see that. "We can't carry it up," he said. "But we can attach a cable and winch it to the surface."

"No," she said, turning toward him. "It's too big to come from the *Nighthawk*. To speed up development, we took the landing gear from the smaller X-37. It gave us more interior space and less weight, but it made the *Nighthawk* look odd when you saw it sitting on the ground. Like a big dog with short legs."

She pointed back through the canopy. "The diameter of that wheel is too large. The strut is too long, even though it's broken off."

"We're looking through curved glass," Kurt said. "It magnifies things."

Emma glanced at him and then back through the canopy. She scanned the wheel first and then turned her attention to the wreckage out beyond. "There's too much debris," she added. "Too much material all together. I'm telling you, this isn't the *Nighthawk*.*"

"Then what is it?"

"I don't know," she admitted. "Some other plane that crashed. Maybe it's that missing airliner from Malaysia. Maybe it's an old military transport that came down years ago."

Kurt shook his head. "The wreckage is pristine," he said, quashing that theory. "It's recent. If this material had been down here any length of time, it would be corroded and encrusted with marine life. The craters in the sediment where each piece made an impact would be filled in like footprints in a snowstorm. Besides, we heard this plane hit the water — it came down within twenty minutes of Vandenberg losing contact with the *Nighthawk*."

"I'll take your word for that," she said. "But you have to take mine as well. The debris we're seeing is not from our vehicle."

Kurt hadn't heard of any crashes in this part of the world. But there was no point in arguing. He clicked on the radio. "*Reunion*, are you getting all of this?"

"The video feed is good," Joe said. "Looks like you've hit the mother lode."

"According to my copilot, it's fool's gold," Kurt said. "I'm going to haul some of the debris up for you to inspect; maybe you can figure out what kind of plane this came from."

"Sounds good," Joe said. "Look for something definitive."

Kurt scanned around them for a smaller piece of debris that might reveal the make and model of the wreck. "What about that circuit board?" he said, pointing to a length of wiring attached to a green computer panel.

"Good idea," Joe said over the radio. "The electronics might be traceable."

Kurt maneuvered the *Angler* into position, overshot just a bit and then cut the throttle, allowing the sub to drift back over the target.

With the thrusters off, the *Angler* was utterly silent. In the sudden quiet, he noticed something he hadn't heard before: a vibration in the water; a low, repetitive hum, coming from somewhere in the distance.

Emma heard it, too. "What is that?"

It sounded like a ship to Kurt. He got back on the radio. "*Reunion,* are you on the move?"

"Negative," Joe replied. "We're full stop. Half the crew are out on deck, sunning themselves. Why?"

"Do you see any traffic?"

There was a slight delay before Joe replied again. "Also negative. There's not a ship on the horizon."

Despite that fact, Kurt was certain they were hearing a ship's propeller.

"If it's not up there . . ." Emma said.

She didn't have to finish. Kurt was thinking the same thing. He deployed a hydrophone. It wasn't a true sonar receiver — in fact, it was just a basic microphone encased in a waterproof container designed to record whales and other sounds of sea life — but by turning it a few degrees at a time, he was able to get a better fix on the strange hum.

Heard through the speakers, the sound was deep and ominous, and growing louder by the moment. "It's coming from behind us," Kurt said. "And it's coming this way."

Kurt nudged the thrusters and slowly spun the *Angler* until it was pointed in the direction of the approaching hum. He switched off the normal light, leaving only the UV system in place. Still they saw nothing.

"Maybe we should get out of here," Emma said.

A sharp ping exploded through the water, reverberating in the hollow confines of the *Angler* like someone had struck the side with a hammer.

Emma put a hand to her ear. Kurt marveled at a ripple in the silt, caused by the power of the invisible sound wave.

"Someone just painted us," Kurt said, meaning the sonar ping had found them and probably registered back to whatever submarine had issued it.

"Searching for wreckage like us?"

"Maybe, but you don't need a sonar pulse like that to search for wreckage," Kurt replied. He left unsaid that powerful sonar pings were normally used to get targeting data for torpedoes.

With a smooth touch, he spun the *Angler* around, looking for the source of the ping. The thrumming sound grew louder, like a freight train barreling down on them.

"What are you waiting for?" Emma asked.

"We have to look both ways before we cross the road," he said, pivoting the nose of the submersible upward and turning the UV light to full intensity while simultaneously glancing toward the monitor.

At first there was nothing. Then, in the far distance a distortion appeared, like a portal to another dimension opening in the deep. Kurt knew it was the swirling water and the tiny sedimentary fragments being forced aside by a pressure wave. Behind the distortion, a shape began to form, emerging out of the darkness.

Huge, wide and bulbous, it was the curving nose of an approaching submarine. Not a small submersible like the *Angler,* or even a svelte attack submarine, but a monster of the deep, grinding toward them, its bow a wall of steel.

It was cruising slowly, perhaps a hundred feet off the seafloor.

"They're trying to run us down," Emma said.

"No," Kurt said. "They're just following the same debris trail we did."

"Then we should get out of the way."

Kurt shook his head. "Moving now would give them our location. As long as we remain still, we *should* appear no different than a rock formation or part of the wreckage."

As Kurt spoke, another ear-splitting pulse came forth. The NUMA submersible rang like a bell and still Kurt held his ground.

A swirling cloud of sediment swelled forth, beneath and in front of the approaching vessel. It made it seem like the behemoth was riding on a cushion of dust.

"Hang on," Kurt said.

The disturbance hit the *Angler* and the small submersible was spun around and swept to one side.

Kurt used the thrusters to straighten the sub out and watched in awe as a mountain of rust-colored steel passed over them, filling the view from one edge of the canopy to the other. It passed by slowly, almost endlessly. The submarine crossing above them was as wide and long as the cargo vessel floating on the surface.

Finally, the propellers came into view.

As they neared, the *Angler* was pulled off the bottom by the turbulence and drawn toward the spinning props. It was swept in close and then spat out behind the passing leviathan, tumbling in the submarine's baffles. Kurt fought to control the ride, but had little power against what was essentially an underwater tornado.

The *Angler* spun and rolled and banged against an outcropping of rock. Several warning lights blinked on. And then everything went black.

Up on the *Reunion,* Joe and Captain Kamphausen watched the events live until the video feed suddenly cut out. Without sound or commentary, it was hard to tell what happened. The last image caught on tape was a shot of the churning brass propellers.

"Did it hit them?" Kamphausen wondered aloud.

Joe picked up the microphone. "*Angler,* what's your status?"

He waited a few moments before making another attempt. "Come in, *Angler.* Kurt, are you there?"

When he received nothing in response, Joe put the microphone down and played the video one more time, studying the blast of sediment and the last, ominous view.

"I don't think the props got them," he said. "A close call, nothing worse. But the communications line must have been cut."

"Why didn't he move?" the captain asked. "He just sat there like a deer in the headlights."

"Kurt doesn't freeze up," Joe replied. "He must have felt it was safer to stay put. A tactic I would agree with. It's very surprising that a vessel that large would be traveling that close to the seafloor."

Joe checked the last burst of telemetry data from the *Angler*'s control systems in hopes of gaining more insight. What he saw concerned him. A list of warning lights had come on right before the line was cut.

"Battery pack," he said, reading off the labels. "Pumps. Gyrostabilizer. They must have hit something pretty hard for all of those systems to go out at once."

Kamphausen offered a grim look. "What exactly does all that mean? Are they drowning?"

"I doubt it," Joe said. "The *Angler* has a strong hull, so I'm assuming they're dry. But they may be facing the submariner's worst nightmare."

"Worse than drowning?"

"Being marooned alive on the bottom," Joe said. "With electrical problems and the pumps off-line, they may not be able to surface."

"Is there any way we can help them?" Kamphausen asked. "Or do we just have to wait and see?"

"Under normal circumstances, this wouldn't be a big problem," Joe said. "I'd just drop another sub in the water, hook a line on them and tow them back to the surface. Failing that, I'd don a hard suit and hook a cable to them and winch them up. But since we don't have either of those things, we're going to have to improvise."

"What about that submarine that almost ran them over?" Kamphausen said. "Judging by the rust on the hull and the general state of neglect, I'd say it was a Russian boat. Is it too much to assume they're after whatever you're after?"

"We'd be foolish to assume anything else," Joe replied.

"Are we in any danger?"

"I doubt they'll torpedo a surface ship like the *Reunion*," Joe said. "That would be inviting war and their rapid destruction from our sub-hunting aircraft. But the depths of the sea are a different story."

"How so?"

"To a large extent, *what happens down below, stays down below,*" Joe replied, co-opting the famous Las Vegas advertising slogan. "They could easily eliminate the *Angler* by ramming it, or hitting it with a torpedo, or by sitting on it and crushing it down into the silt. In all cases, no one up here would ever know what happened. And that, I cannot allow."

Kamphausen scratched his head. "But how can we stop them?"

"By getting them off the bottom before anything else happens."

Kamphausen nodded, looked around as if he was thinking deeply and then turned back to Joe. "I've got nothing."

"Fortunately, I've got an idea," Joe said. "But it's going to take a little work. I assume you have a few generators on this ship."

"Several."

"Show me to the largest one you've got. And have your engineering team meet us there with a complete set of tools."

Kamphausen looked at him suspiciously.

"Don't worry," Joe said. "I'll put it all back together when I'm done."

Nine hundred feet below, Kurt and Emma sat in darkness. The huge submarine had passed over the top of them and continued on into the dark. The turbulent ride had slammed them against a ledge of volcanic rock, tripped a few circuit breakers and lit up several warning lights on the panel before shutting off all the lights.

Using a flashlight, Kurt found the main panel, pushed the circuit breakers back in and brought the *Angler* back to life. "No real damage," he determined.

"Listen," Emma said.

The hydrophone was still picking up the sound of the propellers, but the intensity level had waned. Before long, it ceased altogether.

"They've come to a stop," Kurt said.

"Better than having them double back."

"Couldn't agree more," Kurt replied. "But what are they doing down here in the first place? Considering the size and shape of that sub, I make it out as a Russian Typhoon, a ballistic missile submarine. Not exactly cut out for search-and-rescue work."

"Maybe it was the nearest vessel they had with sonar capability," Emma suggested.

Kurt wasn't so sure. He straightened his headset and tried to reach Joe. "Joe, are you out there? I'm hoping you got the number of the truck that almost ran us down."

There was no answer. Not even static. "I think the Typhoon cut our line as it passed overhead," Kurt replied. "We've lost communications with the surface."

"Maybe we should count ourselves lucky and head up," she suggested. "See if Joe can identify this aircraft and let everyone know this is a dead end."

Kurt considered that, but a curious mind and a sharpened sense of suspicion ran in his family just like the silver-gray hair he'd inherited at a young age. "That would be the smart thing to do," he admitted. "But something doesn't make any sense here. Did you report this location to anyone?"

She shook her head. "I haven't told a soul."

"Neither have I. So, there couldn't be a leak."

"What about our *partners* on the *Reunion*?"

"I can't imagine a Russian agent being stowed away on a refrigerated agriculture ship I chose at random," he replied. "And even if we were *that* unlucky and someone up there did pass our location to the Russians, what are the odds they would have a Typhoon submarine within a few hours' sailing time of our location?"

"Astronomically low," she said. "The few Typhoons they have left spend most of their time in port, and when they do sail, they rarely venture far from home."

Kurt knew that, too. He also knew the Typhoons were in the process of being retired from service. "By all rights, that sub should not be here."

"Maybe we should worry about it another day," Emma said. "They've already scanned the debris field with their sonar. If we're lucky, they'll bring their salvage fleet out here and spend a few days recovering aircraft parts off the bottom before they realize this wreckage doesn't come from the *Nighthawk*."

Kurt was one step ahead of her. "That's just it," he said. "I think they already know."

His hand went back to the console and he raised the volume on the hydrophone. A new sound was emanating from the dark, a pulsing noise that sounded more like water running through a pipe.

"Bow and stern thrusters," he said. "They're keeping station out there in the dark. I suggest we go find out why."

16

"Are you afraid they'll see us?" Emma asked, commenting on their stealth approach.

"Submarines like the Typhoon don't have windows to look through," Kurt said, "but they might have cameras or ROVs and submersibles of their own to deploy. They also have passive listening devices that are highly sensitive. Hugging the bottom will absorb any sound we make."

They both fell silent and Kurt continued tracking toward their target by making small adjustments to the hydrophone. When a rock formation appeared on the video screen, he weaved around it. When they came to a slope of sediment piled up against a wide ridge, he put the *Angler* into an ascent.

They tracked the slope upward and came over the top.

"Look," Emma said.

Kurt looked up from the screen. An eerie blue glow loomed in the distance.

With enough light to navigate by, he switched off the UV system and retracted the *Angler*'s namesake boom. Continuing over the ridge and down the other side, they approached the lighted area.

From a distance, the glow was nothing more than a shimmering orb of water, dark blue in color and revealing no details. As they moved closer, it turned green, and eventually took on a yellowish tint similar to natural light.

Because of the total darkness surrounding them and the weightless state of the submarine, it felt as if they were approaching a strange planet in the depths of space.

As they closed in, Kurt cut the throttle and allowed the *Angler* to drift. "Our friends have set up shop."

The glowing orb had become a swath of daylight that ran for several hundred feet. It was cast by row after row of high-powered floodlights on the underside of the Typhoon. The bulk of the huge submarine remained hidden in the inky black water, but the seafloor beneath was lit up like a stadium. The reflected light illuminated the underside of the Typhoon and the maroon-colored paint the Russian Navy preferred to use below the waterline.

Several pod-like shapes were visible beneath the keel.

"Divers in hard suits," Kurt said.

They were descending toward the seafloor like tiny probes dropped from an alien vessel. Their destination was a large concentration of wreckage, including an upturned wing and the T-shaped tail of a large aircraft.

"Vertical stabilizer," Emma said. "Fuselage section over there. And that looks like an engine pod. I told you this wasn't the *Nighthawk.*"

A clanking sound came through the hydrophone and then a hiss of bubbles.

"Pressure door opening," Kurt said. "Most likely, the lockout room where those divers came from or a compartment from where they can release an ROV."

More clanking sounds rang out through the hydrophone and a narrow slit of light appeared in the underside of the Typhoon. It grew wider as a pair of huge doors in the bottom of the hull drew back from each other. They locked in place, leaving a hundred-foot opening in the bottom of the submarine. As Kurt and Emma watched in amazement, a huge clamshell bucket descended from the center of it, its jaws stretched wide.

191

The bucket crashed into the wreckage with abandon. Sediment swirled in the light, and as the hydraulic jaws closed, the screech of rendered metal cried out through the water.

Kurt watched intently as the tail section of the aircraft was hauled up into the open bay of the submarine. "The Russians have built a submersible version of the *Glomar Explorer.*"

The *Glomar Explorer* was the most famous salvage vessel in the world. Built by the CIA, using the celebrity status of Howard Hughes as a cover, it had performed its secret task once, and only once, pulling most of a sunken Russian submarine off the bottom of the Pacific in 1974.

Disguised as a mining ship, the *Explorer* had moved into position, lowered a cradle, and hauled up three-fourths of what had been the K-129, bringing the wreckage through a huge door in the bottom of the hull and hiding it in what the engineers called the *moon pool.*

Russian spy ships watching from several miles away never knew what happened. When the truth leaked, the Russians were furious. They were also embarrassed and put on notice that anything in the sea was fair game. They'd maintained a large salvage fleet ever since — a substantial portion of which was currently sailing for the Galápagos — but this Typhoon, this huge submarine converted into a clandestine salvage vessel, was something new.

At least it was new to Kurt. "You guys at the NSA know anything about this?"

"This is a surprise. But it makes perfect sense, if you think about it. Take the missile tubes out and the Typhoon has huge storage capacity. It can move about undetected, dive to twenty-five hundred feet and pluck things right off the bottom, all unseen by the world's satellites."

"Wish we'd thought of it," Kurt said. "While we're tracking their surface fleet and telling ourselves we have several days before they get here, these guys are already on scene. Which begs the question: Exactly what scene is this? If this wreckage isn't the *Nighthawk,* then what are we looking at? And why are the Russians so interested in it?"

"Maybe we should get a little closer and find out," she said.

"Look who's become a risk taker," Kurt replied, grinning.

"It's a risk-reward scenario," she said. "A few photos of this Typhoon will help soften the blow of not finding the *Nighthawk* out here."

Kurt bumped the throttle forward once more. "Who am I to stand in the way of shameless self-promotion?"

"I assure you," she said, "I'm thinking purely of the national interest."

Kurt suppressed a laugh — on the odd chance it might have carried through the water to the Typhoon's hydrophones.

The closer they got, the louder the racket became. As they watched the effort from the darkness, it became clear that haste was the priority. As soon as the retrieval bucket deposited a load of wreckage in the Typhoon's cargo bay, it was run back out, repositioned and dropped once again. There was no caution to the work and no attempt to preserve or protect any technology they might be recovering.

The reason dawned on Kurt. "They're not trying to *salvage* anything. They're trying to haul it away and hide the evidence before anyone else finds it here. Which means —"

"This is a Russian aircraft," Emma said, finishing his thought. "Maybe it's a recon flight that went down while searching for the *Nighthawk*."

Kurt shook his head. "This crash happened almost simultaneously with the *Night-*

hawk's disappearance."

"A chase plane, then," Emma suggested. "The Russians have tried that before."

By now, they were near enough to make out gearing and teeth on the inner part of the wing. He was maneuvering to get the camera focused when a brief flash caught his eye.

Kurt shut off what remained of the interior lighting and waited. A full minute ticked by before the light made another appearance. It was quick. Here and then gone. A white spark in the dark water of the sea.

"Low-powered strobe light," he said.

"Black box," Emma suggested, referencing the nearly indestructible data and voice recorders common on most military and commercial aircraft.

"Let's see if we can get at it without drawing too much attention to ourselves."

He eased the submersible forward with a deft touch, traveling past that shattered wing and holding station near a tear in the forward part of the fuselage. The curved body of the aircraft had been opened and peeled back. The section beneath it was exposed. The tiny strobe flashed again from within.

"See if you can reach it."

Emma went back to the controls and

195

extended the arm to its maximum length. "No," she said. "Can you get any closer?"

"Hang on," Kurt said. He backed off and moved forward again, using a quick burst of the throttle. The *Angler* bumped against the wreckage, scraping against it and pushing a section of the airframe out of the way.

When the strobe flashed again it was brighter and closer and they were all but inside the airframe. Emma extended the arm once more. The claw at its end opened. The lower half slid underneath a metal handle on the housing of the data recorder and Emma closed it down tight.

"Got it," she said, retracting the arm.

The black box — which was actually orange and covered with gray Cyrillic writing — came out of its slot with a little effort. Once it was clear, Emma retracted the arm and dropped it into the starboard cargo container.

"Good work," Kurt said.

He put his hand on the throttle and prepared to back out but paused when the sound of the Typhoon's thrusters surged through the water with a different timbre.

Emma looked up. "The Typhoon is repositioning."

Kurt already knew that. He could see the

lighted swath of ocean floor moving toward them.

He reversed thrust, trying to back out of the open section of the fuselage, but instead of moving in a straight line, the *Angler* was yanked to the side and pulled around.

"We're caught on something," he said, craning his head around to see what had hooked them.

"I can see it from here," Emma said. "The frame around the retrieval container is snagged on the wreckage."

Kurt moved the sub forward and then backed up again, trying to pull free. But it was no use. The *Angler* was hooked.

A third try did nothing to free them, and the wreckage around them began to brighten as the peripheral light from the Typhoon reached the area.

Kurt had no choice. He rotated the thrusters and forced the *Angler* back into the wreckage, crashing down and shutting everything off.

"What are you doing?" Emma asked, in shock.

"Hiding," he said. "It's the only choice we have."

The light around them grew brighter, filtering through gaps in the airframe like morning sun through high windows. The throbbing sound of the Typhoon's thrusters grew until the submarine appeared directly above them, rotating slowly until it was aligned into the current once again.

The maroon hull was marked with long scars of corrosion and algae while the lighted gap of the cargo bay shimmered with a sterile white glow.

Two divers in hard suits traveled up toward it, ascending with smaller pieces of debris in their nets and vanishing into the flooded hold. A moment later, the huge bucket reappeared. It traveled on rails in the cargo bay ceiling, stopping and locking into position almost directly above the *Angler.*

"This is not good," Emma whispered.

Kurt couldn't have agreed more.

The bucket remained stationary for what seemed an eternity, its clamshell jaws opening slowly and locking into position. Finally, with nothing more than a pitiful squeak, it began to drop.

There was no mistaking its destination. The huge bucket was dropping straight for the wreckage pile and the NUMA submersible hiding in it.

17

The outstretched jaws of the retrieval bucket plunged downward, crashing into the wreckage surrounding the *Angler.* Metal screeched as it was torn and twisted. A cloud of silt erupted from the impact site and the *Angler* tilted over to one side.

With the teeth of the bucket embedded in the silt below, the powerful hydraulic struts activated. The jaws were forced together, burrowing through the silt, until they slammed shut beneath the heap of tangled metal.

The powerful winch in the Typhoon's cargo bay was engaged and the steel cables pulled taut, straining against the suction created by the sediment. The resistance didn't last. With a sudden lurch, the latest collection of wreckage was pulled from the seafloor to begin its journey upward.

Watching from the outside, the divers in hard suits saw nothing to differentiate this load of material from any other. It was just another stack of twisted metal being hauled away, with a long trail of silt pouring from the gaps and streaming in the current.

As the bucket neared the opening in the Typhoon's hull, a maneuver called *the shake* was performed. The ascent was halted and the jaws were opened a few inches. The tension on the cable was released and the bucket allowed to fall several feet before being stopped.

Each time the crane operator shook the bucket, a new cloud poured from the bottom. After several shakes, there was little sediment left. The jaws were closed once again. The winch was reactivated and the load drawn into the cargo bay.

Once it was fully retracted, the bucket began to move horizontally. At a predetermined position, it stopped and dumped the latest pile of wreckage on the inner deck.

Inside the *Angler,* Kurt and Emma were thrown about. They remained in their seats. When they were finally dropped inside the Typhoon, both of them were amazed to be alive. The claws had gone under and around them. The hull hadn't been punctured or even scratched; the acrylic of the canopy was free of cracks.

"Look at the size of this hold," Emma

said, gazing around.

"Used to be the missile bay," Kurt said. "In their original configuration, Typhoons carried twenty-four extremely large ICBMs. The largest ever deployed to sea."

As Kurt spoke, he got his bearings. The bay was filled with water, which could be pumped out once the heavy doors were closed. At the moment, they were facing aft and tilted over at a thirty-degree angle. To get free, they'd have to rise up, make a U-turn and then dive out through the opening. Assuming, of course, that they *could* get free.

Leaning across the cockpit, Kurt spotted the offending piece of wreckage. "I think I can cut us loose."

"Better be quick," Emma said. "There's not much wreckage left down there."

Kurt moved an acetylene torch into position. At the touch of a button, it snapped to life. He brought it up against the bent metal spar that had snagged them. The flame burned bright blue and the metal flared, red and molten, dropping away in burning fragments.

As he worked, the Typhoon repositioned itself and the retrieval bucket descended once again.

Emma watched the gearing above them

spin. The cable let out for several seconds and then came to a rather abrupt stop. "Now would be a good time," she urged.

Kurt continued to burn through the length of metal, watching small bits melt and fall off. It seemed to be taking forever, as if the metal was made of something other than aluminum.

The gearing above began to spin as the cable was reeled in to bring the next load of wreckage on board.

"Hurry, Kurt," Emma urged.

"I'm cutting as fast as I can."

The torch finished its cut and a large triangular piece fell away. The *Angler* was free.

Kurt switched over to the throttle, tilted the thrusters and poured on the power. The *Angler* rose up out of the junk pile, shedding metallic debris and the coating of silt it had acquired.

Once they were above the wreckage, Kurt spun the submersible in a half circle and accelerated toward the open gap at the end of the cargo bay. They reached the edge, dove downward underneath the bucket just as it shook loose its next great cloud of silt.

Momentarily blinded, Kurt kept the throttle wide open. When they emerged on the far side, they were in the clear, headed for the darkness and safety beyond.

Sitting in the operations room of the Typhoon, Captain Victor Tovarich of the Russian 1st Salvage Flotilla watched the operation unfold on several screens, each linked to cameras on the underside of the Typhoon. An additional screen was divided into four quadrants and displayed the video feed from cameras mounted on the divers' hard suits.

He was proud of his men and his great machine but anxious to complete the project. He turned to his second-in-command. "Progress report."

"Eighty percent of main wreckage recovered," the officer replied.

"Any sign of the *Nighthawk*?"

"No, sir," the officer replied. "I'm afraid not."

"It has to be here," he said, walking over to the monitor to study the grainy picture that was coming in. "We know they had it in their grasp."

"Permission to speak freely?" his First Officer said.

"Of course."

"If the *Nighthawk* is not with the bomber, we should stop wasting our time on this recovery and get back to searching for the American craft."

Tovarich resisted the urge to smile. His First Officer was a charger. He wanted the glory that came with plucking the American space plane off the bottom. He wasn't alone. "I share your desire, Mikael. But they've decided in Moscow that this craft is a priority."

The officer nodded.

"Besides," Tovarich added. "It could still be here. There was always a chance that the pilots managed to hold on to the *Nighthawk* even as they lost control."

"A blind man's chance of catching a sparrow."

"Perhaps," Tovarich agreed. "Only an airman could come up with such a plan. We should salute their bravery. Which reminds me, we'll need to search the wreckage in the cargo bay and recover the bodies."

He reached over and tapped a button, switching one of the monitors to an internal camera view. "Have one of the divers report to . . ."

Tovarich froze midsentence. Something on the screen caught his eye. A flickering light: *fire.* His first concern — that they'd brought something combustible on board — vanished as the firelight snapped off, but his confusion grew worse as he saw movement in the wreckage. "What in the name of . . ."

Tovarich watched in disbelief as a white submersible with a broad red stripe rose out of the tangled metal and spun around. It came forward, heading right toward the camera, and then dove out through the open cargo bay doors, but not before Tovarich noticed the letters *NUMA* prominently displayed on the top of the submersible.

Rushing to the tactical section of his control room, Tovarich grabbed the sonar operator. "We have an uninvited guest out there," he said. "American submersible. Find them!"

The sonar operator worked feverishly, pressing the earphones to his head and listening for the tiny, electric-powered submersible. With all the background noise, it proved impossible.

"It's no good, Captain. Too much interference from the salvage team and the thrusters."

Tovarich turned to the navigation officer. "Thrusters off. All stop. Shut down the salvage operation."

The positioning thrusters were turned off and the vibration they produced began to fade. As the Typhoon began to drift, the work outside came to a halt as well. No one dare move.

"Anything?" Tovarich asked.

The sonar operator continued searching. Finally, a signal emerged.

"Small craft," he said. "Bearing zero-four-five. Depth seven-fifty and rising."

"I want a positive range-and-firing solution," Tovarich said.

The tactical officer looked surprised. "Sir?"

"That's my order. Lock on and fire!"

Out in the dark, racing as fast as they could and heading for the surface, Kurt and Emma listened through the hydrophone as a strange silence grew up in their wake. "They've shut down the thrusters," Kurt said. "It means they're listening for us."

He considered shutting down as well and drifting on the current, but if he did that, the Russians would just resort to active sonar and would find them eventually. The only way to be safe was to reach the surface. He doubted the Russians would do anything once they were out in the open.

He angled the nose of the sub higher and watched as the depth went below seven hundred feet. They still had a long way to go when the sound of the Typhoon's main engines coming back to life reached them.

The heavy pinging of a sonar sweep caught them seconds later, followed by the sound Kurt was dreading: a sudden rush of compressed air as a torpedo was thrust into the water to track them down and destroy them.

18

The NUMA submersible was maneuverable, but not very fast. Certainly not in comparison to the torpedo homing in on it.

"Use this to control the hydrophone," Kurt said, placing Emma's hand on a large dial. "Keep it focused on the torpedo. We need to hear it coming if we're going to have any chance to avoid it."

"Torpedo?"

"Shouldn't have told you that," Kurt said.

A different kind of sonar found them next: rapid clicks with short intervals and a higher-pitched sound.

"It's locked onto us," Kurt said.

They'd put about a mile between themselves and the Typhoon by the time they were discovered. At that distance, and considering the comparative speeds, they might have forty seconds before getting obliterated.

"Can you take evasive action?" Emma said.

"We're making eight knots," Kurt said. "Nothing we do would be considered evasive. But we're not out of options."

He reached past Emma to the cargo controls. "If we can create a diversion, we might survive."

Kurt had loaded the flight recorder into the right-hand cargo container. But the left-hand container was filled with nothing of real value, just junk from the wrecked bomber. Pressing one button, he unlocked the clasps that held it to the side of the *Angler.* Turning a pair of valves to full open, he inflated a pair of yellow bags attached to the container. The rush of bubbles drowned out all noise for several seconds and the bags expanded like hot-air balloons. They rose toward the surface and lifted the cargo container free.

At almost the same instant, Kurt blew the air from the ballast tank and pointed the submersible straight down, hoping the wall of bubbles and the ascending cargo container would draw the torpedo off course.

For several seconds, the water was too turbulent to hear anything, but as the disturbance cleared, Emma refocused the hydrophone. The sonar pings from the torpedo had changed pitch, becoming weaker.

"It's headed for the container," Kurt said. "It's lost us."

He kept the nose of the submersible pointed down and the throttles full open, trying to put as much distance between the torpedo and themselves as possible.

"It's still going to hurt when it explodes," Emma said.

She wasn't wrong. Ten seconds later, a white and orange flash lit up the dark water as the torpedo obliterated the cargo container. The explosion caused a shock wave that slammed the *Angler* and sent it tumbling end over end.

With his ears ringing, Kurt stabilized the sub. "Now to make them think they hit us."

He shut down the thrusters and blew the ballast tanks. The little sub righted itself and began moving upward, headed for the surface propelled by buoyancy alone.

"I'm borrowing a play out of the old U-boat textbook," Kurt said. "They would make their escape *after* the depth charges went off because the water was so turbulent, it was impossible for sonar to hear through for several minutes."

"Won't they just ping us again?" Emma asked.

"Maybe," Kurt said. "But I'm betting they'll just listen for wreckage first. And it'll be a while before the water settles down enough for them to hear anything. By then, I'm hoping to be on the surface and out in the bright light of day."

The elevator ride picked up speed as the last drops of water were forced from the tanks. Kurt and Emma sat in silence, eyes locked on the slowly unwinding depth gauge.

"Anything?" the Typhoon's captain asked.

The sonar operator was listening, but all he could hear were the bubbles and cavitation left over from the explosion. It had rendered the passive sonar temporarily useless.

He waited and listened, keenly aware of the captain standing over his shoulder.

"Well?"

"Bubbles," the sonar operator said. "A moderate volume of released air traveling toward the surface. That would indicate a hit."

"Any wreckage?" Tovarich asked.

"Wreckage?" the tactical officer said. "Captain, that torpedo is designed to take out warships and American attack submarines. There won't be enough left of that

211

submersible to qualify as wreckage."

Tovarich understood, but he was a cautious man. "Humor me," he said. "Use the active sonar. I want to be sure."

The sonar was adjusted, another ping was released and the return echo examined. The results astonished everyone on board. "Target zero-six-one," the sonar operator said. "Depth one hundred and twenty feet and headed for the surface."

"Can we get them before they get there?"

The tactical operator made a few quick calculations. "No, sir," he said. "They'll be up top before we can fire."

Tovarich hesitated. He had standing orders not to allow any interference in the salvage, but he'd also been given similar — and now conflicting — orders to keep the mission clandestine. "They know too much," he said finally. "Load and fire. And, this time, you'd better not miss."

19

Joe Zavala sat in the cockpit of the Air-Crane as it rested quietly on the helipad near the bow of the *Reunion*. Captain Kamphausen was in the crane operator's seat, working the winch controls and reeling in a long section of cable. At the far end was a jury-rigged contraption Joe and the *Reunion*'s engineers had built to pluck *Angler* off the bottom of the sea.

"Are you sure this electromagnet is going to work?" Kamphausen asked.

"I used the best coils from your main generator," Joe said. "With the power from the Air-Crane's aux unit, it should have plenty of power."

Still believing the *Angler* might be stuck on the bottom, Joe's plan was to find the submersible with the side-scan sonar, lower the magnet down on a cable and stick it to the steel hull of the sub. That done, he'd reel them in.

Kamphausen, who'd worked cranes for half his years at sea, would do the honors while Joe piloted the Air-Crane. He shut down the winch as soon as the final length of cable wrapped itself around the drum and the magnet locked in place. "Now all we have to do is find them," he said.

Before Joe could reply, a deep, echoing thud reached them from the port side. Joe turned to see a momentary bulge on the surface of the sea. The circular displacement rose up and then fell back, releasing a tower of white water and foam from its center.

"Looks like someone else found them first," Kamphausen said.

Joe turned around and rushed through the preflight in record time, hitting the starter and getting the rotors moving above them. "Kurt and Emma must be on the move."

"How do you know that?"

"Because there's no other reason to shoot at them."

"At least we don't have to get them off the bottom," Kamphausen said.

"I have a feeling they're still going to need our help," Joe said.

As Kamphausen clicked his seat belt and the rotors flicked past at ever-increasing speed, Joe pulled on a headset and changed the frequency on the number one radio. He'd sent one of the small boats out on the water trailing the side-scan sonar and trying to pinpoint the location of the *Angler* without giving it away to the Russians. "*Survey 1,* did you catch that?"

The replay came loud and clear. "We saw it on the surface. No idea what caused it, though."

"Do you still have the Typhoon on the scan?"

"Yes, but the latest return is blurred."

"The Typhoon is moving, too," Joe concluded. "They wouldn't be doing that unless they were chasing something."

He turned his attention back to the instrument panel. Everything was operating in the green. With a firm twist of the throttle, Joe commanded full power. The weight came off the landing gear and the orange helicopter rose from the deck. With a kick of the rudder, Joe turned the nose to starboard and accelerated toward the widening circle of white water in the distance.

The *Angler* continued to ascend, moving upward at two hundred feet per minute. Kurt watched the light grow around them and Emma tried to pick up something, anything, on the hydrophone.

"It's blown-out," she said.

Kurt wasn't surprised; his ears felt as if they'd almost blown out as well. "Never mind," he said. "Just get ready to abandon ship in case they fire another torpedo our way."

She pulled a life jacket on as Kurt continued to pilot the submersible. They could see the surface now: a shimmering, waving mirror of silver that meant freedom.

As soon as the sub breached the surface, Kurt grabbed the radio. "*Reunion,* this is *Angler,*" he said. "We're on the surface and need *immediate* pickup. Do you copy?"

"Let's just hope our antenna didn't get blown off," Emma said.

Kurt pressed the transmit switch again. "*Reunion,* this is *Angler,* do you read?"

Joe was cruising across the water at an altitude of three hundred feet when he heard the radio call. Seconds later, he spotted the white and red submersible bobbing in the swells.

He turned the volume up. "Kurt, this is Joe. I have you in sight. We'll be on you in thirty seconds."

"Thirty seconds?" Kurt replied. He sounded shocked.

"We're already airborne. We thought you

might need help."

Joe brought the Air-Crane onto a matching course, setting up to grab the *Angler* off the water. As he finished the turn, he noticed something else: a long white trail of bubbles coming in from the west. "Don't look now but you have a torpedo heading your way."

"We'll bail out," Kurt replied.

"Stay put," Joe said. "I think I can get you before it hits."

"You'll never hook on in time," Kurt said.

"We don't need a hook," Joe said. "We have a magnet."

The submersible was moving, but it was ponderous on the surface. The white line of bubbles from the torpedo was tracking quickly toward them.

Joe cut in front of it, brought the Air-Crane down closer to the water. "Lower the magnet."

Kamphausen let out fifty feet of cable. The heavy, bell-shaped electromagnet trailed out behind them. He aimed for the red strip across the top.

"Activate the magnet," Joe said. "Full power. We're only going to get one shot at this."

"Coils are powered," Kamphausen shouted. "Electromagnet is live!"

From the corner of his eye, Joe saw the compass spin wildly as it picked up a new source of magnetism. They were thirty feet above the waves and closing in on the submarine at a shallow crossing angle. The torpedo trail was coming from directly behind them. Kamphausen could see it; Joe couldn't.

"It's going to be close," he said.

Joe slowed as he came in behind the sub and matched its course. The magnet skipped across the water, and the cable scraped across the sub's back. The magnet came free of the water, hit the stern of the small sub and bounced.

It looked as if the impact might cause it to skip over the top, but the powered side of the magnet was drawn toward the flat iron spine of the submersible. It snapped onto the hull with a solid clunk. The winch strained and let out several feet of cable before the brake locked it tight. The Air-Crane was pulled downward as the tension on the cable threatened to whip the helicopter into the sea, but Joe countered the effect and the *Angler* surged forward, riding high in the water for a moment before pulling free. It swung forward underneath the Air-Crane, shedding curtains of seawater behind it.

Joe was too busy stabilizing the Air-Crane to worry about the torpedo. Kamphausen held his breath as it passed underneath.

Nothing happened. No explosion. No detonation. The torpedo didn't even turn to acquire a new target. It just continued on a straight line and traveled off into the distance.

Kamphausen watched it go and gave it a mock salute. "Good riddance," he said.

Joe laughed and turned back toward the *Reunion* with the *Angler* flying beneath them.

Nine hundred feet below, Tovarich and the rest of the Typhoon's crew waited for a detonation that never came.

"What happened?" Tovarich asked finally.

"Nothing, sir," the sonar operator replied.

"I know that already," Tovarich said, the fury barely restrained. "What went wrong this time?"

"Nothing, sir," the tactical officer said. "Torpedo still running straight and true."

"So it missed?"

"No, sir, it . . . it was right on target . . . It's just . . ." he replied, baffled by the situation.

"It's just *what*?" Tovarich demanded.

"It's just that the American submersible is gone."

The captain stared at his sonarman in disbelief. "What do you mean *gone*?"

"It's no longer in the water, Captain."

Tovarich hauled the man out of his seat. He'd begun his career as a sonarman. He'd show these two amateurs how it worked. He snatched the headset and listened intently, adjusting the frequencies, the bearing and the sensitivity settings. He heard what they heard: the torpedo running but not the submersible.

"Give me an active ping!"

The emitter sounded almost immediately and the return came moments later. The torpedo was there, running off into the distance, as was the stationary freighter he assumed the NUMA submersible to be working from. But the submersible itself was gone.

Tovarich pulled the headset off. "Detonate the torpedo," he said. "And return to the crash site. Once the cleanup is finished, set course for the deep. I'll be in my quarters. Alone."

20

Kurt, Joe and Emma said their good-byes to the crew of the *Reunion* a few hours later. To their surprise, it was a warm send-off, despite the fact that no diamonds had been recovered. With the ship back on course and scheduled to make its delivery on time, even the fruit company rep stopped worrying. He took the ream of paperwork he'd been preparing for NUMA's lawyers and tossed it overboard.

Kamphausen, in particular, appeared sad to see them go. He all but crushed Joe in a bear hug. "Haven't had this much excitement in years," he insisted.

With Joe at the controls, the Air-Crane lifted off and turned east, headed for Guayaquil once again. Emma was in the copilot's seat and Kurt sat in the jump seat between the two of them.

Little was said as the flight progressed. Emma seemed pensive even before they took off and grew quiet during the flight, staring out the window for long stretches.

Kurt tapped her on the shoulder. "Are you okay?"

She turned his way. Her eyes suggested she was troubled, but the look was quickly covered. "Just disappointed," she said. "We're back to square one."

He nodded. "In a single day's work you uncovered a pair of top secret Russian projects. That's got to be good for something — at least a smile."

"Our mission was to find the *Nighthawk,*" she said.

"Relax," he said. "We'll find it."

She glanced at her watch. "We'd better."

As she turned back to the window, Kurt considered her demeanor. She played it like she was feeling disappointment, but Kurt saw it differently. It was stress. She looked as if she was carrying the world on her shoulders and that the world was getting heavier.

He unlatched his harness, folded up the jump seat and moved aft. Their backpacks rested there, along with a hard-sided suitcase in which the flight data recorder from the Russian bomber had been stored. Next to the case lay an assortment of refreshments and a parting gift from the crew of the *Reunion:* a fruit bowl covered with plastic wrap. It held limes, apples, oranges and, of course, an assortment of kiwis.

Kurt grabbed an orange and then paused. He glanced over his shoulder toward the cockpit. Emma was still staring out the window. Joe was busy flying.

He hesitated for only a second and then did what he felt needed to be done. Finished, he returned to the cockpit with refreshments for everyone.

An hour later, they were on the ground. Two cars waited for them on the airport ramp. Standing in front of one vehicle was Rudi Gunn. Climbing out of the second were a pair of men in dark suits.

"Friends of yours?" Kurt said to Emma.

"Not friends," she said. "Colleagues. I recognize the guy on the left. He works for Steve Gowdy. A personal right-hand man."

Kurt had expected something like this. He grabbed the luggage and climbed out through the door.

The three groups met on the tarmac. Names were exchanged and ID badges flashed until everyone had been introduced.

Emma handed over the hard-sided case. "Inside, you'll find a flight data recorder from a supersonic Russian bomber. Modified *Blackjack,* by the look of the wreckage."

The lead agent, whose name was Hurns, took the case. "What about the submarine?"

"Extensively modified Typhoon," she said, handing over a portable hard drive. "Photos and video are on here. We got some very clear shots."

Hurns nodded. "The brass are going to be thrilled. At this rate, you'll be a legend before you turn forty."

His words didn't seem to affect Emma in the least. "We all have our jobs to do," she said. "I'm staying on with the NUMA group until this mission is complete. Tell Steve I'll contact him as soon as I have anything else."

Hurns nodded. Carried the case to the trunk of the car and placed it inside. "We'll leave you to it," he said.

As the two agents from the NSA drove off, Rudi Gunn took over. He leaned against the side of his car with his arms folded and a stern look on his face. He addressed Kurt. "So what's this I hear about NUMA going into the vegetable business?"

"*Fruit* business," Kurt corrected. "It's an interesting story. If you'd like, I'll tell you on the way."

"On the way to where?"

"Consulate building," Kurt said. "We need a secure satellite link so we can test a theory I've come up with."

Rudi glanced Joe's way.

"First I've heard of it," Joe said.

Emma shot Kurt a suspicious glance, but he just smiled.

"Okay," Rudi said. "I'm game. But this better be good. We're already getting a lot of flak from the NSA about your *methods.*"

"Give me a few hours and judge for yourself," Kurt said.

Rudi raised an eyebrow of suspicion and opened the driver's door. "I will."

At the American consulate building in Guayaquil, Rudi spoke to the ranking official and clearance to use the communications suite was soon provided.

A quick look at the room revealed a high-tech masterpiece: consoles everywhere, flat-panel displays, computers and keyboards, even a virtual reality headset. All connected through encoding and decoding machines.

Kurt explained. "During my stint with the CIA, I had to use the consulates a few times. I was always impressed by the amount of technology they packed into one small space. It was often better than the stuff we were using on the outside since it didn't have to be portable."

Joe and Emma sat down wearily. It had been a long forty-eight hours. Only Kurt seemed to have any spring in his step.

Rudi remained guarded. He hadn't slept much. When he wasn't deflecting questions about NUMA commandeering a cargo ship or fighting off pressure from Steve Gowdy and the NSA to rein Kurt in, he'd been ducking calls from the fruit company and NUMA's general counsel. So far, they had nothing to show for all the commotion. Eventually, order and sanity would have to be restored, if only to satisfy Rudi's own sense of discipline.

Kurt placed his backpack on the central table and unzipped the main compartment. He pulled out a scuffed and dented piece of equipment. It was a dull-orange color and plastered with Russian writing on all sides.

"What is that doing here?" Emma asked, jumping from her seat.

"I pulled it out of your case while we were flying," Kurt said.

"Obviously," she replied. "But why? I was ordered to send it back to the lab. It's NSA property now."

Kurt held up a cautioning finger. "Actually, based on the law of Admiralty, this flight data recorder is the property of NUMA . . . Or, perhaps, the Russian Air Force, since it would be hard to prove they'd abandoned it or relinquished an ownership interest in it. But, as we're not sending it back to Moscow, I took it upon myself to assert NUMA's claim."

Joe clenched his teeth and shrank down in his seat a bit.

Rudi sighed and looked up at the ceiling, perhaps wondering why the gods had placed Kurt Austin in his life.

Emma just stared at him. "Gowdy is going to flip out."

"We're protecting him," Kurt said. "There's a leak in his department. The bomber and the Typhoon prove it."

"And you know this *how*?" Emma asked.

"Think about it," Kurt said. "The *Nighthawk* goes off course and vanishes. At the same time, in the same vicinity, a Russian supersonic bomber falls out of the sky and crashes into the sea. We mistake one crash for the other and race to the location only to find a top secret Russian submarine *already on the scene.* That's not a coincidence."

Emma sat back. "No, it's not. But I don't see how that indicates a breach of security."

"Don't you?" Kurt said. "To reach the search area when it did, that submarine had to leave Murmansk several weeks ago. And it's not the only vessel to end up in the right place at the right time. There are two separate fleets, one Russian, one Chinese, both steaming across the Pacific at flank speed right now. Both made up primarily of deepwater search-and-salvage vessels, both within a day's sailing of a crash site that didn't exist forty-eight hours ago, despite the fact that their home ports are *ten thousand miles* to the east."

"The fleet movements are suspicious," Emma admitted, "but explainable. Both units were on maneuvers, training exercises. The Chinese and Russian liaison teams informed us about them months ago. It's a little thing we do to keep from starting World War III."

Kurt didn't back off. "Of course they informed you months ago. Because they knew the *Nighthawk* was going to go down months ago."

"How could they know that?"

"Because they're the ones that brought it down."

"Brought it down?"

He nodded. "By hacking the *Nighthawk*'s command system. Codes that are jealously guarded by your NSA friends at Vandenberg. Which means the NSA has a mole, a very highly placed one, and that gives me every good reason not to share this flight data, or anything else, with them."

She went silent. Kurt let the words sink in.

"You're out on a very long limb here," Rudi said. "Even if some of those assumptions are true, it doesn't . . ."

"No," Emma said, interrupting him. "Kurt's right."

All eyes turned her way.

"It's the only thing that makes sense. We've never been able to figure out why the *Nighthawk* went off course in the first place. One technician noted that *Nighthawk* was having a problem trying to process *conflicting* commands. It made no sense at the time. We assumed it was a computer glitch. But the bomber, the Typhoon, the salvage fleets conveniently on the scene — it all suggests the Russians and/or the Chinese reprogrammed the *Nighthawk* and tried to get it to splash down in the ocean where they could pick it up with ease."

Rudi said, "But if that's the case, why wouldn't their fleets be *in* the crash zone instead of several days' sailing from it."

"Because we brought it back early," she said. "The storm off Hawaii was tracking toward the California coast. It was expected to hit during the initial landing window. We didn't want to risk dealing with the weather, so we moved the reentry up five days.

Without that change, both salvage fleets would be within a hundred miles of the Galápagos Islands chain just waiting for the *Nighthawk* to drop out of the sky and into their hands."

"Even the location makes sense," Joe added. "Aside from the terrain around the Galápagos, the sea is ten thousand feet deep for hundreds of miles in every direction."

"And the bomber?" Rudi asked.

"Probably a chase plane," Emma said. "The *Nighthawk* is coated in third-generation stealth materials. It's completely invisible to radar. But coming through the atmosphere, its skin heats up to three thousand degrees. A supersonic bomber with an infrared tracking system could follow it for miles, zeroing in on its heat signature and following it until it slowed to landing speed and parachuted softly into the sea."

Kurt nodded. "Exactly what I was thinking. But something went wrong. And even though the bomber went down, there might be a clue to the *Nighthawk*'s whereabouts on the data recorder. A clue we don't want broadcast to Moscow or Beijing."

"What if someone has found it already?"

"They haven't," Kurt said, "or their fleets would have turned around."

Emma nodded. "All right," she said. "Do your magic. Send the data back to NUMA and let's find out what the Russians were doing."

Kurt presented the black box. "Can you tap into it?"

Joe nodded. "Dataports look fairly standard. I'll do some quick tests and then send the information to Hiram. Max will be able to decipher it better than we can."

As Joe went to work, Rudi stepped out to make a call and Kurt took a seat next to Emma. The color had returned to her face. "You like the game?" Kurt said.

"I like to win," she replied.

"So do I."

They sat for a moment. "So what did you give them anyway?" she asked.

"Who?"

"My colleagues, Hurns and Rodriguez. When I lifted that case, there was something heavy in there."

Kurt leaned back in his chair and put his feet up. "A very nice parting gift. One I'm sure they'll appreciate on their long flight home."

The NSA-owned Gulfstream was halfway to Houston before Agent Hurns let his curiosity get the better of him. On this mission he was a courier, assigned to pick up and deliver a package. He wasn't supposed to open it and have a look, but he couldn't help himself.

He suggested as much to Rodriguez.

"I'm game," his partner said.

They left their seats, walked aft and lifted the metal-sided suitcase onto a table. With quick fingers, Hurns popped both latches and opened the case.

His face went blank. "What the heck is this?"

Rodriguez stared over his shoulder. "It appears to be a bowl of fruit," he said, reaching in for a ripe kiwi.

A handwritten note was tucked in between two oranges. It read:

Feed these to the mole.

Best regards,
Kurt Austin

21

Washington, D.C.

Hiram Yaeger had been part of many daring operations during his time with NUMA. But when the data from the black box was finally decoded, he could not help but tip an imaginary cap to the Russians for the sheer audacity of what they'd attempted.

With the full details revealed, he waited in the video conference room at NUMA headquarters while the satellite connection to the consulate building in Guayaquil was secured.

The room was a mix of the old world and the new. Paintings of tall ships lined the walls while a mahogany table from a nineteenth-century yacht dominated the center of the room. It was surrounded on three sides by comfortable chairs, though one had been removed for Priya, who came into the room in her wheelchair. On the remaining side lay a wall of flat-panel screens on which the team in Ecuador soon appeared.

"Good to see you all," Hiram said.

"Looking forward to being enlightened," Rudi replied.

Hiram nodded. "I have a feeling you won't be disappointed."

He pressed a button on the remote and another flat-screen display lit up. It was divided into three sections. The main part displayed a video image, taken from the Russian bomber's camera system; the second part of the screen displayed an overhead map view; and the third section displayed the bomber's cockpit and instrument panel as seen from a high-mounted camera over the pilot's shoulders. Their helmets and shoulders were partially in view.

"Are you seeing this on your screen?" Hiram asked.

"Yes," Rudi said.

"Fantastic," Hiram said. "The Russians use one recorder to collect all vital information instead of two separate recorders for voice and data like the FAA requires. Their system worked well, but we only have the last twenty minutes of the flight. I think it'll be enough. For your convenience, Max has translated all the voices into English."

The lights dimmed and the presentation

began. The initial image was a gray-scale infrared video. On the right side were various numbers, indicating speed, course and altitude. In the distance, a tiny white dot flared and dimmed while tracking lines indicated it was above the bomber and thirty miles distant.

"Target acquired," the translated voice said. *"Vehicle speed four thousand one hundred. Engaging scramjets."*

"Did he say *scramjets*?" Emma asked.

"He did," Hiram replied. "We double-checked the translation. They're using a different acronym, but the operation is the same. The bomber was powered by supersonic ramjets capable of taking them up to Mach 6."

As the scramjets came to life, the video image began to shake and buzz. The Mach number climbed and the voices of the pilot, copilot and engineer were almost overridden by the ever-increasing roar of the engines.

The pilot called out the milestones. *"Passing Mach 3 . . . 3.5 . . . Mach 4 . . ."*

The acceleration continued for another minute and then slowed.

"Speed locked in at Mach 5.1."

The copilot spoke next. *"Surface temperature within tolerance."*

"He's referring to the outer skin of the aircraft," Hiram said.

Emma nodded. She was the aviation expert. She understood instinctively. "At Mach 5, the leading edges of the nose, wings and tail would be suffering tremendous heating. Regular steel would melt. The aircraft skin would have to be made of a special alloy, probably using extensive amounts of titanium."

"Which explains why the alloy detector and the magnetometers locked onto the wheels and internal parts first," Joe replied. "More iron, easier to find."

"Exactly."

The video continued to play. *"Course matched,"* the pilot's voice said. *"Releasing controls to the computer."*

The small dot they were tracking on the cameras grew larger as it moved closer until it became obvious they were looking at the *Nighthawk.* But they weren't catching up to it; they were allowing it to catch up to them.

"At this point, the bomber is in front of and below the *Nighthawk,"* Hiram said. "Max, display the course lines."

On a second part of the screen, the satellite view of the South Pacific and the South American coast sharpened. Two icons appeared, one red, one green. Thin lines stretched out behind them.

"The red line is the Russian bomber," Hiram said. "The green line is the *Nighthawk.*"

The two lines soon merged, with the Russian bomber slightly ahead of the unmanned spacecraft.

"Course matched," the flight engineer's voice called out. *"Distance two miles and closing."*

Another voice sounded on the cockpit recorder. *"Signal jamming complete. Vandenberg has been blocked.* Nighthawk *is all yours."*

"Roger that, Blackjack 2."

"A second bomber?" Joe asked.

Hiram nodded. "Approximately a mile ahead of the first."

On the infrared video, the *Nighthawk* continued to grow larger and move closer. A distance indicator and a series of vertical and horizontal bars appeared on the video feed.

"Range one thousand feet and closing," the copilot called out.

The *Nighthawk* approached steadily, looming ever larger in the video. The camera tracked it moving past the bomber's tail and into a position directly above the Russian aircraft. At thirty-nine hundred miles an hour and ninety-one thousand feet, the two aircraft were now traveling in perfect formation.

The copilot's voice was calm. *"Speed matched. Course steady. We're in position for the capture."*

"Deploying windbreak," the pilot said.

A series of small spikes emerged from the back of the Russian bomber. They created a vortex and a low-pressure area across the bomber's spine that drew the *Nighthawk* downward. It dropped slowly, kissing the Russian plane gently. It was immediately trapped by a series of clamps that sprung up from the bomber's fuselage. They grabbed the *Nighthawk*'s wings and locked it in place.

"Contact made. Snares in place," the copilot said.

"Deploying secondary windbreak," the pilot announced.

A triangular wedge of metal rose up in front of the captured spacecraft. It deflected the wind around and away from it. A vapor trail streamed from the top of the windbreak, traveling up and over the nose of the delta-wing craft and back. The ride was smooth.

"They grabbed it," Emma whispered.

"They snatched it right out of the sky."

"I can't believe there's no turbulence," Kurt said.

"The atmosphere is so thin at that altitude, there isn't any turbulence," Emma said.

"But they're traveling at four thousand miles an hour," Rudi pointed out.

"Not in relation to each other," Emma replied. "We dock spacecraft in orbit all the time. On TV, it looks like they're barely moving, but in reality they're whipping around the Earth at 17K. In the sixties and seventies, the *Apollo* and *Gemini* pilots eyeballed it. I'm sure these guys have the most advanced computers in the Russian catalog at their disposal."

"Docking complete," the pilot reported. *"Tell Moscow we have the* Nighthawk."

The sounds of a celebration could be heard on the tape, and the next few minutes were routine. A call went out to the second bomber. Tests were done, systems were checked and rechecked. All this time, the *Blackjack 1* continued on the same course, traveling at the same incredible speed.

"Reducing power," the pilot said finally. *"Inform Caracas we'll need refueling."*

"We're not sure if he means Caracas, Venezuela," Hiram said, "or if that's a code name for a refueling aircraft."

"I'll bet on the former," Rudi said. "The Russians have plenty of friends where Hugo Chávez used to rule."

As the aircraft slowed, there was a noticeable drop in the background noise. The speed fell below Mach 4 and then below Mach 3. At Mach 2.5, the bomber began a shallow turn to the north and, for the moment at least, it seemed as if the Russians had pulled off the world's greatest hijacking.

A flicker ran through the video, followed by a garbled communication.

A rhythmic vibration grew up and the aircraft began to shudder. Before long, the cameras were trembling.

"Inertial dampers failing," the copilot said. *"Vibration reaching critical."*

"Where is this coming from?"

"We're getting a strain on the lockdown bolts," the flight engineer called out. *"It's the* Nighthawk; *there's a flutter in the control surfaces."*

The pilot's next response was unintelligible. He was grunting and breathing hard as he fought the controls.

A call went through the radio. "Blackjack 2, *we have a problem.* Nighthawk *is trying to go active. I repeat, the* Nighthawk *has woken* up. *Falconer, use the alpha codes. Shut it down.*"

The return call was far calmer. *"Are you certain,* Blackjack 1? *We show no activity. Our board is green. You should not be having any issues."*

The pilot shouted his response. *"I'm telling you that damned thing is trying to break free. Boost your signal and order it to shut down — now!"*

Whatever *Blackjack 2* did in response, the vibration only grew worse. The sound of alarms filled the cockpit. Warning lights came on all over the board.

"Hydraulics," Priya said. "Vertical stabilizer . . . Inertial dampers."

The pilot's breathing was labored. His words marked by cursing and desperation. On the external video feed, the *Nighthawk* could be seen shaking violently in its locked-down position. Its own flight control surfaces could be seen fluttering. Ailerons moving up and down. Rudder snaking back and forth.

And then it was gone.

In the blink of an eye, the captured aircraft ripped free of its moorings and peeled away, taking a chunk of the bomber's fuselage with it. Hydraulic fluid and white vapor streamed from the gaping hole it left behind.

"Mayday! Mayday! Mayday!" the pilot called out. *"We have an emergency situation."*

Despite his frantic efforts, the plane rolled over slowly and began corkscrewing dizzily toward the ocean. Mercifully, the camera failed a short time later. From that point, only the audio remained, filled with desperate shouts and garbled radio calls, until even the pilots went silent and all that could be heard was the aircraft's computer warning the pilots repeatedly to *Pull up . . . Pull up.* And then suddenly everything stopped.

Utter silence filled both rooms.

"We think they blacked out," Hiram said.

"Why didn't they eject?" Emma asked.

No one knew the answer.

The Russians might have been their political adversaries and opponents, but the pilots were just men doing their jobs. Men taking a tremendous gamble, and almost pulling it off, before paying with their lives.

"You can't help but admire their guts," Kurt said, breaking the silence. "If it wasn't our plane they were trying to steal, I'd be sitting here wishing they'd succeeded."

Everyone around him nodded.

"Any idea what went wrong?" Emma asked.

Hiram replied. "As long as the Russian

bomber continued on the *Nighthawk's* original course, all went well. As soon as the pilot turned away from that course, the *Nighthawk* went active again, attempting to steer itself back onto the initial heading. That started the vibration which led to separation and the crash."

"Why would it do that?" Kurt asked.

"We think the Russians hacked the navigation system," Hiram replied. "They reprogrammed it to head south and rendezvous with the bomber, but they forgot to shut the inertial navigation system off before they commenced the turn to the north."

"*Alpha code* is the NSA term for a reboot command. The equivalent of hitting the *Ctrl–Alt–Delete* buttons on your computer. It's supposed to break everything and reset the operating system."

"Any idea what they meant when they called out to the *Falconer?*"

Emma hesitated for a moment and then spoke. "I'm not sure," she admitted, "but several years ago we received intel suggesting that the NSA's space program had been penetrated. Either by a mole working at Vandenberg or through a Trojan horse computer program. There was no way to confirm the information and there were few details in the lead itself. Just a suggestion that vast amounts of data were being passed on to either the Chinese or the Russians. Other than that, we had only the code name."

"Falconer," Rudi said, "interesting choice. A falconer trains raptors to fly free and then return to him."

"The concept was lost on no one," Emma assured him, "as that's exactly what we were trying to do with the *Nighthawk*. Even so, a thorough investigation revealed no evidence that the agency had been compromised. The idea was written off as a red herring. You'd be surprised how much bad and false information is passed along. Most of it deliberately. We do it, too. All part of the game."

"Something tells me your boss might want to reopen the investigation," Rudi said.

"Agreed."

Kurt glanced at the dark screen and then back at Emma. "Well, whoever he was, he failed. The real question is, why? Everything appeared to be firmly in hand."

"Maybe a stray signal got through from Vandenberg?" Joe suggested.

"We don't think so," Hiram replied. "They were using the second bomber as a mobile transmitter, blasting a high-powered signal at the *Nighthawk* from close range. A setup like that would effectively drown out anything the NSA tried to send through."

Emma agreed. "Assuming the time on their clock was accurate, we'd already lost total contact with the vehicle when they caught it. It wasn't our doing. It must have been the autonomous programming. Not that it matters at this point." She looked Kurt's way. "For whatever it's worth, you were right about one thing: the NSA and Vandenberg have been compromised. If the Russians have the alpha codes, they have everything."

"Not everything," Kurt reminded her, before turning back to Hiram. "Any idea where the *Nighthawk* went after this?"

"We're working on that now," he replied. "But it's difficult to say for sure. The intercept changes all the calculations. The Russians gave it a nine minute piggyback ride at Mach 5, keeping it at full speed and above ninety thousand feet when it was supposed to be slowing and descending. That helpful little boost added seven hundred miles to the maximum glide path. Complicating matters are several video frames where the *Nighthawk* appears to be turning and shedding tiles, suggesting it was damaged as it broke free. All of that could affect the course, speed and glide path."

"I'm sure you have something," Kurt prodded.

Hiram nodded. "Max, show us the new course probability cone."

An image appeared on the screen. This time, the Ecuadorian coast was much larger and closer. A widening yellow cone curved toward it, crossing southern Ecuador and continuing inland over the mountains and jungles of Peru.

"It could be anywhere in that area," Hiram said. "Or any other area if the flight controls were damaged."

"So we *are* back to square one," Emma said.

"Not quite," Priya said. She wheeled over to a keyboard and tapped away on it for a few seconds. "We have this. It's a video that was released on Peruvian television."

The recording played for all to see. Shot by an amateur, it went in and out of focus but captured a glowing object crossing the night sky like a fireball. There was some shouting in the background and then the object disappeared beyond the top of a nearby hill.

The camera panned around, briefly capturing the edge of a solar panel and a pile of jumbled stones that looked like the ruins of a Neolithic building. A voice spoke off-camera. *"A sign from the gods,"* it said in accented English. *"The end must be near."*

A few grins broke out among the NUMA staff, but Emma's lips remained tightly pursed. "Who filmed this video?" she asked. "And where?"

"According to the television network, it was taken by a Peruvian archaeologist named Urco. He's currently working in the Andes on a dig connected to the Chachapoya, the Cloud People of Peru."

"Is there any way to authenticate it?" Kurt asked.

"No," Priya said. "It was shown a few hours ago. But it was allegedly filmed just before dawn on the morning of the *Nighthawk*'s disappearance. We've double-checked. The time frame is right and the location is within the *Nighthawk*'s newly extended glide path."

Rudi spoke next. "Any chance the video is a hoax?"

"A hoax of what?" Emma said. "No one in the outside world knows the plane is missing."

Priya added to that thought. "If you notice, the man in the video doesn't claim he's seen a spacecraft. The text accompanying the video calls it a *meteor sighting.*"

"Can you calculate altitude and speed

from the video?" Kurt asked.

"Not without more information," Hiram said. "Even if we could get a rough estimate, it wouldn't do any good without a precise direction."

Joe chimed in. "If we knew where he was standing and the exact location of that cliff dwelling behind him, we could get an accurate directional fix."

Kurt nodded, glanced around the room and then asked the question on everyone's mind: "Do we have any other leads?"

Both rooms held silent.

"Then it's agreed," Kurt said. "Let the Russians and Chinese search the Pacific. We'll go inland and see if this archaeologist can point us in the right direction."

"I say we move with all possible speed," Emma added. "We're not the only ones with access to Peruvian TV."

22

Chinese spy trawler
Off the coast of Ecuador

Daiyu stood in the control room of the Chinese trawler. The swells had vanished and the sea was as dark as pitch. Everything quiet and still. Too quiet for her. Unnerving.

For three days, they'd kept the American vessel *Catalina* under surveillance. Over the last twenty-four hours, it appeared as if the crew of that ship had begun search-and-recovery operations. Daiyu had been planning an underwater reconnaissance mission to see what they'd found when the Ministry called it off.

General Zhang appeared on a video screen. "The recovery effort of NUMA vessel *Catalina* has been determined to be a diversion."

"So we've been wasting our time," Daiyu said. There was an edge to her voice; it was always there, even speaking to a superior like Zhang. It was half the reason she'd been posted to such a backwater place.

"So it would appear," Zhang replied. "But that's not the only news. We have new information that suggests the *Nighthawk* escaped capture by the Russian bomber and did not come down at sea. A possible sighting has been reported over the mountains of Peru."

"So our Russian friends failed to do their part," she replied. "I'm not surprised. You cannot trust a bear to dance with a sparrow."

"Nor can you trust it to share its meal with you," Zhang added. "This is a blessing in disguise. Had the Russians succeeded, they would have taken the American aircraft home with them and given us as little as possible. Now we have a chance to take it all."

Daiyu nodded. "As it should have been from the start."

She well knew that General Zhang felt the same way, though he would never say it. A slight curl of his lip was all she received. "A helicopter is being sent," he said. "It'll be on deck within an hour. Be ready."

"We shall," she replied.

"Do not fail your country," Zhang said

and signed off.

Jian stood at her side. Where Daiyu was excited, he appeared solemn, apprehensive. "Is something wrong?"

"The Americans will not be easy to eliminate," he said. "Our men had the advantage of surprise in Guayaquil, but they still failed. By the time we make contact, the Americans will be on guard."

"There are methods beyond brute force," she said. "If we can't take them by direct action, we'll set a trap. All targets are susceptible to one form or another. If they're ready to run at the slightest sign of us, then we'll let them run headlong into disaster."

23

Guided missile cruiser Varyag

The storm had passed. Or, rather, the Russian Cruiser *Varyag* and salvage vessels accompanying it had passed through the worst of the weather. No one was happier about the sea change than Constantin Davidov. For the first time in days, he was sitting to a full breakfast without worrying that it would come back up.

Rear Admiral Borozdin sat across from him, his eggs smothered in hollandaise sauce. It kept the powdered taste down and passed for a delicacy in the Soviet Navy.

"You look different today," Borozdin said between forkfuls of egg. "I can't quite put my finger on it."

"Yes you can," Davidov said. "I'm not three shades of green."

Borozdin laughed. "Yes, of course, that's it."

A knock at the Admiral's door brought a

courier. "Captain Tovarich reporting on the satellite link," the courier said.

"Have it patched through to us in here," Davidov suggested.

Borozdin nodded to the courier and moments later they were listening to Tovarich.

Though his voice sounded tinny and distant, the signal was clear enough to reveal disappointment. "Recovery operations are complete," Tovarich explained. "We've pumped out the cargo bay and combed through the wreckage. Unfortunately, there's no sign of the American craft."

"How can that be?" Davidov asked. "*Blackjack 1* reported the *Nighthawk* as captured and locked in long before the emergency."

"I'm aware of that," Tovarich said. "But a preliminary examination of the wreckage reveals that the lockdown bolts have been sheared clean through. The *Nighthawk* must have broken free as the bomber lost control."

Davidov sat back in frustration. Things were not going according to plan. When he'd dissolved the partnership with China and left Beijing, he'd done it thinking he had a bird in hand. At that moment, he'd been certain that Russia — and Russia alone — knew the whereabouts of the

American craft because only Russia knew where the bomber had gone down.

"I'm afraid there's something else," Tovarich added.

Davidov looked up. "More bad news?"

"Of a sort," Tovarich said. "During the recovery operation, we encountered an American NUMA team in a small submersible. They seem to have arrived and surveyed the site just before we did. Their presence not only compromised the secrecy of this vessel but the airborne mission itself."

"How so?"

"We have reason to believe they took *Blackjack 1*'s flight data recorder. We've searched the wreckage and the surrounding area. Despite detecting a signal when we first arrived, it's nowhere to be found. The only logical explanation is that the Americans have it."

"NUMA," Davidov grumbled. This wasn't the first time the American nautical organization had thwarted a Russian effort.

Across from him, Admiral Borozdin grew tense. "If the Americans have the black box, they won't have any problem piecing together the entire mission. They'll know we tried to hijack their craft out of midair."

Davidov waved off the concern. "It's of little consequence. They can't reveal or complain about our actions without exposing their own secrets. The bigger issue — the only issue — is what happened to the spacecraft."

The submarine captain assumed the question was for him. "I have no answers, at this point."

"Continue the search," Davidov ordered. "Follow the last-known course. I want updates every hour."

Tovarich signed off, and Davidov found he'd lost his appetite. His silver fork rattled against the Admiral's fine china as he put it down. "We had it," he said. "We had it in our hands."

Borozdin put his own knife and fork down and took a drink of water. "Even if the *Nighthawk* broke free, it should have come down nearby."

"Not necessarily," Davidov said. "Considering the speed and altitude at which they were traveling, it could literally be anywhere."

Borozdin nodded. "What orders did *Blackjack 2* have?"

"Its primary job was to override the signal from Vandenberg," Davidov said.

"And in the event something went wrong?"

"To track the *Nighthawk* as long as possible and report final course, altitude and speed."

"Do you have any reason to think they did otherwise?"

Davidov bristled. "I have no reason to think anything, Sergei. We never heard from them again."

"They were Russian officers," Borozdin said. "Highly trained. No doubt handpicked for their proficiency, loyalty and bravery. Unless you sent cadets up on your most secret of missions, I think we can assume they followed orders as long as possible. Right to the end."

Davidov settled back. "Fine. I agree. What good does it do us? We still don't know where they are."

"We know where they aren't," Borozdin noted. "They're not in the sea."

Davidov froze. For the first time, he realized Borozdin was not just toying with him. "How can you be so sure?"

"Because the Americans would be pulling them out of the water already."

"I think you overestimate —"

This time, Borozdin cut him off. "We are loath to admit it, but their technology is far superior to ours."

"Sergei, it doesn't help —"

Borozdin would not be interrupted. "I've

been thinking about this for a while," he continued. "I don't know how the Americans found *Blackjack 1* so quickly, but they did. They heard it, or saw it, or found it with a drone or with remote sonar or some other method we know nothing about. Whatever the case, they were on-site and picking the bones of our dead before we could get there, and we knew *exactly* where the plane had gone down. But now they're searching grids again. Back and forth, east and west. If *Blackjack 2* hit the water, they would have found it just as easily as they found *Blackjack 1.* But they haven't found it, which tells me it didn't come down in the ocean."

Davidov considered this. "So you think it made landfall. How does that help us?"

"If *Blackjack 2* was following the *Nighthawk* as ordered and then crashed on dry land, it stands to reason that the *Nighthawk* made landfall."

It was a leap, but there was logic to it.

"And if we can find the wreckage of *Blackjack 2,*" Borozdin continued, "even if it's burned to a cinder in the jungle somewhere, it will still be an arrow pointing us in the direction of the *Nighthawk.*"

Davidov warmed to the idea, in part

257

because it was all they had. "We need satellite data and we need it immediately."

24

Somewhere in the mountains of Peru

A long, pointed cone stuck out horizontally from beneath a tarp. It stood a dozen feet off the ground and was unmistakably the nose of a high-speed aircraft. Streaks of blackened oxidation swept back from the tip that suggested it had been through a fire, but the soot-colored stripes were caused by friction with the air and the heat of traveling at five times the speed of sound.

Several men with reddish brown skin hauled lines connected to the tarp and pulled it forward until it covered the entire aircraft.

"Stake that down," someone yelled. "I'll not have another windstorm pulling it free."

While the first group of workers pulled the tarp taut, a second group moved into place with sledgehammers. With repeated blows, they pounded long spikes deep into the ground. When they'd finished, the tie-down rings at the edge of the tarp were hooked to the spikes and locked down.

As the men worked in the chilled mountain air, white vapors streamed from their mouths and noses. They wore colorful coats of alpaca wool, while the man who supervised them was dressed in modern black garb and wore a balaclava over his face.

"Two more spikes here," he said.

As the section he'd pointed to was secured, another man came up to him. He had his long sleeves pushed up to the elbows, exposing an old scar that ran the length of his forearm. "We've doubled the number of stakes," he said. "And the men are cutting more branches to lay across it."

"Have them cut slits in the tarp as well," the man wearing the balaclava said. "Up high."

"But won't that expose —"

"It will keep the tarp from lifting. Aerodynamics. Trust me, my friend. This is my business."

The second man nodded. "Do you think we've been noticed?"

"I checked the satellite tables," the man in the balaclava said. "Fortunately, we're in a remote part of the mountains. No one is flying spy satellites over this area. Not yet, at least. But, we can expect that to change soon. Another exposure could ruin every-thing."

"But you want them to find the bomber?" the second man said, unsure and trying to follow his master's lead.

"Oh, yes. But on our schedule, not theirs."

The man with the scar on his arm nodded and turned away, walking toward the forest. He made a whirling motion with his hand and chain saws roared as the men began cutting down branches and felling entire trees, all of which would be dragged forward and used to disguise the landed treasure.

The man in the balaclava was pleased. With the aircraft covered again and the camouflage work progressing, he ducked under the edge of the tarp and walked beneath the bomber's sharply swept wing. He passed the squared-off engine pods and continued forward beneath the fuselage, careful not to bump any of the antennas or aerodynamic probes that stuck out beneath the plane. With its sharp edges and armored exterior, the aircraft seemed to him like a sleeping dragon. One that would wake and breathe fire soon enough.

He arrived at a ladder that dropped from the center of the fuselage just behind the nose gear. He climbed it slowly, arriving in the darkened crew compartment. Another of his men was inside. He wore fur-lined boots and a colorful poncho over his shoulders.

"What about them?" the man asked in his native tongue. "Another night like the last and they'll freeze to death."

He was referring to the Russian pilots, bound and gagged and sitting on the floor of the aircraft. Three nights in the frigid plane without food or much to drink had taken most of the fight out of them. A swath of dried and frozen blood beside them where another crewman's throat had been cut served as a warning not to argue.

"They bring disease," the man wearing the balaclava said. "But we'll need them when the time comes. Take them to the cave."

The man in the poncho whistled down to several others and the prisoners were soon being taken down the ladder and hauled away.

With the tarp covering the aircraft, it was dark in the cockpit, but it would be darker for the prisoners in their cave. And darker still for the world to come.

"Keep everyone on alert," the man in the balaclava replied. "Things will happen at a rapid pace now. The lure has been set. The trap will not remain empty for long."

25

Ecuador

They parted ways at the airport — Rudi boarding a flight for Washington to put out a growing series of political brush fires, Kurt and Emma boarding the NUMA Gulfstream for a ninety-minute flight to Cajamarca, Peru, where they would meet up with Paul and Gamay.

Joe would follow in the Erickson Air-Crane, but the helicopter's lumbering pace and the need to stop for fuel along the way meant it would be nine hours before the Air-Crane reached Cajamarca. It was a long delay, but if they were lucky enough to find the *Nighthawk* — or major pieces of it — they'd need some way to haul it out of the jungle or off the mountains.

Shortly after takeoff, Emma used the encrypted satellite linkup to contact Steve Gowdy and give him a status update.

The NSA chief was blunt from the word

go. "So, what was all that business with the fruit bowl?"

"Complimentary gift," Kurt said. "We send one out to all the VIPs."

"You're not helping," Emma said.

Kurt put up a hand and remained quiet for the rest of the call while Emma explained their new theory and vouched for Kurt's belief that the NSA had a leak.

On-screen, Gowdy's eyes narrowed, but instead of anger or defensive bluster, he said simply, "Falconer. I thought we'd determined that to be an unfounded rumor."

"Listen to the tapes," Emma suggested. "As they say, dead men tell no lies."

Gowdy nodded. "I'll start an immediate investigation. But if there is a mole in here somewhere, then you'd better be careful. Your move to Cajamarca might be front-page news already."

"We haven't reported it to anyone but you," Emma replied. "But we'll keep our eyes open."

"You're going to need more than that. I'm sending Hurns and Rodriguez back down to help you out. Don't brush them off this time."

Emma shook her head. "No deal," she said. "If the Falconer is real and has a contact inside the NSA, it could be anyone.

Even one of them, for all we know."

"They're field agents," Gowdy said. "They have no access to Vandenberg. They weren't even on the project until after the *Nighthawk* went missing. They're clean, I promise you."

Emma sighed and looked at Kurt. He shrugged. With a little luck, they'd have the *Nighthawk* in hand by the time the two agents arrived.

"I still don't like it," Emma said.

"And I don't care," Gowdy said. "They can stand by in Cajamarca in case you need them, but I'm sending them."

She couldn't argue with that. "Fine. Anything else?"

"Just be quick about this," Gowdy said. "We're running out of time."

Kurt saw a look pass between the two of them. Even on a video screen, even from five thousand miles away, it was obvious and intimate — the acknowledgment of something unsaid.

Without another word, Gowdy signed off.

As the screen faded to black, Emma sat quietly.

Kurt looked on. It was now obvious to him that she was concealing something — probably on direct orders from Gowdy — but, as the saying went, a lie is a lie is a lie. And, in this business, the lack of information tended to get people killed, people like Kurt and Joe.

They touched down in Cajamarca thirty minutes later and Kurt stepped from the plane into the brisk mountain air. Cajamarca sat at nearly seven thousand feet. This time of year, the midday temperatures hovered in the fifties. Quite a change from the steamy subtropical heat of Guayaquil. It was also overcast and, as any skier could attest, the difference between clouds and sunshine at high elevations was far more pronounced than at sea level.

Pulling a black sweater over his head, Kurt moved down the stairs and signed a rental car agreement for a burnt-orange four-wheel drive Range Rover Sport. It sat on the ramp beside the plane, where it would be easy to load up. As Emma swept the vehicle for bugs, Kurt walked inside the small terminal, where he spied a pair of friendly faces.

Paul and Gamay Trout had been airlifted in from the *Catalina* and then flown up commercial, arriving shortly before the NUMA jet.

"Great to see you guys," Kurt said, giving both of them warm hugs.

"Glad to be back on the A-team," Paul said. "Not that it wasn't fun dumping millions of dollars of equipment over the side of the ship, but we're looking forward to being used as something other than a distraction."

"Shall we go meet your new friend?" Gamay asked, shouldering her backpack.

"Not yet," Kurt said. "I have a change of assignment for you."

The look of suspicion appeared in practiced unison. Gamay dropped her pack. "What is it now? Shopping for alpaca sweaters?"

"I need you to do some research," Kurt said. "Find out everything you can about the *Nighthawk,* and I don't mean the surface-level stuff. They're hiding something from us, something big."

"What makes you think that?" Gamay asked. "Other than your general distrust of the NSA."

"For one thing, they seem on the verge of panic," he replied. "It's felt like that to me right from the start. Losing the *Nighthawk* would be bad, but even at its worst all that would do is give whoever found it technologies they're probably already trying to develop."

"It is the most advanced aircraft in the world," Paul reminded him.

"Was," Kurt corrected. "The thing has

been floating around up in space for three years. And they didn't design and build it in a day. At best, it's five or six years old. The plans were probably drawn up a decade ago. Even if the Russians or the Chinese found it in one perfect piece, they'd still have to take it apart, reverse-engineer every component and then build the factories and facilities to duplicate what we already possess. What we possessed years ago. By then, we'll be on to the next technological leap."

Paul nodded. "Like stealing a used car and watching the owner get a new model to replace it."

"Couldn't have said it better myself," Kurt said.

"It's still a big loss," Gamay pointed out.

"If you saw their faces, you'd think it was the end of the world."

Gamay nodded. Paul did the same.

"And it's not just our friends at the NSA; the Chinese and the Russians have gone over the top as well."

"An opportunity comes up to get your hands on the adversaries stuff, you take it," Paul said. "We always have; can't blame them for that."

"I don't," Kurt said. "But it's not done like this. There are unwritten rules to the game. Boundaries that stop it from turning into outright war. None of those seem to be in effect here. The Chinese tried to kill us before we got to square one and the Russians tried to torpedo us twice. The second time, on the surface for everyone to see."

"So the stakes are higher than they appear," Paul said.

"Which is interesting, considering how high they seemed to begin with," Gamay said.

Kurt nodded. "And we're the only ones in the dark. That needs to change. I want to know what they're hiding. And I want to know as soon as possible. I need you to find out what you can by linking up with Hiram and Priya on the satellite. I'm sure they can dig something up."

"And then what?" Paul asked.

Kurt checked his watch; it was a long drive to the archaeological site. "We'll be out of satellite coverage on the way up the mountain," Kurt said, "but we should have a signal by the time we get there. That gives you four hours."

"Four hours to do the impossible," Gamay said.

Kurt was already on his way back out of the terminal. "It's more time than I usually give you."

"That doesn't make it okay," Gamay

called out.

Kurt pushed through the door and let it close behind him, crossing to the Range Rover and climbing into the driver's seat.

Emma was in the passenger seat. "Aren't your friends joining us?"

"I need them to look into something," Kurt said. "They'll fly up with Joe, once he arrives."

"So, it's just the two of us on a romantic drive in the country," she said with a grin.

Kurt smiled and turned the key. The engine came to life instantly, the finely tuned machine a symphony to his ears. "Hope you brought a picnic basket."

"Of a sort," she said, opening the lid of a small plastic case.

Kurt peered inside. He saw a night vision scope, a black 9mm pistol and a belt with several spare magazines. Underneath, he saw a survival knife and several small demolition charges.

"You forgot the wine," he said.

"That's your job," she joked.

Kurt laughed. He might not have brought wine, but the back of the Range Rover was filled with hiking equipment and tackle, if they needed it. In addition, he'd brought his own weapon: a Heckler & Koch HK45. The weapon was a lightweight tactical .45

270

caliber pistol; it had a ten-round capacity, a mini-flashlight on the lower rail and tritium sights.

He had brought three spare magazines, each loaded with a separate type of ammunition. The first carried soft-tipped hollow-points; the second carried a mix of standard shells and mini-tracers, specially fabricated by a gunsmith Kurt knew. The third magazine held solid steel slugs coated with a thin layer of titanium and propelled by a more powerful blend of gunpowder; they traveled at higher velocity, and the titanium jacket kept them together at impact.

Kurt had never used them but was told they could punch through an inch of armor plating or two inches of regular steel. He was also warned that the pistol kicked like a mule when fired. He hoped he wouldn't have to find out, but they'd already been attacked twice and he wasn't interested in going a third round without punching back.

He dropped the transmission into drive and pulled away from the aircraft.

"So what's with the explosives?" he asked, getting his bearings and looking for a spot to exit the ramp.

She closed the lid and put the box away. "If we find the *Nighthawk* and can't haul it

271

out of the jungle, I have orders to blow the electronics package and the propulsion system."

It made sense. But he took everything she said with a grain of salt now. From the size of the charges, he estimated each to be the rough equivalent of a grenade. "Those should do the trick," he said, pulling through the gate. "Next stop, La Jalca and the Fortress in the Clouds."

Daiyu stood on a low hill watching the burnt-orange SUV as it left the airport. The color and the metallic gloss made it easy to spot, especially against the gray road and the dusty mountains.

She tracked the vehicle as it passed through the airport's main gate and moved east. When it shifted into the right-hand lane and moved onto the mountain road, she lowered her binoculars and picked up a radio.

"Target moving," she said, speaking into the radio. "Route 6A, as expected. We'll follow at a distance. Be ready at the intercept point."

"Affirmative," a voice replied.

She clipped the radio to her belt and walked to a white Audi A8. Jian sat at the wheel, his broad shoulders filling the cockpit of the sleek car.

She climbed in the passenger's side, slammed the door and nodded. "Go."

26

The route from Cajamarca wound its way eastward, climbing higher into the mountains as it went. Paved at first, the road surface changed to a combination of gravel and hard-packed clay after an hour of driving. As the footing worsened, Kurt dialed back the speed. They continued to climb, curving around the switchbacks, while ducking in and out of patchy fog.

The higher they went, the cooler it got. Passing eight thousand feet, they found spitting rain. At nine thousand feet, they were in the clouds. At ninety-five hundred, they finally broke out into the sunlight.

A wide valley appeared on the left, its floor a thousand feet below. Successive layers of jagged mountains rose up behind it. The visibility was twenty miles or more.

"Welcome to the Andes," Kurt said.

From this point on, the road clung to the shoulder of the mountains. It grew narrower out of necessity and, in certain spots, had been cut right into the cliffside, requiring the cars to drive beneath an overhang of solid rock.

While the terrain to the right-hand side changed often, the view to the left was constant, nothing but a sheer drop.

"They might have splurged on a guard-rail," Emma said.

"And ruin the view?" Kurt replied, laughing.

Instead of a barrier, the road sported a low curb, painted in alternating blocks of black and white. Not only wouldn't it stop anything larger than a model car, hitting it would be like catching one's foot on a tree root — more likely to tip a vehicle over the edge.

"Just be glad this isn't an English colony," Kurt added. "Otherwise, we'd be driving on that side."

The mountain bulged outward and the road bent out around its waist, offering a view back in the direction they'd come. They were on the leeward side now and the slopes were tawny brown and spotted with patchy scrub brush and a smattering of gray rock. All of it tied together by the zigzagging ribbon of route 6A.

Kurt stole a quick glance. Emma shifted

in her seat and took it all in.

"How much traffic do you think this road gets?" she asked casually.

"Not much," he said. "We've passed two trucks and an old Jeep in the last hour. Why?"

"I count three cars following us," she said. "Two black, one white. By the dust they're kicking up, I'd say they're moving a lot faster than they should be."

Kurt set his jaw. "I was hoping we'd left all that behind."

Emma reached into the "picnic basket" at her feet. She pulled out the 9mm Beretta, made sure it was loaded and switched the safety off.

Kurt drove faster, but there wasn't a turnoff until they hit the plateau. If the cars behind them proved to be trouble, they'd have to deal with them here and now.

It took several minutes but the trio of vehicles finally appeared in the rearview mirror. Between the vibration from the road and the dust streaming out behind them, it was a blurred image, but it was all Kurt needed. The two black cars were staggered up front in an attacking formation, the white car trailing a short distance behind. All of them charging up the hill in a cloud of dust.

"Here they come."

Emma slipped out of her seat belt and lowered her window. Holding the Beretta on her lap, she poked her head outside and risked a look. She could see little inside the dark interiors, but when a man popped out through the side window, she knew what was about to happen.

He brought a submachine gun up and opened fire. Emma ducked back into the Rover as a series of tiny explosions raced along the dusty slope to the right. The first shots went wide, but a second burst clipped the driver's side-view mirror and shattered it. "So much for our relaxing drive in the country."

Kurt mashed the pedal to the floor. The supercharged engine answered and the Range Rover surged ahead.

For a moment, it seemed they might leave their enemies behind, but the cars following them were also high-performance models. They had the horses to answer and they quickly closed the gap.

Kurt crouched low on the wheel as another spread of bullets punched angry holes in the sheet metal. One blasted out the taillight, while another hit the rear window, rendering it a mess of cracks and fissures that was impossible to see through.

Emma leaned out the window to return fire. She hit the lead BMW with several shots, but it drifted to Kurt's side and the back of the Rover blocked it from her view.

She turned in her seat and aimed for the back window. "Cover your ears."

There was no hope of that, but Kurt appreciated the warning. She opened fire, blasting out the remnants of the back window with her first shot and empting the rest of the magazine into the nearest chase car. It dropped back for a moment but soon came on again.

Kurt pulled the .45 out of his shoulder holster and handed it to her. "Try this."

Emma took it and aimed. The first shot almost knocked her out of her seat. She righted herself and fired three more times.

The armor-piercing shells found their mark. Steam and smoke blasted from the punctured engine block of the BMW as its radiator exploded. The car swerved toward the cliff and then back the other way, going up the slope at an angle, rolling over onto its roof and then sliding back onto the road and coming to a stop just short of the cliff's edge.

The other cars passed and left it behind.

"I like this," Emma shouted over the noise. "Can I keep it?"

"Get rid of the two cars and it's yours."

Emma climbed between the seats and into the back for a better spot to shoot from while Kurt did his best to present an elusive target. He kept the gas pedal pinned to the floor as long as possible, thundering toward each turn and then tapping the brakes before cutting the wheel and hitting the gas again.

On one inside turn, they banged an over-hanging rock. It put a huge downward dent in the roof. A sharp outside turn came up quicker than Kurt had expected. As Kurt hit the brakes, the Rover started skidding.

Kurt released his tight grip on the steering wheel and stepped back on the gas. He'd raced in off-road rallies both in cars and on dirt bikes; he knew that getting through a turn like this required power to the wheels.

They hugged the edge, sliding and drifting and threatening to tip. From Kurt's position, all he could see was the drop, not an inch of road left. As if they'd gone over the edge and were already airborne. And then the heavy tread bit into the road once more, the tires spat dirt and the Rover surged back to the inside of the curve.

"That was close," he shouted. "Almost found out if man was truly meant to fly."

Emma didn't reply. It was so loud inside the Rover that she didn't hear him. She was perched on the backseat, holding the .45 in a police grip with two hands.

The cars had fallen back as they refused to take the turns at full speed. But instead of closing in on the straightaway as they had before, they held their distance this time.

Emma watched the passenger emerge through the sunroof of the lead car, the upper half of his body visible. He brought out a long weapon with a pointed end.

"Go faster," she called out.

"Can't go much faster," he replied.

"Go faster, Kurt! They have an RPG."

In the white Audi, Daiyu could see the Americans accelerating and weaving left and right, trying to present a difficult target. "That's it," she urged under her breath. "Speed up."

She pressed a button on the headset she wore. "Push them," she urged. "Push them harder."

"We have no shot," one member of the kill squad called back.

"It doesn't matter," Daiyu replied. "Push them to the limit. We're almost there."

The car ahead of them accelerated and Daiyu switched channels. "Thirty seconds," she said. "Be ready to detonate."

"*Ready,*" another voice replied.

"Blow the bridge as soon as they come out of the tunnel."

Up ahead, Kurt was almost shocked to still be alive. Unfortunately, a long, straight tunnel loomed in front of them where this section of road had been carved into the side of the mountain. The overhanging rock closed down on the left and the road soon became dim and dark.

"They're coming again," Emma said as the lead car began to close the gap.

"I see that," Kurt said.

"The road is getting narrower."

"I see that, too."

Emma put the empty .45 down and grabbed her Beretta, ejecting the empty magazine and reloading. Kurt kept the pedal down as they roared through the tunnel. The growl of the engines reverberated off the walls. Headlights blazed behind them, daylight appeared in the distance. At any second, Emma expected to see the flare of the rocket coming their way.

But they raced out into the sunlight again still in one piece. The wall to their right softened into a hilly slope and the road angled downward toward an iron bridge that crossed a narrow chasm and looked as if it had been built in the forties or fifties. As they charged toward it, a series of detonations erupted along the bridge. Two larger blasts followed, one at each end.

Iron bent, rivets exploded and the bridge buckled and fell, collapsing in on itself and dropping into the depths of the gorge.

Traveling slightly downhill, on loose footing, at high speed, Kurt knew instantly that they couldn't stop in time.

He jammed his foot on the brake pedal, bled off half the speed and then turned up the embankment, skidding, bouncing and nearly flipping the Range Rover in the process.

Traveling uphill, the Rover slowed rapidly and Kurt regained control. What had been a desperate maneuver to avoid a thousand-foot swan dive now became a possible way out.

He dropped the transmission into a lower gear and kept climbing. With a deft touch, he turned away from the gorge and traversed the slope at an angle. The four-wheel drive kept them moving, spinning the wheels in the soft gravel, bouncing them over the rocks and powering through the thorny bushes that clung to the incline.

Emma held on in the backseat. They were

climbing so sharply that it felt like she would slide out the back. But the engine of the Rover was in the front, which kept the weight forward, and every time Kurt felt the front wheels lifting, he pulled off the gas for just a second.

They were still climbing the hill when their pursuers came out of the tunnel at a much slower pace. Emma watched as they stopped in the middle of the road, looking up at their escaping prey.

At first, they appeared confused, and the man holding the rocket-propelled grenade launcher steadied himself and aimed, leaning against the back edge of the sunroof.

Emma was faster, raising the Beretta and raining a hail of bullets down on them. She emptied the entire magazine, peppering both cars with multiple shots and hitting the rocket man in the shoulder.

He twisted with the impact and squeezed the trigger.

The RPG fired. Its smoke trail stretched upward across the terrain, drawing a line from the road below directly across the top of the Range Rover and into the ridge above them. It detonated amid a wall of weathered rock.

The mountain shook and a long section of the ridge broke loose and came tumbling toward them.

Kurt turned the wheel, angling to the right and fighting against gravity. He couldn't turn any sharper without rolling the vehicle, but even that would be better than being crushed in a landslide.

Fist-sized rocks bounced their way, pounding the doors and smashing the windshield. A wave of dust engulfed them. They pulled clear just as half the mountainside roared past behind them.

Daiyu stared upward from the passenger seat of the white Audi as man-made thunder echoed through the canyon. When the smoke from the explosion cleared, she spotted movement, but it wasn't the American Rover tumbling and burning, it was the mountain itself. With gathering speed, a large mass of gravel and heavy rock was surging their way.

"Move!" she shouted.

Jian slammed the car into reverse, looked over his shoulder. The transmission whined as the car sped backward. A hail of gravel pinged off their hood as they rushed into the tunnel.

The BMW driver reacted too slowly. Instead of backing up, he tried to turn, and his car had just begun moving when the main body of the avalanche thundered across the road, a tsunami of stone and sand. It hit with surprising speed, launching the car off the cliff like a child's toy swept angrily from a table.

The landslide continued for another few minutes. The large rocks settled first, but the sand and gravel continued to pour down, filling the entrance to the tunnel, until dust choked the air and all that could be seen was a hazy beam of light coming from the Audi's front end.

High above, Kurt and Emma had skirted the landslide, avoiding the worst of the damage. They picked their way upward toward the next section of the road, surging onto it with a final effort.

"I didn't think we were going to survive that," Emma announced.

Stabilized on flat ground once again, Kurt stopped to look back. "Never entered my mind."

"Think that's the end of them?"

Looking down the embankment, he saw nothing but an impenetrable cloud of dust. "No idea," he said. "Doesn't matter which way; even if they're gone, we'll have others to deal with soon enough."

As Emma returned to the front seat, Kurt

thumped the shattered windshield with his palm. It fell away, peeling off the A-pillars like matted paper. Able to see clearly now, he donned a pair of sunglasses, put the Rover in gear and continued on.

They were twenty miles from La Jalca and every minute counted.

27

Kurt drove the rest of the way at a reduced speed because the suspension had been damaged in the climb and was groaning with every mile. An hour later, they were nearing the ruins.

"This is the turn," Emma said.

Kurt pulled off the road. The new track was little more than two ruts in the ground, with a long furrow of stray grass standing knee-high between them. It took them into a narrowing valley past small herds of grazing animals and terraced fields abundant with crops. Both sights suggested a large community nearby, though Kurt saw no houses.

"I thought this was an archaeological site," he said.

Emma nodded. "As did I. Seems more like a working farm."

As they continued into the valley, the ridges and peaks grew higher and the gorge became narrower. When an encampment of tents appeared in the distance, Kurt pulled over and parked.

"I suggest we walk from here," he said. "I don't really want to start off by explaining how our vehicle ended up like this."

Emma laughed. "You might want to practice that speech; you still have to turn this thing in."

They climbed out of the battered Rover, pulled backpacks over their shoulders and began a short hike.

On foot, without the roofline of the SUV interfering, the view was spectacular. The excavation was taking place in the closed end of a box canyon. Three high peaks dominated the landscape, towering above the ridgeline around them. The cliffsides were honeycombed with caves and marked with several distinct layers of construction. They were also covered with a scaffolding of vertical and horizontal ropes. Another set of wires stretched across the sky like power lines, spanning the canyon from one peak to the next.

"Quite a setup," Kurt noted.

Emma nodded but didn't reply. To her, the canyon felt tight and compressed — the kind of place a Western gunfighter might find himself surrounded and ambushed. She kept close to Kurt, aware that the Beretta in her pack would not be easy to reach if something did go wrong.

As they neared the tents, a group of men came out to meet them. They stood in the path, arms folded, eyes squinting, mouths tight.

"Hola," Kurt said, thrusting out a hand toward the closest of them. "My name is Kurt Austin. I'd like to speak with Urco, if I could."

The man stood like a statue. He was shorter than Kurt but well built, with muscular forearms and bulbous shoulders. He had a different look from the Peruvians Kurt had known; broader and shorter, with a wider face; more indigenous, less European. His skin was a darker, copper shade and his eyes seemed larger.

He neither responded to the words nor reached for Kurt's hand.

Kurt lowered his arm and glanced at Emma. "Maybe you'd better try."

She repeated the greeting in Spanish. Adding something about them being interested in archaeology and the Chachapoya and mentioning that they'd seen Urco on the Internet.

This brought some chatter among the group, and the burly man nodded. *"Me llamo*

Vargas," he said, unfolding his arms and pointing to the cliff top. "Urco," he said, before adding in English, "Up there."

Vargas led them to the base of the cliff. Several ropes dangled down from above.

"I'm not great with heights," Emma said. "Maybe I'll just wait here."

Looking at a climb of several hundred feet, Kurt wasn't all that excited himself. "I don't suppose he could come down?"

Vargas just stared.

"Never mind."

Kurt was given a safety harness and led to the nearest rope, where Vargas handed him a pair of well-used work gloves. They were loose and worn smooth — not exactly fit for gripping a nylon rope.

"To climb?" Kurt asked, making a hand-over-hand motion.

Vargas shook his head. "No . . . fly."

He placed Kurt's hands on the rope and then snapped the safety harness to a hook using a heavy carabiner.

Kurt saw instantly what was about to happen. He gripped the rope as Vargas released a cast-iron clamp attached to a second rope.

A heavy weight suspended up above began to fall and Kurt — whose rope was attached to that weight by means of a pulley — was lifted off the ground and hauled upward.

The initial launch was sudden, but after that the ride was smooth.

He passed small dwellings carved out of holes in the stone. Open rooms were empty except for ladders that went from one level to the next.

Above them, he passed a row of stone figures carved into the living rock; they looked almost bird-like, but with enlarged heads and human bodies and features. They reminded him of Egyptian hieroglyphs.

Higher up, in smaller niches and openings, he saw mummified bodies and weaponry; spears and morning stars. These were the mountaintop burial sites of the Chachapoya warriors.

He was approaching the block, tackle and pulley arrangement, which had allowed him to ascend so quickly, when Vargas applied the brake. He came to a stop ten feet from the crest of the mountain. A ladder affixed to the cliffside on his right led the rest of the way.

"You've made it this far," a voice boomed from above. "Now comes the tricky part."

Kurt looked up to see a face peering over the edge at him. It was weathered and creased from years in the sun, topped by shaggy dark hair and half covered by a gray beard as thick as wool on a sheep. Gleeful, dark eyes focused on Kurt. The man chuckled as he pointed to the ladder.

"I see it," Kurt said.

"And you see the dilemma?"

Kurt saw that, too. The ladder was several feet beyond his reach. And even if he could stretch out to touch it, he would have to disconnect the safety harness from the rope in order to transfer to the bottom few rungs.

He looked down for a moment and then wished he hadn't. "Now I know what the window washers on the Freedom Tower feel like."

He swung his feet toward the ladder, pulled them back in the other direction and then swung them again. The rope began to move, sliding side to side with his motion. On the third arc, Kurt stretched out and grasped the metal frame of the ladder. Pulling himself over to it, he set his feet, wrapped one arm around the closest available rung and then disconnected the harness. Keeping his gaze skyward, he climbed to the top and pulled himself onto solid ground.

The man with the gray beard offered a slight bow. "I congratulate you. It takes most people several minutes before they figure out how to do that. And even then, many are reluctant to let go of the rope.

Indeed, one reporter who came to interview me last year flat out refused. He just mumbled a few questions from the harness and then asked to be lowered to the ground as quickly as possible."

The man allowed himself a belly laugh.

Kurt chuckled and turned to take in the view. They were standing on a platform in the sky, the highest spot for miles around. A major valley loomed to the east and north while the teeth of lower ridges loomed to the west. "That reporter missed out," he said. "Reminds me of a spot called Eagle's Nest in Colorado."

"There was a time when eagles made their homes on this aerie," the man said. "Long ago."

Kurt noticed that the man spoke English far better than Vargas had. "Since you're the only one up here, I'll assume you're Urco." He offered a hand. "Kurt Austin."

The man looked at Kurt's outstretched palm and offered an uncomfortable grin. "I am Urco," he said without moving. "Pleased to meet you."

For the second time, Kurt pulled his arm back. "Not too fond of shaking hands around here, are you? Is it some custom I'm unaware of?"

Urco shook his head. "I'm afraid we

are . . . germaphobes . . . of a sort."

"Really?" Kurt said. "You live out in the wild, dig around in the dirt, unearthing dead bodies, and you're afraid of germs?"

"I know it sounds strange," Urco replied, "but, in a way, it's the bodies that remind us to be wary. These dwellings and burial chambers are from the last stronghold of the Chachapoya people. They held out against the might of the Inca for centuries. They even resisted the conquistadors after Pizarro and his one hundred and sixty-eight men defeated Atahualpa and his six thousand Inca warriors. Unfortunately, their next enemy was one they could not defeat."

"Disease?" Kurt said.

Urco nodded. "Smallpox. It ravaged the settlements, killing nearly everyone it found. Those who stayed died. Those who fled brought the disease with them, spreading the plague to other villages. I've found writings that describe a traveler coming home to a village of two thousand people to find no one alive. Most had died horribly, covered with pustules. Others had killed each other when fighting and chaos set in — as they always do when social order breaks down."

Urco waved his arms about in a sweeping gesture. "This place was a nation once. And then it was gone."

Kurt nodded. He knew the grim statistics. European diseases had hit the New World hard. South America fared the worst. According to many experts, smallpox, influenza and measles wiped out ninety-five percent of the indigenous population.

Urco continued. "The men and women who work on this project are all descendants of the Chachapoya. Some nearly pure-blooded. Others, like myself, have a mix of European and indigenous genes. Of course, we're not really afraid of disease anymore, but avoiding the touch of outsiders is one way we remind ourselves what happened to our ancestors."

"I assure you," Kurt said. "I've had all my proper shots and inoculations."

Urco stared at him for a second and then began to laugh. He waved Kurt over and sat down, leaning against a slight rise in the ridge that acted like a natural chair even if it was made of stone. Beside him was a laptop computer. A wire from the computer led to an exterior antenna propped up and pointed at an almost flat angle to the northwest.

Kurt recognized the antenna as a type used to communicate via satellite. "Checking your e-mail?"

"Yes, actually," Urco said. "The satellite we use is very low on the horizon this time of year. You can't get a signal from the valley floor. So I come up here every day. Sometimes twice a day. I tell the workers I'm conversing with the gods. They remind me to check my battery level or the gods will never hear me."

"I'm very impressed with the dig," Kurt said. "I assume all the ropes are to keep you from damaging the excavation sites."

"Partly," Urco said. "The Peruvian government owns the site and they won't permit us to set foot in the burial areas — something I agree with. As a result, we have to learn what we can by looking in from the outside. That means being suspended midair like an acrobat. I must admit, it sometimes makes things tricky, especially if the wind gets up, which it often does. But after a while, it becomes second nature."

Kurt studied the setup. Three high summits around the valley acted like the points of a jagged crown. The face of each peak was adorned with a rope and pulley system like the one that had lifted Kurt. The scaffolding ropes were offset from these, and the third set of taut cables stretched from one peak to the next. Highest to middle. Middle to lowest. And from there, back down to the camp below.

The heavy ropes reminded Kurt of the recreational zip line operations marketed to tourists all over the world.

"Your people use these lines to get from peak to peak," Kurt said.

"Precisely," Urco said. "They allow quick access from one crest to the next without having to go all the way down and back up again. I make the circuit at least twice a day myself, inspecting the work. It's a one-way journey, of course — since those crests are lower than this one. But it's quite exhilarating."

"I can imagine," Kurt said. "I'd like to try it."

"You're more than welcome to," Urco said. "But something tells me you didn't come all this way to talk about ropes and zip lines."

"No," Kurt admitted. "I'm looking for some information. But I'm not a reporter. I work for the American government, for an agency called NUMA."

"Ah, yes," Urco replied. "I know of this organization."

"You do?"

"When your work is dependent on grants, you become very familiar with the world's governmental organizations. Over the last ten years, I've applied to every department, of every agency, in every country, in the Americas. Or so it seems. I've petitioned NUMA several times. I'm afraid you've always turned me down."

"That's unfortunate," Kurt grunted.

Urco laughed. "Not to worry. It's all part of the business. But tell me, why would an organization that studies the sea be interested in the mountains of Peru and the people who lived there?"

"It's complicated," Kurt said. "The other night, you posted a video of a meteor crossing the sky. We wanted to know more about it. Can you tell me what you saw? When exactly it happened? Which direction you were looking?"

"It was very early in the morning," Urco said. "I get up before dawn each day. The sunrise is my affirmation. That morning, we were going to film a new chamber we'd uncovered. I was checking the cameras to make sure the batteries were charged. As I went about my routine, I looked up and saw a light in the sky. At first I thought it was a star, but it was moving with great speed. I had the camera in my hand, so I pointed and filmed. Pure serendipity. I'm not even sure the video was focused."

"It was slightly blurred," Kurt admitted,

"but not too bad, considering the circumstances. Which way did it travel?"

Urco pointed to the north. "It came in from that direction, crossed over the clearing and continued south."

The time interval was right, but the direction seemed off. Although Hiram had suggested the *Nighthawk*'s right wing appeared to be damaged. That might account for the change.

Kurt chose his next words with care. Urco was obviously a man of great intelligence. He was worldly even if the people who worked for him were relatively simple. Kurt had found truth worked better with such people, better than even the most carefully crafted lies. "What if I told you it wasn't a meteor in the sky that morning?"

Urco's face scrunched up, his weathered skin wrinkling, the beard shifting, but hiding any true expression. "I would have to agree with you," he said. "Up here, one sees shooting stars on a regular basis. No city lights to blind us. I posted the video as a lark, but as the day wore on I couldn't stop thinking about it. I must admit, my later impression was of something larger and closer. Lower to the Earth, I think."

"I think so, too," Kurt said. "I believe you saw an experimental American spacecraft that reentered the atmosphere and went off course. We — and by that I mean NUMA and the United States government — are very interested in finding the crash site. If you help us now, I can promise you, with a high degree of certainty, that you'll never be turned down for a grant again."

Urco nodded as if considering the possibilities. "Perhaps we can help each other," he said. "Have you ever heard of my theory?"

"Afraid not," Kurt said.

Urco didn't take offense. "It's called *Civilization Wave Theory.* It's adapted from a field known as cataclysmic evolution, which is the belief that a new form cannot prosper until the existing, dominant form subsides. Mammals, which rule the planet today, were nothing more than scurrying rodents for the first hundred million years of their existence. Surviving only because they were beneath the dinosaur's majestic notice. But after the Chicxulub meteor impact, the dinosaurs fell. In the blink of an eye, the entire playing field was leveled; indeed, tilted toward small animals with warm blood and fur. And so the rise of the mammals began."

Kurt nodded.

"My theory suggests that civilization

changes in much the same way. Nothing new can rise until the old, dominant power is swept away. Usually by a catastrophe beyond its control."

"For instance?"

"Being a man of the sea, I'm sure you're familiar with the sudden collapse of the Minoan empire."

"Of course," Kurt said. "After dominating the Mediterranean for centuries, the Minoans were weakened by the tsunamis that hit their island after the eruption of Santorini."

"Precisely," Urco said, "but they weren't wiped out. They still existed. They hung on for centuries in a diminished capacity. But the effect was a changing of the playing field; it was now tilted toward other civilizations of the region. The Mycenaean civilization in particular. Something that would never have happened were it not for the cataclysm."

Kurt nodded again.

"You see the same thing here," Urco told him. "Originally, the Chachapoya were more powerful than the Inca, but catastrophe struck them from the outside — not once, but twice."

Kurt settled in; he loved a good history lesson. "How so?"

"At the end, it was the diseases," Urco

admitted. "But long before that, these people faced another catastrophe. You can find the evidence in a body of water known as the Lake of the Condors, fifty miles from here."

Kurt had heard something about Lake of the Condors when reading Urco's website. "There are Chachapoya ruins there as well."

"Indeed," Urco said. "Extensive ruins in the cliffs all around it. Everyone knows about these. But what I found is different. Evidence that a major settlement had once thrived on the valley floor, stretching from one side to the other and up into the foot-hills."

"This, I hadn't heard," Kurt said.

"Few have," Urco insisted. "Thousands lived within the walls of this city, which made it a very large settlement for its day. They were protected by a strong warrior caste, with some of the finest weapons of the time. I assure you, these men shrank before no one, and for several centuries the Chachapoya were the power of the region, taking tribute from other groups. But then the disaster came upon them."

"What happened?"

"The city was built in the sheltered area between the mountains. It received its water from the snowmelt and a mountain lake, higher up in the range," Urco said. "A massive earthquake in the eighth century released the contents of that lake all at once. A fifty-foot wall of water crashed into the city in the dark of night. It drowned the city. The people were trapped. They died by the thousands. It was Noah without any warning from God. Pompeii without the ash. By daybreak, there was nothing left. The wealth was gone; the warriors were gone. *The city itself was gone.* The reign of the Chachapoya, unbreakable at sunset, was swept away by morning. And in its aftermath the Inca began their storied rise."

Kurt had no idea if there was any merit to the tale, but he found it fascinating. "Were there any survivors?"

"A few hundred," Urco said. "Those who'd lived higher up in the hills. When they tried to rebuild their civilization, they did things differently, constructing their dwellings in the cliffs instead of on the valley floors, where they felt they'd be safe from any future disaster. At first it was simple logic, but as time went by it became their way, their religion. They became the *People of the Clouds.*"

"Can't say I blame them," Kurt added.

"Indeed," Urco said. "Who could sleep on

the low ground after surviving a night like that?"

"Sounds like you've got it all worked out," Kurt said. "What do you need us for?"

"To help me prove it."

"By exploring the lake," Kurt surmised.

Urco nodded. "The Peruvian government has given me a permit but denied all my requests for funding or help. They have a vested interest in not diminishing the appeal of the mighty Inca. And I lack the funds to mount a submerged expedition myself. But I tell you, at the bottom of that lake is a flooded city the likes of which no one has ever seen."

The idea of unearthing something that would change the accepted history appealed to Kurt, but they had a more pressing issue. "I'm sure something could be arranged," he said. "You help me, I'll help you."

Urco stroked his bushy beard. "I was hoping we could do it *the other way around.*"

"The problem is, time," Kurt said. "I *have* to find this missing aircraft before I do anything else. I don't say this lightly, but everyone here is in danger until that plane is found."

Urco looked at him with a powerful gaze. "Why would *we* be in danger?"

"Because NUMA isn't the only group

looking for the missing aircraft. Agents from several other countries are after it as well. They've tried to kill my partner and me several times already. Including on the way up here."

"On the way up here?" Urco asked, suspicious.

"We were attacked on the road," Kurt said.

"They could still be following you."

"Not unless they can fly," Kurt said. "But others will come. And they're not the kind of people who are interested in striking deals. They won't hesitate to torture or kill everyone here to get what they're after."

Urco sighed and looked away. "I put nothing past selfish men," he said. "My research has shown it's our nature to fight and oppress. But how will helping you protect us? Wouldn't these other groups be more likely to resort to violence if they knew *we* had chosen sides?"

"All they care about is the missing aircraft," Kurt said. "Once we have it, they'll have no reason to be here. The danger will be gone."

Urco took a minute to ponder Kurt's words. Finally, he looked Kurt in the eye once again. "Nothing good happens to small people when they get in the way of the great powers. Better that this thing is found and taken away so we can continue on with our lives."

"So you'll help us?"

"I will. What do you need?"

"Only for you to show me where you were standing when you took the video. Once we match up the surrounding peaks with what's on the recording, we can extrapolate the precise direction of the craft and make a good estimate of its speed and altitude. With that information, we'll be able to find the landing site in a matter of hours and haul it away."

"And once that's done?" Urco asked.

"I'll make sure it's well known that we've recovered the vehicle intact," Kurt promised. "I'll even tell the world where we found it so that anyone who wants to look for themselves can bypass you and go straight to the crash site."

Urco stroked his beard. "Very well," he said. "Then I will help you gladly. But first . . . we eat."

28

The mountain road to La Jalca had been blocked. The bridge was gone; its twisted metal frame now lay at the bottom of the canyon while the road itself was covered with a swath of gravel, boulders and rock ten feet deep — remnants of the avalanche unleashed by the errant Chinese missile.

The man who'd fired that missile was gone as well, but Daiyu and Jian had escaped by driving back into the shelter of the tunnel and staying put until the rumbling ceased. They sat in darkness until the choking dust began to settle and a small gap of light appeared near the top of the tunnel.

"We should go back," Jian suggested. "We have a helicopter waiting in Cajamarca. We should make contact with command, secure reinforcements and fly to the ruins. Take them from the sky."

Daiyu shook her head. "We go forward," she insisted. "Not back. If we keep up a good pace, we can reach La Jalca by mid-night. Take them in their sleep."

"We're at a disadvantage now," he argued. "The kill team is gone. The Americans know we're following them."

"If anything, they think we're dead," she replied. "That gives us the advantage. And remember, our mission is to prevent the Americans from finding the *Nighthawk* at all costs. Driving all the way back to Caja-marca, reaching out to General Zhang and waiting for more support, will take far too long. We must go forward. You start clearing a way through and I'll gather the weapons and supplies."

Jian stared at her for a moment and then did as ordered. He stepped from the car, climbed onto the rubble pile and began dig-ging with his bare hands. The loose gravel was easy to move and the small boulders and rocks were no match for his great strength. He tossed them aside with ease and before long he'd dug enough of a channel for them to squirm through.

He emerged into the fresh air, covered from head to toe in dust. Daiyu came out behind him, handed him a backpack and pulled on one of her own. As she scanned the slope for a safe route to take, Jian picked his way to the edge of the cliff, looking for the other car.

"Don't bother," she called out. "They're gone."

He knew that. He looked anyway. It was a long drop. There was no sign of the car at the bottom, just a sloping pile of rock that had buried it.

As Jian stared into the abyss, Daiyu looked upward. A trick of the inner ear, caused by tilting the head backward, exaggerated the grade of the hill. Even knowing that, she was impressed that the Americans had managed to climb it without flipping their vehicle or rolling back down the hill. She'd underestimated them, something she would not do again.

She turned to Jian. "Ready?"

He nodded.

She pointed to a trail on the right. "This way looks to have better traction. Follow me."

The climb was more perilous on foot than in a vehicle. Thorny bushes and high-mountain cacti clawed at them mercilessly. Loose rocks shifted with each step, threatening to turn their ankles and send them sliding back toward the road below, while the air at nearly ten thousand feet was thin enough to leave them light-headed. By the time they reached the roadway above, they were scratched, bleeding and breathing hard.

Daiyu stood with her hands on her hips. Though the temperature was cool, she was sweating in the sun.

"Rest here for a minute," she said, taking a drink of the water and handing the bottle to Jian. "I'm going to scout ahead."

While Jian drank, Daiyu walked along the road. It continued upward and curved to the left. Beyond that, it flattened out. They were near the top. The plateau lay ahead of them.

As she waited for Jian to catch up, she caught the sound of an engine in the distance. Squinting against the glare of the afternoon sun, she spied a small box truck coming toward them. It was old and worn, a workhorse that showed the wear and tear of too many runs in the mountains. Dented in places, it listed to one side, trailing oil smoke from its exhaust pipe. Still, it would be far better than walking the rest of the way.

She waved it down.

With her long hair set in a ponytail and a backpack over her shoulders, she looked like any other hiker on a trail.

The truck stopped beside her and the passenger window rolled down. A man with rough black hair and a dark face looked out at her. He had small, dark eyes. A similar man was at the wheel. Both were more native than European.

"Are you all right?" the passenger asked in Spanish.

"I need some help," she replied, also in Spanish. "The bridge is out. It collapsed. There must have been an earthquake because there was a rockslide as well."

The men looked over the dashboard. Down the slope, they saw the rubble covering the road and the empty span where the bridge should have been. What they didn't see was Daiyu pulling a Chinese-made pistol from her jacket.

She fired three shots before either of them reacted. All three hit the passenger.

She yanked the door open and pulled him out. He landed dead at her feet as the driver threw his hands up.

"Get out," she ordered.

He fumbled for the door handle and unlatched it, falling from the truck in his haste. It wasn't fast enough. Daiyu shot him, a single bullet to the head that killed him instantly.

By the time Jian reached her, she'd dragged both dead men to the edge of the bank and shoved them over. They tumbled a short distance and then slid limply down the slope until catching on separate bushes halfway to the bottom.

"You didn't have to kill them," Jian said. "They could have been useful. They might have had information."

She put the pistol away. "Bringing them along would be a distraction. And by leaving them here, we'd risk the chance of someone spotting them and setting them free."

She climbed behind the wheel as Jian took the passenger's seat. After a precarious three-point turn, she got the truck moving back toward La Jalca.

The poor truck never topped twenty miles an hour going uphill, but once they were out on the flat top of the plateau, it picked up speed until they were traveling close to forty.

Daiyu checked the time. Instead of reaching La Jalca at midnight, they'd be there by dusk. They might just catch the Americans after all.

29

Cajamarca, Peru

The streets of Cajamarca were cold and wet. A brief spell of rain had left mud in the gutters and puddles everywhere. Rain in the mountains was always a cold rain. The damp got into the bones. Paul and Gamay would have preferred snow.

Walking along the sidewalk, Paul pulled his coat around him and flipped up his collar. "I think someone is following us," he whispered.

"The guy in the colorful poncho," Gamay said. "I've seen him three times since leaving the airport."

It might have been a good way to blend, as many of the natives of Cajamarca wore similar ponchos in the cold months, but the pattern was unique and Paul and Gamay both had an eye for fashion.

Catching sight of the man in the reflection of a store window, Paul nodded. The pattern was the same; the fur-lined boots were the same. The man was the same.

"What do you say we get off the main street," he suggested.

"If it means somewhere warm . . ."

"How about this place," Paul said, pointing to a brightly painted Internet café.

Gamay read the sign. "Strong java, stronger Internet, 4K video. Let's go."

They stepped inside, watched through the glass as the man passed by and saw him return a moment later. Instead of coming in, he sat at the bus stop across the road, apparently content to watch.

Paul was fine with that. He and Gamay moved deeper into the narrow building. Thankful for the warmth, as much as anything.

The café was busy, the coffee, computers and young people creating a perpetual buzz. They found a spot with access to both the front and back doors, logged on to a computer and spent a few minutes browsing.

"Do you think our friend is going to sneak in anytime soon?" Paul asked.

"Doubt it," Gamay said, "but we'll see him if he does."

"In that case, I'm going to make a phone call."

He stepped away from the desk, found a

ladder to the roof and climbed it. Popping out through a trapdoor, Paul climbed onto the roof and lowered the door gently behind him. He wasn't looking to escape; he just needed a clear view of the sky.

After linking up to the NUMA communications system, Paul was patched through to Hiram Yaeger. He got right to the point. "Kurt needs you and Priya to hack into the NSA's database."

Of all the staff at NUMA, Hiram Yaeger was the least afraid to flout authority — it was half the reason he kept his hair long and wore decidedly non-corporate clothes to work. But he was surprised to hear this request from one of NUMA's most buttoned-down officers. "Who are you?" he asked. "And what have you done with Paul?"

"Very funny," Paul replied. "I'm serious. Kurt has reason to believe they're hiding something regarding the *Nighthawk* and its mission. Good reason. And since he's the one out there risking his life —"

He must have been on speakerphone because Priya chimed in. "I'm not an expert in such matters, but isn't that frowned upon . . . or perhaps illegal?"

"It's not exactly encouraged," Hiram admitted. "But we've done it before and never really gotten more than a slap on the wrist."

"Apparently, the NSA is more forgiving than their reputation suggests," she replied.

"Preventing a worldwide catastrophe with the information we borrowed might have had something to do with that," Paul said.

"I have no problem with this," Hiram said. "You know that. But we have been warned. Maybe I should run it by Rudi or Dirk."

"And ruin their plausible deniability?"

"Good point," Hiram said. "Okay. We'll give it a shot."

Paul knew that meant it would get done. "Kurt wants the information as soon as you can get it. Preferably, before his romantic Sunday drive gets the best of him."

Hiram promised to do his best and the call ended. Paul looked around to find a large crow staring back at him from another section of the roof.

"Thank God, you're not a parrot," he said.

The crow cawed and spread its wings. It flew off to the south, and Paul climbed back down into the warmth of the café.

"Get through?" Gamay said.

He nodded and checked the clock on the wall. "Joe is still several hours away."

Gamay had already purchased a steaming cup of soup and an alpaca hat. "Yep," she said, settling in and tapping away on a keyboard. "Looks like this café is our temporary home."

Back in Washington, Hiram and Priya were left to figure out the details of their latest hacking scheme.

"Whether we should do this or not is one thing," Priya said. "But how we do it is the more important question."

"You're not worried?" Hiram asked.

"Worst thing they can do is deport me back to Merrie Olde England. And while I can't stand all the rain, you and Rudi will be the ones who go to jail."

"Not likely," Hiram said. "But it isn't going to be easy to break their code. Each time Max and I have hacked the NSA, they've responded by raising their game. Their security is quite good."

"We could overwhelm them with a brute force attack," Max suggested over the speakers.

Hiram looked up — as he often did when speaking to Max. "Let's try something less reminiscent of Genghis Khan."

Priya was already tapping away at her computer. "The NSA may have built the *Nighthawk* in secret, but they didn't design it from scratch. Design cues were taken

317

from the space shuttle and the X-37. Ms. Townsend even said something about the *Nighthawk* using common parts from the X-37. If that's the case, NASA probably shared data on the construction process. And that means we might be able to hack into NASA instead of the NSA."

"Great idea," Hiram said.

"I prefer the word *brilliant.*"

"Then *brilliant* it is," Hiram replied. "To collaborate with NASA, our friends at the NSA would have set up a secure and authenticated connection. If we do as you say and break into NASA first, we can get into the NSA computers through the back door and they might think they're just sharing data with the Johnson Space Center."

Max chimed in. *"I assign a seventy-three percent chance of success to the plan. And if they do discover the hack, they'll investigate NASA first, giving us more time to make a run for it."*

"Without legs, you'll be going nowhere," Hiram said. "I'm afraid they'll melt you down for scrap."

"I could get wheels," Max suggested. *"Like Dr. Kashmir."*

For an instant, Hiram felt awkward, but Priya laughed. "Trust me, Max, having wheels isn't all it's cracked up to be."

Hiram laughed as well. "We'll talk about your mobility issues some other time, Max. Let's break into the space center's network and see if their computers are still on speaking terms with the National Security Agency."

It was the better part of the day before Priya and Max were able to gain access. Eventually, they had to go through the systems at Cape Canaveral and the Jet Propulsion Laboratory before discovering a link to the NSA database. Shortly, they were receiving copious amounts of information on the *Nighthawk*'s design, test flights and mission parameters.

Priya and Hiram looked at what they could but relied on Max to determine what was important or not, as they soon had over a thousand pages of information.

As Max continued to sort things out, Priya found herself studying the technical papers related to the *Nighthawk*'s construction. "Look at this," she said, waving Hiram over to her desk.

He peered down at the image on her computer.

"These are the blueprints and design specs for the X-37." She pointed. "And these are the plans for the *Nighthawk.* See anything interesting?"

Hiram pulled his glasses off, cleaned them with a soft cloth and put them back on. "They're very similar. Almost identical."

"The only real difference is size," she said. "If we scale an original set of plans up, they match. Same engine, same navigation system, same wing design, same heat shield. In fact, aside from a coating of stealth material that burns off on reentry, the heat shield is not much different than the tile system used on the space shuttle since the eighties."

"So much for the technological leap forward they keep claiming," Hiram said. "It's little more than an updated version of an older vehicle."

He stood up and addressed Max. "Are you sure we're looking at the correct plans?"

"Affirmative," Max replied.

"How certain are you?"

"There's a 99.98 percent probability that the plans you're looking at match the vehicle that was launched and is now being sought in South America."

"That's pretty certain," Priya said.

Hiram agreed. "It doesn't make sense. The Russians took an immense risk to grab it. They exposed their secret Typhoon submarine, in an attempt to retrieve the wreckage from where they thought it had crashed, and both they and the Chinese seem willing to risk a war to find it."

"With the attempts on Kurt and Ms. Townsend so far, I'd say a skirmish has already begun," Priya added.

Hiram nodded. He looked over the plans once again, double-checking the propulsion specifications and the structural blueprints. "If it isn't the machine that matters, then it has to be something else. Something related to the mission."

"Perhaps it collected one of our spy satellites. Or one of theirs."

"Maybe one of each," Hiram said. "That would get them hot under the collar."

"If we knew where it went, we might learn more," she suggested.

"Max, what can you tell me about the *Nighthawk*'s mission profile?"

The computer voice responded instantly. *"The NSA launches the* Nighthawk *out of Vandenberg on a modified Titan booster. The vehicle inserts into a polar orbit and stays aloft for extensive periods of time. Seventy-five days on the first launch, eight hundred and fifty-one days on this latest mission."*

"And yet," Hiram said, scanning through the page count, "we seem to have far more data from the first mission than the second. Are you holding something back on us?"

"Mission 1 was a test mission," Max said.

"Data from all phases of the mission was freely shared with NASA. Mission 2 was an operational event. Fully classified. Only pre-launch data and orbital track information was provided."

"Can you match up the *Nighthawk*'s orbital track with known satellites?"

There was a slight pause — unusual for Max, considering how fast her processing speeds were. *"The* Nighthawk *made 14,625 complete orbits and one partial orbit before reentry. At no time did its path intersect with the position of any known satellite. Available data suggests the* Nighthawk *maneuvered* specifically *to avoid any orbital convergence."*

"Anything else unusual about the path?"

"For ninety-one percent of its time in space, the Nighthawk *remained in the Earth's shadow."*

"So the *Nighthawk* was staying out of sight," Hiram said. "Can't hijack another satellite when you're hiding in the dark and avoiding them like the plague."

"I'm not sure it could retrieve something if it wanted to," Priya said. "Look at this. On the initial blueprints, the cargo bay is an empty space, just like the cargo bay on the shuttle. But on the last set of prelaunch schematics, the entire bay has been filled with equipment."

Hiram's curiosity grew, he pulled up a chair and settled in beside her. "What kind of equipment?"

"Cryogenic storage containers, advanced lithium batteries and a bank of devices called *Penning traps* — which must use powerful magnets because the control center and the propulsion bay have been electromagnetically shielded to prevent magnetic interference."

"Penning traps," Hiram said, trying to remember where he'd heard that term before.

"According to the schematic, they take up the whole bay."

Hiram nodded. He was suddenly very grim. The truth was coming to him and he didn't like it one bit. "Max, can you correlate the *Nighthawk*'s orbit with evidence of the northern lights?"

"Affirmative," Max said. *"The* Nighthawk *was present in a northern polar orbit during all major flares of the aurora borealis. It was also present over the South Pole during the major and minor flares of the aurora australis, otherwise known as the southern lights. Its positioning indicates direct emersion within the vortex point of the Earth's magnetic field."*

"Vortex point?" Priya asked.

"Where the lines of the Earth's magnetic

field converge above the North and South Poles, before they dive down into the Earth."

By now, Priya had picked up on his tone. "Do you know what they're doing?"

"Testing a theory," he said. "A very dangerous theory."

She looked at the schematics again, running her finger across the imaginary Penning traps. The term itself gave her the answer. "They brought something back. Didn't they?"

Hiram nodded. "I'm afraid so," he said. "And it's something far more deadly than any satellite could hope to be."

30

La Jalca Canyon, Chachapoya ruins

By dusk, the cooking fires had been stoked and several long wooden tables set for a communal meal. Urco introduced Kurt and Emma to the rest of the volunteers and insisted that their arrival was cause for celebration.

Before the food was served, Urco led the group in a traditional invocation. "It's a Chachapoya prayer," he explained. "It cautions us not to begin the feast until all the guests are present and accounted for."

"Another way to remember the people whose world you're excavating?" Emma asked.

"Precisely," Urco said. "We even live like them. In ancient times there was far less trade than today. Each society, each village, had to be self-sufficient. And so are we. We catch rainwater in barrels, grow manioc in the southern section of the clearing. We have the llamas in the corral."

"Adorable animals," Emma said.

"I wouldn't get too attached to them," Kurt whispered.

"Why?"

"I think you're about to eat one."

She looked ill for a second.

"You can't be self-sufficient in everything," Kurt said.

Urco disagreed. "I assure you, we are. As are all the villages our volunteers come from. I tell you, the rest of civilization could cease to exist and we would never know it."

"I can understand the desire to live that way," Emma said. "But wouldn't all the effort put into growing crops and raising animals be better used here, at the dig site? If the food was shipped in, it would leave you more workers to handle the other chores."

"The road to civilization is both long and treacherous," he said. "Both in the real and metaphorical sense. Being self-sufficient keeps us from being dependent on that road in any form. And since I've recently heard that it was closed . . ."

Kurt laughed and took a drink of water.

A moment later, the food was served: bread made from manioc flour, some type of diced vegetable and what looked like venison. The aroma was heavenly.

"Enjoy it, my friends," Urco said. "As soon as we're done, I'll show you what you came to see."

Kurt nodded, buried the impatience he felt and enjoyed a hearty and unusual dinner. As things were cleared away, Kurt and Emma went back to the Range Rover to collect a few items they would need and then rejoined Urco near the bank of solar panels. "We use these to power our modern equipment."

"So you're not dependent on civilization," Emma said, "but you are beholden to the sun."

"True," Urco replied. "But the sun is far more reliable. Five billion years and counting. Something tells me modern civilization will never match that."

"So this is where you were when you saw the light in the sky?" Kurt asked.

"Yes," Urco said. "I came up the trail from our tents and checked the flashlights. We were going to look into a newly discovered cave that day, so we needed as much light as possible. Satisfied that everything was fully powered, I came over to this stand where our video cameras were connected to their chargers."

He led them to a cradle where two cameras were supported and attached to the power station via cables.

"I picked up this one," he said, grabbing it. "Turned it on and waited. As it powered up, I happened to see a flicker of light in the sky. Once I realized it wasn't a star, I brought the camera up and filmed it."

He held the camera up to his face, showing them how he'd done it and pretending to track the fiery target across the sky. "It went from north to south," he said, tracing the arc with his fingers. "It vanished behind those peaks."

"Did you hear anything?" Emma asked.

"Like what? An explosion?"

"Anything at all," Emma said. "Explosion, popping, the sound of jet engines."

"Nothing," Urco said. "You can hear the audio on the recording. Just me huffing and puffing."

Kurt studied the sky, black and punctured with stars. A slight glow from the new moon gave them just enough light to see the outline of the mountains. "Let's do it."

She placed her laptop computer on a nearby table and began tapping away. "Can you set up the tripod for me?"

Kurt unfolded the legs of the aluminum tripod. "Where *exactly* were you standing?" he asked Urco.

"Right about here," Urco said, moving several feet to his right.

Kurt extended the legs of the tripod, attached the camera to the central mount and raised it up until it was resting at the same level as Urco's eyes. That done, he connected an HDMI cable from Emma's computer to the camera and switched it on. "All yours."

Emma nodded and continued to tap away at the keyboard. Kurt slid behind her and watched as she replayed the original video, pausing it several times. When it finished, she ran it all the way through once again.

"We need an exact distance from here to the peak." She handed Kurt a laser range finder.

Kurt turned it on and pointed it at the jagged ridge until he got a reading. "Seven hundred and forty-two feet."

She typed it in and two outlines appeared on the screen, one displaying the peaks as they appeared through the NUMA camera and the second displaying the peaks from the video Urco had taken.

At Emma's command, the camera moved left and right and then back to the left. She tapped the up arrow and the camera tilted just a bit. The computer took it from there and fine-tuned the image until the two outlines merged exactly. "That's it."

At the touch of a button, Emma received the heading of what they assumed to be the *Nighthawk.*

"What about speed and altitude?" Kurt asked.

"For that, we'll need to match this with the new descent profile your friend Hiram is working up."

Emma tried to initiate a satellite linkup, but it failed.

"It's the mountains," Urco said. "You'll have to go up top."

"You mean, on those ropes?"

"It's the only way to get a signal," Urco explained. "How do you feel about a night ascent?"

She sighed. "Worse than I did about a daytime's."

Hidden in the dark among the same type of scrub trees that had scratched their exposed skin, Daiyu watched Kurt through a spotting scope. He was talking with the woman and the bearded man. She focused on his lips, trying to make out what he was saying.

"What are they doing?" Jian asked.

"They're calculating something," she said. "They're using the video we were told about to get a bearing on the *Nighthawk.*"

"We should be doing that," Jian suggested.

She and Jian had arrived just after sunset, ditching the truck near one of the fields and hiking the last few miles on foot. They'd made a study of the camp and were trying to decide how best to get at the Americans without having to fight their way through the forty Peruvian men and women of the archaeology group.

"They're trying to connect to their satellite," she said, reading Emma's lips, "but they can't get a signal. They're going to higher ground."

She put the scope away and looked to Jian. "This is our chance. We have to get that computer."

31

Urco led Kurt and Emma to the base of the second peak and, with a wolf whistle, called several of his people over. "I'll go first," he said, stepping into the harness for the ride to the top.

As he disappeared upward into the night, Kurt glanced at Emma. "You don't have to go," he said. "I can send the data."

She shook her head. "I'd never live it down."

"In that case, think about it this way: it's so dark, you won't be able to tell how high you are."

"That doesn't help," she replied.

A double flash from high above told them Urco was safely on the mountaintop. When the harness dropped out of the dark, Kurt grabbed it. "Ready?"

Emma exhaled and nodded. "Here," she said, handing him the computer. "My hands are shaking already. Won't do us any good if

I drop it."

Kurt took the laptop as she strapped herself in and gave the thumbs-up signal. "Top floor, please."

Emma was pulled upward into the dark. Because she was lighter, she rose faster. From Kurt's angle, she almost seemed to be flying.

His turn came moments later. With the harness around him, he held the rope with one hand and gripped the computer with the other. After the initial liftoff, he turned to look out over the camp. Only the fires near the center of camp and a few lights dotted here and there.

He glanced upward. A soft glow surrounded the rigging at the top. It came from the flashlights that Emma and Urco carried, but it was dim and very far away, like a boat on the surface waiting for him to return from a night dive.

As he neared the crest, the lights converged on him. On this particular peak, there was no need for a ladder to make the final ascent; instead, Kurt continued up until the top of the harness tapped against the pulley above him and his feet were level with a broad wooden platform. He stepped onto it with ease, disconnected the harness and handed Emma the computer.

"You should have had that reporter meet you up here," he mentioned to Urco.

"Then he might never have left," Urco replied.

"That was quite enjoyable," Emma said to Kurt. "I don't know what you were worried about."

Kurt laughed at that and took a look around. There was a marked difference between this peak and the one he'd met Urco on earlier. For one thing, it was smaller — a dance floor instead of a football field. It had also been improved. Wooden planks had been nailed together and anchored in the stone. They covered most of the surface. Though some ground remained visible at the edges, the decking sloped away so sharply, it would have been treacherous to stand on.

On Kurt's right, two plastic storage bins had been nailed to the deck. On his left, a well-braced rig held the zip lines coming to and leading off of the platform. Beyond was nothing but pitiless black.

"Love what you've done with the place," Kurt joked.

"The terrain made it necessary," Urco said. "The ground here is too uneven, and terribly weathered. It made for poor footing, so we built this platform."

Kurt moved across the creaky boards to a spot beside Emma. She'd taken a seat near the very center and had already flipped the laptop open and was booting up.

As she worked, a brief schematic appeared, depicting the horizon line, the constellations and the track of several NUMA satellites. The computer chose the satellite with the strongest signal.

"Locked in," Emma said. "Beginning transmission."

"I saw your vehicle," Urco said out of the blue. "You seem to have gone through a great deal just to get here. You must want this airplane back very badly."

"We do," Emma admitted.

"It makes sense," Urco replied. "We all want back what we once had."

A message popped up on the screen. *Download complete. Processing data.*

As the computer began combining the data, it displayed a series of calculations. Emma stared as the numbers danced, but Urco acted blithely uninterested, and Kurt had a sudden impression of danger.

He caught a sound in the wind and then heard a squeak from the rigging beside him. He turned to see the zip line from the higher peak tensing and moving. He glanced out into the night and spotted a dark shape rushing toward them.

"Look out!"

A stocky man with square shoulders came flying in on the line. He let go of the T-bar as he crossed the threshold and barreled into Urco.

Another figure appeared out of the dark right behind him. This one, a lithe woman, landed with cat-like grace. She whipped out a pistol, targeted Emma and pulled the trigger all at once.

The shot went wide only because Kurt lunged forward and knocked her arm to the side. With one hand on her wrist, Kurt took her to the ground. Several shots fired, but they drilled harmlessly into the wooden deck.

She counterattacked by slamming a knee into his midsection. The bony impact struck with surprising power, but all Kurt cared about was the pistol. He kept her wrist locked in his grasp and banged her arm on the flooring until the weapon came free.

She stretched for it with her other hand, but he punched it away. It slid off the deck and out into the dark.

In the meantime, Urco struggled with the second attacker. They rolled toward the edge, oblivious to how close they were to falling, as they grasped each other and traded punches.

Emma sprang toward them, wrapping her arm around the assailant's thick neck, pulling him back. He reared up, arching his back and reaching for her in vain.

Kurt kept his focus on the woman. She'd gotten loose, hopped to her feet and pulled out a knife with almost inhuman speed. He dropped to the ground as she slashed at him. The blade cut the air above, and he spun on his side, sweeping her feet out from underneath. She landed hard on her back, her head whiplashing into the deck. She made an odd noise and went limp, dropping the knife and rolling over onto her side.

Since the woman appeared to be unconscious, Kurt turned his attention to the melee at the edge of the platform.

By now, the big man had thrown Emma off his back, gotten to his feet and doubled Urco over with a shot to the solar plexus. A brutal shove sent Urco tumbling off the platform and onto the weathered slope of the mountain. He slid, grabbing for anything he could reach, but his hands found only loose rock.

Emma dove for him, stretching out her arm. "No," she shouted.

She missed by several feet and Urco continued downward, his fingers scraping across the ground, until he vanished over the edge.

Kurt knew he had to take this wrecking ball of a man out or they would all follow Urco to their deaths. He jumped toward the man and hit him with a leaping kick. Both feet connected with the small of the man's back and he stumbled off the deck, vanishing into the dark. A soft thud marked his end seconds later.

"Help me," a voice cried from down below. "Please."

"It's Urco," Emma shouted.

They rushed to the edge. Kurt noticed one of the excavation's scaffolding ropes twisting back and forth. "Hold tight," he shouted, "we'll pull you up."

Kurt found a spot to anchor his feet, gripped the rope with both hands and leaned back. Emma joined him, and Urco rose, one foot at a time.

When he cleared the edge and could assist them using his feet on the slope, the archaeologist all but charged back onto the platform. "Thank you," he said, falling at their feet. "Thank the gods."

He rolled onto his back, breathing heavily. "Ms. Townsend, your fear of heights is well founded. I'm thinking of taking a similar position —"

He stopped midsentence, interrupted by movement and the sound of steel wheels spinning, as one of the T-bars zoomed away down the zip line.

They turned in unison. The woman was gone.

"She took the computer," Emma pointed out.

Kurt didn't hesitate. He grabbed the other T-bar, connected it to the rope and launched himself after her.

32

Kurt leapt into the dark and was instantly flying. He gripped the T-bar, brought his knees up and felt the acceleration as the rollers spun ever faster.

This line led from the middle peak down to the first, a distance of three hundred yards and a drop of two hundred feet. It wasn't overly steep, which played to his advantage. Being heavier, and having taken a running start, Kurt closed the gap with the fleeing computer thief.

He crashed into her and wrapped his legs around her waist. She squirmed and twisted loose, then spun and managed to kick him in the shin.

With his momentum used up, they were now traveling at similar speeds. Considering that neither one of them wore a safety harness, her next move was wildly dangerous. She took one hand off of the T-bar and slashed at Kurt with the knife.

The first hack made a small cut on his arm, drawing blood. A second try missed and Kurt kicked the knife out of her hand before she could try again.

She was traveling backward now, fending him off with her feet. She didn't see the end of the line coming and crashed onto the next platform with an ugly tumble.

Kurt hit as hard. The impact sent him sprawling, but he was on top of her before she could move. Holding her to the ground, he bent her arm up behind her back. "I don't like to hurt women," he said, "but I'll break your arm if you don't stop fighting."

"Damn you," she said. "I'll kill you."

"You had your chance," he replied, upping the pressure.

She must have been incredibly limber because, even lying facedown, she managed to kick him in the back with her heel.

At that point, Kurt had had enough. He grabbed her by the hair and slammed her head forward, banging her face on the ground. She went limp, out cold.

Not trusting her to stay that way, he tied her up. By the time he was finished, Urco and Emma were sliding down the zip line toward him.

"You got her," Emma said, undoing her harness.

"And the computer," Kurt replied, opening the laptop to see if it had been damaged.

As the flashlights illuminated the woman, Kurt saw that she was Asian. Most likely, from mainland China.

"Looks like all three powers are now accounted for," Emma said.

The computer screen lit up, the soft glow illuminating Kurt's face, as the program resumed its calculations. He stared, watching as the lines on the map slowly converged to mark the *Nighthawk*'s final resting spot.

"No way!"

"What is it?" Emma asked.

He turned the computer around, displaying the map to Emma and Urco. A blinking pin marked the crash site.

"Lake of the Condors," Emma said.

Urco's eyes grew wide in the dark.

Kurt grinned at the irony. "Looks like you're going to see what's at the bottom of that lake sooner than we thought."

33

It was too dangerous to move at night. The road to the lake was every bit as treacherous as the drive up from Cajamarca. The woman they'd captured insisted that others would come for her.

"She's probably bluffing," Kurt said. "But we're far more vulnerable on an open road in the dark than here."

Both Urco and Emma agreed. Instead of driving out, they stoked the fires around the camp and borrowed a page from the Chachapoya, taking to the high ground and pulling up all the ropes. If there were Chinese agents or assassins out there, they'd have to scale the mountains by hand to stage an assault.

"We're not supposed to use these caves," Urco told his volunteers, "but they belonged to your forefathers, so they should be yours, not the government's."

Kurt went higher, heading up to the tallest peak. Alone, he made a satellite call to Rudi Gunn, who had returned to Washington. He got the good news first: Joe and the Trouts had arrived in Cajamarca. Then came the bad.

"You were right," Rudi said. "The NSA has been hiding something. And it's big, even though it's actually very small."

Kurt listened as Rudi explained what Hiram and Priya had found. The explanation was detailed, highly technical and riddled with physics, but Kurt got the basics. "That's worse than I thought."

"Worse than any of us thought," Rudi said. "Want us to send you more resources?"

"No," Kurt said. "It would take too long to get everything in place. Speed and stealth are our best friends, at the moment. If we're right about the *Nighthawk*'s location, we can salvage it tomorrow and get the cargo out and off to wherever the NSA intended to store it. In the meantime, I'm starting to feel like Humphrey Bogart in *Treasure of the Sierra Madre* — suspicious of everyone and everything."

"Can't say I blame you. We haven't heard from the Russians since you and Joe got back on dry land, but I doubt they're going to give up. And I'm certain we haven't seen the last of our Chinese friends. According to Central Intelligence, they have an army of agents in Peru and Ecuador. Don't be surprised if reinforcements show up when you least expect it."

"Which is why I need to change the plan."

"What did you have in mind?"

Kurt was thinking back to the service records of the Special Projects team. Considering who to choose for a difficult task. "I'm going to send you a set of specs," he said to Rudi, "Relay them to Joe and the Trouts, and tell Gamay I'm sorry but she's going to miss the raising of the *Nighthawk.*"

"Understood," Rudi said. "I'll look for your message."

Kurt said good-bye, cut the link and slid the phone into his pocket. He was ready to head back down when the pulley squeaked as someone came up on the rope. A moment later, hands appeared at the top of the ladder.

He was expecting Urco, but the determined face of Emma Townsend popped up over the edge instead.

Kurt helped her off the ladder. "This is a surprise."

She moved toward the center of the peak. "Turns out sitting in a creepy cave with mummified bodies is worse than scaling heights in the dark."

Kurt laughed. He found the caves claustrophobic himself. "I think it's time we leveled with each other," he said. "I know how it works. I know you're not at liberty to say much, so I don't blame you, but at this point I need the truth."

"You *have* the truth," she said.

"I have part of it," Kurt said. He sat down, picked up a stone and ran his finger over the smooth surface; the color was faded on one side but deep and rich on the other — two sides to every story. "When we first met, I wondered why they sent you with us," he explained. "It really made no sense. You have a reputation as a troublemaker in the NSA — a trait I happen to admire — but one that makes you an odd choice to go with the group most likely to find the missing plane."

"Don't flatter yourself," she said. "Or build me up to be something I'm not. They sent everyone they could find. Everyone they could get their hands on."

"Sure," Kurt said. "But we were on the scene three days before anyone else, which gave us a big lead. That, along with our well-earned reputation for finding missing things in the ocean, is why they put you with us. Because if we did find it, they needed someone along for the ride who knew exactly what we were recovering. And even among the shadowed halls of the NSA, very few know what's really going on here. But between that Doctorate in Physics and your ties to NASA, you have to be one of the few."

She didn't deny it. Nor did she admit anything. "Time is of the essence," she said. "The Russians and the Chinese —"

"Aren't interested in the *Nighthawk,*" he said. "They want the cargo that it's carrying. They want what it brought back."

She went as silent as a stone.

"I know about the Penning traps," Kurt said, "along with containment units, the cryogenic equipment and the entire system you built to harvest and store antimatter. That's why the *Nighthawk* had a polar orbit. That's why it stayed in the dark, where the temperatures in space are closer to absolute zero. That's why it was up there for three years, because it's a very slow process."

He let that linger and wondered if he would have to press her further. Finally, she came around.

"Not *anti*matter," she said. "A different form of matter. A few scientists call it by the rather awkward name: *un-matter.* We prefer to call it *mixed-state matter:* long-chain molecules made of equal parts of regular matter and antimatter."

That was news. "I thought matter and antimatter annihilated each other the instant they touched."

"Normally, they do," she said. "But at temperatures close to absolute zero, molecular structures break down. Matter no longer holds a physical shape and, instead, acts more like a wave than a solid particle. In that condition, matter and antimatter can mix without destructive results, the way two waves of different frequencies can exist superimposed on each other. Using magnetic force and cryogenics to confine and control this mixed-state matter, we realized it could be stored indefinitely. It wasn't long before a member of our research team suggested there might be naturally occurring pools of mixed-state matter floating high above the poles, held stable within the magnetic field."

"So you built the *Nighthawk* to go test that idea."

"And we discovered a relative abundance of it."

"A relative abundance?"

"Far more than we expected," she said. "Filaments of the material, spinning in what are essentially magnetic bubbles. Fractions of an ounce, in most cases, but enough to be worth retrieving. So we spent a year modifying the *Nighthawk,* and we filled the cargo bay with a more advanced type of Penning trap, which we call a *containment unit,* and we sent it up again to collect what we could find."

"And now it's sitting at the bottom of a lake," Kurt noted. "And those containment units are running on battery power. What happens when the batteries run out?"

"You know what happens," she snapped. "A very large explosion."

He did know that. He just wanted to hear her say it. "How large?"

She spoke without emotion. Clinical and cold. It was the dry tone of a distant scientist, not someone who might be vaporized at any instant. "Eight ounces of antimatter exposed to an equal amount of matter will cause an explosion the equivalent of a ten-mega-ton bomb detonating. Our best estimate puts the load on board the *Nighthawk* somewhere in the range of two hundred kilograms. Almost four hundred pounds."

"Four hundred pounds!?"

"Approximately," she said. "If it all reacted simultaneously — and once some of it reacts, it will all react — the explosive force will be nearly eight thousand mega-tons, or eight giga-tons. The blast will be five times larger than the combined effect of detonating every nuclear weapon in the world's combined arsenal in the same place at the same exact time."

Kurt just stared at her. He didn't know whether to laugh at the stupidity of what they'd done or curse them for their arrogance. "And you brought this material to Earth willingly? Compiled it all in the same place? Are you people insane?"

"What would you have us do?" she asked. "Once we figured out this material was up there, it wasn't going to be long before the Russians and the Chinese made the same discovery. Would you rather they had it? Do you want the designers of Chernobyl playing around with this stuff? The builders of the already crumbling Three Gorges Dam?"

"Of course not," Kurt said. "But what's to stop them from retrieving their own supply?"

"The fact that we took it all," she said. "It accumulates very slowly. It'll be a thousand years before there's a harvestable amount floating around up there again."

"Great," Kurt said. "Maybe civilization will have dragged itself back from the Stone Age by then."

"You think I don't know the danger?" she

said. "Do you think it doesn't weigh on me?"

He looked up at the dark night sky. The stars were bright out here, so far away from the nearest city. Tiny balls of fusion, which the Earth would become for a brief instant if they didn't find the *Nighthawk* and keep the containment units functioning.

He turned back toward her. "At least I finally understand why you were all so certain the *Nighthawk* came down in one piece."

"We knew the core had to be intact or we'd have all seen the results already."

"How much time do we have?"

"Seventy-two hours," she said. "Maybe less. It depends how much light is reaching the solar panels on the wings."

"And if the containment units or the cryogenic system fail early?"

"A Nebraska-sized hole in the Andes," she said. "A hundred trillion tons of rock instantly vaporized and blasted into the atmosphere. A ninety percent reduction in photosynthesis and biological activity. No one will have to worry about global warming anymore because the Earth will be in frigid darkness for at least five years."

Not a pleasant scenario, he thought. "And if we get it back to the United States?"

"The material will be split up into thousands of tiny samples, each no more than half an ounce. They'll be stored in a labyrinth of underground facilities that the NSA has been building for the last three years. A failure at one site will be no worse than a small bomb going off in an underground test location because there will be no other material for it to react with."

All emotion had left Kurt. There was only one thing that counted now. "Then we'd damn well better find it and get it locked down."

"My thoughts exactly," she replied.

34

Astaccato thumping echoed through the high mountain pass. Ground-dwelling animals looked up nervously and then darted away as a thundering orange machine flew between peaks and its great whirling shadow passed over them.

Joe Zavala was at the controls of the Air-Crane once again. The big helicopter was slow and stable, but it wasn't the easiest bird to control in a crosswind. As a result, he was more focused on the flying than the scenery. At least his passengers were enjoying the view.

"Now, this is a view fit for the gods," Urco's voice called out over the intercom.

Joe glanced back for an instant. The cockpit of the Air-Crane was packed. Kurt sat in the copilot's seat while Emma, Urco and Paul Trout sat on the jump seats behind them.

"It's too bad we couldn't see it at sunrise,"

Urco added.

In fact, Joe had seen plenty of the mountains at sunrise, making another run that only he, Kurt and Paul knew about. It had pushed back their arrival at La Jalca. "Sorry about that," Joe said. "We were slightly delayed."

"Are we trying to make up time by flying through the mountains instead of over them?" Paul asked.

"Talk to Kurt," Joe said. "I just go where I'm told to."

"The Chinese agent claimed she had more support out here," Kurt said. "If so, the Air-Crane slowly crossing the sky in a nice straight line would be like a big orange arrow pointing to the crash site."

"Not to mention a tempting target," Emma said.

Joe banked to the right, rounding another peak and taking them out over the plunging valley on the far side. "Besides," he added, "this is a lot more fun."

The mood in the helicopter was upbeat. They were close to finding the missing craft and averting disaster. That hope had given everyone a burst of adrenaline and a second wind.

"Even if they did spot us, it would take forever to get here," Urco promised. *"The*

road to the lake is very poor; it makes a goat path look like the German autobahn. It was built by the Inca seven hundred years ago and hasn't been resurfaced since."

They could see the path from where they were. A long, thin pencil line scraped into the side of the highlands. It curved in and out of the various hills and then began to drop, leading from the high plateau down to the valley and eventually to the lake.

Lake of the Condors sat at the foot of a plateau. It was fed by a river that snaked down from the mountains, entered a gap in the bluff and then shot forward over a ledge and down into the lake.

The drop was two hundred feet, not particularly high for a waterfall, but it poured out of the overhanging rock with substantial force, filling the narrow upper end of the pear-shaped lake.

From the air, it appeared static, a standing wave covered by a veil of spray that sparkled in the sun. Cliffs surrounding it stood like battlements, and the hills sloped downward from there.

"Get your cameras out," Joe said. "I'm going to buzz the falls while I look for the best spot to set us down."

They crossed the lake at an angle, giving everyone a great view of the waterfall. Down below, the mirror surface of the lake reflected the blue sky, the green of the hills and white of the clouds, but the water itself was a dark, inky black.

"The water level is fairly low," Paul said. "There's a lot of empty beach around the lower half of the lake."

Joe saw what Paul was describing: dried silt and stones fifty feet wide encircled that section of the lake. Beyond, a rushing stream took the outflow of the lake on its continuing journey toward lower ground and the Pacific Ocean.

Urco pointed out several features, having been to the lake before. "You cannot land over there," he said, pointing to a flat area. "Too soft. Sometimes a swamp. Best to land up high on the rocks."

Joe nodded and turned back toward the hills. He found a raised section that looked solid and flat, circled once and put the Air-Crane down on top of it.

Thirty minutes later, they were on the water, cruising across the lake on an inflatable Zodiac. A compact sonar emitter trailed out behind them while a receiver designed to pick up the *Nighthawk*'s beacon — if it was still transmitting — dangled over the side.

While Joe drove the boat, Kurt kept his eyes on the sonar display. The scan showed a flat-bottomed lake filled with sediment and averaging about sixty feet deep. Here and there, small outcroppings of rock appeared, though nothing to indicate a city had ever existed at this location.

"I'm not seeing any skyscrapers," he said to Urco.

"The ruins lie beneath the silt," Urco explained. "As we get closer to the waterfall, you'll see some of them jutting out where the current has scoured the sediment away."

"Have you been down there?" Kurt asked.

"I don't dive," he said. "But some of my people do. I should learn, though. Up on the surface, grave robbers and the elements have taken away so much of what we could discover. But down there, preserved beneath the mud, lie untouched treasures from the past."

Kurt nodded. He was more interested in an untouched aircraft from the present, but he understood Urco's excitement.

While Kurt and Urco kept their eyes on the sonar scanner, Emma and Paul were working with the underwater receiver. She wore a headset and was listening for a signal. Paul was directing the receiver by hand.

"Anything?" he asked, operating with the skills of a man who'd grown up adjusting the rabbit ears on his TV.

Even with the headphones on, Emma was straining to hear a tiny electronic beep over the wind and the outboard motor. "Not yet."

Paul held the unit steady, twisting a lever that turned the submerged receiver five degrees at a time. "How about now?"

She shook her head.

Kurt stole a glance her way. Tension lined her face. If the *Nighthawk* wasn't here, they were in major trouble and all but out of time.

He looked back at the sonar display. For the first time, the underwater profile of the lake had begun to change. Small mounds became noticeable and then block-like structures protruding through the silt. The depth was increasing as well.

Kurt looked up; they were nearing the waterfall. The force of the drop and the outflow of water had carved a deeper pool at this end as the current scoured away the sediment and deposited it farther out in the lake.

"You see?" Urco said, pointing to squared-off sections of the screen. "Streets, avenues, buildings — it's a city. A drowned city."

Kurt wasn't so sure. He'd seen rock formations that looked man-made before. The Bimini Road off the Bahamas came to mind, as did the Yonaguni ruins near Japan, a place that many thought was a submerged temple complex even though geologists insisted it was nothing more than a formation of stratified granite.

He chose not to burst Urco's bubble, at the moment. "We'll have to dive on it to get a better look," Kurt said. "But I won't deny it's plenty interesting."

Urco grabbed him by the shoulders and shook him with appreciation. "You won't be disappointed."

By now, they'd come close enough to the waterfall that the overspray was drifting across them. Kurt wiped the screen of the laptop and covered the keyboard.

He glanced at Joe. "Nothing on this pass. Take us back around."

Joe nodded and turned the wheel. But instead of turning in front of the falls, he guided them in behind it. Because of the overhang of rock high above and the speed with which the water was traveling when it flew off the edge, there was a thirty-foot gap at the bottom.

The Zodiac cruised into that gap and sped between the curtain of water and the cliffside. The rock wall was dark and wet and pockmarked with caves.

"More burial chambers," Urco said, pointing. "I would like it if they remain undisturbed."

Kurt studied the dark caverns as they sped past. "Understood," he said.

The next leg took them down the middle of the lake. They hadn't gone far when Emma held up a hand. "Slow down," she said. "I'm picking up something."

Joe cut the throttle back, the boat settled and all eyes fell upon Emma.

"Ten degrees to the right," she requested.

Paul turned the lever and stopped.

"Ten more?" she asked, and then, when he'd done that, added, "Back five."

Emma held both hands against the headphones, pressing them to her ears. She looked out over the water and pointed. "That way. Slowly."

Joe nudged the throttle and the Zodiac moved forward at a speed just above idle. At Emma's direction, they made a wide circle and then a narrower one, homing in on the signal.

Finally, Emma held up her hand once more and Joe brought the Zodiac to a stop.

As the boat settled, Emma pulled the headphone jack out of the receiver so everyone could hear the signal . . . *Beep* . . . *Beep* . . . *Beep* . . . Steady and low.

"It's here," she said, a wave of relief washing over her face. "The *Nighthawk* is here."

35

With their dive gear on, Emma slipped into the water with Kurt and Joe. They would make the first dive together, though once the *Nighthawk* was physically located, Joe would dry off and prep the Air-Crane for the big lift.

As she descended into the water, Emma noticed the chill in her bones. The water came mostly from snowmelt and the temperature was a frigid fifty degrees. Even wearing heavy, 3:5 wet suits with attached hoods, full-face helmets, boots and gloves, it could be felt.

While the cold was something planned for, dealt with and otherwise ignored, the visibility was a different problem. The water was full of floating sediment stirred up by the waterfall and decomposing plant matter washed down from higher elevations. There was perhaps ten feet of visibility and, at thirty feet, even powerful lights looked as if they were nothing more than glowing candles.

Emma used a light meter to check the incoming energy from the sun. *"This isn't good,"* she announced over the helmet-to-helmet communications system. *"With the water so murky, the system will be charging at fifteen percent efficiency. That won't do much for the batteries. The sooner we raise it, the better."*

"We have to find it first," Joe said. *"Which wouldn't be too difficult, except we're looking for a black aircraft, sitting at the bottom of a black lake."*

They were kicking lazily and descending slowly.

"The upper surface of the wing has a reflective strip built into it," Emma said. *"Hit that with your light and you'll have no problem spotting it."*

The lake was eighty feet deep in the center and at least seventy feet beneath the Zodiac. Emma was two-thirds of the way down before the beam of her diving light reached out and found the bottom.

The silt was dark, the color of coal, but flecked here and there with just enough quartz to sparkle like a black gemstone. Tiny rills in the sediment looked like the ridges of a huge fingerprint.

"Spread out a little and drift with the current," Kurt suggested. Most of the lake would be free of any appreciable current, but they were still getting a little push from the waterfall and for that reason had gone into the lake upstream of the target area.

Emma did as Kurt suggested, feeling a surprising pang of isolation as Kurt's and Joe's lights dimmed with the distance.

She concentrated on the task at hand, scanning back and forth, looking for any sign the *Nighthawk*'s tail or the reflective strips glued to the upper surface of her wings. But the first item of consequence was a blur of color, orange and white, billowing gently along the bottom.

Emma felt her heart rate quicken. *"Contact,"* she said. *"Parachute."*

She moved toward it and found both of the *Nighthawk*'s parachutes lying on the bottom, half buried in the silt. The free sections were wafting like sea grass as the water flowed over them.

As Kurt and Joe converged on her, she grabbed ahold of the settled nylon and hauled on it. The line was taut.

"Still attached," she said. She pulled herself forward, making her way down the line arm over arm, until a bulky shape came into

view. Kurt and Joe swam in behind her. Their lights played across a midnight black curve. Stamped on the side in low-resolution gray were the letters *USAF.*

With all three of their lights pointed down on it, the craft came into view. It was resting solidly on the bottom, its belly and the lower half of its wing touching the silt. Though she'd seen it plenty of times before, it still appeared surprisingly small.

"Finally," she said.

"How's it look?" Kurt asked.

Emma drifted over the top of it, checking for damage. *"The fuselage and payload bay are still sealed,"* she said. *"The wings seem to have some gouges where the Russian clamps locked onto it, but nothing catastrophic."*

She swam forward, arriving at the nose. With her gloved hand, she brushed a layer of silt from a panel on the side of the aircraft. It revealed an electronic touch screen display protected by a scorched plate of transparent Kevlar.

Tapping the panel, she brought it to life. It offered a bright glow in the dark water. Three bars indicated the condition of the cryogenic system: all were solidly in the green. Another section of the screen indicated that containment units were operating as planned while the final part of the display indicated the power supply in a yellow condition.

"One battery pack has already failed, but the others are compensating," she said.

"Is this a problem?" Kurt asked.

"Only if another pack goes down. Even as is, we should have at least twenty-four hours to get this thing topside, get the containment units out of it and plug them into the portable fuel cells."

"No reason to wait," Kurt said.

Joe floated over beside them. *"What about opening the cargo bay and removing the containment units without ever lifting the aircraft? It would save time and eliminate the danger of something going wrong with the lift. Not to mention prevent any satellite from spotting the* Nighthawk *once we get it up on the surface."*

Emma shook her head. *"It's too risky in the aquatic environment. All the electronics are sealed and self-contained, but we can't be certain of their condition. Between the vibration of the launch, three years in space, the heat of reentry and the Russian attempt to capture the aircraft, there may be internal damage on a small scale. Loose connections. Gaps in the insulation. If we get everything wet and end up with a short —"*

"The lake goes up along with a big chunk of

northern Peru," Kurt said.

"*Exactly,"* she replied. *"No shortcuts. We have to raise it and get it onto dry land before we do anything else."*

36

The rattle of the gas-powered air compressor carried across the lake from the stern of the Zodiac, a jarring disturbance into an otherwise peaceful setting.

Paul Trout sat beside it, keeping an eye on the compressor and the line that ran over the edge and disappeared into the water. Fifty feet away, a circle of bubbles boiled and churned as the excess air rose up to the surface.

For now, Paul was alone in the boat. Kurt, Joe and Emma had gone back down to prepare the *Nighthawk* for lifting, while Urco had volunteered to go ashore, where he was scouting around for a solid place to set the aircraft down.

Squinting across the lake, Paul could just see the Peruvian. He was higher up on the slope, moving behind a section of tall grasses, thrusting a staff down into the ground in an effort to determine if the soil would hold the *Nighthawk*'s weight.

Using a handheld radio, Paul reached out to him. "Urco, this is Paul."

"Go ahead, Mr. Paul," Urco replied.

"Wondering if you're having any luck out there?"

He saw Urco turn his way and wave. *"The shoreline is too soft and muddy to hold much weight. And even back here, away from the edge, it's marshland. I'm going to make my way to higher ground."*

"Roger that," Paul said. "Keep us posted."

Urco waved and moved off, carrying his staff. Paul watched until Urco was out of sight. Perhaps other eyes were watching him, too, Paul thought. And then he turned his attention back to the compressor and the pressure gauge.

Down below, Kurt was holding the business end of the air hose and feeding it underneath the *Nighthawk.* The compressed air blasting out through the front acted like a drill bit, scouring out the dark silt. The power of Kurt's arms acted like a hydraulic press, forcing it forward.

With each shove, another burst of bubbles and sediment came flowing backward and out toward Kurt, billowing forth in a dark, swirling cloud. As the sediment churned around him, Kurt kept feeding more line into the opening. *"Anything yet?"*

Joe's voice came back slightly distorted as if he were standing in a deep tunnel. Joe was on the other side waiting for the line to pop out. *"Not yet. Keep pushing."*

Kurt worked the line back and forth and gave it another shove.

"I'm seeing bubbles," Joe announced. *"You're almost there."*

Kurt gave the line one more push and felt it move freely. The billowing cloud of silt that had been streaming back toward him relented.

"Got it," Joe said.

"Phase one complete," Kurt said. *"Time for you to do some work, amigo."*

On the far side of the *Nighthawk,* Joe grabbed the tip of the air hose and pulled it toward him. Using a length of wire, he hooked one of the lifting straps to the valve and tugged hard to make sure it was secure.

"Strap one attached," he said. *"My job is done."*

"That was quick," Kurt said. *"Maybe I should rethink the division of labor on this project."*

Joe laughed, watching as the hose and the attached strap were pulled back beneath the

Nighthawk, moving one arm's length at a time.

While Kurt and Joe placed what would eventually be four braided nylon straps beneath the aircraft, Emma inspected the wings, examining every blemish she found. Many of the outer tiles were damaged. She found hairline cracks and plenty of chips and scrapes, even several spots where the tiles had been torn off completely, presumably when the *Nighthawk* broke the grasp of its Russian captors. But the high-strength alloy beneath was untouched.

"The wing doesn't appear to be compromised," she announced. *"It won't have taken on any water."*

"Good to hear," Joe replied. *"We're fairly close to the max lifting capacity of the Air-Crane already. We don't need a few tons of lake water to make it worse."*

"Agreed," Emma said. *"I'm going to check the hardpoints for corrosion and pitting. Would hate for something to break loose just as we claimed victory."*

As she swam across the top of the aircraft, the air hose broke through the silt once again, releasing a swarm of fine bubbles that swirled up around her. For an instant, it was like swimming in a glass of champagne.

She didn't want to get ahead of herself but imagined they'd soon be raising glasses to celebrate the victory.

37

La Jalca Canyon, a half mile away
A half mile away, in the dark throat of a barren cave, there was no sense of victory or even hope for the men imprisoned in it. Only cloying darkness, cold, bone-aching dampness and noise. Constant, unending noise.

The bulk of the waterfall dropped downward just beyond the mouth of the cave. Its tumbling white water hid everything beyond, causing vertigo to anyone who stared into it for too long and blocking out all semblance of detail.

What it hid from the eyes it hid also from the ears as its endless roar echoed off the stone walls, drowning out soft speech, clear thought and even the din of modern men out on the lake.

The two men sitting in the cave hadn't heard the approach of the helicopter this morning nor the outboard motor of the

Zodiac nor the excited shouts of discovery that came shortly afterward. Not even the endless rattle of the air compressor could penetrate the wall of sound that shielded them. It was isolation of the body, soul and mind and it had taken its toll already.

After days in this condition, they were numb to it. They sat with their backs to the wall, their knees up and their heads down; an upright version of the fetal position. Their hands were chained in front of them while their ankles were bound together and hooked to heavy iron weights that made walking a difficult task.

Days of growth covered their faces while a layer of grime covered their uniforms. Beneath the dirt, oil and dust could be seen the double-headed eagle of the Russian Air Force and the squadron patch depicting the great claw of a flying raptor grasping another bird from the sky. A star on one man's shoulder indicated his rank as Major. A set of wings on his chest overlaid with measuring tongs indicated he was a test pilot.

He stared in the darkness, weakened by the cold and a lack of food, but in his mind churned thoughts of revenge. So dark was his mood that it took him a moment to notice a shaft of light appearing in the back part of the cave.

The light came down from the surface, through a narrow vertical chute that the two Russians had been forced to descend at gunpoint days before. After reaching the bottom, they'd been chained up and then abandoned by their captors, who had climbed up the shaft, pulled up the rope and blocked out the light by sliding a trapdoor across the top.

The appearance of the light meant the door had been moved aside. It meant something would change. Good or bad, Major Yuri Timonovski welcomed that.

"Someone's coming," he said.

The second man looked up, his eyes bloodshot and jittery. "Maybe they're going to feed us."

"Or kill us," Timonovski replied. "I'd take either at this point."

The end of a rope dropped down the shaft, hitting the ground and curling up like a snake. The hanging part writhed back and forth as someone descended it.

Timonovski stood, ready to face whatever was about to come his way. His legs ached, his back hurt, and he waddled awkwardly in the direction of the intruder, dragging the weights with him.

The weights didn't keep him from moving but were enough to prevent him from climbing. And they made jumping into the lake a suicidal notion. Something he might consider if circumstances did not improve.

Boots appeared at the bottom of the shaft and a rangy man with a heavy beard dropped the last few feet into the cave. Timonovski recognized him instantly: the Falconer, the man they'd been working with since day one. The man who'd promised to deliver the *Nighthawk* to them by hacking its guidance program and overriding the American directives coming from Vandenberg.

Timonovski also knew him as a betrayer. He was certain the Falconer had done something at the last minute that caused the *Nighthawk* to break loose from *Blackjack 1*. And when he'd attempted to break off pursuit and head for the refueling rendezvous, the Falconer had slit the throat of Timonovski's copilot, pulled a snub-nosed pistol and threatened the Major and his flight engineer with death if they didn't do as he ordered.

After following the *Nighthawk* down and watching it parachute into the lake, the Falconer had directed them to a narrow landing strip seven miles from the lake. A group of armed men waited for them and, after being taken hostage, any hopes of escape vanished.

"You're awake," the Falconer said as he came closer. "Excellent."

They spoke English to each other, the only common language between them.

"It's impossible to sleep in here," Timonovski said.

"Some people find waterfalls soothing."

"Not when they're right on top of your head."

The Falconer shrugged.

"I see you're alone," Timonovski said. "Have you run out of friends?"

"On the contrary," the Falconer insisted, "I am collecting them by the handful as I once collected you."

Major Timonovski could barely stand the arrogance, but he could do nothing about it. "What do you want from us now, Bird-caller?"

"I've come to feed you," the bearded man replied. He shrugged off a backpack, unzipped the top and placed it in front of his captives.

The Major kept his eyes from it, but he couldn't keep the aroma from his nostrils. Perhaps starvation heightened the senses.

Still sitting, the flight engineer scrambled toward the backpack and began plucking items out of it. A plastic container filled with soup came first, bottles of water with added electrolytes were next, followed by a couple of wrapped items.

"Sandwiches," the engineer said, unwrapping one.

Timonovski found his mouth was watering. "Is this some kind of trick?"

"Not at all," the Falconer said. "You'll need your strength if you're to fly out of here."

"Fly?"

"You can pilot a helicopter, can't you?"

"Of course," the Major said. He'd flown everything in the Russian inventory. "Do you have one?"

"My new friends do," the Falconer said.

He nodded toward the lake, invisible beyond the mouth of the cave. "What you can't see — one of the many things you can't see — are American agents submerged in the water and securing the *Nighthawk* as we speak. They're preparing to remove it from the depths. Once they do, I shall take it from them and you will deliver it to the runway where *Blackjack 2* now waits. You will finish your mission, refuel over Venezuela as planned and cross the Atlantic, returning to Russia as great heroes."

Timonovski was stunned. "I don't understand. Now you want us to take it back to

378

Moscow? But we already had it. You're the one who set it free. If you hadn't woken it up after *Blackjack 1* captured it —"

"Had I let you proceed, I wouldn't have been able to extract the full payment I desire. But now the price to be paid will be equal to the pain. Indeed, it's much higher than you can possibly imagine."

"Blood money," the Major said.

"All wealth is blood money," the Falconer said. "In one form or another."

Major Timonovski just stared.

"If you prefer, I can leave it to the Americans and leave you both here to rot away while going mad from the noise."

"If this is a trick —"

"Then you will endure it because you have no choice in the matter."

Timonovski fumed. The Birdcaller was in complete control. But even that had its limits. Even this master manipulator had to deal with gravity. "We'll never get off the ground," he said. "The runway is too short, the *Nighthawk* too heavy. We'll never clear the trees with that thing on our backs."

The bearded man cocked his head. "Leave that to me."

He turned, walked back to the rope and wrapped his hands around it and began to pull himself up. The rope vanished moments later and the column of light was cut off.

Gray darkness and white noise engulfed them once again.

"You should eat," the flight engineer said. "Whatever happens, we will need our strength."

Timonovski ignored him for a moment, pondering the situation, before giving in to the lure of the food. He didn't believe a word of what the Birdcaller promised; somehow, it would be another lie, he was certain of it. But it seemed far better to die on a full stomach than to starve.

38

Off the coast of Ecuador

The Russian salvage fleet was now within a hundred miles of the Ecuadorian coast, though they had yet to discover any sign of either *Blackjack 2* or the American space plane.

It seemed to Constantin Davidov that the race had been lost. The sudden drawdown in American naval activity suggested they'd found it.

Alone in his cabin, Davidov considered returning to Russia and facing the consequences of failure. A knock at the door startled him.

"Come in."

It was one of the Admiral's staff. "A message has come in," he said. "The Admiral wishes you to meet him in the communications room."

Davidov hurried to the communications center.

"It's from the Falconer," Borozdin said.

"He's alive?"

"It would appear," Borozdin said. "And since we've found no sign of *Blackjack 2*'s wreckage, we must assume the crew and the aircraft are fine as well."

"Then where have they been?" Davidov snapped.

"Maybe this will tell you."

Borozdin handed him a note. It was all code. The Falconer's code. Davidov translated from memory and stared at the curious message. It was cryptic even after it had been deciphered. "Is this it? Is this the entire communiqué?"

"That's all we received," Borozdin replied. "It came in with the Falconer's identification marks. The message is from him."

"That, I do not doubt," Davidov replied. "The man is nothing if not obtuse."

He stared at the page again. "The numbers are obviously map coordinates," he said. "But the message . . ."

It read:

Full delivery.
Bring gold. Coins only.
The price has doubled.

Beware, Americans are watching.

RATO.

You have eight hours

"Full delivery," Borozdin said. "Does he mean the *Nighthawk* itself?"

"I suspect he does," Davidov replied.

"That seems doubtful," Borozdin said. "You yourself said the Americans must have it by now. Their fleet actions confirm it. It's a money grab, pure and simple. He'll ambush you and take payment for what he could not deliver."

Davidov rubbed his chin thoughtfully. "I'm not so sure," he said.

"Why is that?"

"RATO," Davidov said almost to himself. *"Rocket-assisted takeoff.* It's a plan we discussed if one of the bombers captured the *Nighthawk* but was forced to land. A contingency to get it, and the *Nighthawk,* back in the air together. If he's requesting RATO, maybe he has the *Nighthawk* after all."

Borozdin shook his head. "Only you still believe in him, my friend."

"I believe nothing," Davidov said. "But I must not fail, not now, not after all this. Is the satellite sweep of Ecuador and Peru complete?"

"Nearly."

"And these coordinates?"

Borozdin looked the numbers over and then moved to a computer terminal and typed them in. "Rudimentary airfield on a high plateau," he said. "Completed by a Chinese mining company three years ago. Abandoned."

"Do we have a recent pass?"

Borozdin accessed the satellite scan. "Yes," he said.

"Bring it up and zoom in."

Borozdin used the cursor to draw a box around the airfield and tapped ENTER. The resolution changed and the photograph resolved. "No sign of the *Nighthawk,*" he said.

"What's that?" Davidov said, pointing to a distorted shape at one end of the airfield.

Borozdin zoomed in once more and shrugged. "Hard to tell."

Davidov disagreed. "It's an aircraft. A large delta-wing aircraft, hidden beneath a tarp. That's *Blackjack 2.* I have no doubt."

"If it is, then where are the crew? Why haven't they contacted us?"

"Who knows? It's a very remote area," Davidov said. "A miracle they even found that airfield to set down upon." He stood. "I need to speak with the quartermaster. And,

God protect me, I need a helicopter to get me to Peru."

"You're not seriously going to fly out there with a suitcase full of gold?"

"I'm going to do exactly that," Davidov said. "I'll take four of your commandos with me."

Borozdin clearly thought the idea was dubious, if not suicidal. But he was a sailor, a man trained to act when circumstances were in his favor and to flee when they weren't. The intelligence service worked differently — they took chances, enormous and sometimes near-suicidal chances. It was their character and their nature and the whole reason behind the attempt to capture the American spacecraft in the first place.

Borozdin offered a more plodding solution. "We have an Antonov 124 cargo plane waiting in Havana," Borozdin said. "Why not dispatch it with a hundred men on board? It's designed for heavy lifting and short fields. It will easily be able to land there, pluck the *Nighthawk* up and carry it away. And you won't have to expose yourself to this treachery."

The Antonov 124 was a four-engine, heavy-lift transport. It would be perfect for the job. But getting that large aircraft into Peru unnoticed would be near impossible.

"You forget the balance of the message," Davidov said. "The Americans are watching. I have no choice. I will ride in one of your infernal helicopters to the coast. We can charter a small turboprop aircraft to take me from there."

"And if the Falconer double-crosses you?"

"Others will hunt him down," Davidov said. "A fact I will remind him of when I see him."

39

Kurt and Emma were back in the water. They'd positioned four straps beneath the *Nighthawk,* two at the front, two at the back. The straps were spaced so that the aircraft's center of gravity was directly between them.

While Emma attached lifting bags to the ends of each strap, Kurt filled them with air. Known as parachute-style bags because the bottom end remained open even after they were filled, they arrived in a compact folded state but expanded into teardrop shapes the size of a small car.

To keep the strain balanced and prevent the straps from slipping toward one side or the other, Kurt moved from spot to spot, partially inflating one and then swimming to the other side and inflating its counterpart to equalize the buoyancy.

When he was finished, eight inflated yellow bags floated around the sunken craft, jostling against one another in the current.

Still, the *Nighthawk* hadn't budged.

"Air bags filled," Kurt said. *"Straps are tight."*

"And it hasn't moved an inch," Emma's voice announced.

Kurt hadn't expected it to. *"The lifting bags aren't enough to pull it from the bottom,"* he said. *"But they'll help the Air-Crane overcome the suction effect created by the layer of silt."*

Salvage teams called this additional effort the breakout force. Depending on the texture of the sediment, it could be a small or large problem. Kurt expected the latter.

At first, it looked as if the *Nighthawk* had touched down without lowering its landing gear and had come to rest on its wide, flat underside. A quick investigation proved otherwise. Burrowing beneath the nose, Emma had found the landing gear not only down and locked but sunk directly into the sediment like the spikes on the bottom of an athletic shoe. Because of this, and the large surface area now in contact with the silt, the breakout force would be huge. Almost as much as the weight of the *Nighthawk* itself.

"I was hoping it might break loose just a little," Emma said.

She was floating above him. The light

strapped to her shoulder illuminating the side of the *Nighthawk* and the hardpoints near the nose. Kicking steadily, she guided a steel cable with gloved hands, connecting it to an attachment point and testing the assembly with several solid pulls. That done, she moved to the other side of the aircraft to connect the second hook.

Kurt looked toward the surface. The Air-Crane hovered somewhere above them, hidden by the silt in the water. Kurt could just make out the dull thumping of its rotors as the sound reverberated off the surface of the lake.

"Lifting cables secured," Emma announced as she swam out through the forest of yellow bags.

"Looks like we're ready to go," Kurt said.

"I'll inform Joe," Emma said.

She swam toward the surface, navigating what was now a maze of cables and straps above and around the downed aircraft.

When she disappeared behind the inflated yellow bags, Kurt was left alone on the lake bottom. "Moment of truth," he whispered to himself.

It would only be the first of many. But, if they didn't get that craft off the bottom, nothing else mattered.

Hovering above the lake in the Air-Crane, Joe kept one eye on the gauges and one on the surface of the lake below.

He could just see the circular tops of the yellow air bags through the dark water. They were bunched together and stationary. They looked fully inflated.

"It won't be long now," he said. "Are you ready?"

The question was meant for Paul, who sat behind him in the crane operator's seat. "Yes," Paul said. "I've become an expert at operating cranes over the last week. I even know how to throw a submersible like I was casting for a fish."

Joe could hear the mischievous tone in Paul's words. "I heard how you launched the *Angler* from the deck of the *Catalina*," Joe said. "A neat trick. At this point, it's all about reeling in a big fish and not letting it get away."

"I'll try to restrain myself."

Joe made another scan of the gauges. The engine temperature was running high, not in the red zone yet but getting there.

Hovering wasn't easy on the turbines, it meant less airflow to cool the blades. It meant the engine had to work harder and hotter. And even though he was only fifty feet off the lake's surface, the altimeter read ninety-four hundred and change. That meant the air was thin, the rotors getting less bite of air with each circular sweep.

Joe had studied plenty of crashes during his flight training. It was a way to learn from the mistakes of others. As he recalled with a certain morbidity, a great many of those crashes came when operating *hot, high* and *heavy.*

The old-timer who'd taught him to fly had insisted that was not a place any pilot ever wanted to find himself, but Joe had no choice. The Air-Crane was already hot and high; as soon as they pulled the *Nighthawk* free of the water, it would be very, very heavy.

He tapped the temperature gauge, thankful for the breeze that was helping cool the turbine. "Come on," he whispered. "Let's get this show on the road."

"Do you see any dye?" Paul asked.

Kurt and Emma had dye capsules with them. Red to indicate a problem; green to give the all clear and show Paul and Joe the exact flow of the current, so they could align themselves with it as they lifted.

"No," Joe said. "But someone's coming up."

A diver appeared on the surface. In the full suit and helmet, it was impossible to tell which one. The diver flashed a light on and off three times, offered a thumbs-up, and then broke open the green dye capsule.

Joe responded by toggling the landing light on and off. The diver acknowledged and went back down. "Cables are in place," he said. "Ready to lift."

"Finally," Paul replied. "Hauling in the slack."

As Paul manipulated the controls, the cables began rising out of the dark lake. One led to the nose of the *Nighthawk* and one to a spot near the tail.

Joe felt weight on the helicopter as soon as the slack was taken up. "Lock it there," he said. "I'll do the rest."

As Paul locked the winch, Joe added power slowly. This was the most dangerous point: the lift itself. Manipulating the controls with a light touch, he pulled up, allowed the Air-Crane to settle and then pulled up again.

The cables strained and stretched tight, shedding water each time, but after several attempts, the *Nighthawk* remained stuck in the silt down below.

"Come on, baby," Joe whispered. "Don't play hard to get."

He pulled harder and longer on the next try. The rotors thundered above him. The turbines howled. The swirling pattern on the water below swept around and around, but despite continued attempts, the *Nighthawk* would not break free.

A yellow warning light came on indicating high temperature in turbine number one.

"It's no good," Paul shouted from behind him.

"It's got to come loose soon," Joe said.

Joe relaxed the power and watched the temperature stabilize just below the red line. "One more try," he said. "I'm going to full power."

Down below, Kurt and Emma could tell the Air-Crane was struggling. The cables had groaned and creaked with each successive pull while the drumming of the rotors rose to a crescendo, but the black spacecraft never moved.

"Is it caught on something?" Emma asked.

"It's the suction," Kurt said. *"Get under the wing. Dig out as much silt as you can."*

Emma swam for the tip of the right wing and began digging with her gloved hands, scooping at the muck and pushing it out behind her.

Kurt swam to the tail, shoved the air hose beneath the fuselage and opened the valve to full. He fed it in, trying to build up an air bubble that would spread across the underside of the plane and break the effect of the suction.

When he'd pushed the hose in as far as possible, he left it there and swam to the left wing.

Diving beneath it, he began digging out the black silt with his arms and shoveling it away. Reaching deeper and deeper, he was soon beneath the craft — where he'd be trapped and crushed if it rose and then settled.

The sound of the rotors torquing up to full power came again. The cables strained. Kurt stretched deeper and deeper beneath the plane, pulling at the muck with his long arms.

Suddenly, a wave of bubbles surged across the underside of the aircraft. It rose with surprising abruptness and Kurt heard a sucking sound, like the last of the water going down a drain.

He and Emma were pulled in beneath the *Nighthawk* along with the tons of water that were rushing into the space the aircraft had suddenly vacated.

In the swirl of bubbles and sediment, it was impossible to make out anything aside from the light on Emma's shoulder.

Kurt grabbed her arm and pulled.

They kicked hard, swimming together through a storm of swirling black water. After the initial surge, the *Nighthawk* was settling back. Kurt felt his flippers hitting against the underside of the plane as he kicked out from under it. By the time he turned around, the aircraft was rising again, traveling upward through the water, moving slowly but surely. A fountain of bubbles pouring from the air hose chased it toward the surface.

"Let's get topside," Emma said. *"I want to be there when it lands."*

Kurt nodded and the two of them swam toward the Zodiac's anchor line and then began moving slowly upward.

By the time they emerged into the bright sunshine, the black tail of the *Nighthawk* had broken the surface. It looked like the dorsal fin of an oversized shark or killer whale.

The yellow air bags appeared next, breaching and flopping over on their sides, deflating slowly as the trapped air came out through the open collars.

Above it all, the Air-Crane howled as it began the next stage of the epic lift, hauling the space plane from the grasp of the water and up into the air.

The nose came up first, and then the rest of the craft. Sheets of water poured off the *Nighthawk*'s wings and mud sloughed from the extended landing gear in heavy, dripping globs.

Floating beside the Zodiac, Kurt and Emma watched in awe as the Air-Crane began a slow pivot and moved off toward the firm section of higher ground that Urco had picked to land it on.

Emma pointed to the center of the lake. Silt and foam swirled in an effervescent circle where the *Nighthawk* had been lifted free. The air bags were left behind, sagging on the surface as they slowly deflated.

"We'll clean up later," Kurt said. "Let's get to shore and see this thing land."

Emma removed her fins, tossed them into the boat and grabbed the cargo net they'd set out as a makeshift ladder. She pulled herself upward and flipped up over the edge with surprising speed.

Kurt heard a shout of surprise as she entered the boat and the distinct sound of a struggle. He pulled himself up and spotted a man in the boat wrestling with Emma.

Lunging forward, half in the boat, Kurt got a hand on the assailant, but before he could do any more, a powerful set of arms wrapped around his legs and pulled him back down into the water.

40

Joe felt a strange oscillation through his hands. The Air-Crane was swaying one way and then the other as they headed for the landing area.

"Is that thing moving?" he called out.

"It's trying to," Paul said. "It's torquing to the right and then swinging back to the left. Each time, it moves a little more."

Joe understood instantly. The downwash created by the six-bladed rotor overhead was a minor tornado. That airflow was catching the *Nighthawk*'s vertical stabilizer. It pushed the tail to the left and that swung the nose of the aircraft to the right. When it could twist no more due to the tension on the lines, it swung back in the other direction. A movement that was slowly becoming circular.

The *Nighthawk* continued to sway as they crossed the shallows and then the muddy, barren shoreline. A hundred yards ahead, on higher, firmer ground, Joe saw Urco waving a make-shift flag.

Outlined by tall grasses, the spot Urco had found was flat, rocky and almost circular. It looked like a natural landing pad.

Joe continued toward it, ignoring the yellow temperature light that had come on once again and working the rudder pedals to keep the Air-Crane stable.

Finally over the clearing, he turned the nose into the wind and hovered.

"Come to the right," Paul said.

"How far?"

"Ten feet."

Joe eased the Air-Crane over to the right, staring through the clear Plexiglas foot well at the ground below.

"That's it," Paul said. "Let her down slowly."

"No time for that."

Joe relaxed the pressure on the controls and allowed them to descend, trying to lower the *Nighthawk* gracefully and quickly. It was a partial success. The craft hit with a minor crunch, landing harder than Joe had hoped. The lines went slack and the strain on the engine was reduced.

"*Nighthawk* on solid ground," Paul said.

"Cut it loose."

Paul disconnected the line and metal cable

fell to the ground.

The Air-Crane rose upward in response. Freed of all the weight, it felt nimble. Joe powered back as soon as he could, but the yellow warning lights continued to glow. "We need to get on the ground or we're going to void our warranty."

Easing away from the *Nighthawk,* Joe aimed for the far edge of the clearing and brought the Air-Crane down for a landing.

The wheels hit with a trio of thumps. Joe powered down to idle but kept the engine running until it had cooled enough to bring the temperature down.

"Hot damn," Paul said. "Let's go take a look."

Joe checked the temperature gauge one last time. It was settling nicely. A second light that would warn of metal shavings in the oil system had never come on. The engines were undamaged. One break in their favor.

He shut everything down, unbuckled his harness and followed Paul out the door. Cutting across the clearing, they found Urco, crouched beneath the aircraft's nose, clearing mud from the landing gear. He looked up as they approached.

"How'd we do?" Paul asked.

"Excellent," Urco said. "Exactly as I

hoped you would."

There was something odd about the response. Before Joe could put his finger on it, he saw movement in the tall grass. His first thought was that it was Kurt and Emma coming up from the beach, but, instead, a handful of men pushed through the high grass and out into the clearing. They held weapons in their hands, rifles and shotguns.

Joe turned to make a break for it. But it was too late. A second group of men had come in from behind them.

"Don't fight," Urco said, standing up and leveling a pistol in Joe's direction. "There's no need for you to die."

41

Kurt had been pulled back into the water, a surprising sensation. He'd recovered by kicking hard and pulling his legs clear. No sooner was he free than he felt something heavy wrap around his neck and pull tight. At first he thought it was a metal chain, but he came to realize it was a diver's weight belt.

He grabbed at the belt and pulled, but it was being twisted tight by whoever had swum in behind him. As he struggled with the first attacker, a second diver moved out of the shadow beneath the Zodiac. This one wore a gray wet suit and a squared-off mask. He carried an eight-inch knife, which he thrust toward Kurt.

Using the man behind him as leverage, Kurt twisted to the side. Instead of puncturing his rib cage, the knife only skewered his buoyancy control device, or BCD, sending a flood of bubbles into the water. Before the man could strike again, Kurt kicked him in the face, shattering his square mask and knocking his regulator free. A second kick caught him in the teeth and sent the man fleeing toward the surface.

One down, Kurt thought, *one to go.*

The weight belt was choking him.

As he struggled, both Kurt and his assailant were sinking fast. They grappled all the way to the bottom, where they crashed into the sediment with surprising force.

With somewhere to plant his feet, Kurt gained back some control. He fired an elbow backward into his attacker. The grip loosened but the man grabbed Kurt's main air line and ripped it free.

Kurt felt the helmet pulled to the side, saw a second explosion of silvery air bubbles and was tackled and forced down into the silt before he could do anything about it.

Kurt was on his back. His attacker — whom Kurt recognized as Urco's associate Vargas — was holding him down, pressing him into the sediment as if to bury him. It was a simple strategy. Kurt would black out before long.

Holding his breath, Kurt reached for his own knife, but Vargas kicked his wrist and knocked it free.

In desperation, Kurt fired a punch upward, hoping to catch Vargas in the neck, but the blow was deflected by one of the man's large forearms. A second punch hit Vargas in the solar plexus but did nothing to make him back off.

As Kurt fought, the struggle took on a surreal appearance: sediment swirled around them; the light strapped to Kurt's wrist flicked this way and that. Kurt sensed his muscles growing weary from lack of oxygen. He saw Vargas pull out his own knife and raise it for a lethal blow. It came plunging down hard. At the very same moment, Kurt thrust his knee upward, slamming it into the man's groin.

Both impacts occurred simultaneously.

Vargas spit out his regulator and doubled over in agony. Kurt felt the impact of the blade and watched the water around them churn red in the light.

With a last desperate grab, Kurt reached upward and grabbed Vargas's mouthpiece and snapped it off with a twist.

Vargas reacted with instinctive panic. He pushed off the bottom with both feet, launching himself toward the surface and leaving Kurt behind in a swirling haze of crimson water.

42

Urco stood in the clearing in complete control. Everything was proceeding as he'd designed it.

The *Nighthawk* had been freed from its watery pen and laid at his feet, while agents from each of the competing nations had become his prisoners: the American men and women; the surviving Chinese agent at La Jalca, where she remained in chains until he chose to summon her; and the Russian bomber pilots, in a high cave behind the waterfall.

They were captives now but would soon become his servants — though they didn't know that just yet.

Glancing across the water, he could see his divers in the Zodiac. "Give me the radio," he said to one of his men.

A walkie-talkie was handed to him. "Vargas," he said, pressing the talk switch down. "Do you read?"

It didn't take long for a voice to answer. *"I'm here,"* Vargas grunted.

He sounded like he was in pain.

"What happened?"

"We have the woman," Vargas said. *"But I had to kill Austin. He fought too hard. I gutted him and left him on the bottom. I had no choice."*

Urco received that news with a trace of disappointment. He'd come to respect Austin in the brief time they'd known each other. The man had offered him the truth about the *Nighthawk* instead of insulting his intelligence with a lie; he'd reacted with introspection instead of arrogance when Urco pointed out the devastation caused by the European viruses to the indigenous population.

"Very well," Urco said. "Bring Ms. Townsend to me. I require her services."

"On our way," Vargas replied.

Urco clipped the radio to his belt and turned his attention to the survivors. They were on their knees with their hands behind their heads. Urco's men stood behind them with various weapons drawn.

"Kurt is dead," he announced.

Neither of the men batted an eye.

"He didn't have to die, but he chose to fight. I hope you take it as a lesson."

He walked back and forth, listening to the sound of the Zodiac approach. When he noticed that Zavala was eyeing him every step of the way, he approached the helicopter pilot, crouching down in front of him for a better look.

Zavala had a quiet intensity about him. From his features, hair and skin color, Urco could tell he had a large amount of Central American DNA in him.

"Where are you from?" Urco asked.

"New Mexico," Zavala replied.

"And your parents?"

Zavala was not the hostile sort; his confidence came from within and he appeared less than threatened even in this situation. "Why would you want to know?"

"Call it *hereditary curiosity,*" Urco said. "I find many people in this world don't know who they really are. Just by looking at you, I can tell you have European blood in your veins — like I do — and while you're at ease here, your soul is of the Americas. We are cousins. I would suspect to find that much of your blood is from the Olmec and the Maya."

Zavala did not look away or argue. He was a master of his own emotions. "My blood is red," he replied. "Like everyone else's."

Urco pursed his lips and stood. "We shall see."

By now, the Zodiac had reached the shore. Emma was marched up through the weeds and out into the clearing. She still wore her wet suit. Her mouth was taped.

"Remove that," Urco said.

"She spits," Vargas said angrily.

Urco expected she would be trouble. He knew how fiery she could be. He looked her up and down. She was . . . *different*. Age and time had changed her, of course, but there was something more. The weight of knowledge; the invisible burden? He bore it, too. Perhaps he could use that to his advantage, but first he needed her to understand how truly powerless she was.

He turned to Vargas. "Go get the other boat and begin phase two."

As Vargas left, Urco reached out and gently removed the tape from her mouth. "My apologies for such harsh treatment."

She stood, defiant, casting a challenge at him with her eyes, not seeing but posturing. He accepted that. It was to his benefit that she be blind with rage. At least a little while longer.

"What's the meaning of this?" Emma demanded. "Who are you working for? The Russians? The Chinese?"

"Of course you're confused," Urco told her. "Why wouldn't you be? Right now you're wondering which of your great enemies has corrupted the little servant you found at La Jalca? It must be one of them, musn't it? Since the rest of the world is filled only with pawns to be moved by the players of the great game. Isn't that what your time at the NSA has taught you?"

She pulled back, no doubt because none of them had ever mentioned the National Security Agency.

"To answer your question," he continued, "I work for neither the Russians nor the Chinese but for all of humanity."

Her gaze tightened and the fine lines around her eyes deepened, enough to suggest he had her thinking. That was good.

"And at this juncture," he added, "humanity requires your help."

"I won't help you do anything."

"Yes, of course," he said, waving an indifferent hand. "You're required to say that. Duly noted, but I assure you, *you will help me.* In fact, you'll literally spring to your feet to do it."

Without waiting for a reply, he walked over to the *Nighthawk*. The craft was still dripping muddy water from the landing gear. It appeared larger in the clearing but low to the ground, thanks to those stubby legs.

Arriving beside the nose, Urco found the touch screen panel he was looking for. He tapped it until it came to life and then entered an alphanumeric code. A green indicator flickered and a small door opened just aft of the touch screen panel.

Reaching in, he grasped a recessed handle.

"Don't," Emma said.

He ignored her and pulled the handle, first to the side and then down. As he released it, the sound of hydraulic actuators powering up became audible. A pressure seal between the cargo bay doors released with a hiss and they slowly began to open.

As the doors locked in place, Urco stepped up on the wing and gazed into the interior. In contrast to the black outer hull, the cargo bay was done in a gleaming, sterile white.

"You don't know what you're doing," Emma insisted. "If you're not careful, you'll kill us all."

"Perhaps you'd like to show me, then? Prevent me from tinkering?"

Emma was led up beside him. They stood together gazing down into the interior of the payload bay. A maze of power packs, wires and cylindrical tubes were lined up front to back. The arrangement was perfectly symmetrical.

"Two by two," Urco said, pointing out matching components with the words *Cryogenic Containment Unit* stenciled on top.

"You don't understand," she said.

"Don't fool yourself more than you already have," he replied. "We both *understand* exactly what we're looking at. Mixed-state matter. The most powerful reactant known to exist, gathered for the first time in vast quantities."

Emma turned toward him. "And I suggest you leave it alone."

"I suggested the same thing a decade ago," he shot back. "But it's too late for that now, isn't it?"

She stared at him looking confused. He hoped the little riddles were getting to her. He needed her to be off balance.

"Disconnect the first containment unit and hook it up to one of the fuel cells you've brought along," he said. "That *was* the next step, wasn't it? Search for the plane, but take the cargo and blow the rest to scrap metal."

"We never intended to blow anything up, just to —"

"Come now," he said. "You were *never* going to carry an eight-ton load over the mountains and all the way back to Cajamarca. The strain that would place on the helicopter would have been dangerously high, not to mention the strain on credibility when the Peruvian officials got wind of it. They'd want to know what it was, why it was here and why they hadn't been informed in the first place."

He turned and whistled to another group of his men. They went into the Air-Crane and came out carrying a suitcase-sized device; it was one of the fuel cells Joe and Paul had been given in Cajamarca.

Emma looked crestfallen. The exact look he was hoping for. "We would have come back for the rest of the craft," she said.

"You may still get that chance," he replied. "In the meantime, you will detach the first containment unit, hook it to that fuel cell and make certain it's safe enough to be transported."

"Transported where?"

"Stop asking questions," he said. "You can easily guess where."

She shook her head. "I won't do that. It's too dangerous. All of this is too dangerous."

He could have chosen to threaten her friends at that moment, but he had no intention of wasting time. Most likely, they would all be willing to die rather than cooperate. How dreadfully boring, he thought.

No, there was a much easier way.

He turned back to the cargo bay, looking for a piece of equipment with a shape he knew by heart. "Power converter," he said. "Connects the battery pack to the containment unit. Steps up and intensifies the current in order to run the cryogenic pump. Each of the units has one of its own. Thankfully, they're still operating."

"Yes, but —"

Ignoring her, he pulled out a pistol, extended his arm and fired a single shot. The power converter connected to Containment Unit 1 was punctured instantly.

"No!" she shouted.

It was too late. The damage was done. Warning lights started to flash in the cargo bay and on the exterior panel.

"Release me," she shouted.

He cut the tape from her wrists and she climbed over the low sill and into the cargo bay. She crouched beside Unit 1, scraping frost from the outer edge of the panel. Despite a layer of thick insulation, the surface temperature was still forty degrees below zero. The lights showed a complete power disconnect. They had sixty seconds to get the unit hooked up to the replacement pack.

"Bring me one of the fuel cells!" she called out.

"No," he said. "Disconnect the unit and remove it. We'll hook up the power cell out here."

She looked at him, terror in her eyes. There was no arguing. She turned back to the unit and went right to work. He could see her running through a mental checklist. One he knew well.

Switch to internal power.

Remove the voltage regulator.

Disconnect power delivery cord.

Shut off cryogenic exchanger and wait five seconds for the fluid to cycle.

He could see her counting. When she got to 5, she reached beneath the unit. Four latches held it in place. Three of which were easy to access. The fourth, Urco knew, lay in an awkward spot.

He cocked his head to watch as she stretched and winced, trying to pull the latch free with her fingers. With a snap, it came loose. When she brought her hand out, it was bleeding.

She ignored the blood, stood quickly and moved to one side of the unit.

"Help me," she called out. Each unit weighed a hundred and forty pounds. Powerful magnets and cryogenic tubes filled with slush helium accounted for most of the weight. But inside the tubes and magnetic bottles lay the supply of exotic and deadly matter. Twenty-five pounds of it in each of the eight units.

At her request, Urco climbed into the cargo bay himself. He donned a pair of gloves and grabbed the frame of Unit 1. They lifted together, heaving it upward and carrying it over the lip. Two of his men took it from there and set it down on the wing.

"Please reconnect the device," Urco asked calmly.

Emma climbed out of the cargo bay, hopped off the edge of the wing and rushed to the fuel cell that had been brought out to them.

Urco imagined a clock was ticking in her head: *But there was plenty of time.*

She flicked through a series of switches on the side of the fuel cell and watched as it came to life, making energy instantly.

She grabbed the power cord and rushed to the containment unit but ran out of cord a foot shy of the connecter.

Urco stood absolutely still; neither did any of his people move. But Joe Zavala did. He jumped to his feet, dashing past the man who was guarding him, grabbing the fuel cell and carrying it closer. Urco grinned at the cooperation.

Emma connected the cord. In quick succession the amber lights blinked out and the entire panel went green. The power was back on. The frozen slush began to circulate again. The antimatter would remain suspended in the magnetic bottles, held safely at a temperature near absolute zero.

Urco smiled and clapped loudly at their efforts. "Excellent work. I trust we won't have to go through this again."

Emma's chest heaved as the effort and the adrenaline had sent her heart pounding. She looked up at him and shook her head. "No," she said. "I'd rather not."

He grinned. Another battle won. The pretense that they could resist him was gone. Wiped from their thoughts. It no longer mattered what he intended to do with the antimatter. Whether he planned to sell it to the Russians or to the Chinese or to auction it off to the highest bidder in a worldwide contest.

It didn't matter whether he promised to free them, kill them, or keep them prisoners until the end of time. None of that mattered. Any and all outcomes were preferable to a world of darkness brought on by the mixed-state matter escaping its magnetic

prison and exploding all at once.
He owned them now. He owned them all.

43

Daiyu sat in darkness. She'd been placed in the back of the same truck that she'd hijacked on the mountain road. Her hands and feet were bound with cord, cinched tight by men used to tying off knots that climbers' lives depended on. Despite hours of trying, she could neither loosen the bond nor pull free.

She'd chafed her wrists bloody from the effort before switching tactics. Sliding herself across the wooden floor of the trailer, she'd gone back and forth until she found a rough spot where a nailhead had worked loose from the planks.

Flipping over, she'd positioned her hands near it, writhing in the dark and rubbing the cord across the nail until her muscles cramped from the effort. Collapsing onto her side, she felt for the edge of the rope. It was damaged and fraying, but she couldn't tell if it was enough.

She relaxed, waiting for the painful spasms in her back to pass, so she could begin again.

She would get out. They would not stop her. She would complete her mission. And if she got the chance, she'd kill every one of the Americans and their new Peruvian friends in the process.

Breathing deeply but otherwise still, she caught the sound of voices approaching outside. Heavy boots were scuffing against the dry soil of the mountain road.

She instantly redoubled her efforts, grinding the rope across the exposed nail with maniacal intensity.

It had to snap. It had to.

She heard the key hit the padlock and then the handle being thrown over. An instant later, the door slid upward and the white light of day poured in, blinding her.

As she shut her eyes against it, two men climbed into the vehicle, grabbed her by the feet and pulled.

"No," she grunted, kicking at them. She was so close to freedom.

The men hauled her out and set her on the ground. With a pull and twist, the knot on her legs came undone. Thoughts of running vanished when she tried to stand and fell to the ground on numb legs that

419

couldn't even support her weight.

She looked upward at the men, squinting in the light. They were only silhouettes. Two standing above her, a third off to the side. A forth shadow just beyond.

The fourth man spoke English to them. "What happened to her? Where did the bruises come from?"

To her surprise, there was a familiar tone to the voice.

"She fought with the American," one of the Peruvians replied.

"Pick her up."

They grabbed her arms, lifted her and allowed her to lean against the bumper of the truck. The man who sounded familiar came into view. It was Lieutenant Wu, General Zhang's aide.

"Black Jade," he said quietly. "The General is astounded to hear that you have been . . . subdued so easily."

Embarrassment flooded through her, the sense of failure peaking so strongly that she could not look at him.

"Untie her," Wu ordered.

Why these men were taking orders from the lieutenant, she couldn't guess. But with a nod from the third member of their group, they did as he asked.

The sudden release of her hands brought

both great relief and a new wave of pain as she brought her arms in front of her for the first time in hours.

Her hands were caked with dried blood, her wrists rubbed raw from the effort. The cord that had held her captive was frayed within a few strands of breaking. The Peruvian men looked at it suspiciously.

Wu laughed. "You're lucky I arrived," he said to the Peruvians. "She would have killed you all."

They scoffed at the statement, but that didn't make it any less true.

"Can you walk?" Wu asked.

Daiyu tested her legs. They were tingling with pins and needles, but she would show no more weakness. She nodded and stood.

"Come with me," Wu said, turning and strolling down the path.

She followed awkwardly, listening as the Peruvian men closed up the truck behind her. The door slid down with a rattle before slamming against the stops. Angry words were exchanged among them.

Daiyu focused on Lieutenant Wu. "Did General Zhang buy my freedom?"

"Yes and no."

"I failed you," she whispered. "I'm not worthy of being ransomed."

Wu laughed lightly. "The General said you

would react this way. He also said to tell you he can find diamonds and gold in the ground; that he can either buy or steal them, if he must. But a good operative, one such as yourself, is far harder to come by."

She felt a wave of pride at the compliment. But it did not change what had happened.

"At any rate," Wu added, "it's not you alone that we've paid for but the *Nighthawk*'s cargo."

Her eyes grew wide.

"There is much you don't know," he said, leading her around a bend.

A sleek helicopter sat in the road up ahead. It was guarded by two men with assault rifles. Men from home. Allies.

"How did you find me?"

"You recall the name Falconer?"

"The Russian asset."

"Our asset," Wu insisted, "though the Russians think he belongs to them. Falconer was on the second Russian bomber, in charge of overriding the American commands from the Vandenberg. He was supposed to abort the capture of the *Nighthawk* and direct it back toward our fleet. Where we would grab it once it hit the water."

"Obviously, he failed," she said.

"Partially," Wu replied. "Whether that was

by design or happenstance, we cannot say. But as it turns out, the man lives. He contacted us, told us where to find you and where to find the *Nighthawk.*"

"But the Americans are already there," she said. "With the man from this camp."

"Yes," Wu said. "The Falconer. They are one and the same."

As she put it all together, she began to laugh. "And to think, I almost killed him."

"You couldn't know," Wu said. "The man has been operating as a triple agent. But the final act is now upon us. General Zhang secured your release with gold. And now, for a pittance in rough-cut diamonds, we will take possession of the cargo."

A pittance might be fifty million dollars, in Zhang's terms. But it was truly nothing compared to what they were receiving.

They arrived at the helicopter. The side door was pulled back. A body covered in plastic lay on the floor.

"Jian," she said. *Her brother among the children who had never been born.*

"A casualty of the operation."

She and Wu climbed in, the armed commandos followed and the pilot began the start procedure. A heavy pack was tossed out to one of the Peruvian men who followed them. It clinked like a bag of loose change.

"Krugerrands," Wu said.

The Peruvians opened it. One was satisfied, but another was frustrated. An argument broke out, in their native language. It was hard to follow with all of them speaking at once, but she understood enough.

She killed them. We should not be letting her go.

It's been arranged.

I don't like it . . . deserves to die . . .

The sound of the helicopter starting drowned out the rest. But Daiyu could read lips. She focused on the leader of the Peruvian men.

Of course they deserve to die.

Don't worry. They will.

44

Kurt's face was bathed in yellow light. The strange hue and intensity was all he could see no matter where he looked, but it wasn't the afterlife.

After being dragged to the bottom of the lake, Kurt had been on the verge of blacking out when his furious counterattack coincided with the assailant's attempt to plunge the diving knife into his ribs.

The sudden cloud of the red that erupted seemed to leave no doubt who'd gotten the worse end of the deal. As Vargas had pushed off the bottom with both legs and soared up toward the surface, both he and Kurt had every reason to believe that the blade had plunged home.

Kurt's initial thought was that his blood was surprisingly bright. Still, with his main airline ripped out, getting the secondary line attached to the valve on his helmet took precedence over finding a wound and stopping the bleeding.

He'd grabbed his backup line, brought it up to the quick connect port on the side of the helmet and snapped it into place.

A slight hiss told him gas was flowing and he immediately started breathing rapidly, trying to expel the carbon dioxide that had built up in his lungs.

With air flowing, he searched for his wound. By the time he found it, the swirl of red color around him had begun to thin. The water turned pink and then went clear once again.

Either he was out of blood or . . .

It turned out that he hadn't been impaled. The blade had only sliced a thin crease in his skin. He was bleeding, but the outpouring of crimson came from the red dye capsule, which had taken the brunt of the impact. The knife had split it in two and flooded the water with enough coloring to make it seem like an artery had been gashed open.

Kurt had found the dye capsule, tossed it away and looked upward. He could just make out the bottom of the Zodiac and two figures clinging to it.

Adrenaline urged him to surface and make an immediate attempt to rescue Emma, but the odds were against surviving another battle with the two divers. Not without much oxygen in his tank. And even if he could overcome them, there was still the man in the boat with Emma as a hostage.

If a frontal assault wouldn't work, he thought it might be time to try the stealth approach. *They think I'm dead. Let them keep thinking it, until we make our counterattack.*

He detached the dive light he'd carried, placed it down in the mud and swam from the scene.

If anyone was looking down from the Zodiac, they would see only the stationary light. The diver in the black wet suit, moving in the depths of the black lake, would be as hard to spot as the *Nighthawk* had been.

He moved calmly across the bottom, found the spot where the *Nighthawk* had been resting and pushed off the bottom. Rising upward and exhaling slowly as he went, Kurt emerged from the dark lake into one of the yellow lifting bags. The voluminous air bag lay on its side, like an oversized Portuguese man-of-war that had washed up on the beach.

Hidden within, Kurt removed his helmet to breathe, unzipped a waterproof pouch on the sleeve of his wet suit and pulled a small transmitter free.

Keeping the compact radio clear of the water, Kurt turned it on and switched to a prearranged frequency. He pressed the transmit button and spoke calmly into the microphone.

"Gamay, this is Kurt," he said.

A hushed voice came over the radio, imbued with a slight, scolding tone. *"Kurt, I thought they'd killed you. I was about to move in on my own."*

Tired of being ambushed, Kurt had decided the NUMA team could use a guardian angel to watch over them. With Joe needed to fly the helicopter and only Paul and Gamay to choose from, Kurt had picked Gamay for several reasons.

Most importantly, she was a crack shot. Good with a pistol, but an expert with a rifle. She was also smaller, more agile and more athletic than Paul. Attributes that would help her hide and move from spot to spot without being noticed.

Joe had flown her in early this morning, dropping her off on a high ridge, before heading to La Jalca to pick up Emma, Urco and himself.

Dressed in camouflage and carrying a rifle, Gamay was out there now. "What's your position?"

"I'm on the second ridge east of the landing

zone," she said. *"I can see the clearing, most of the lake and the waterfall."*

"What about Joe and Paul?"

"They're in the clearing. They were sur-rounded as soon as they landed. The Night-hawk *is down safely. So is the Air-Crane. Paul and Joe are being held just across from it."*

"And Emma?"

"They have her working on something," Gamay said. *"I can't tell exactly what it is. But they've opened the* Nighthawk *and begun unloading it. Other than that, all seems fairly calm at the moment."*

"Was it Urco?" Kurt asked, fairly certain that he knew.

"It was," Gamay said. *"How'd you know he couldn't be trusted?"*

"I didn't know," Kurt admitted. "But a few odd moments were enough to cause concern. For one thing, he had his satellite antenna aimed low and to the northwest. There's no reason for an archaeologist working in a deep canyon in the Southern Hemisphere to be using a satellite so low on the horizon to bounce his communications. Based on the angle, it had to be a Northern Hemisphere bird out over the Pacific. He'd also claimed to be the cameraman who shot the video of the *Nighthawk* crossing La Jalca, but I noticed that he was a lefty. He writes left, eats left, and yet the footage was filmed by someone holding a camera in their right hand. I couldn't see any reason to lie about something like that, but it was definitely suspicious."

"Your intuition is spot-on, as usual," Gamay said.

"Not quite," Kurt said. "I truly thought we'd be safe until we pulled the containment units out of the *Nighthawk.* I also thought you'd spot anyone coming down the Inca road or up through the valley. What happened?"

"That part of the plan didn't work," she said. *"I haven't blinked in hours. The road in from La Jalca has been empty. The road out to the south has been empty. Nothing has arrived or departed this valley on foot or by wheel or wing since you guys landed."*

He understood the implication. "Which means Urco's men were already here, waiting for their moment to attack. I thought their numbers looked a little light this morning. Must have driven over last night."

"I counted six down in the clearing, plus the three on the water," she said.

"Ten, including Urco," he noted.

"Do you think that's it?"

"No reason it shouldn't be," he said.

"They've shown their hand. Now it's our turn."

"If I circle to the south, I'll have a clear shot at everyone and everything in the clearing," she said. "If you can move in at the same moment, we can catch them in a cross fire."

It was a good plan. The problem was, the beach. With so much open land running from the edge of the lake to where the tall grass began, Kurt would be seen and shot long before he got into the fight.

"I'll have to circle around as well," Kurt said.

"Circle around where?"

"To the only place I can get out of this lake without being spotted," Kurt said. "Unfortunately, that means a trip through the washing machine. I'm just glad the *Nighthawk* didn't land in Niagara."

"I've always assumed you were crazy," she said. "This proves it."

"It's the only way to get behind them," he said. "Should be okay, if I skirt the edge."

"You might want to hurry," Gamay said. "If you are where I think you are, you have a boat headed straight for you."

"Roger that," Kurt said. "If the situation changes and the others seem to be in imminent danger, take action without waiting for me. I'll contact you as soon as I'm back

431

on dry land."

Kurt shut the radio off, slipped it back in the waterproof pouch and zipped the pocket shut. With the growl of the approaching boat to spur him on, he pulled his helmet back on and dove straight down, beginning the most dangerous swim of his life.

45

Kurt descended twenty feet before moving horizontally and passing under the approaching boat.

Rolling over on his back, Kurt watched the wake of the small boat flare out around the air bags and slow. The yellow bags began to move. The occupants of the boat were gathering them in.

Putting space between himself and the cleanup crew, Kurt continued toward the rolling thunder of the waterfall.

As he approached it, the current around him became more turbulent and confused. The falling water dropped into the lake with so much force that it continued downward in a column until it hit the bottom, spreading out in all directions. It scoured away all sediment and loose debris, forming a deep well known as a *plunge pool,* often filled with heavy boulders resting on hardened rock.

Others called this pool the *washing machine* because the downward force of the water caused swirling vortices all around it. They led outward, up and then back down. Horizontal drums of churning liquid.

Water surged away from the falls in general, but get too close and Kurt would be sucked right into the washing machine and shoved downward into the plunge pool.

Unfortunately, to many daredevils who'd gone over Niagara Falls in various barrels, capsules and other vehicles, getting caught in the washing machine at the bottom of the falls had proved more deadly than going over them in the first place. Once they got trapped inside the vortex, it was incredibly difficult to get out. Several attempts ended in disaster when the homemade conveyances survived the drop only to be pinned at the bottom and held there until the occupants ran out of oxygen.

Kurt had no intention of getting into the washing machine. His plan was to swim around the edge of the falls, stay far enough out to avoid trouble and surface behind it. It was a good plan in theory, but the upper end of the lake narrowed so tightly around the falls that it proved difficult.

Pushed outward at first by the churning water, Kurt found himself forced upward as well. Swimming harder, he made a little progress but was still being pushed back nearly as fast as he went forward.

Tired of being caught on a liquid conveyer belt, and well aware that he might be seen at any moment, Kurt angled more directly toward the falls, charging into the semicircle of water that boiled upward from below.

Straining every muscle in his body, he began to make progress. All at once, the outward pressure of the water waned and he was moving forward.

Too far, too fast.

He changed direction and fought the pull of the eddy, trying to use the momentum he'd gained to slingshot around it. Despite his powerful stroke, the vortex had him. He was dragged toward the thundering wall of falling liquid and pulled downward in the grasp of an underwater storm.

There was no fighting it now; he had to go with the flow. Surrounded in the swirling white foam, Kurt was forced deeper and deeper. Even after slowing through seventy feet of water, the column hit bottom with surprising strength.

Kurt was slammed downward and shoved sideways into the rocks. His shoulder took one hit, the aluminum cylinder on his back took another.

He was pushed into a large boulder and then swung around back in the other direction, where he crashed into a pile of rocks worn smooth by the constant tumbling action beneath the falls.

He could feel the water hammering him, pressing him into the stones. His fins were ripped off; water forced itself into a gap where the helmet sealed around his neck, filling the helmet with frigid liquid, cutting off his air supply and chilling his face in the process.

Kurt had ahold of one large boulder — he clung to it and pulled himself along. The water pressed him downward; there was no swimming, only crawling.

He scraped across the two boulders, then pushed up against the wall of stone behind the waterfall and caught under a ledge for a moment. Bracing himself, he refused to be held in the trap. He found a foothold and pushed himself outward and up.

Suddenly, he was on the far side of the vortex. Instead of crushing him downward, it carried him up on a rapidly ascending elevator.

He breached the surface in a swirl of foam on the back side of the falls.

Kurt lunged forward and pulled himself onto the rocks. He was battered, bruised

and exhausted, but the risk had paid off.
He was now hidden behind enemy lines.

46

Joe Zavala had been taken down to the rock-strewn beach. His hands were bound with a zip tie, and while his feet were free, his boots and socks had been taken away to make it more difficult and painful should he try to escape or fight.

Paul sat on Joe's left, tied and bound in a similar fashion. Emma was on his right, also restrained. Though many thoughts were competing for Joe's attention, Kurt's death was not at the top of the list. Joe had heard the words, felt the pain they carried and then locked the thought away in some distant corner of his mind. After so many risky adventures together, both of them knew a day like this might arrive. In Joe's position, Kurt would have done the same.

"We're going to get out of here," Joe said. "I'm not sure how, but we're going to break free."

"And then what?" Emma asked.

"Depends on the manner of our escape," Joe said. "If we can get to the Air-Crane, we'll fly. If not, we go on foot or by boat on the river. There are rapids downstream, but we could navigate them in the Zodiac."

"They have to slip up at some point," Paul said.

"They will," Joe assured him. "Until then save your strength and do everything you can to lull them into thinking they've won."

"It's not about us," Emma said. "I know you want to escape, but there's a far bigger danger here."

"One we can't prevent without first getting free. You can't give up," Joe urged.

"Getting free will require fighting," she explained. "Most likely, shooting. All within a stone's throw of the frozen supply of mixed-state matter. One stray bullet could set off the disaster. If it means preventing that, I'm fine giving up."

One of Urco's men came out of the tall grass, where he'd probably been listening. His approach killed off any further conversation. He moved in behind Emma, cut her loose and stood back. "Come with me," he said. "Urco wants your help."

Emma stood and was led away. Joe sensed she was close to despondency, but then she didn't know there was still hope. She hadn't been privy to Kurt's backup plan. He had wanted it that way. And now, seeing how much power Urco had over her, and how deeply the fear of a disaster had clutched at her heart, Joe was glad he'd kept the secret. He could imagine Emma telling Urco what she knew all in the interest of preventing a catastrophe.

As Emma and the guard left, Joe glanced at Paul.

Paul nodded. He was ready. Joe was ready, too; he'd already been working the zip tie back and forth, twisting his wrists this way and that, in order to weaken the plastic. Before long, it would be weak enough to snap.

Then Joe would rest, waiting for the sound of a rifle firing from somewhere high in the rocks.

Gamay would take out several of their captors before the men knew what hit them. Joe and Paul would spring into action at the same moment and, with a little luck, the tide would be turned.

47

As soon as Kurt's strength returned, he began moving across the rocks behind the waterfall. Not planning to get back in the water, he shed his cumbersome air tank, damaged helmet and deflated BCD. Hooking them together, he tossed them in the water. Empty, the aluminum cylinder would float, but the deflated BCD, with its integrated weights, would drag them down.

They vanished and Kurt continued on foot, looking for a place to start his climb. He would have to climb upward and then over, where the ridge was thick with foliage thanks to the constant overspray from the waterfall.

Climbing it would be easy; getting there was more difficult. The footing behind the waterfall was treacherous. Kurt watched every step. Halfway in, he noticed something that didn't belong in a pristine mountain lake. A sheen of discoloration lay across the wet rocks. Even in the flat light, he could see all the colors of the rainbow.

Oil and water, he thought. Or, more likely, gasoline.

It vanished where the churning water mixed it into the depths but clung to the stones, leading like an arrow into the mouth of a large cave.

That second boat had to come from somewhere.

Kurt picked his way to the mouth of the cave, gazed around the edge and into the darkness. He saw nothing and heard only the echo of the thundering waterfall, but the slick of petrochemical color beckoned him to enter.

He eased back into the water and swam into the cave. The farther in he went, the darker it became, but his eyes adjusted and he began to make out the details. Eighty feet back, the cave jagged to the right and widened; around the bend lay outlines of a camp.

Gas cans, propane canisters and a cookstove sat beside a group of plastic crates that looked exactly like the ones he'd seen at La Jalca. Bedrolls and wool blankets were laid out on a higher section. Spare oxygen tanks for the divers leaned against the cave wall. Beside them sat a stack of boxy items covered with plastic liners.

The camp was empty. Not exactly a surprise, considering the activity out on the lake and in the clearing where the *Nighthawk* had been placed.

"More burial chambers," Kurt whispered, thinking of Urco's statement when they'd cruised near the waterfall. *"I would like it if they remain undisturbed.* Of course you would. Your men were hiding back here."

Kurt swam to the edge, climbed out of the water and began to pick through the offerings. He found a pair of binoculars and a flashlight but left them where they were since they would obviously be missed.

He dug into one of the plastic boxes and found a container filled with strips of dried beef. Realizing how hungry he was, he took a sample and chewed on it as he searched the rest of the cavern.

He found no guns or knives, but one of the bins had several boxes of ammunition in it. Another was empty except for cut lengths of color-coded wire. A third held bricks of orange clay that were wrapped in clear plastic. The alphanumeric code *S-10* had been written on the outside of each.

"Semtex," Kurt muttered, using the brand name of the compound. "What would you be doing with Semtex?"

The orange clay was a plastic explosive. Manufactured in the Czech Republic, S-10 was the latest version. It was similar to American-made C-4. Each of the bricks would be powerful enough to obliterate a car.

Kurt counted the supply. Assuming the crate had been full, at least half the explosives were already missing.

Finding no other weapons, Kurt pulled one of the bricks free and tucked it into a pocket. Without a blasting cap or an electrical charge, it would be difficult to set off, but it still might come in handy.

Closing the lid on the explosives crate, he moved to the back of the cave, rifled through another box and then moved over to the plastic tarp and the stack of equipment it covered.

Moving a rock that held the tarp down, Kurt peeled the material back and found himself staring at a rectangular piece of equipment that looked incredibly familiar.

Fuel cell.

Not only was it a fuel cell, it was identical in size, shape, design and color to the ones Joe had flown in on the Air-Crane. It was even marked the same; stenciled writing on the outer case read *Type 3 Hydrogen Fuel*

Cell, Property of the United States Government.

Kurt touched the control panel, his fingers gliding across a bank of switches until he found the power button. He switched it on and received an immediate indication that it was working and producing power. A display lit up, indicating fully pressurized reservoirs of hydrogen and oxygen. Enough for twenty-six hours of continuous operation.

Under the next tarp was an identical unit. Behind them lay two more. Marks on the ground suggested two other units had been there and were now missing. Looped power cords, neatly banded together sat in a crate beside the units.

Why were they here?

"Explosives without detonators," Kurt said to himself. "Replicas or stolen fuel cells, what are you up to Urco?"

The sound of an outboard motor approaching echoed down from the mouth of the cave. Kurt switched off the fuel cell, covered it up and placed the flat rock back on top.

The buzzing motor grew louder and then cut out as a light played across the water. Kurt retreated quietly into the recesses of the cave and took cover.

Peering out over a rock formation, he watched a gray inflatable with three men in it pull around the bend and drift to the shore. It bumped against the rocks, stopping beside the cookstove.

Two of the three men got out. They carried the deflated yellow air bags and stuffed them one on top of another into a gap in the rocks. That done, they went directly for the fuel cells.

"Cuántos?" the first one said.

"Llevar todos," the second one replied, pulling up the tarps. *"Una para los americanos, una para el chino, los otros son para los rusos, y para los amigos de Rio."*

He laughed as he finished.

"Y los explosivos?"

"Estan dentro," the man replied. *"Boom!"* he said, chuckling further.

The other men laughed as well. They selected one of the fuel cells, tested it, as Kurt had, and then switched it off.

The man in the boat grew impatient. *"Vamanos."*

The men onshore got moving. They carried all four of the fuel cells to the small boat, loaded them inside and then climbed aboard and pushed off.

As soon as they were clear of the rocks, the outboard was lowered back into the

446

water and started with a hard pull. It coughed out a fog of blue smoke as it came to life and the men eased out of sight, heading toward the mouth of the cave.

Kurt waited until he'd heard them speed away and then cautiously stepped from his hiding place. He didn't speak much Spanish, but some of the words were obvious to him.

His mind went to the Semtex he'd found and the joke that had brought out a round of laughter.

"Los explosivos," Kurt whispered. *"Boom!"*

48

Emma followed her guard as he walked across the beach, cut through the grass and traveled up into the clearing where the *Nighthawk* sat. On the far side, Urco stood among the containment units.

Two of the eight units had been removed. They now rested on the stony ground, each of them connected to a fuel cell.

"Check these over, please," Urco said.

"What am I looking for?" she asked.

"I want to be sure everything is functioning properly and that they're safe to move."

It was a simple task. She crouched beside the units and did a quick diagnostic review, all the time wondering why he'd bothered to say *please*.

"The magnetic bottles are stable," she said. "The cryogenic systems are operating within accepted parameters. The fuel cells are generating clean power."

"Good," Urco said.

She stood. "I assume you want me to remove the other units?"

"In time," he said. "For now, we should discuss your role in things."

"My role?"

He only smiled and said, "Walk with me."

With little choice in the matter, she nodded. "Lead on."

They left the guard behind, entering a path cut through the foliage that twisted toward higher ground. Machetes had done the work; freshly cut stalks and fallen blades of the long grass lay across the ground. They'd been trampled down by a fair amount of foot traffic already.

"Are we entering some kind of maze?" she asked.

"We're already deep inside one," he insisted. "Working together is the only way out."

"We *were* working together," she replied, "right up until the point where your men attacked us, killed Kurt and took the rest of us hostage."

"Not *hostages,*" he said, "*captives. Captured thieves,* actually."

"Excuse me?"

"You're a thief," he said. "A well-dressed, Stanford-educated thief. Your entire organization has larceny in its heart and, by extension, the nation you serve. But you've been caught — red-handed, as they say — in the middle of the greatest robbery the world has ever known."

"You're the one who took the —"

"No," he said, turning on her and cutting her off. "I only relieved you of the stolen goods. It was you and your government that engaged in this theft. *You* chose to fly this craft up into the heavens and gather the mixed-state matter from the magnetic field. *You* chose to bring it home to your hidden bunkers at Vandenberg, where you and your people would hoard it for your own purposes."

"We only did that because —"

He wouldn't let her speak. "There are five separate treaties governing activities in outer space," he snapped. "The United States is a signatory on each and every one. Three of them were drafted by American statesmen. Collectively, they forbid every activity you've so recently engaged in, from the militarization of space to the national appropriation of any part of space or any celestial body, such as the Moon."

As he railed at her, she recalled the ethical arguments internally discussed at the NSA prior to the mission. Arguments put forward and then so easily swatted aside. "We

450

claimed nothing," she said. "We merely retrieved free-floating particles."

"Are you really going to play the lawyer with me?"

She fell silent and he turned and led her out of the grass and onto a plateau. From here, they looked over the lake seventy feet below. In the distance, the waterfall fell, with its hushed and ceaseless voice.

He turned back her way and bore down. "Like everything else in space, these *free-floating particles* are reserved as part of the *common heritage of all mankind.* They belong to everyone on Earth and to no one person or government in particular."

The furor in his voice surprised her. *Why,* she thought, *should he care about such things? How would he even know about them? Or about the wording of some obscure treaties?*

"Who are you?" she asked.

"You still don't recognize me?" he said, sounding almost disappointed. "Fortunately for me, I suppose. I feared you might spot me when we dined together beneath the cliffs of La Jalca."

He reached to the side of his face as if to scratch at his ear but instead of scratching began to pull at his beard, slowly removing the portion on the right side of his face. His skin was burned beneath it, not terribly disfigured but scarred and hairless.

"The other side of my beard is real," he replied, "but I can grow nothing over here."

An indentation in his jawline told her the bone had been broken and never healed correctly; a portion of it might have been removed.

"It was the crash and the fire," he explained.

Suddenly, the pieces came together for her. *This* man was involved in hacking the *Nighthawk*'s control system. He knew about the NSA mission and the antimatter. He was well versed in the international treaties regulating the use of space. And he knew her.

"Beric?" she said.

"So you *do* remember."

She barely recognized him even now. Years had passed. Age and scars had changed his face. His eyes held no kindness, only bitterness and twisted anger. "I don't understand? How? Why? Your plane exploded. They told us it was a terror group. They told us we were all in danger."

"I was in danger," he insisted, as he raised his voice. "And the terror group was based in Washington, D.C. Ironically enough, you now work for them."

"The NSA?" she said. "Why would they want to harm you? Surely you can't believe what you're saying."

"I have proof," his voice accusatory as he moved closer to her. "And what's more, *they had a motive.* If you recall, I was involved in the initial studies that determined the possibility of antimatter getting trapped in the magnetic field. I was the one who suggested it might be a more stable form of *mixed-state matter* — if it remained cold enough. The head of the program came to me shortly after I submitted my findings. He said they'd been discussing a plan, not just to search for the antimatter *but to actually harvest it.* I objected strenuously. They insisted the purpose was peaceful, but when the funding is coming from the military and the National Security Agency, that stretches credibility just a bit."

Her head was spinning, but she took in every word.

"We shall use this for propulsion to push rockets to Mars in eight weeks," he said in a false voice. *"To the outer planets in less than a year.* Even to deep space. But it wasn't long before *someone* mentioned the possibility of a weapon."

His voice growing louder, he shook his

head in disgust. "I threatened to go to the press. To put the information out on the Internet. To tell the whole world, no matter what they did to me. I knew what you're probably discovering right now: it is a mistake, a Pandora's Box we've brought into our homes and managed to hold shut only by the thinnest of margins."

She saw it now. It *was* a mistake. A disaster in the making. She wished she'd never been a part of it.

"I was threatened with deportation, should I speak a word — thirty years in solitary confinement. I agreed to keep quiet, but they watched me constantly. It seems my word wasn't enough. On that short flight to New Orleans they made their move. My plane exploded over the Gulf of Mexico. It left me like this. I ended up clinging to an abandoned oil rig, my face a cake of blood. I found a life raft the next day and waited for the tide. I made it to shore under cover of darkness. And I chose to remain hidden. I knew if they found me, I would be dead."

She stared at the scarred complexion, wondering how he'd survived and who had stitched him back together so badly. *A doctor with a gun to his head, perhaps. Or maybe he'd done it himself.* His affect was hideous; he sounded paranoid. She wondered if he'd blown up his own plane to fake his death. Was he so deranged that the difference between good and evil was lost on him? "So you came here and began plotting revenge?"

"At first, I only wanted to survive and disappear," he insisted. "I created Urco. As I learned more and more about the destruction of man by man, it became clear to me."

He hesitated; taking a step back, he changed the subject. "Why did you leave NASA and join the clandestine world of the NSA?"

"Because of what happened to you," she whispered. "After your death, and the endless news of terrorism and war in other parts of the world, I realized that most of the planet was filled with evil. And that evil must be fought at every turn."

"You were a pacifist," he said.

"So were you."

He nodded slowly and reapplied his beard. "It seems we've both realized the truth. *Pacifism* in a violent world is another term for *suicide*. Only the evil and violence I see resides in government buildings and ivory towers."

"There's a difference between governments and terrorists."

"Only in the scale of their atrocities," he insisted. "Learning that was the key to everything. Despite my desire to simply leave it all behind, I soon learned that the *Nighthawk* project had been transferred to the NSA and that the unthinkable was going to be attempted. I began to obsess over ways to expose it without exposing myself. Ways to prevent what you might do. Eight long years has led to this."

"And what exactly is *this*?" she asked. "How is it better? The whole world put at risk so you could take the mixed-state matter away from us and give it to the Russians? That's your solution? Hand the most powerful substance ever known to a nation that invades its neighbors, crushes any form of freedom or human rights and poisons its detractors with radioactive isotopes?"

As he stepped toward Emma he said, "You're so focused on winning. You fail to see the forest for the trees. You fail to understand my position even as I shout it at you. *All governments are evil. All power corrupts.* Of course I'm not working for the Russians. Or for the Chinese. Or for the Americans." His voice grew tighter and louder. *"They, and you, are all working for me."*

The statement rang of such megalomania, she could hardly believe it had come from his mouth. "What are you talking about?"

She tried to step back but was frozen by the depth of hate in the eyes that bore deeply into hers. "I needed allies," he said smugly. "*I* made them a deal. I would hack into the NSA's system and divert the *Nighthawk* into their clutches *if* they would provide the means to collect it."

"You're the Falconer," she said.

"I see you've heard the name."

It made perfect sense now. She realized they'd played right into his hands. "You designed the automated computer system that operated the X-37 and we used it virtually unchanged in the *Nighthawk.* No wonder you were able to hack into it and redirect the aircraft. No wonder we never found a mole. You were operating remotely the whole time and we weren't looking for a dead man."

"Your mistake," he said arrogantly. "One of many."

"How'd you do it? How did you get past the encryption?"

He stepped so close to Emma, she could feel his hot breath. "NASA left a huge back door open to your project," he said. "It was so easy to hack, I thought it might be a trap. I received data from every division like clockwork. I probably had more information about the program than any single person actually working on it. And when you decided to bring it back a week early because of the storm, I was literally the first to know."

Their betrayal was complete. "But why? To what end?" She hesitated. "What's the point of all this?"

He stared back at her, his eyes never blinking. She saw him now. The same man but changed, deranged by some mad desire. "Balance," he said. "I gave the Russians a choice, I gave the Chinese a choice and now offer you the same one."

"Which is?"

"To fight me," he taunted. "Or to work for me. And, by extension, to work for the *common heritage of mankind.*"

She wasn't sure where this was going, but it was not something to refuse out of hand. It might give her a chance to seek help. "I have no idea what you're getting at."

"It's very simple," he said, his voice teeming with vengeance. "I intend to undo what you and your nation have done. Obviously, I can't give the mixed-state matter equally to all the world's citizens or even to each nation or a large group of them. Few have the technological capability to handle it. One part to the Russians, one part to the Chinese, one part to your government and the rest to another group of my choosing."

She could hardly believe what she was hearing. Was he serious? Her mind drifted back to the Beric she had known and some of his causes. Not only was he a pacifist like her but also an *antinationalist,* of sorts. He'd written an article he'd titled *Duty of the Commons* that argued ownership of anything by a nation-state was the cause of wars and strife. It tied in with what he was suggesting now. "You want us to share this?"

"Far better that than one country hoarding all of it," he said.

"Who are you to make such a decision?"

Urco stepped back and smiled. "The only one who can," he said smugly, "since I now control the entire stock."

She struggled to process the situation. It was all too new. He was unstable, delusional and perhaps even certifiably insane, but he was also brilliant, devious and determined. And, at the moment, in an unquestionable position of control.

"Cooperating with you would be considered treason," she explained.

"Better to live in prison than to die in a cataclysm."

She looked away. She didn't want this. Didn't want to help him in any way. But no matter from what angle she approached it

459

at, the answer was always the same: *What choice did she have?*

His plan sounded like madness, but even that was preferable to Armageddon. "How will I take *our* portion back to America? Will you let us fly it to Cajamarca?"

"No," he said. "You will explain what is occurring to your friends and then you'll drive in a vehicle that I possess."

"How can I drive when the bridge is out?"

"There's another route," he said. "A shorter route that goes to the south and then through the pass. It avoids the highest of the mountains. It has its own steep cliffs, yes . . . but I trust you'll drive with the requisite caution."

She glanced to the north as the sound of a helicopter approaching became audible.

"That will be the Chinese agents," he said. "I require your answer."

She looked him in the eye once more. "Fine," she said. "I'll do as you ask. I have no other choice."

460

49

The sound of the helicopter drifted across the open beach.

"Airborne tow truck to haul away our *Nighthawk*?" Paul suggested.

Joe scanned the horizon for the source of the clatter; he spied a black speck in the distance. "Not a heavy-lifter, by the sound of it. Something faster and more maneuverable."

"Help maybe?"

"Even less likely," Joe said. He could hear Urco's men running around and making preparations. "But if it preoccupies our captors, I'll take it."

Joe considered whether this might be the moment to break free, but Emma's return with two guards at her side quashed the idea.

"On your feet," one of the guards said, waving a pistol.

Joe stood wearily. Paul did likewise.

The black speck continued to grow larger, and descend, as it came closer. It crossed the lake at two hundred feet and passed over the beach, whipping the tall grasses behind them into a swirling frenzy. It continued on, landing higher up on the plateau, several hundred feet away.

"Are we done standing at attention," Paul asked, "or are we going to do something?"

Surprisingly, Emma replied, "Urco wants you and Joe to carry the containment units up to the plateau."

"And if we go on strike?" Joe said.

"Please," Emma said. "Just do as he asks."

Joe could see the strain on her face. He also noticed that she stood *behind* the two guards, not in front of them. As if *they* were taking orders from *her.*

Reluctantly, Joe held out his hands. The man pulled a knife, slid it between Joe's wrists and pulled upward. The zip tie broke with a sharp snap. So much for all his work weakening the plastic. No doubt, he'd have to start again.

Paul's restraints were cut free as well and the two men followed Emma into the grass and up toward the *Nighthawk.* Urco's men followed a few steps behind.

"You've earned their trust pretty quickly,"

Joe whispered. "Tell me there's a reason for that."

"There is," she said. "I'm doing whatever I can to avoid disaster."

She went on to explain the situation as quickly as possible.

"You know it's going to end badly," Joe said.

"There are degrees of *badly,*" she said. "But it's the lesser of two evils at this point."

Joe understood her reasoning, but he wasn't buying in. The lesser of all evils would be if they could escape, subdue or kill this madman *and* secure the mixed-state matter. A long shot, but he still intended to pull it off.

They entered the clearing, rounded the nose of the *Nighthawk* and found Urco standing in front of the containment units.

He pointed to the first unit. "You two will carry that one up to the helicopter on the plateau. Ms. Townsend will carry the fuel cell. I trust you understand what happens if you drop it."

"Don't worry," Joe said. "Though it might help us to keep our footing if you gave us our boots back."

"Help you to escape, maybe?"

Joe shrugged. It was worth a try.

He and Paul were handed gloves. They set

themselves on either end of the first containment unit and grabbed the handles. Joe could feel chilled air coming off the frosted pipes as soon as he got close to them.

"Ready," Paul said.

"Up," Joe replied.

They lifted simultaneously. The unit was hefty, but the weight was distributed evenly and the lifting bars were well positioned. They picked it off the ground with ease and were directed toward the freshly cut pathway.

Joe was at the front of the unit, walking backward and looking over his shoulder to see where he was going. Paul was at the back. Emma walked beside them, lugging the portable fuel cell and keeping the cords from getting tangled.

They arrived at the top of the path a minute later. Four of Urco's men stood there waiting, surrounding the helicopter at various distances. Three held assault rifles, one held a shotgun.

Urco walked past them and began conversing with a petite woman. Even from a distance, Joe could see her physique was well muscled.

"That's the woman who attacked us at La Jalca," Emma whispered. "She said her name was Daiyu."

Joe could see why she'd turned out to be such a handful.

After a nod from Urco, Daiyu walked over to inspect the containment unit. Like him, she had armed men at her disposal. One stood in the helicopter and two others were on the ground with her. They carried short-barreled submachine guns, held at the ready to spray everyone and anyone with a hail of lead.

"A hard bargain is being struck here," Paul noted.

"So much for honor among thieves."

"And this is what we've been after all this time?" Daiyu said, running a finger across the frost on the outer casing. "How am I to be sure there's anything in this metal box?"

"You could open it up and look inside," Urco suggested. "Though your brain cells will be vaporized before they process anything you might see."

Daiyu cut her eyes at him. "My country does not play games."

"I know more about your country than you might," he said. "I know your orders from Zhang are to take possession of the containment units and leave the diamonds without confrontation. I receive fifty ounces of them now, and another fifty upon your scientists confirming that the antimatter is

465

stored inside. If you want to haggle, we can do that, but every minute on the ground here increases all of our risks. So if you have an issue, state it; otherwise, take possession and close the deal or turn it down and leave."

She glared back at him, the fury barely suppressed in her eyes. "If you're lying, I will hunt you down personally."

"You would never find me," he said. "But, have no fear. You're getting what you asked for. To make sure I get what I want, Vargas will travel with you."

"Acceptable," she said. "Have them load it up and bring the second unit. The sooner we get out of here, the better."

Joe and Paul were urged forward. The pilot helped them lift the unit into the helicopter and then secured it to the floor. Emma made sure the fuel cell and the power cords were strapped down tightly.

That done, they moved off to collect the second unit and they carried it back at double speed.

Joe's initial reaction to Emma's cooperation hadn't changed, but the sooner the Chinese agent and her gunmen left, the quicker he could get back to planning an escape. And by taking one of Urco's most intimidating henchmen with them, the

Chinese had unknowingly helped out.

With the second unit loaded aboard, the black helicopter powered up and took off. Even as it left, he and Paul were given a new order: loading another of the containment units into the back of an old Toyota Land Cruiser that Emma was slated to drive.

Emma strapped the unit and the fuel cell down tightly. "I'll contact Urco as soon as the unit is safely airborne," she said. "He's promised to release you at that point."

Joe knew that wouldn't happen. And from the sound of her voice, Emma knew it, too.

"I'd say wear your seat belt," Joe replied. "But I'm assuming you'll be driving carefully."

She offered a sad look, closed the door and waited as another of Urco's men climbed in the passenger side to make sure she did as she was told.

Joe stepped back as the engine came to life. Still under guard, he and Paul watched as the old Land Cruiser moved off down the dirt road that led south.

Three of the eight containment units were gone, four remained in the *Nighthawk* and one sat in the clearing, awaiting another purchaser.

Perhaps more importantly, two of Urco's

467

men were gone. Two of the biggest and strongest.

As he and Paul were led back to the beach under guard, Joe glanced at the sun. It was falling toward the horizon now. The time to act was soon.

50

From her spot on the ridge, Gamay watched. Wearing high-desert camouflage, she had wrapped a tawny scarf around her head and neck to complete the disguise. She carried a modified Heckler & Koch G36 assault rifle. It had an extended barrel, a high-powered scope and two fold-out legs to steady it for long-range shooting.

This particular weapon had come from a target-shooting enthusiast they'd found in Cajamarca. It wasn't a sniper's rifle, but it was lightweight, accurate and the best they could procure on short notice.

Staring through the high-powered scope, she'd watched the helicopter's arrival and departure; sighted the old Toyota, as it drove off to the south; and followed Paul and Joe, as they were marched back to the beach and placed under guard again.

Not long after that, a white Jeep Cherokee came rumbling down the path. It pulled off the road and several men climbed out of it. They wore blue flight suits. They spoke with Urco and were led over to the Air-Crane.

With each passing minute, Gamay felt the danger grow. Whatever Urco was up to, he would soon have no need for hostages.

She pulled back the sleeve of her camouflage jacket. Kurt had been silent a long time. Had he been anyone else, she'd have assumed he was drowned by now. Still, she couldn't wait much longer.

"Come on, Kurt," she whispered. "This is no time to be late."

Having moved to a firing position, Gamay was more exposed, but she hadn't seen the slightest sign of anyone looking for her.

Finally, the tiny speaker in the earbud came to life. *"Gamay, this is Kurt."*

"Who else would it be," she said. "Glad you didn't drown. A lot has happened since you went on radio silence. By the look of it, Urco's dispersing the mixed-state matter. Selling it off piece by piece. The Chinese landed and took off with two units. Emma drove out of here with another unit in the back of a Land Cruiser."

"If this was about money, he could have named his price and any one of the three countries involved would have paid it. But instead he wants us all to pay — in blood."

470

"What do you mean?"

"I found replicas of the fuel cells in a cave where Urco's people were hiding. I also found a crate of Semtex that was several bricks short, but I couldn't find a single detonator. That tells me the rest are already in place — most likely, in the fuel cells."

"In the fuel cells," she said. "But if he blows them up —"

"He gets a catastrophe," Kurt said. *"Which is exactly what he wants. A catastrophe for the Americans, the Russians and the Chinese. Or, more likely, for the entire industrialized world."*

"What purpose could that possibly serve him?"

"Payback," Kurt said. *"For what the industrial powers did to the indigenous tribes of South America five hundred years ago. For what he feels they're still doing today. By dispersing the mixed-state matter the way he is and then detonating it, he can strike a crushing blow to China, Europe, America and whoever else he blames for the fate of the native people. He can set industrialization back a thousand years in most of the world while his people are safe in their mountain pastures, living a technology-free life."*

Gamay listened as Kurt explained his theory. "The Chinese are already gone," she

471

said. "Emma's out of sight as well."

"We stop Urco first and get to them after."

A flash of light caught Gamay's eye. A dull whine reaching her on the wind.

She looked back through the scope. The two men in the blue flight suits were still in the Air-Crane. The rotors had begun to turn, moving slowly, reflecting the sunlight.

She could see that the cables leading to the *Nighthawk* had been reattached. The cargo bay had been sealed shut.

"You'd better hurry," she said. "I think the Russians are about to take the rest in the Air-Crane."

"I thought I heard it starting up," Kurt said. *"I'm on the move now. Wait for my signal and then drop the hammer. Get the men guarding Paul and Joe first. Once they're down, fire at will. Take out everyone you can, but don't risk hitting the* Nighthawk. *And, remember — I'm the guy in the black wet suit."*

51

Having finished his climb, Kurt moved across the upper part of the landing area of the plateau, darting from one patch of scrub foliage to another in quick, crouching movements.

He was halfway across when the Air-Crane lifted off, rising on a whirlwind of dust, blinding anyone who was foolish enough to open his eyes and look into it.

As it gained altitude, it drew up the same steel cables that had been attached to the *Nighthawk* in the water. They snaked across the ground, rising slowly, until they were taut with tension and the black spacecraft came up slowly off the ground.

The two linked aircraft rotated until they were pointing to the southeast. Finally, they began to move, traveling so cautiously at first that they barely appeared to be making any progress.

With all eyes on the departing craft and

no chance that he would be heard, Kurt rushed in. He charged the nearest of Urco's men, tackled the man in a flying leap and slammed him to the ground. A short scuffle ended when Kurt landed a knockout punch.

He grabbed his radio. "I'm in the clearing and armed. Open fire."

Gamay had been waiting for a call, tracking the men who were guarding Paul and Joe. Taught to shoot by her father at a young age, she'd been around guns all her life. And though she preferred to avoid violence, she'd shot at attackers and been shot at more than a few times during her years with NUMA. It was the nature of the job. Still, as she steadied the barrel and aimed at the men in the clearing she realized this was something she had never done before.

The discomfort vanished as one of the men pulled out his pistol and moved in behind Joe.

Gamay exhaled and pulled the trigger.

The rifle cracked. The man with the pistol dropped to his knees and fell over on his side. Before he hit the ground, Gamay adjusted her aim and fired again, this time hitting the guard that was standing over by Paul.

She saw him tumble, pulled the trigger

again for good measure and then switched her sights to a third target. By now, the men were racing in all directions. Her fourth shot winged one of them; her fifth may or may not have struck home as another of Urco's crew dove back into the tall grass.

Down on the rocky beach, Joe heard the rifle shot and thought it sounded like deliverance. He pulled and twisted the new zip tie that had been wrapped around his wrists. It hadn't been weakened as much as the prior one, but he'd been working on it.

Another shot rang out and then another. The men around them were falling dead or running for safety when Joe finally snapped the restraint.

He immediately grabbed a sharp-edged rock he'd been eyeing and rushed over to Paul.

With a quick pull, Paul was cut free. Joe tossed the rock aside, exchanging it for the pistol in the dead man's hand.

Joe pointed to the ridge that he assumed Gamay to be firing from. "Get to the bottom of the bluff."

"Where are you going?"

"To find Urco."

Paul turned over another of the men Gamay had shot and retrieved a weapon of his own. "Let's go."

As Gamay fired from the high ridge, Kurt came in low and fast. He'd taken out two of Urco's men, commandeered a shotgun and rushed forward with it. He wanted to capture Urco, but his surviving men were making things difficult.

Kurt shot one of them as the man sprayed a clip of bullets up at the hills, hoping to hit the sniper.

Rushing past the dead man, he pumped the shotgun and fired at a man who'd taken cover in some bushes. The blast ripped the bush to shreds and left the man lying on the ground, bleeding.

Kurt rushed over to him and kicked the rifle from his hand. "Urco?"

The man pointed, his finger extending unsteadily toward the path that had been hacked in the grass.

Kurt glanced in that direction and noticed something being thrown toward them from up above. He sprinted and then dove away, launching himself into the grass just as the brick of Semtex detonated.

The explosion rang in Kurt's ears, momentarily flattened the field of green stalks and rained dirt on him for several long seconds. He was far enough away to avoid serious injury.

The man who'd pointed to Urco was not so lucky.

Kurt was about to move forward when someone tapped him on the leg.

He spun around with his weapon. But instead of enemies, he saw the smiling face of Joe Zavala. Paul Trout was just behind him.

"For a ghost, you're made of surprisingly solid material," Joe said.

Kurt grinned. "And easy to sneak up on," he said. "Glad to see you both. Believe it or not, I think we're winning, primarily thanks to Gamay's shooting."

"She'll be hard to live with after saving us," Paul said. "But well worth it."

"How many of them are down?"

"Four down below," Joe said.

"And I took out three," Kurt said.

"That leaves only Urco," Joe said. "Trust me, I've been counting them obsessively."

Kurt pointed to the high ground. "He's up there. But I have a feeling he'll be lobbing bombs at us if we move his way."

"Maybe Gamay can hit him from her position," Paul suggested.

Kurt pulled out the radio, gave Gamay a status report and made the request.

"He's up there, all right," Gamay insisted.

"And he's alone. But he's not defenseless."

"We got a taste of the explosives," Kurt said. "I'm not interested in a second course. Can you hit him?"

"Maybe," she replied. *"But there's a problem with that plan."*

"Which is . . . ?"

"He seems to have anticipated this," she said. *"He's crouched behind the last of the containment units. And he's got his pistol up against the housing as if it was a living human hostage."*

Just then, Urco's booming voice called out to them. "This violence has gone on long enough," he shouted. "Throw down your weapons. Or I'll destroy us all."

52

The battlefield went silent in the wake of Urco's words. Kurt glanced at Joe. "Apparently, we're not winning . . . yet."

"We could rush him from three sides," Joe offered.

"The last thing I want is for him to panic."

The radio came alive with Gamay's voice. *"I might be able to get a head shot if he moves,"* she said. *"But if I miss . . ."*

"Even if you hit him square, he might squeeze that trigger," Kurt replied. They had to try something else. He handed Joe the radio. "I'm going to walk up there."

"He'll shoot you down."

"Hopefully," Kurt said. "And when he does, you guys drop him."

Joe looked at Kurt quizzically.

"Clue Gamay in," Kurt said. "Once I get moving up the path, you two move through the grass. I'll try to keep him talking as long as possible."

Kurt stood slowly. He raised the shotgun over his head with both hands like a surrendering soldier. Carrying it high, he walked out of the grass, across the clearing and up the snaking path to the higher ground.

He arrived at the upper clearing and found Urco crouching behind the last containment unit with the pistol up against one of the cryogenic tubes.

Kurt tossed the shotgun away as soon as they made eye contact.

Urco stared. "Austin," he said quietly. "And in far better condition than I was led to believe."

"Disappointed?" Kurt asked.

"Surprised. Vargas does not often fail at his tasks. Nor does he lie. Not to me. He said you were bleeding out at the bottom of the lake."

"Don't be too angry with him," Kurt replied. "He cut the red dye packet in my vest. Must have thought he'd sliced me deep. An accidental deception. Unlike the one you've created for the world. I have to hand it to you, not many people have the guts to manipulate the three most powerful nations on Earth."

"I took advantage of an opportunity," Urco said. "Nothing more."

Kurt shook his head. "It's a little late for false modesty, don't you think? You pulled the strings. We danced. You wanted the *Nighthawk* raised and you got us to raise it for you. You needed someone to pluck it out of the air for you and you convinced the Russians to build a pair of hypersonic bombers to catch it for you. When they needed money — cash-strapped as they are — you manipulated the Chinese into partnering up with them. And you did it with nothing but words. Unless I'm mistaken, you have no money, no political power, no weapons, nothing but that brilliant mind of yours."

Urco was too smart not to see Kurt's flattery for what it was, but he was also too full of himself not to hang on every word.

"I've fought with terrorists, foreign governments and even billionaires with private armies at their beck and call," Kurt added. "And I honestly doubt that I've ever met a more dangerous man. Congratulations, Urco. Or should I call you the Falconer?"

Urco's chin rose at the sound of the name. Intrigued, his gaze hardened on Kurt. "So you know a thing or two as well. Tell me, where did you hear that name?"

"From the cockpit voice recorder we found in the wreckage of *Blackjack 1,*" Kurt said. "It survived, even if the pilots didn't. You were on *Blackjack 2;* you were the reason the *Nighthawk* suddenly came back to life again when the Russians thought it had been shut down. And you ignored their pleas to reboot the system with the alpha code. That's why the camera footage from La Jalca was filmed by someone using their right hand. Because you weren't there to film it yourself."

Urco stared at Kurt and then nodded.

"A brilliant scheme," Kurt continued. "You parceled out just enough information to lead us all along by the nose. The part I couldn't understand until recently was, why?"

"Avarice affects even the purest of hearts," Urco responded.

Kurt had him talking. It was now a conversation. That was Kurt's advantage. He began to walk slowly as he spoke. "Greed is not your game. If it was, you could have contacted any one of the three nations and demanded a huge sum be transferred to a numbered account in return for the *Nighthawk*'s location. After all, you were the only one who knew where it was. But you didn't. You teased us all along, brought us all in close. As you said at our dinner the other night, the feast cannot begin until *all the guests are present and accounted for.* You didn't sell the mixed-state matter. You gave it away, a portion to each nation that sought it."

Urco became agitated at Kurt's accusations. "I was paid in gems."

"All part of the act," Kurt said. "A nice touch in your little drama of revenge. But wealth will do nothing for you when the world comes crashing down. I know what you have in mind. I saw the replica fuel cells in the cave. I found your explosives."

Urco seemed unnerved by the fact that Kurt had uncovered so much. He held the pistol against the containment unit, but his eyes were focused on Kurt.

"What's the point in hiding the truth?" Kurt said, pressing harder. "This is the end. Either the end of your world or the end of ours. Do you really want to go out pretending you did this for money? That's the motivation of an industrialist, of a conquistador, of Pizarro and Columbus and every other European who came to the New World. Do you want to throw your lot in with the people who decimated the Inca and Chachapoya?"

"*Decimated,*" Urco repeated angrily, his voice rose sharply. "The term means *to kill one in ten.* The Europeans and their filth

483

didn't leave one in ten alive. Their plagues wiped out ninety-five percent of those who lived here. They raped and enslaved the rest. Polluted our blood with theirs. For three-quarters of a century, we've labeled the evil actions of the Nazis and the purges of Stalin with terms like *Holocaust* and *genocide,* but they were nothing compared to what happened here!"

Urco's sudden furor unbalanced him as Kurt had hoped it would.

"No one alive today had anything to do with that," Kurt said, moving closer.

"It's still occurring today," he shouted. "You point to the past as if the murder and dislocation of the innocent happened once and then ended, but it continues even now. Every hour of every day. Not just here or in the Amazon but in Africa, Asia, the outback of Australia and the cold expanses of the Arctic. The last vestiges of the original peoples are threatened by the *children of the machine.* There is no hope of accommodation. The way industrial people spread like a virus, there will soon be no room left for any other way of life. It has to be stopped. I am the one to stop it. And this is the only way."

"One bomb for America, one bomb for China, one for someone else and the rest —

the vast majority — to make Europe into an inferno as the Russian bomber passes over it. Is that your idea of revenge?"

"Justice." Urco seethed. "Long delayed. An eye for an eye. One genocide for another."

"You can't think you won't be affected here."

"We live off the land, as do all the children of the soil. You live off the energy of automation and mechanical power. That reliance on industrialization will be your undoing. Without equipment to do their bidding, the children of the machine will starve; they will die of thirst and of heat and of cold. They will destroy one another fighting over what's left. The children of the soil will simply return to what they've always known."

Urco went cold and the conversation ended.

Kurt edged closer.

"That's far enough," he said. "One more step and I'll kill us all." Urco pulled the hammer back and cocked it. The fate of the world now hung on a hair-trigger response of a man who was literally shaking with anger.

"No," Kurt said. "I don't think you will."

"Don't test me," Urco said. "I am more than willing to die."

"Oh, I'm sure you are," Kurt said. "But your plan . . . You're not thinking this through. You can't pull that trigger now. Your other bombs are too close. This one is too powerful. It's a thousand Hiroshimas, maybe five thousand. If you set it off, the shock wave and fireball will engulf the Russians in our stolen helicopter. That will set off a second reaction. The combined effects of which will obliterate Emma Townsend on the road to Cajamarca, triggering a third explosion.

"Even if the Chinese have somehow transferred their containment units to a long-range transport headed for Asia, they can't have gone far. Certainly not far enough to escape the effect of three small suns igniting a hundred miles away. The same shock wave you intend to use on the industrial civilizations of the world will swat that plane out of midair. The gamma rays and EMP burst will fry the circuitry and melt the containment unit. One way or another, that fourth ticking bomb of yours will go off. It *will* be a cataclysm, but it'll be South America that bears the brunt of the disaster and the *children of the machine* who come to render assistance."

Urco's jaw clenched as Kurt spoke. It was possible he'd already thought it through.

Was it even possible that he'd never considered it? But he saw it now, saw it exactly how Kurt had laid it out for him.

Kurt took another step. The only thing he needed to do was prevent Urco from firing by accident.

"Stay where you are!"

"It's over, Urco!"

"I will pull this trigger," Urco shouted. "It will still be a cataclysm. And it will affect your society far more than it affects those who live in the jungles, the tundra or the distant plains."

Kurt was close enough now that he could see the flaring of Urco's nostrils and the wildness in his eyes. He watched a bead of sweat run down his temple and his knuckles turn white on the pistol grip.

"You've got one move left," Kurt said. "One shot. It's either the bomb . . . Or me."

Urco was shaking with fury. A second drop of perspiration trickled down his face. It ran down his beard and stopped for the slightest instant before dropping onto the containment unit. It hit and froze instantly on the supercooled pipe. "Damn you!" he shouted.

With a shift of his shoulders, Urco snapped the pistol upward, swinging it toward Kurt.

Kurt dove away as two shots rang out almost simultaneously. One near and one sounding off in the distance.

Urco was thrown to the side by the rifle shot, which hit him in the ribs beneath his outstretched arm. He crashed to the ground, still grasping the pistol. Joe rushed forward, leapt on top of him and punched the gun away before he could attempt to fire again.

Kurt looked up from where he'd landed. Urco's shot had missed. The barrel had stuck momentarily to the frost-covered cylinder of the containment unit. He rushed over to assist Joe.

"He's bleeding out fast," Joe said.

They tried to stanch the bleeding, but the bullet had gone through his body. Too many organs had been hit and damaged. Too much tissue had been torn up.

Kurt gave up trying to save Urco and attempted to force one last answer out of him.

"You're going to die," he said. "Don't take half the world with you. Tell me how to stop what you've set in motion."

Urco gazed at Kurt blankly.

"We'll come back here. We'll help your people and the other people. You're not wrong about what's been and is being done, but you have to help us first."

Urco looked at him. "I almost . . . believe you," he said in a whisper. His eyes were unfocused. "It's too late," he said. "What goes up . . . will never . . . come down."

53

Urco died without saying anything more. Joe and Paul gathered up the dead and the two survivors. Gamay came running from her hiding place and embraced Paul.

"My compliments to your shooting instructor," Joe said.

"I'll tell my father," she said, then turned to Kurt. "That was some game of brinksmanship."

"I figured he'd put so much into his plan that he'd do anything but short-circuit it now."

"What if you'd been wrong?"

"Simple math," he said. "One obliterated continent is better than four."

"Marginally," she said.

"You'll get no argument from me," Kurt replied.

"Any idea where this last unit was supposed to go?" Paul asked.

"I heard Urco's men mentioning something about Rio," Kurt said.

"Considering how much deforestation is occurring in the Amazon, it would make sense to wipe out the largest city on the continent in hopes of putting a stop to it," Joe said. "But now what?"

Kurt was grim. "We've won the battle, but we're losing the war. We need to warn the Chinese and the Russians and get in touch with the NSA."

They searched both the camp and Urco's men for any form of long-distance communication. All they found were short-range walkie-talkies, their own satellite phones, which had been destroyed, and Urco's computer with its bulky satellite antenna.

After twenty minutes of trying, Paul said, "I've seen this before. It's a multistep security program. Even if we could get past the first level, there's probably a second layer of encryption to get through before we can access the satellite communications suite."

They pressed the two survivors for information, but they could get nothing out of them.

"We don't have time for this," Kurt said. "We'll have to do this the old-fashioned way. Up close and personal."

"We've only got one vehicle and three

mega-bombs to chase down," Joe noted.

"We'll have to split up," Kurt said. "You and I will go after the Russians. Paul, you and Gamay take that Jeep Cherokee and see if you can catch Emma."

"She has an armed escort," Paul noted.

"Then deal with him."

"What about the Chinese?" Gamay mentioned. "They've got to be airborne by now."

Kurt glanced at his watch. There was nothing they could do about the Chinese at the moment. "It's a long flight to Beijing; maybe we can figure out how to defuse the bombs and talk to them before they land."

Without wasting any time, they carried the last containment unit down the path and out to the narrow dirt road where the Cherokee waited. After loading and securing it, Paul and Gamay got moving. There were no good-byes. Time was too short.

As Paul and Gamay drove off, Kurt and Joe set about to chase down the Russians. The first problem was, knowing where to find them.

"They flew directly over that notch in the ridge and kept on going," Joe said. "I can't see any reason they wouldn't be flying in a straight line to whatever destination they had in mind. And considering the weight and control problems I encountered carrying the *Nighthawk,* they can't seriously hope to get too far."

"I think I know where they're going," Kurt said. "Remember the audio from the first bomber's crash? The pilot of *Blackjack 1* was in a panic when the *Nighthawk* began to break free. He was shouting for the Falconer to use the reset codes on the *Nighthawk.* He was calling to *Blackjack 2.*"

"And Urco was the Falconer."

Kurt nodded. "Which means *Blackjack 2* did not crash. It landed safely, and probably in the near vicinity. All we have to do is find the closest airfield."

"There is one," Joe said. "About seven miles from here. When I was planning our route, I saw it on the map."

"That's a long hike," Kurt said. "We'd better get to it."

"We don't need to hike it," Joe said. "At least not all the way. The river passes within a mile of the runway. We can take the Zodiac. It'll save us hours."

54

The seven-mile flight of the Air-Crane would be its last, thought Major Timonovski of the Russian Air Force. The big helicopter was struggling to carry the load in the thin mountain air. The engine temperatures were in the yellow before they'd made it halfway. But with the *Nighthawk*'s nine tons of mass slung beneath them, Timonovski did not dare speed up.

"Red light on engine number two," the flight engineer said.

"What is it?" Timonovski asked.

"Metal shavings in the oil pan. The main rotor — its transmission is coming apart. We need to put this bird down."

Timonovski heard the strain in the engineer's voice but shook it off. "We're almost there," he said.

He could see the outline of the runway up ahead. *Blackjack 2* was there, no longer covered in the shroud of netting and tarps that the Birdcaller had wrapped around it. Another aircraft was there on the runway as well. A small turboprop.

Ignoring the warning lights, Timonovski brought the orange helicopter and the stolen American spacecraft over the last line of trees and down toward the hard-packed airstrip. A man on the ground flashed a light at them in Morse code.

"So the Birdcaller tells the truth, for once," he said. After so many lies and tricks, Timonovski half expected to be met by American agents or perhaps the Chinese. "Contact them on the low-frequency channel."

The flight engineer dialed up the correct frequency and engaged in a rapid-fire conversation. "They want us to land the *Nighthawk* on top of the bomber," he told Timonovski. "Can we stay airborne that long?"

"I would rather put it down on the side of the runway, but once we land this helicopter, it will never take off again."

"That's what I thought," the flight engineer said. "What should I tell them?"

Timonovski didn't hesitate. "We chance it."

He angled toward the sitting bomber, pulled up next to it and put the helicopter into a sideways slip. With a deft touch, he eased them over the resting bomber until they were centered and began to lower the American craft toward it.

The first attempt ended in failure as the swirling downwash of the rotors continued to twist the suspended craft. The second attempt was no better.

"I can't keep it lined up," Timonovski said.

"We need to put it down," the flight engineer said. "We're going to lose the gearbox any minute."

"One more try," Timonovski said.

This time, as he moved in, the men from the ground crew appeared on the back of the bomber. They grabbed the *Nighthawk* with their bare hands, hooked ropes around the nose and tail and used their combined weight to arrest the twisting motion. With their help, Timonovski steered the *Nighthawk* into position and felt it bump softly against the armored spine of the bomber.

"Down and locked," the flight engineer said. "I'm releasing the cable."

With an audible snap, the cables were disconnected. The Air-Crane rose quickly in response — and did so with dark smoke pouring from the transmission housing.

A horrible grinding noise soon drowned out the roar of the engines and Timonovski knew they'd lost the gearbox.

"Hold on," he shouted, angling away from the bomber, the *Nighthawk* and the ground crew.

The smoking helicopter peeled off with what little power remained and then began to fall. Timonovski did what he could to counter the loss of control, but the craft had become unstable. They hit near the shoulder of the runway.

The impact bent the right landing strut and the Air-Crane went over. The rotors struck the ground and shattered into deadly fragments, most of which flew mercifully into the trees.

As the helicopter came to rest on its side, Timonovski shut down the engines and cut the fuel. He turned to see the flight engineer bailing out through the door.

By the time Timonovski pulled off his seat belt and caught up with the engineer, half a dozen members of the ground crew had closed in around them. One was spraying foam from a fire extinguisher toward the engine compartment. Black smoke belched from the vents, but there was no flame.

"Evil things," said a voice among the crowd.

The Major spied Constantin Davidov. To have the head of the directorate out in the field was a rare sight indeed. The old war-horse was beaming as he rushed forward.

"Evil things?" Major Timonovski asked. "What things would those be?"

"Helicopters," Davidov explained. "Unnatural, noisy and ugly. Little more than torture devices, in my opinion."

The Major didn't know about Davidov's long ride from Kamchatka to the cruiser *Varyag* in the *Carrier Pigeon*. But he knew better than to question the boss. "If you say so."

"I do," Davidov replied, "But they have their uses."

"And their limits," Timonovski replied. "As do we all." He pointed to *Blackjack 2,* with the *Nighthawk* sitting proudly on its back. "We'll never get off the runway. The field is too short. The trees too high. I told the Birdcaller as much."

"And he listened," Davidov said. "I've brought the RATO boosters. With the rockets to assist us, and a few of those trees chainsawed to the ground, we'll make it without a problem. The ground crew are attaching the boosters as we speak."

Timonovski squinted. He could see the ground crew hooking up the stubby missile-like canisters to the hardpoints beneath the bomber's wings. It was a complex process.

"It seems the Falconer thought of everything."

"Yes," Davidov agreed. "It seems he did."

55

Emma's route to Cajamarca took her through a wide valley and then up through a narrow pass. At first the road was flat and hemmed in by the mountains, but as they came out of the pass the road began to look like the one she and Kurt had dealt with on the way up. Only now it was dusk and growing darker by the moment.

She had the high beams on, along with the small fog lamps under the bumper and two auxiliary lights mounted on the roof rack. They lit the road well enough, but the drop beyond the narrow shoulder was nothing more than a dark void.

"When this is over, I'm moving to Kansas," she said.

"What's Kansas?"

The question came from Reyes, the escort Urco had sent with her. He sat in the passenger seat, cocked to the side and holding a 9mm pistol in his hand.

If she drove too fast or too slow, he gave her a dirty look and then complained. Right now she must have been doing fine since he was leaning back and the Beretta was resting on his lap, aimed roughly at her thigh.

"Kansas," she said, "is a very flat part of America. None of these mountains to climb or cliffs to fall off."

His brow furrowed.

"Never mind," she said. "I can imagine how that sounds to someone who lives here."

He said nothing, leaned forward to glance at the speedometer and then leaned back again.

"Are we on a schedule?" she asked.

He didn't reply. Maybe they were.

"Urco didn't need to send you along, you know."

"I'm here to make sure you do as you promised."

"Why wouldn't I?" she asked, rounding a curve. "It's, literally, the only sane thing to do."

He shrugged.

"And, anyway, what would you do if I refused? Or changed my mind?"

She was just talking, just making conversation on the long drive and perhaps hoping to make him see her as a human being instead of a target. But she'd hit a nerve.

"I shoot you and drive there by myself."

"Really?" she said, surprised and not surprised all at the same time. "And then what? Just going to hand over the containment unit and tell my colleagues you're a Good Samaritan who picked it up on the side of the road? For that matter, how would you even find them without me?"

The answer came to her even before she'd finished asking the question. "Oh, you have a phone," she said. "You have *my* phone."

At almost the same moment, both of them realized that he'd given something away.

A phone could deliver help. It could summon a rescue team to the lake and military units to swarm over Urco and his followers. *Her* phone could turn the entire situation on its head.

"Pull over," he said.

"No," she said. "It's okay. Let's just drive to Cajamarca."

"Pull the car over!"

From there, everything happened in a flash. Reyes shouted again and leveled the pistol at her head. She realized this might be her only chance to act and slammed hard on the brakes. The sudden deceleration caused his extended arm to swing forward. His hand smacked against the dashboard and the pistol discharged into the windshield.

As the glass shattered, Emma swung her right arm toward him. Her hand was stiff, her fingers outstretched. The edge of her palm caught him in the throat, a perfect backhand to his Adam's apple.

The blow crushed his windpipe and Reyes dropped the pistol.

Her foot went to the accelerator, slamming it to the floor. He fell back now, thrown off balance again.

As he reeled in the seat, she reached down for the pistol, trying to pluck it off the floor. Her fingers brushed it, but before she could pick it up, he did the unthinkable, lunging for the steering wheel and pushing it hard to the right.

The wheels turned sharply. The Toyota skidded and then went over on its side. The windshield blew out and the old SUV slid toward the far edge of the road and the cliff beyond. It went halfway over the edge and crashed headlong into a gnarled tree that grew from the side of a steep slope and stopped.

The impact knocked Emma unconscious. Whether it was seconds or a minute or more, she didn't know. When she woke up, she was lying on her side and pinned by the steering wheel. A hissing sound could be heard, and she was surrounded by a cloud of steam that was venting from the Toyota's shattered radiator.

Reyes was nowhere to be seen. And with the damaged windshield completely missing, she assumed he'd been ejected.

"That was foolish," she grunted, angry at herself. Angry at him as well, wherever he was.

She twisted around, felt a spike of pain shoot through her ribs and laid eyes on the containment unit. It remained in place, strapped down as it had been.

Emma stretched far enough to reach the control panel. As her fingers touched the screen, it lit up. The indicators were all green. Power was still flowing through the unit. The magnetic bottles were intact and the cryogenic system was still operating.

"Thank God, they didn't give this contract to the lowest bidder," she whispered.

For obvious reasons, the units were incredibly durable and well made. They'd been designed to survive years in space, cosmic radiation, extremes of heat, cold and pressure, not to mention the turbulence and vibration of reentry and landing or even a minor crash.

Fortunately, the one car accident was not

more severe than those conditions.

All Emma had to do was get out of the Land Cruiser, find her former guard and hope that the phone in his pocket had survived his ejection and landing in the road.

She pushed against the steering column that had been loosened by the blow against the tree until she was able to shove it far enough to slide her legs free. Then she pulled them up toward her and eased into a sitting position.

With the Toyota over on its side and the front windshield gone, the easiest way out was forward. Sitting where the driver's window had been, she swung her legs forward. They stretched through the empty space where the windshield had been and touched . . . nothing.

Emma froze. Her legs were dangling as if she was sitting on a swing . . . or a ledge. She looked beneath her. There was ground against the cabin where her side window had been, but it fell away near the front edge.

She leaned forward, grabbing the seat belt for stability. As the steam from the radiator began to dissipate, the rooftop lights played out into the darkness, touching the ground three hundred feet below.

The Land Cruiser was already pointed downward at an angle. The only thing keeping it from dropping was the gnarled tree it had run into.

Emma pulled her legs back in and shifted her weight to climb out the top. A barely audible crack from the tree trunk and a subtle shift in the Toyota's position told her that moving was a bad idea. She went still, wondering how long the tree would hold.

56

Kurt and Joe made excellent time in the Zodiac. They ran with the engine wide open and the current at their backs. A few sets of minor rapids caused little problem and they'd soon traversed twelve miles on the looping river, enabling them to move nearly seven miles as the crow flies — or the *Nighthawk* flew.

"This is as close as we're going to get," Joe said, navigating based on his memory of the chart and the time.

"I'm ready," Kurt said. "Let's go on foot."

Kurt had changed into regular clothes, and both men were wearing their boots. As soon as Joe beached the Zodiac, they leapt off and began a hike that would be more of a sprint than a walk.

Darkness had fallen, the night air had cooled dramatically and the stars had come out. They shone up above like diamonds on black velvet. Using the stars to navigate,

Kurt and Joe continued to cross the rocky ground, moving toward the airfield.

A few yards behind Joe, Kurt felt his knees begin to ache from old football injuries.

"You're getting slow in your old age," Joe needled.

"While some of us were sitting around all day, I was working," Kurt said.

"Floating on the lake in an inner tube doesn't count as work where I come from," Joe said.

"I've basically created my own kind of extreme triathlon," Kurt insisted. "Swim under a waterfall, climb up a sheer cliff and now a 2K uphill run in the rarefied air at ten thousand feet of altitude."

"Under a waterfall?" Joe said. "Why didn't you swim around it?"

"I tried," Kurt admitted. "Not as easy as it sounds."

Joe laughed. "I just hope all this running is worth it and we haven't missed our flight."

Kurt was hoping that, too. There was no way to know until they got there, but having lived near several air bases during his time in the Air Force, Kurt knew how far the roar of military jet engines carried. "Unless they launched while we were in those rapids, I think we'd have heard a supersonic bomber taking off; I'm sure they'll need full afterburners to do it."

A droning sound rolling across the plateau stopped the conversation. Both Kurt and Joe slowed down to listen.

"Turboprop," Joe said, turning until he was facing the sound. The droning grew louder and picked up an odd resonance as a second engine came online.

"They may have switched planes," Kurt said.

The hike turned into a dead sprint, and with the sound of the turboprop to hone in on, they never wavered. They were still rushing toward the edge of the airstrip when the small plane clawed its way into the night sky, banked to the northeast and flew off into the dark.

"If we get to the Air-Crane," Joe said, "we can use the radios. And get them back before they get too high."

Both men kept running. They arrived at the outskirts of the airstrip, breathing hard and dropping down beside a pine tree for cover.

The Air-Crane was visible across the field, lying on its side and smoking. "The radios probably still work," Joe said. "But the antennas might be sheared off."

Kurt pointed to a second outline in the gloom, darker than dark, sinister in shape.

Blackjack 2 was still there, with the *Night-hawk* perched on top.

"They wouldn't have bothered placing it so carefully if they were going to leave it behind."

57

Paul drove as fast as he dared in the Jeep Cherokee. Considering the cargo he was hauling, the type of road and the utter darkness of the moonless night, he was being positively reckless at forty miles per hour.

Sitting beside him, dividing her attention between the portable apocalypse machine they were carrying and the map, Gamay seemed to want him to go faster. "I can only hope Emma is being as careful as we are," she said. "For a variety of reasons."

Paul had seen the map earlier. He knew it was a race they couldn't win. "We'll never catch her. The last forty miles into Cajamarca are paved and relatively flat. Once she hits that section, we'll be left in the dust."

"Maybe we can flag down another car or truck," Gamay suggested. "If we're lucky, they might have a radio or a phone."

"It would have to be a satellite phone up

here," Paul said. "But maybe as we get closer to town." He glanced over at the map. "Coming in from the south, she still has to drive through most of the city before she gets to the airport. That might give us some —"

A shout from Gamay cut him off. "Paul, look out!"

Paul looked up. A man's body lay in the road, crumpled and broken. Paul hit the brakes, veered around it and brought the vehicle safely to a halt. The body was behind them now, but what loomed ahead was even more surprising. A vehicle tipped over on its side, its front end dangling over the edge of the cliff and held up by the Y-shaped trunk of a tree.

Paul put the transmission in park and grabbed the door handle. As he swung it open, he felt Gamay's hand on his.

"We're not on some backcountry road, Paul," she said. "We don't have time for this."

There was cold reason in her voice, but only because she hadn't realized what Paul had already ascertained. "It's Emma."

Gamay's eyes lit up. She looked at the stricken vehicle and nodded.

Paul and Gamay jumped out of the Cherokee, rushing toward the overturned Toyota.

The front end was out over the cliff, jammed into the gnarled trunk of the tree. The back end was up in the air, and the entire vehicle was pointing downward as if it were ready to slide off the edge.

The engine was ticking and pinging, while fluids dripped everywhere. The entire balancing act looked so precarious that Paul's first instinct was not to touch anything.

"Emma!" he called out. "Are you in there?"

"Hello?!" a female voice replied from inside the vehicle.

"Emma, this is Paul," he shouted, easing around the side. The angle of the vehicle and the condition of the ledge made it impossible to get at the front end. "Gamay and I are here. We're going to get you out of there."

"Forget about me," Emma said, her voice suddenly firm. "Just get the containment unit out. Pull it out through the back. It's a miracle it hasn't gone off-line already. But trust me, I'm staring into the abyss, and if we fall into this canyon, it's all over."

Paul moved around to the back end of the SUV and pulled the hatchback open. The door moved slowly and awkwardly, and even that small shift had consequences. The vehicle rocked forward and then back before settling.

"There's a small problem with that plan," Paul said, studying the situation. "If we remove the containment unit, the center of gravity will move forward, and unless that tree is a lot stronger than it looks, the whole thing will go over with you inside."

"I know that," Emma said. "I've been sitting here for a long time thinking about it. But there's no other choice. There's no other way. Every time I've tried to move, we've slid farther down. Please, just get that thing out of here before we go."

Emma might have been willing to throw away her life, but Paul wasn't so quick to give up. "All we need is more weight on the back end," he said. "I weigh at least as much as the containment unit and twice as much as you. If I climb on the back bumper . . ."

"The problem is the tree," Emma said. "It's already splitting down the middle; the extra weight might snap it and send us down. Just get that damned thing out of there and let me go."

"We can pull it back," Gamay said. "We could use the bungee cords that are holding down our containment unit and the jumper cables we found in the back of the Cherokee."

"It's not going to be enough to pull a five-thousand-pound vehicle uphill," Paul said. "But it could be enough to keep it from sliding down."

"Someone will still have to get in there to disconnect the ropes they used to tie their unit down," Gamay replied.

"*Someone*'s already in there," Paul said. "She can loosen everything on her way out."

Inside the Toyota, Emma listened as Paul explained the plan. It required her to climb over the seats, unhook the nylon rope she'd used to secure the dangerous cargo and wrap the rope around the containment unit several times. Then crawl out the back hatch with the ends of the rope in her hands.

It sounded plausible. And it saved her a trip she didn't want to take. "I can do that," she said.

The light around her changed as Gamay moved the Cherokee into position. She held still while Paul laced the jumper cables and the bungee cords through parts of the overturned vehicle and then did the same on the front bumper of the Jeep.

She felt the Land Cruiser rock back to a flatter angle as the Jeep inched backward and pulled everything taut.

She looked back through the vehicle. Paul

was standing there, shrouded in the light.

"You're up," he said.

Despite a primal urge to get out of the doomed vehicle, Emma simultaneously found herself afraid to move a single muscle. For half an hour, she'd been sitting there listening to creaks and groans coming from both the tree and the Land Cruiser. Sitting still had been her only defense; a part of her didn't want to give that up.

She took a deep breath, steeled herself to do what she had to do and nodded to Paul. "Here goes."

She twisted around to face backward. The vehicle rocked ever so slightly.

She found a spot for her feet, pushed off and shinned into the back.

The Toyota shifted again, not rocking but sliding.

Emma heard the sound of wood splitting and felt her heart pounding. Through the back hatch she saw Paul grasping onto the bumper and pulling as if it were a tug-of-war.

The movement slowed and then stopped and the only sound was the trickle of pebbles and sand sliding out from underneath the SUV and falling down the slope.

"It's okay," Paul said. "We've got it. Keep moving."

She inched forward and eased around the side of the containment unit. "Now for the ropes."

Disconnecting the ropes was fairly easy. And once they were untied, Emma was able to loop them around the containment unit and the attached fuel cell. One loop, two and then a third. That was all the excess length they had.

She pulled it tight, tested the weight and looked up toward Gamay and Paul. "Ready?"

"Whenever you are," Paul replied.

Emma took a deep breath. To get to the back hatch, she had to use her legs. She edged around the unit, put her feet on the back of the passenger seat and pushed.

The force caused the seat back to fold forward.

Emma slid. The containment unit slid. The Land Cruiser tilted downward at a steeper angle and she heard the tree splitting down the middle. She grabbed the seat belt to keep from falling out through the gap and crawled upward once again.

"Hurry!" Gamay shouted.

Emma moved as fast as she could.

The Toyota began to slide forward. Two of the bungee cords snapped.

Emma was climbing at a fifty-degree angle

now, each move worsened the slide. As she neared the top, Paul let go of the bumper and reached in with his long arms. She tried to hand him the ropes, but instead of grabbing them, he clamped his hands around her wrists and pulled her out.

She hit the ground just as the tree split in half.

She turned to see the Toyota sliding off the edge and into the dark. She set her feet and pulled on the ropes with all her might.

As the back end of the Toyota vanished, the containment unit popped free and landed on the edge of the dirt road. With Paul and Gamay's help, she pulled it safely onto level ground.

A resounding crunch followed far below as the Land Cruiser hit a small ledge and tumbled farther down.

The three of them sat there with the ropes clutched tight in their hands like the exhausted winners of an epic tug-of-war.

Only now did it dawn on Emma that Gamay hadn't been with them earlier. "What are you doing here?"

"I came to rescue the boys," Gamay said.

No less confused, Emma crawled to the side of the containment unit to check the readings one more time. Even after the latest bump, everything remained in the green.

"Let's just get this thing on a plane and get it back to the States."

"Not," Paul said, "until after we remove the bomb."

58

Kurt stared at the runway from the edge of the tree line. He could barely believe their luck. *Blackjack 2* was still on the ground, though a pinprick of light moving back and forth suggested it wouldn't remain for long.

"Flashlight," Joe said. "Probably the copilot doing a last-minute inspection before takeoff."

Without warning, one of the bomber's turbines came to life with an electric whine. The sound blossomed into a throaty roar, and a wave of blue fire appeared behind the bomber.

Then twin sets of landing and taxi lights came on. The four blindingly bright beams lit a wide swath of ground up ahead and directly in front of the plane.

"We need to stop that plane from taking off," Kurt said.

"We can get to the plane easy enough," Joe replied. "But then what?"

"We reason with them," Kurt said. "Explain Urco's plan and point out the danger they face."

"And if they ignore us?"

Kurt pulled out the brick of Semtex. "Then we reinforce our argument Teddy Roosevelt style. Let's go."

They stepped out of the tree line, moving cautiously at first and then picking up the pace as the second of the bomber's four engines came to life. The pilot on the ground could be seen hastening his final inspection and then rushing toward the nose gear and the ladder that led up into the plane.

"We're about to miss our flight," Joe said. He rushed ahead as the copilot vanished up into the aircraft's belly.

Kurt sprinted to keep up, but he'd exhausted so much energy, his muscles would not respond.

The ladder began to retract. Joe jumped onto it and the ladder groaned with the weight.

Kurt rushed up seconds later, leapt and caught the bottom rung.

"Add ladder climbing to your Ironman," Joe shouted over the roar of the engines.

Arm over arm, Kurt pulled himself upward until finally he could get a knee on the bottom rung. As soon as he did, the plane lurched forward and began to move.

The movement caused Kurt's knee to slip and he was back to dangling by his arms. Behind him, two of the four engines were screaming in full voice. Their square intakes loomed like mouths ready to devour him, should he fall.

"Come on," Joe said. "Stop playing around."

Kurt pulled himself up, got his knee on the bottom rung and moved higher. As soon as Joe could reach him, he leaned out and grabbed Kurt by the shoulders, yanked him upward and into the plane.

With their weight off of the ladder, it finished retracting and the hatch shut and sealed behind it.

They were in the dark as the bomber turned back into the wind, then the remaining engines came to life and the plane began to roll.

Finally, the floor shifted beneath them, the nose came up and the monstrous bomber, with its wings swept wide, soared up into the air.

"We really have to work on your foot speed," Joe shouted.

"My speed?" Kurt yelled back. "I was counting on you holding the door for me."

The ladder well was dark except for a dim light coming from the inner hatch up above. It was glowing an ominous red.

Joe tested the hatch and shook his head. "It's locked from the other side."

59

The rest of the trip to Cajamarca was uneventful. Along the way, Paul and Gamay explained to Emma what she'd missed. It was a roller coaster of emotion. Hearing that Kurt was alive sent her spirits soaring.

In the end, all that mattered was finding a way to stop the bombs from detonating. Meeting up with NSA agents Hurns and Rodriguez at the airport was the first step.

"We have additional fuel cells on the aircraft," Hurns said. "Is there any chance the containment units themselves have been tampered with?"

Emma shook her head. "The entire unit is sealed. Any tampering or attempt to hide something inside would have caused the mixed-state matter to react. That's why Urco chose to rig up the replica fuel cells."

"Then all we have to do is switch them out and dispose of the bombs."

"Except that we need the bombs," Emma

replied. "The Chinese have been airborne for hours. And barring some incredible stroke of luck, the Russians are flying by now as well. Based on what Urco told Kurt, the bombs are rigged to detonate when the planes descend. The only chance they have is if we figure out what type of detonator they've been connected to, how and why it will go off and, more importantly, how to disarm them."

"Not likely to find a bomb disposal expert in Cajamarca," Hurns noted.

"I know," Emma said. "But we can pipe one in. All we need is a 4K video feed and a high-speed Internet connection. And someone can guide us through step by step."

"Where are you going to find that at this hour?"

Paul spoke up. "We know a place," he said, "where the caffeine never stops and the Internet is strong."

After switching the fuel cells at the airport and watching the NSA Gulfstream take off, Paul, Gamay and Emma drove into town. Calls had been made, cooperation arranged and the buildings around the Internet café evacuated.

They'd set up shop in the back of the café, under the lights where they could stream the 4K video feed back to Washington,

D.C., and the NUMA headquarters building. Their only safety devices were a twelve-gauge shotgun and a cast-iron pot the café used to cook soup.

In front of a camera, Emma took the fuel cell apart. Her audience watched from the NUMA conference room, where Rudi, Hiram, Priya and a bomb disposal expert named Collin Kane, who stared at one of the high-definition displays and told them what to do next.

"Connect that gray wire to the metal leg of the table," Kane said. "Make sure the unit is grounded. You don't want a static spark."

Emma moved cautiously, doing as she was told.

Paul and Gamay were outside, a hundred yards away, watching on a video feed. If Emma blew herself up, they would use what they'd seen and take the next bomb apart — hopefully, learning from her mistake.

"Where do I start?"

"You're going to have to reach in and see if you can free the explosives from the case or if they're attached."

She grounded herself by touching the leg of the table and then reached in and put her hand on the Semtex. She pulled it slowly from the inside of the unit, stopping halfway out. "It's hooked to a pair of wires."

"Do not remove them," Kane warned. "Most likely, they're instant arm-and-detonate wires designed to prevent what we're trying to do."

She found there was enough length to pull the explosives out and set them on the table without disconnecting the trailing wires.

"What next?"

"Using a sharp knife, cut away as much of the Semtex as possible without touching the wires. Take each section you remove and separate it from the rest. When you've cut it down as far as possible, we'll test the detonator."

Emma took a sharp knife and did as instructed. It felt like she was cutting into an apple.

She took the sections to the far side of the room.

"Now you'll have to test the detonator," Kane told her.

"How?"

"It appears to be a touch screen; tap the front."

She tapped the detonator and the screen lit up. The scrolling numbers disappeared and a password screen appeared.

Kane suggested a few ways to get around the password screen, but each was blocked.

On the third attempt, the screen went dark. Two numbers appeared. A green number read 50000; the second number it flashed was a steady 26000.

Suddenly, the first number began to decrease, rolling down like a clock.

"What's happening?"

"A second precaution on their part," Kane said. *"A fail deadly."*

Emma stared, tapping the screen, trying to stop whatever she'd done to trigger the countdown.

"Get rid of it," Kane said.

Emma tried to stop the countdown.

"You've got to secure it now."

"It's still attached to the case."

"Use the shotgun," he said.

Emma grabbed the shotgun, aimed at the detonator and its scrolling numbers and pulled the trigger.

The twelve-gauge blast obliterated the fragile electronic device and scattered the remnants of the Semtex and the fuel cell across the room. There was no explosion, but the room filled with acrid smoke.

Emma lowered the shotgun and sighed.

"Ready to try again?" Kane said.

Emma nodded. "Let's get the second unit in here."

60

Constantin Davidov sat in the copilot's chair watching the pilot and flight engineer run through their tasks. *Blackjack 2* was performing flawlessly. "How's our payload doing?" he asked.

The flight engineer looked over his board and cycled through the video cameras that were pointed at the *Nighthawk*. "Payload secure. No sign of any flutter."

All of them were concerned about a repeat of what happened to *Blackjack 1*.

"Change course to three-five-zero," Davidov said.

Major Timonovski glanced back at him from the captain's seat. "Three-five-zero? That will take us to Cuba. I thought we were refueling over Venezuela and heading home."

"That was the original flight plan, but this aircraft has been through a great deal since then. There is too much risk. We are to land at Manzanillo. An Antonov 124 transport will meet us there. It's large enough to carry the *Nighthawk* internally. It will be safer that way. And it will allow us to move unseen by American eyes."

The pilot nodded and set in the new course.

"Have you ever been to Cuba?" Davidov asked. "Either of you?"

"Not I," Timonovski said.

The flight engineer shook his head. "Nor have I. Have you been there, comrade?"

"Many times," Davidov said. "The first when I was a young man. A thousand years ago, it seems."

They smiled at that. And Davidov was glad to see their spirits perking up. Both men had appeared so gaunt when they'd arrived at the airfield that Davidov had wondered if they were fit to fly. The Falconer had badly mistreated them. Once they got back to Moscow, Davidov would have to decide what to do about that. In the meantime, he wanted to reward the men for a job well done.

"You'll stay in Havana for two weeks, recuperating. Then you'll bring *Blackjack 2* home and we'll put it in a museum. It is my hope you will find the women and weather as comforting as I once did."

"Will you be staying with us?" the pilot asked.

"No," Davidov said. "I'll be transferring to the Antonov to accompany our prize safely home. It's high time we put this operation to —"

Davidov swallowed the last word. Perhaps it was the change in his posture, but he thought he'd felt a subtle thud reverberate through the metal floor. As he waited, the vibration came again and then once more.

Now that he'd clued in to it, Davidov could feel it continuously: . . . *Thud* . . . *Thud* . . . *Thud* . . . A few seconds between each impact.

He pulled off the noise-cancelling headset he wore. The whistle of air over the skin of the bomber became instantly louder, but so did the dull, repetitive impact. "Is the *Nighthawk* secure?"

The flight engineer ran all his checks once more. "No strain on the lockdown bolts. No sign of flutter. It's secure and behaving perfectly."

Davidov continued to detect the vibration. "Do you feel that?"

"Feel what?"

"Something's broken loose," Davidov said. He reached over and pulled the engineer's headset off. "Listen."

The weary flight engineer cocked his head, straining to hear the sound. A life around jet aircraft had dulled his hearing, but he picked it up just the same. He put his hand on the control panel and then slid it downward until it touched the floor. "It's inside."

Davidov felt so, too. "We can't afford a system failure. Not now."

The flight engineer checked his board. "Everything's operating perfectly. It has to be something we don't have a sensor on. I'll go look around."

The engineer slipped out of the shoulder straps, grabbed a flashlight and stepped to the cockpit door. Opening it, he stepped through and into the aft section of the airplane.

Davidov followed, grabbing a flashlight of his own.

The aircraft was huge, larger than the American B-1, which it was based on. It had a cavernous bomb bay and other empty crawl spaces.

He watched as the flight engineer checked one inspection panel after another and then lingered near a small crane that was used to hoist material up through the bomb bay doors. "Anything?"

The engineer was a long way back. He

turned around and shook his head.

The banging was closer now, Davidov could feel it through his feet. "What about the landing gear?"

He turned, looking for an inspection port, and heard another bang, far louder than the rest. He swung back around to see the egress hatch in the floor burst open.

He pointed his flashlight toward it and saw a man with silver hair pop up through the open hatchway. He had a large pistol in his hand. An American HK45.

"In the name of Saint Peter!" Davidov exclaimed.

"Actually, my name is Austin," the man said, climbing out onto the deck. Another man popped up after him. "And this is Zavala."

Davidov was familiar with the names. "NUMA."

Austin nodded and stood while Zavala tossed out a metal bar he'd used to bash open the sealed hatch and then climbed free.

"You guys really should have a handle on the inside," Austin said in a droll American attempt at humor. "Or at least a doorbell."

"What are you doing on my plane?" Davidov blurted.

"We're here to prevent you from making a

very big mistake," Austin said.

Davidov felt a wave of anger growing in him, but he realized the opportunity at hand. The Americans had been focused on him this entire time. They hadn't seen the flight engineer sneaking up on them from the other direction.

"The mistake is yours," Davidov shouted.

The flight engineer lunged at them, swinging the flashlight. Zavala saw him at the last moment and dodged the blow. He threw a quick counterpunch and knocked the weary engineer to the ground.

The distraction lasted just long enough. Davidov sprinted forward, rushed into the cockpit and then turned and slammed the door shut. It pressure-sealed tightly.

"What happened?" Timonovski shouted.

Davidov pressed against the door, looking through the small round peephole in the center. "We have boarders," he said.

61

Kurt ran forward and banged against the bomber's cockpit door while Joe prevented the flight engineer from interfering. "Listen to me," he shouted. "We're not here to fight you. We're all in danger."

From its thickness and the small size of its circular peephole in the middle, Kurt could tell he was leaning against a pressure door. He hoped the men on the other side could hear him through it and over the sound of the engines.

"*You* are most certainly in danger," a voice shouted back.

"I know what you think. You've won," Kurt said. "You've got the *Nighthawk* and the mixed-state matter, but trust me, you're getting more than you bargained for. It's a sucker's prize. A Trojan horse. The Falconer lied to you. He lied to all of us."

The next words came over an intercom. *"What do you know about the Falconer?"*

Kurt turned, located the intercom and pressed the white button next to it. "That he's a liar and a master manipulator. That he played you, us and the Chinese against one another."

"Of course he is," the voice replied nonchalantly. *"That's the business. In the end, he gave us what we wanted."*

"No, he gave you what *he* wanted," Kurt replied. "Enough rope to hang yourself and a billion others. The *Nighthawk* is nothing more than a giant bomb now. A mixed-state matter bomb powerful enough to obliterate half of Europe and set the rest of it back to the Stone Age. It's rigged to blow once you exceed a certain altitude and then descend back below it."

"How would you know this?"

"He told me as he was dying."

"A deathbed confession? Do you really expect me to believe that?"

"Not a *confession*," Kurt said. "A *boast*. He said we couldn't stop it. That what went up would never come down."

Silence followed. Kurt glanced back at Joe and the flight engineer.

Joe shook his head softly. "We're still not winning."

Kurt turned back to the intercom. "Who am I speaking with?"

"My name is Constantin Davidov," the voice replied. *"I'm head of the Directorate for Technical Resources Acquisition."*

A spy, Kurt thought. A thief. "Listen to me, *Comrade Davidov,*" Kurt said. "If the Falconer wanted you to have the *Nighthawk,* why not just call you when he found out where it went down. He knew the location from day one."

"Because he needed you to raise it for him," Davidov replied.

"Why would he need that? Is raising a small aircraft from the bottom of a shallow lake beyond the capabilities of the Russian salvage fleet?"

"The difficulty came with the location," Davidov replied. *"Our ships are not equipped to scale mountains."*

"We did it with four people and one helicopter."

"Congratulations," Davidov replied. *"That proves nothing."*

"He imprisoned your pilot and flight engineer. What possible reason could he have had for that?"

Silence.

Kurt turned to look at Joe. He had the flight engineer subdued and the man wasn't fighting. If anything, he looked like he might be on their side.

"Tell him," Kurt urged.

"It's true," the engineer shouted. "The Falconer lied about everything. Every step of the way."

"I will not take advice from a hostage," Davidov said.

"At least stop climbing while we talk," Kurt urged.

"I'm sorry," Davidov said, *"but your reputation for perseverance and deception precedes you. Save your breath. There is nothing you can possibly say that will cause me to release the* Nighthawk *into your custody."*

"Looks like the reasoning portion of the evening has ended," Joe said.

Kurt agreed. He reached into a pocket and brought out the brick of Semtex he'd taken from Urco's cave. He held it up in front of the peephole for Davidov to see.

"You know what this is," Kurt said. "Either you open that door or I'll blow it off its hinges."

"You'll blow the plane apart."

"That's going to happen anyway."

Inside the cockpit, Davidov stared at the explosives in the American's hand. The fish-eye effect made it seem larger than it was, but the amount would be more than enough. There was only one alternative.

"Prepare for rapid decompression," he

said to Timonovski. "And then open the bomb bay doors."

"They'll be sucked out of the aircraft," Major Timonovski said. "The engineer will go with them."

"Yes," Davidov replied. "That's the idea."

"What if the American is right?" the pilot said. "Falconer murdered my copilot, he did nothing when the *Nighthawk* was breaking *Blackjack 1*'s spine. Nothing."

"Do as I order!" Davidov commanded.

Timonovski stared back at him and then shook his head.

"Then I'll do it myself." He stepped away from the pressure door and lunged for the bomb bay controls.

62

Rudi Gunn sat in NUMA's communications room with Hiram Yaeger, Priya Kashmir and Collin Kane. They were now part of a globe-spanning web of satellite links.

One screen showed the White House Situation Room where the President had convened his Security Council. A second screen displayed Paul, Gamay and Emma at the Internet café in Cajamarca. The Vandenberg control room appeared on the third, where Colonel Hansen and Steve Gowdy were standing by. The fourth connection went all the way to China, where General Zhang of the People's Republic sat and scowled.

As the conversation progressed, with all its requisite arguments, denials and disagreements, Rudi had the sense of a runaway train with five different engineers in the cab, none of whom had their hand on the tiller.

Finally, the group managed to get down to business. Zhang admitted that the Chinese had two of the *Nighthawk*'s containment units on board one of their long-range aircraft and gave away its transponder code.

The path was instantly picked up. Much farther along than anyone had expected.

"Are you sure this is the right aircraft?" someone asked.

"The HL-190 has super cruise ability," Zhang said. *"It can travel long distances at supersonic speeds."*

The aircraft was five hundred miles northwest of Hawaii. Its altitude was listed at fifty-one thousand feet. Its speed at more than a thousand knots.

"We know all about the HL-190," Gowdy said. *"Ever since you stole our engine designs."*

"And improved on them," Zhang said.

The President's chief of staff broke in with a calming tone. *"Gentlemen, we need to work together now or there won't be anything left to argue over. Ms. Townsend, please explain what you've discovered."*

"We've taken both bombs apart," Emma said. She stood calmly on the screen but looked exhausted. *"The first attempted a self-*

destruct when we made a mistake. The second detonator was neutralized. Once it was removed from the explosives, we discovered a USB access port used to program it. Hiram and Priya took it from there."

Hiram cleared his throat. "The device is a combination GPS receiver and altimeter. It becomes active once the aircraft exceeds a certain threshold speed and climbs above a specific altitude. It will detonate when they descend below the threshold altitude again or arrive at their destination."

"What speed?" General Zhang said. "What altitude?"

"One hundred and twenty knots," Hiram said. "Twenty-six thousand feet."

"Unfortunately," Priya added, "your aircraft has already exceeded both parameters."

On-screen, Zhang nodded. "I can see that. How do we stop it?"

"Your people will have to disarm the bomb before they begin their descent."

"Why not just dump the fuel cell out the door and be done with it?" Zhang suggested.

"Because of the power requirements of the cryogenic system and the magnetic bottles holding the mixed-state matter," Emma said. "It requires an extremely pure flow of power. Tiny surges or fluctuations could be disastrous. You can't just plug the unit into a cigarette lighter."

"Don't patronize me," Zhang snapped. "It wasn't my people who brought this curse down on us."

"But it was your people who tried to steal it," Emma shot back. "If they hadn't interrupted the flight, the material would already be safely stored in underground facilities."

"Yes," Zhang said. "Yours and yours alone."

Again the President's chief of staff cut in. "Please!" he urged. "None of that matters at this point. We're all damned lucky that the containment units didn't explode in Peru. And we're fortunate, General Zhang, that your aircraft is still out over the Pacific and not coming in for a landing. That gives us time. We can argue over who the mixed-state matter belongs to later. But first the bomb must be disarmed without damaging the fuel cell."

"How is that to be done?"

"It's a fairly simple process. We're prepared to transmit the schematics of the fuel cell, along with everything we know about the detonator, the power demands of the cryogenic unit and the design of the Penning traps. All we ask in return is that your aircraft change course to a more northerly route."

"Why?"

"Should your agent fail, it's important that

the detonation take place as far from civilization as possible."

"Perhaps I'll order the pilot to turn for California or Hawaii," Zhang replied testily.

"I promise you," Colonel Hansen said, jumping in. "If that aircraft deviates toward any landmass, American or otherwise, it will be shot down."

Zhang shook his head. "You are too easily baited, Colonel. Of course I have no intention of doing any such thing. Transmit the information. I have no wish to argue about this again."

"Turn the aircraft first," the chief of staff said.

A brief stare-down ensued.

"Very well."

With that, Zhang's screen went dark. And the four remaining links in the network lapsed into silence.

It fell to Emma to break it. "What about the Russians?" she asked from the screen. "What about Kurt and Joe? Have we heard from them?"

"All we know is that the Blackjack and the Nighthawk are airborne," Colonel Hansen said. "A satellite pass forty minutes ago showed the rural airfield to be empty. We've launched AWACS from Pensacola and Corpus Christi to look for the bomber's radar signa-

ture. Several squadrons of F-22s are being readied to intercept."

"Intercept?" Emma asked. *"Why would we need to intercept it?"*

"To protect ourselves," Hansen said. *"If the Russian government doesn't believe our claim and they or the pilot act rashly — the way Zhang threatened to a minute ago . . . well, we're dealing with a hypersonic aircraft, covered in stealth materials, that could make it from the coast of South America to Atlanta in twenty minutes. We can't allow that. So we have to find it first and be ready to act when we talk to Moscow."*

"But why would they act rashly?" she asked.

Rudi knew why. Everyone in the room and at the White House and out at Vandenberg knew why. He suspected Emma would have easily guessed the reason if she weren't exhausted.

He jumped in and explained. "Because they've almost certainly exceeded the speed and altitude thresholds that will prime the detonators. And unlike the Chinese plane, there is no physical way for the occupants of the bomber to get at the *Nighthawk* and disarm them."

Understanding washed over Emma's face in high-definition. Understanding and grief. *"There's no way to stop it,"* she whispered to herself. *"The pilots are dead men. And if Kurt and Joe are on board, they're dead men, too."*

63

The HL-190 transport represented the state of the art of Chinese aerospace industry. Intended first as an aircraft to fly dignitaries around the world, its interior was trimmed in high style. Active noise cancellation created a superquiet cabin. The air kept at a perfect seventy-two degrees and fifty-one percent humidity by a high-tech system that had twenty sensors spaced throughout the plane. The soft leather seating and lushly carpeted floor were designed specifically to caress the bodies and feet of those used to sitting down and giving orders.

Daiyu had no use for any of it. If not for the remarkable speed with which the aircraft flew, she'd have rather flown back to Shanghai in a sparse military transport.

To her surprise, the burly man who'd accompanied her from the lake seemed to be of a similar mood. Urco had called the man Vargas. He was as rough-spun as any of the group. If he'd been Chinese, he would have lived in a rural village, pushed a plow and carried heavy loads to and from ox-drawn carts, tossing them in and out as if they weighed nothing.

He'd remained awake for the entire flight, and she wondered if this was the first time he'd ever flown. His eyes appeared to be pricked open and slightly bloodshot as if he'd taken a powerful stimulant. After five hours in the air, he'd said no more than a dozen words.

Only when the plane banked to the right did he speak up. "Why are we changing course?"

"Probably to avoid some weather," she said. *It wasn't likely. At fifty-one thousand feet, the HL-190 flew* above *almost all the world's weather.* "Would you like a drink?" she asked. "It might help you to relax."

She stood up and walked to the bar. "Rice wine? Or maybe you'd prefer gouqi jiu; it's made from wolfberries."

He shook his head. "Water."

She gave him a bottle of Voss.

"Urco must trust you a great deal to send you alone for millions of dollars in diamonds. What will you do with them? And by that I mean what will he do with them since, obviously, you'll deliver the package to him without keeping any for yourself?"

The questions flowed from a combination of boredom and training. It was part of her instinct to divide slaves from their masters.

He stood and glared at her.

She stared back, unflinching, and he decided to take a walk down the carpeted aisle. He stopped and looked out through one window, then went to the other side of the plane and looked out another.

Daiyu didn't need to look; he would see nothing but darkness out there.

"How far have we gone?" he asked.

"More than halfway. You should sleep. It will pass the time faster."

"No," he grunted.

"Suit yourself."

The intercom buzzed. *"Daiyu, please come to the cockpit. General Zhang wishes to speak with you."*

She walked forward, passing Vargas and ignoring his stare.

She entered the cockpit and noticed they were continuing to turn, veering to a more northerly course still. She took a headset from Lieutenant Wu.

"Daiyu," General Zhang said. *"I must congratulate you for the progress of your mission. You've made me proud."*

He sounded very dour for a man offering

congratulations. "Thank you, General, but as you know it is not necessary," she said. "I do as I'm ordered for the nation. It is my mother and father, as you taught me."

"Yes," Zhang said. "And through no fault of yours, it is now in danger."

He went on to explain what he had learned from the Americans. Twice she asked him if he was certain. Twice he admitted he could not be sure the Americans were telling the truth, but he saw no reason for them to lie.

"Our engineers have studied the problem," he added. "They've found no way to use the aircraft's electrical system to keep the containment unit safely powered. The voltage and current do not match. You'll have to remove the explosives from the fuel cell without damaging it."

"And then?"

"Eject them from the aircraft."

That was easier said than done, but if they depressurized the cabin, it could be accomplished.

"There may be a problem," she admitted. "Urco's courier. It's possible he knows of the plan. He seems very grim. Perhaps contemplating what lies ahead."

"Martyrs usually are," Zhang said. "Dispose of him first. We cannot risk any interference."

"It will be taken care of," she said.

Zhang signed off. Lieutenant Wu took the headset back and offered her his sidearm.

She shook her head. "Give me your knife."

With the knife hidden in her sleeve, Daiyu opened the door. Vargas was standing right there.

He lunged first, grabbing her with both hands, lifting her off the floor and throwing her down the aisle.

She landed, sprang back to her feet and rushed back to the cockpit.

Vargas had already plowed forward into the cramped space. He was throwing punches and slamming heads against the wall. With a downward swing of his huge right arm, he clubbed Lieutenant Wu to the ground and then broke his back with a stomp of an oversized foot.

He grabbed the copilot's neck and snapped it with a lethal twist.

Daiyu launched herself at him, aiming the knife for his spine. Even at his size, a severed spine would render him useless. She missed to the right, hitting his fleshy back and plunging the blade as deep as it would go. She twisted it quickly and pulled it out.

Hot blood poured from the wound, but the mountain of a man barely responded.

He turned, backhanded her across the face and went for a choke hold. She threw one arm up beside her neck as a bar. It prevented him from crushing her windpipe or choking the life out of her, but he now had control.

With the power of a hydraulic press, he squeezed her neck and arm until she felt her elbow crack and separate. Excruciating pain shot through her body. She ignored it and brought a knee into his midsection. She might as well have been thumping a rock wall.

He barely reacted, held her tight and reached for her fallen knife. She twisted around in a desperate attempt to break free, came face-to-face with Lieutenant Wu's lifeless eyes and remembered his offer of the sidearm. She thrust her free hand into his jacket, wrapped her fingers around the weapon's carbon fiber grip and —

The knife went into her back.

Daiyu went stiff from the impact, felt the blade being pulled free and then being plunged into her a second time. The second puncture was far less painful than the first. A third was barely felt, as she shuddered and slumped to the floor.

Vargas stood awkwardly; he was bleeding badly from a wound he could not reach. It didn't matter. He knew his own end was near — he'd known it since the moment he'd left the lake. *It was well accepted,* he thought. *At least he would die in the clouds that his ancestors had always aspired to reach.*

He pulled the knife from Daiyu's back, went to the wounded pilot and pressed the bloody blade to his face.

"Call them," Vargas said. "Tell them she did as she was told and then resume course to Shanghai."

"But?"

"Do as I say!"

With Vargas holding the knife to his eye, the pilot got on the radio and made the call. He said everything Vargas had ordered him to say. The Chinese General said some brisk words and then ordered them back on course without emotion.

Vargas watched the pilot turn the aircraft. Urco had shown him on the computer what to look for on the computer screens.

When the plane leveled off again, Vargas smiled and then he cut the pilot's throat.

Lying in a pool of blood, Daiyu understood completely. Vargas was on a suicide mission. And now he'd overcome the only two obstacles he faced: her and Zhang. She was as good as dead, and with Zhang believing the explosives and the detonator had been removed, the Chinese authorities would welcome the aircraft to Shanghai with open arms.

The bomb would detonate as they descended and the matter and antimatter would mix instantly.

Deadly opposites, she thought. *Yin and yang destroying each other, as she'd always believed they would.*

She was the barrier, the only thing preventing the destructive mix. But she would be dead in minutes from the loss of blood. Even if she could somehow kill Vargas, she couldn't crawl ten feet, let alone take the fuel cell apart and disarm the explosives.

Her eyes started to dim, but her other senses remained for the moment and she realized there was something in her hand. *It was Wu's pistol.*

She knew what she had to do. She couldn't stop the explosion, but she could choose where it happened. And out over the sea was preferable to the destruction happening above her homeland.

Vargas was standing there, his hands on the back of the pilot's chair. She aimed at his head and pulled the trigger.

The shot hit home, splattering blood across the windshield.

Killed instantly, Vargas fell forward. His heavy body landed on the control column.

The impact disconnected the autopilot as the computer wrongly assumed that the captain was reasserting human control.

The HL-190 nosed down and began to descend.

Daiyu could just make out the altimeter. They quickly passed below fifty thousand feet. The dials continued to unwind. Forty-nine thousand . . . Forty-eight . . . Forty-seven . . .

64

Kurt saw through the peephole as Davidov made a sudden move toward the control panel. He'd overheard every word and knew what Davidov was planning.

There was no time to shout a warning, no time to do anything but act. With quick precision, Kurt raised the HK45, aimed at Davidov through the door and pulled the trigger twice.

The HK45 boomed and the armor-piercing shells punched through two layers of steel and struck Davidov in the ribs and the thigh. The statesman crumpled to the floor in pain.

"I'm begging you," Kurt shouted to the pilot. "Level the plane off and open the door."

Pushing Davidov aside, the pilot stretched from his seat and released the door. It swung open and Kurt stepped inside. "What altitude are we at?"

"Thirty-five thousand feet," the pilot said.

"Too high," Kurt said. "Almost certainly too high."

As if to prove the point, a sudden flash lit up the coal black sky outside the cockpit windows. It came in a staggered flicker, white-purple and then white-blue. It blinded like a nearby lightning strike would, but it was distant and soundless and so far off that the entire western horizon slowly came to life.

As the glowing color spread higher and farther, it gave way to a darker blue and then a greenish color reminiscent of the aurora borealis. It took on a texture, churning in long filaments, twisting and curling back in on itself in a mesmerizing, hypnotic display.

There was no sound, no shock wave, but the radios soon squealed and the computer screens skewed oddly to the right. On the panel above, whole rows of circuit breakers tripped, one after the other.

By now, Joe and the flight engineer had joined Kurt in the bomber's cockpit. As the flight engineer began resetting the tripped breakers, Joe stared out the window.

"What is that?" Davidov said from his position on the floor. He was in pain but not lethally hit. The double-layered steel door had taken much of the force out of Kurt's shots.

"The Chinese plane," Kurt said quietly.

"The Chinese . . ." Davidov grunted from his position on the floor.

"I told you," Kurt said. "He gave a deadly present to all of us."

Far beyond the horizon, out over the Pacific, a ball of fire, the likes of which no human had ever seen, expanded in spherical shells that stretched fifty and then a hundred and then two hundred miles across before finally fading.

Lightning shot out of the inferno in all directions, along with an electromagnetic storm of X-rays, gamma rays and other forms of ionized radiation. The upper atmosphere was ionized instantly, while down below enough seawater to fill Lake Erie was instantly vaporized. The fire and the shock wave left a circular depression that dented the Pacific to a depth of two hundred feet.

As the shock wave subsided and the ocean sought to level itself, a ring of enormous waves surged into the depression from all sides, eventually colliding and being thrust back outward again.

Several thousand miles away, Kurt, Joe and the Russians were seeing only the reflection of the events. An effect known as a *light echo* filtered through thousands of miles of atmosphere and was distorted by the curvature of the Earth. Yet not one of the five men on board the Russian bomber could take their eyes off of it.

"Something must have gone wrong," Joe said. "They can't have reached China yet."

Kurt helped Davidov up and into a jump seat. The wound to his ribs was broad but not deep; the wound to his leg hadn't hit any vital arteries.

"How far . . . how far away?" Davidov asked.

"Five thousand miles," Joe estimated, "give or take."

"To reach us from five thousand miles away . . ." Davidov said without finishing his thought.

"The Chinese had two units on board," Kurt said. "Fifty pounds of mixed-state matter. We're carrying twice that."

Davidov nodded and gripped the edge of the seat. "Why? Why would anyone want this? What has Russia done to him?"

"It's not going to explode over Russia," Kurt said, "but as you cross Europe."

Kurt explained the rest of what they knew. Davidov seemed more shocked with each revelation.

"We need to use your communications system," Kurt said. "We need to reach our people and find out if there's any possible way to prevent what we just saw from happening again."

65

Reaching anyone from the bomber proved to be difficult. Every satellite over the Pacific had been rendered inoperative, and though they were over the Caribbean, there was a spillover effect. Communication networks were crashing. And most of the Western world's active resources were busy trying to ascertain the extent of the damage.

Finally, after making contact with a Russian communications satellite over the Atlantic and being relayed through a commercial phone exchange in Poland, they were linked into the NUMA communications room.

"What altitude are you at?" Rudi Gunn asked immediately.

"Thirty-five thousand," Kurt replied.

The signal was poor because of the ionization in the atmosphere and the mismatch between the Russian equipment and NUMA's, but Kurt could hear the silence plainly. "We're too high," he said, not waiting for Rudi to tell him that. "We know that. What are our options?"

"There aren't any," Rudi said.

Kurt had expected this. He exchanged glances with the other men in the cockpit. "We figured that, too. We'll turn out to sea," he said. "Do you have a preferred course for us?"

"We do," Rudi said. *"We've picked a spot in the mid-Atlantic as far from any landmass as possible. All aircraft have been ordered out of the area and to land as soon as possible. All ships have been ordered to move away from the location at their best possible speed, though for many of them it won't matter."*

"We can't make the mid-Atlantic," Major Timonovski said. "We don't have the fuel."

"This is an intercontinental bomber," Joe said.

"We had to reduce the weight in order to clear the trees. We dumped ten thousand gallons back there."

"How far can we fly on what we have?" Kurt asked.

"Five hundred miles," Timonovski calculated. "Not much more."

"What about aerial refueling?" Joe asked. "We heard on the cockpit voice recorder from *Blackjack 1* that you were going to refuel near Caracas."

"Yes," Davidov said, "that was the original plan. But when the intercept failed, the tanker was ordered back to Russia. Our plan was to land in Cuba. We would be starting our descent in twenty minutes."

"Could we link up with an American tanker?"

"We use a different type of fuel," Major Timonovski said. "Modified to work with the scramjets."

Kurt looked at the map. They were halfway between Colombia and Cuba. Five hundred miles in any direction wouldn't be enough.

"We can't put sufficient distance between ourselves and civilization to do much good," he said. "We've got to come up with another plan."

Joe offered a desperate thought. "There's a windbreak in front of the *Nighthawk*. If we slowed to the very minimum controllable speed —"

Major Timonovski shook his head. "There is no hatch leading to the top of the fuselage."

"What if we depressurized the plane and cut a hole in the skin?"

"The skin is titanium," Davidov replied. "Double-thick. Even if we could, there's no hope in what you're considering. No matter how we try to secure you, it's not possible to keep you from being swept off the upper surfaces once you're out in the airstream. You'll never be able to get in the cargo bay."

"If we can cut our way out of the *Blackjack,* maybe we can cut our way into the *Nighthawk* from below," Joe said. "Tunnel our way through."

Unknown to the men on the bomber, the communications were being shared with the White House, Vandenberg and the café in Cajamarca. Emma's voice chiming in alerted them to that fact.

"You won't be able to cut into the Nighthawk *from below,"* she said. *"The entire structure is designed to resist the heat and shock of reentry. Even if you had a high-intensity acetylene torch, you'd never get through."*

Kurt found himself smiling. Strange, he thought, considering the situation. But he was glad to know at least she and the Trouts were safe. "What if we use the scramjets?" he suggested. "Instead of conserving fuel, we get this thing up to maximum speed and altitude. How high can this bomber go?"

"One hundred and twenty thousand feet," Timonovski replied.

"The problem is, the gamma ray burst," Rudi told them. *"The higher you go, the*

farther the devastation spreads. At that height, there will be less physical destruction, but the radiation, the shock front and the electromagnetic pulse will cover sixteen times as much surface area. The simulation we've run suggests that you nose-down at maximum velocity. It will concentrate the damage in one area, but it's still going to be bad."

"How bad?" Kurt said.

"The other burst was seven hundred miles from Hawaii. It set off seismometers all over the globe. Hawaii's gone dark. The Aleutians have gone dark. The entire Pacific Rim has gone dark. There are likely to be tsunamis and a hot shock front. If we had any satellites working out there, we'd expect to see fires and damage on most shores, effects the equivalent of a large earthquake, but we were lucky that it was so far away. The majority of the radiation and destructive energy dissipated prior to making landfall."

Kurt looked at the faces around him. Russian and American alike were calm and resigned. "You know how far we can go," Kurt said. "Give us a location when you have one. Until then, we'll conserve as much fuel as possible."

As Kurt spoke, Major Timonovski adjusted the flight setting to its most efficient mode. The wings came forward and the engines powered back. The *Blackjack 2* rose up and slowed down like a ship meeting a large, lazy swell.

It was peaceful, Kurt thought to himself, quiet. Truly, the calm before the storm.

66

Emma stood in the empty Internet café and felt her knees go weak. Not only would Kurt and Joe be killed but the detonation would inflict lethal damage across a large swath of the Americas and the Caribbean.

"This can't be happening," she whispered.

She sat down on the floor, tried to breathe and found her lungs would not draw in any air. "This can't be happening," she said again.

Gamay approached. "Breathe slowly," she urged. "You're hyperventilating."

"I killed them all," Emma said, tears streaming down her face. "Kurt and Joe, and a hundred million more."

"It's not your fault."

"I was part of it!" she snapped, going instantly from despair to anger.

She knew what Gamay was trying to do, but she didn't want to be told how it was going to be all right. It most certainly was *not* going to be all right.

"They're carrying twice the mixed-state matter that was on the Chinese plane. Even from the middle of the Caribbean Sea, the shock wave will cover half the South. Every living soul from Houston to Tampa will be incinerated, irradiated or drowned in a hundred-foot wave. Along with half of Mexico, Central America and every living being on every island in the Caribbean."

Gamay just stared at her. There was nothing to say.

Emma stood and turned away. In her darkest moment, when she would have rather died than be witness to what was about to happen, the defiance of Hurricane Emma flared the brightest. "I will not accept this," she said. "I will not!"

She pulled free of Gamay's attempt at kindness and willed her tired mind back into action. There had to be a way. There had to be!

She went over the properties of the mixed-state matter, the design of the containment units, tried to calculate the minuscule odds that they would survive if the Semtex detonated. But there was no way to stop the reaction; no known way, aside from the frigid cold of absolute zero, to stop matter and antimatter from annihilating each other.

She paced around the room searching for an answer. The frustration boiled over as she bumped a small table. In a fit of rage, she pushed it across the room. It slid with surprising ease, toppled and gouged a line in the painted concrete floor.

Emma stopped in her tracks, staring at a lengthy scratch. It was white on blue, like a vapor trail in the dusky sky.

Paul took a step toward her.

"Stop," she said without looking his way. Something had come to mind.

Vapor trail . . . Contrail . . . The thought lingered in her consciousness. *Streams of tiny ice crystals released by passing aircraft, high in the frigid sky.*

The thought hit with so much force, she almost fell over. "There is a way," she whispered. "There is a way!"

She turned with a snap. "Get Rudi back on the line. I need to talk to Kurt. I need to talk to him now. Before time runs out."

67

The scene in the NUMA communications room had become chaotic. With the impending disaster all but certain, all government assets had been turned toward coordinating the efforts to minimize the damage.

Orders were being sent out, troops mobilized. People directed to shelter underground. Anything and everything that could be thought of and acted upon in two hours was being done.

Highways were closed to southbound traffic. Aircraft were ordered to proceed as far north as possible and land within the two-hour window. Information was relayed to Central and South American countries, though there was no assistance to lend and by morning it would be every man, nation and group for themselves.

Into this maelstrom, Emma's attempt to communicate foundered. No line was free, no satellite communication available. No ear open to listening. Everyone too busy sending out orders and making requests.

Everyone except Priya, who'd moved quietly into the background. She thought she'd be safe, but figured by morning she would have no way to contact her family in London. She decided to send them an e-mail now before the worst happened.

As she sat down at the computer, a blinking icon told her she'd gotten an urgent message. It was from Paul Trout.

Emma thinks there might be another option to prevent disaster. We need to speak with Rudi and NASA Flight Dynamics. CANNOT get thru.

"Rudi," she said, waving him over.

Rudi was in the midst of five different things and had two other staffers talking in his ear.

"Rudi!" she shouted.

He turned.

"Emma needs to talk with you. She says there may be a way to avert the disaster!"

In the cold, dark cockpit of the bomber, Kurt focused on every static-skewed word.

"The Daedalus Project," Emma said. *"Remember I told you about it? We planned to use small nuclear explosions for deep-space propulsion. We thought we might be able to*

571

accelerate a spacecraft to nearly a tenth the speed of light. The explosions occur behind the craft, the shock wave hits what is known as a pusher plate and sends the craft surging forward without destroying it. I believe we can do something similar with the Nighthawk using the mixed-state matter. It won't be one big explosion but a long trail of smaller ones. If we vent the right amount of mixed-state matter through the original intake port, it will create a burst of energy and a continuous wave, accelerating the Nighthawk back into space before the subsequent explosion."

"Won't the mixed-state matter explode the second it hits air?" Kurt asked.

"As long as it remains cold enough, it lives in harmony. In its current condition, it will exit the collection port at 2.7 degrees Kelvin. The air temperature at one hundred and twenty thousand feet is somewhere in the neighborhood of negative eighty degrees. That's still a boiling two hundred and ten degrees Kelvin, and the mixed-state matter will react in less than half a second, but since the Nighthawk will be moving at four thousand miles an hour, that half-a-second delay will create enough space to build a wave rather than blow the craft apart."

Kurt listened intently, visualizing the attempt. "A wave?"

"A fast and powerful one," Emma replied.

"Max and the NASA Flight Dynamics team have done the calculations," Hiram said. "It could work."

Kurt grinned. Major Timonovski and the copilot nodded as well.

"We're not dead yet," Joe said. "You can't imagine how happy that makes me."

Even Davidov was smiling through the pain. "If we survive, a bottle of twenty-year-old scotch for each of you."

"What do we have to do?" Kurt asked over the radio.

"You have to take the bomber up to its maximum speed and altitude and then release the Nighthawk," Emma said. *"Reboot the control system with the alpha code and then download a series of commands that we will transmit to you momentarily."*

"That doesn't sound too hard," Kurt said. "What's the catch?"

"The Nighthawk's *antennas are on the top. They have to be or they would burn off on re-entry. That means you'll have to be above and in front of the* Nighthawk."

"Which means we get hit with the wave as well."

"We could try to use an Air Force satellite," she said. *"But there's so much ionization in the atmosphere that —"*

"No," Kurt said, cutting off the discussion. "We get one shot at this. Let's do it right."

Joe gave the thumbs-up. Davidov nodded enthusiastically. *"Da,"* Major Timonovski said.

The flight engineer nodded as well and switched on the antenna dish they'd used to override the *Nighthawk*'s program seven days ago. After a few checks, he turned to Kurt. "Tell them we are ready."

It took several minutes for the bomber to get up to supersonic speed and climb above eighty thousand feet. There, it switched over to the scramjets.

The burst of power pushed Kurt back into the seat and he listened as Timonovski called out the Mach number and altitude. Because Joe knew how to fly, he'd been given the copilot's seat. Kurt and Davidov sat behind them in the jump seats, and the flight engineer was at the command station where the Falconer had been days before.

"One hundred and nineteen thousand," Major Timonovski said. "Maximum altitude and velocity in five . . . four . . . three . . ."

"Releasing *Nighthawk*," the flight engineer said.

To avoid *Blackjack 1*'s fate, they flew in a parabolic arc, ejecting the *Nighthawk* as they went over the top.

"*Nighthawk* clear," the flight engineer said. "Stabilizer intact."

Once the *Nighthawk* drifted back far enough, Timonovski brought the bomber up above and in front of the unmanned space plane.

"Separation, two miles," the flight engineer said. "Initiating alpha code."

At the press of a button, the information was sent. Now they waited. Finally, a response came in.

"*Nighthawk* up and functioning," the flight engineer said. "Transmitting new orders."

As Kurt watched the others perform their duties, he triple-checked his shoulder harness and gripped the handhold beside the jump seat. There was nothing else for him to do.

"*Nighthawk* confirms orders received and processed," the flight engineer said excitedly. "Initiation in thirty seconds. All systems green." He turned to Timonovski. "Let's get the hell out of here."

Timonovski put the bomber into a turn, banking away from the *Nighthawk*'s course. The turn had to be gradual because of the incredible velocity, but the farther the two courses diverged, the better chance they had of surviving the wave that was about to hit.

The *Blackjack* was pulling hard. Kurt felt the g-forces pressing him down into the seat. He strained to look at his watch. The second hand ticked along the orange face. Each click seemed a lifetime. And then they were all used up.

A flash of blue light filled the sky. Kurt shut his eyes and still saw the glare.

"Hang on!" Joe shouted.

The shock front hit the bomber like a crashing wave. Despite their speed and course away from the *Nighthawk,* the impact was intense as the surge picked the bomber up and shoved it forward.

"Don't fight it," Kurt grunted.

Timonovski did as Kurt suggested, going with the wave instead of turning against it. Still, the ride was violent, the systems inside the cockpit fried out in seconds, the fuselage buckled and, after ten seconds of buffeting, the left wing folded and the plane rolled over into a dive.

Unseen from inside the bomber, the *Night-hawk* had done precisely as ordered, ejecting a tiny stream of the antimatter out behind it. The reaction was nearly instant, but instead of one giant flash, it left a trail of hundreds and then thousands of flashes in a series that lit up the night sky. At the head of this expanding flare of blue light, the tiny black craft was propelled toward space, accelerating at a rate that would have killed a human occupant.

Seen from the ground, the burst of light looked like glowing ripples in a pond, with each circle of light expanding into the others until the interference pattern formed a maddening kaleidoscope of luminescence, streaking upward and outward to the east.

Perspective was hard to come by from down there. And no one who viewed it with the naked eye could really follow the band of swirling light as it lengthened and stretched before terminating in a blinding flash high above the planet.

The experiment had worked. In three minutes, the *Nighthawk* covered just under five thousand miles, accelerating to a maximum velocity of nearly one hundred and seventy thousand miles per hour, the fastest man-made object of all time.

It was still accelerating when the heat and vibration caused a catastrophic failure in one of the containment units, but by then it was far enough from the Earth's surface to be nothing more than a mind-blowing fireworks display in the night sky.

■ ■ ■ ■

The men in the falling bomber never saw it; they were knocked about mercilessly and traveling in the opposite direction.

Inside the cockpit, Kurt felt himself whiplashed one way, then the other. He was certain the plane would come apart at any second. Miraculously, it held together, despite the fact that one wing had been ripped off and most of the tail was gone.

It didn't take long to realize that they were in a nosedive. Light from the artificial sun had temporarily illuminated the Earth and its sea far below.

They were corkscrewing down like *Blackjack 1* had, falling from the sky like a gull with a broken wing.

The spinning motion was disorienting. The loss of pressure threatened to cause him to black out. He remembered the other crew's long descent with only the computer talking.

"We need to eject!" Kurt shouted to Major Timonovski.

The pilot didn't answer. He was still strapped in his seat, but with every move of the plane he was being thrown back and forth like a rag doll.

"Joe, we have to punch out!"

Joe seemed no better than Timonovski. Davidov looked to be awake but too weak to move, and the flight engineer was hanging in the straps, a huge gash to his forehead.

Kurt had no idea how high they were, no idea what would happen if they ejected, but he'd seen the wreckage of the other bomber on the bottom of the sea. That impact he knew they would not survive.

He looked around for an ejection handle. Everything was labeled in Russian. Finally, he spied a red bar with two orange stripes.

He reached for it.

Grasped it.

And with one hard pull, yanked it up and back.

An explosion shook the plane, fire surrounded the cockpit and everything went black.

68

Emma arrived in Washington five days after what they were calling *the event.* It took that long because so much of the world was in chaos. Half the world's satellites were down, most of the communication systems were down, aircraft were being routed by hand and most of those were being used to fly relief supplies to the Pacific.

When she finally arrived in D.C., she discovered that land lines were temporarily back in fashion as a line of two hundred people was waiting to use three working pay phones.

She skipped the line. Found a cab and rode into the city. After a long debriefing with the NSA, she walked across town to NUMA. There she found Rudi, Hiram and Priya.

They had old-fashioned paper maps in front of them. Various areas were outlined in green, yellow and red.

"How bad is it?" she asked.

"Nowhere near as bad as it could have been," Rudi said. "Hawaii and the Aleutians fared the worst, but physical damage was minimal. A sixteen-foot tsunami hit Waikiki, but the larger wave went to the west. Ironically, Japan shielded the Chinese coast, but since they've been preparing for this since the Tohoku tsunami a few years back, they were ready."

She'd been hearing the reports for days. She was thankful.

"Surprised the NSA let you come up for air," Hiram said. "Figured they'd have you working round the clock on the mixed-state matter you brought home."

"It's a huge controversy," she said. "I think they plan to send it all back into space."

"The irony," Rudi said.

"Anyway, they have no more claim over my time," she said. "I've resigned. As of an hour ago, I'm officially unemployed."

"Really?" Rudi said. "Want to help us?"

He pointed to an open spot at the desk.

"What are you doing?"

"Searching for Kurt, Joe and the Russians," Priya said.

She looked at the map: it was the eastern Caribbean.

"The Navy and the Coast Guard are a

581

little busy running emergency supplies to the Pacific Rim, so we figured we'd jump-start the effort on our own," Rudi explained. "We've got NUMA assets, private aircraft and chartered boats on the search. These are areas we've checked. And these are other possible search zones."

"But nothing yet," she said.

Rudi shook his head.

Emma sat down. "I'll help any way I can," she said. "I hate to think of them out there — suffering, fighting off sharks and dying of thirst."

"They're tough and well trained," Rudi said. "I'm sure none of that will be a problem."

69

Kurt narrowed his gaze against the blinding glare of the high-noon sun. "Sharks," he said grimly. "The whole lot of you."

He threw down a hand of cards in disgust, tossing them onto a flat section of wood that was serving as a makeshift poker table.

Across from him, Davidov grinned as he collected a literal pot of gold from the center. "I assure you, I played honestly," he said.

"A spymaster who played fairly," Joe said from the other side of the table. "I doubt it."

"Scrupulously," Davidov insisted. "Is it my fault you have squandered all your chips?"

Kurt leaned back. They were sitting on a pristine white sand beach with the turquoise Caribbean waters lapping at the shore just beyond. Among their few possessions were a rubber raft, a deck of cards, a bottle of twenty-year-old scotch that was nearly empty and a million dollars in Russian gold coins that Davidov had brought along in case the Falconer tried to gouge him further on the price.

They'd survived ejecting from the bomber because, unlike a fighter aircraft, the *Blackjack* ejected the entire cockpit in an enclosed ballistic capsule. They'd landed in the sea, floating down on three large parachutes and then transferred to the rubber life raft. After a day at sea, they'd rowed ashore on the island and set up a small camp.

Two fires burned. The first, a signal fire; the second, to heat water as part of a jury-rigged desalinization system that Joe had designed. It provided several cups of water each hour. Plenty to keep them going. Though none of them wanted a drop until the scotch was used up.

Using a long, jagged stick as a spear, Kurt had caught several fish, which they'd deboned, cooked and eaten with gusto.

Since then, there had been nothing to do but drink and play cards and wait for someone to rescue them. The gold coins were their chips, but after starting with even amounts, Kurt was down to his last ten chips.

"Deal again," Kurt said. "And, this time,

from the top of the deck."

Davidov laughed and shuffled.

As Kurt waited for the cards to be dealt, he grabbed the bottle of scotch, brought it up toward his mouth and then put it back down again. "I think I hear a boat," he said.

"Nonsense," Timonovski said. "You're just trying to get out of the game."

Despite the Russian's doubts, the sound grew louder until a twenty-foot fiberglass powerboat rounded the point and cruised into the empty cove. It came straight toward them and the signal fire, beaching on the sand a few yards from the poker table.

A young man in a red polo shirt and white shorts was at the wheel. He jumped down onto the shore. "What are you people doing here?" His official tone clashed with the outfit and the soft lilt of his Caribbean accent.

"Losing at poker," Kurt said.

The others laughed. The young man seemed baffled.

"You can't be here," he said. "This is private property."

"We didn't have much of a choice," Joe said. "Our plane crashed. We bailed out. This is where we ended up."

"But why did you stay on this side of the island?" the man asked.

Kurt, Joe and the Russians looked at one another, confused by the strange conversation.

"Is the other side of the island more hospitable?" Davidov asked.

"I should hope so," the man said. "They have a Ritz-Carlton over there."

Kurt looked at Joe and burst into laughter. The island was several miles across; the center was all hills and sand dunes; it had appeared completely deserted. It was pitch black at night, without the slightest hint of civilization.

"Don't they have lights at the Ritz-Carlton?" Kurt asked.

"All lights are out since the big flash in the sky."

"Ahh," Kurt said. "That's kind of our fault."

Joe and the Russians laughed at that, but the man in the red polo shirt did not seem amused.

Kurt held out the last of his gold coins. "I offer ten thousand dollars for a ride to the Ritz."

Joe held up a hand as if he were bidding at an auction. "And another ten thousand if you tell everyone you found us at sea."

"Good thinking," Kurt said. "Well worth it."

The man looked at them as if they were crazy. Sunburned, scruffy, ripped clothing and a near-empty bottle of scotch confirmed it for him, but he couldn't leave them there.

He ignored what he must have believed was fake gold and walked back to his boat. "Come on," he said. "I'll take you. But rooms are expensive. They may want you to pay up front."

As they climbed into the boat, Kurt offered a sly grin. He had the scotch. Joe, Davidov, Timonovski and the flight engineer carried the gold. "I'm sure something can be arranged."

ABOUT THE AUTHORS

Clive Cussler is the author or coauthor of more than fifty previous books in five best-selling series, including Dirk Pitt, NUMA® Files, *Oregon* Files, Isaac Bell, and Sam and Remi Fargo. His nonfiction works include *Built for Adventure: The Classic Automobiles of Clive Cussler and Dirk Pitt*, plus *The Sea Hunters* and *The Sea Hunters II*; these describe the true adventures of the real NUMA®, which, led by Cussler, searches for lost ships of historic significance. With his crew of volunteers, Cussler has discovered more than sixty ships, including the long lost Confederate ship *Hunley*. He lives in Colorado and Arizona.

Graham Brown grew up in Illinois, Connecticut and Pennsylvania, moving often with his family. A former pilot and lawyer and later part of a start up health care firm, Graham decided he hadn't had enough different careers yet and decided to become a writer. A huge fan of Clive Cussler, Michael Crichton, Stephen King and television shows like the *X-files* and *Lost*, Graham's first novel *Black Rain* debuted in January 2010. He now co-writes the NUMA® Files series with Clive Cussler. Their second collaboration, *The Storm*, debuted at #1 on the *New York Times* best seller list.